Precisely Terminated by Amanda L. Davis ha[...]
in a book—an exciting journey, intriguing cha[...]
turn, anguish, joy, and, most of all, great writing. The story begins
with gloom, which is perfect for the dystopian setting, but unlike many
dystopian novels, this story doesn't leave the reader in despair. I whole-
heartedly endorse and recommend *Precisely Terminated*. This is a book
that can be enjoyed by anyone and a story no one will soon forget.

    Bryan Davis, author of **the Dragons in our Midst** series

Few debut authors can create a story world and characters that are original and unique, but Amanda L. Davis has succeeded. A page-turning
blend of futuristic and old-world, *Precisely Terminated* pits a young
heroine against a mindless computer with the power to take millions of
lives. I read this book cover-to-cover and enjoyed it immensely. If you
want something out of the ordinary, read *Precisely Terminated*.

    Scott Appleton, author of **The Sword of the Dragon** series

Amanda L. Davis is an exciting new voice in Christian fiction I'm
thrilled to discover. The imaginative adventure of *Precisely Terminated*
kept me eager to turn pages, and Davis' vivid prose places you right in
the midst of the action. A perfect read for fans of *The Hunger Games*
series and other dystopian novels. You'll be rooting for these characters
and clamoring for more in the Cantral Chronicles. Keep 'em coming,
Miss Davis!

    C.J. Darlington, TitleTrakk.com co-founder and author of *Thicker
than Blood* and *Bound by Guilt*

Fantastic! This skillfully written debut novel by Amanda L. Davis will keep you enthralled to the last page. With an extraordinary setting and a compelling story, *Precisely Terminated* is a definite must-read.

Ruth Shafer, Age 19

WOW! *Precisely Terminated* was amazing! Instantly you get to know and love the characters and wonder what will happen next! This book was impossible to put down!

Jacob Fish, Age 15

Amanda L. Davis's dystopian novel *Precisely Terminated* captures the reader's attention from the opening chapter. The three main reasons this book has become one of my favorites is because of the book's dynamic and realistic characters, the fully developed and detailed world, and the powerful examples of self-sacrifice and bravery. *Precisely Terminated* has a cast of characters that display real personalities, and the world in which they live is extremely clear and understandable for any reader. Lastly, this dystopian story demonstrates striking examples of love and self-sacrifice. The reader's admiration for Monica climaxes when, although Monica loses part of her fingers and later nearly her life, she continues on in her desperate search to do what Faye did for her—to save the people of Cillineese from death. Because of the characters, the setting, and the lessons one can learn from Amanda L. Davis's masterful writing, *Precisely Terminated* is a novel all can savor.

Olivia Skelton, Age 15

Amanda L. Davis has delivered masterfully. *Precisely Terminated*'s authentic Dystopian imagery lends itself well to the reader's imagination. Had I not known better, I would not have considered this her first book. With a great storyline and deep characters, Amanda has won my confidence in her writing.

Noah Aresenault, Age 16

Precisely Terminated was fantastic! It tells of an adventure that has hardship but in the end finds new hope and a better future. The strengths of the book are the plot and the details; it showed that Amanda L. Davis spent a lot of time putting details into the story's history and background. The ending was a signal of hope for the characters that there could be a better future.

Anya Herdeg, Age 12

When beginning *Precisely Terminated* my biggest fear was that Amanda L. Davis wouldn't be able to step out of her father's shadow. I feared that her writing style would be a duplicate and wouldn't stand out. Thankfully, all these fears were blown away with an amazing first book that has a fantastic premise, plot, and characters. Amanda L. Davis has crafted a fantastic book. I highly recommend it.

Seth Reid, Age 15

Precisely Terminated is the first book in the Cantral Chronicles trilogy, as well as Amanda L. Davis' first published work; I believe both will go far. Amanda uses flawless technical skill to avoid the pitfalls first-time authors often succumb to, making especially good use of a riveting world-building job that is not lost on the reader. With believable characters, a world as real as our own, and stakes that escalate, this story has all the ingredients for a readers' favorite. Encompassing a struggle against tyranny and the ticking time bomb of reliving the deadly past, *Precisely Terminated* remains a wholesome read in the dystopia genre and one I wish the best of luck to.

Sam Jenne, Age 17

PRECISELY TERMINATED

The Central Chronicles Book 1

TERMINATION POINT

TERMINATION POINT

PRECISELY TERMINATED

TERMINATED

The Cantral Chronicles Book 1

TERMINATION POINT

TERMIN POINT

AMANDA L. DAVIS

LIVING INK BOOKS

PRECISELY TERMINATED
THE CANTRAL CHRONICLES® BOOK I
Copyright © 2011 by Amanda L. Davis
Published by Living Ink Books, an imprint of
AMG Publishers, Inc.
6815 Shallowford Rd.
Chattanooga, Tennessee 37421

First Printing—August 2011

Print edition	ISBN 13: 978-0-89957-896-5	ISBN 10: 0-89957-896-9
EPUB edition	ISBN 13: 978-1-61715-258-0	ISBN 10: 1-61715-258-7
Mobi edition	ISBN 13: 978-1-61715-259-7	ISBN 10: 1-61715-259-5
ePDF edition	ISBN 13: 978-1-61715-260-3	ISBN 10: 1-61715-260-9

Library of Congress Cataloging-in-Publication data applied for at time
of first printing

THE CANTRAL CHRONICLES® is a trademark of AMG Publishers

Cover layout and design by Daryle Beam at BrightBoy Design, Inc.,
Chattanooga, TN
Interior design and typesetting by Adept Content Solutions LLC,
Champaign, IL
Edited by Susie Davis, Sharon Neal, and Rick Steele

Printed in the United States of America
16 15 14 13 12 11 –D– 6 5 4 3 2 1

CHAPTER 1

How nice it must be to sleep so peacefully when doom awaited at dawn. Letting out a sigh, Faye pulled a threadbare blanket from a top bunk and surveyed the many beds and sleeping bodies lined up in the cramped room. How little they all knew, these poor, ignorant laborers. Perhaps they would die unaware of the tragedy about to befall them.

As she folded the blanket and laid it back on the bed, tears welled in her eyes. Why did it have to happen this way? She was only a nursemaid, one slave in the midst of thousands. Why should she die because of one man's actions? It simply wasn't fair. No, it was cruel, inhumane, tragic . . . evil.

She slowly clenched a fist. Fair or unfair, the time had come. The plan had to proceed.

A child cried out from across the room. Faye turned to locate the sound, knocking her elbow against a bunk beside her own. She squinted into the darkness and across the rows of similar bunks along each side of the narrow room. Thin sheets hanging around each one offered the only privacy to be had by the overworked slaves.

Faye pressed a hand on her forehead and blinked away her drowsiness. If only she could have slept for more than a couple of hours. Would she be able to complete her part of the plan? Was there really any choice?

The child yelled again, and the noise rose above the snores of others. Faye weaved through the maze of people lying about the room's floor, trying not to imagine the horror they were soon to face. Each and every soul here would die, including herself. It was too late to save anyone except the chosen refugee. Master Joel's well-laid plans had to be scrapped in exchange for a desperate rescue. He had moved too quickly. Now they had to salvage one life in the midst of the storm.

Faye tripped over someone lying in the aisle. She muttered an apology, but the sleeper paid no mind. Like the others, he was accustomed to poor treatment. The Nobles didn't even provide enough beds for their chattel. Could anyone really be surprised that the heartless Nobles thought so little of killing every inhabitant of this vast city? There were plenty of other cities to rule, mobs of replacement slaves to put into service. Although Cillineese was a major trading hub, the Nobles would scarcely feel the loss.

A petite, blonde woman sat on the floor, cradling a squirming child, her back against the wall. Faye knelt beside her and placed a hand on the small boy's head. "Any news, Kat? Have they found out for sure?" Faye's hands trembled. She never should have allowed herself those precious few moments of sleep, but exhaustion had held sway. Now everything could be lost if she didn't act quickly.

"The uprising has failed." Kat closed her eyes and rested her head against the wall. "They will raise the dome shortly." She rocked the toddler in her arms. "The night-shift dorms are buzzing with the news."

Faye shook her fellow worker's shoulder. "Kat, we mustn't give up now. We can still save a life!" The image of a rising wall burned in Faye's mind. One small child could escape if Master Joel's plan worked. It had to succeed.

Kat pushed herself to her feet. She pointed to the back of the boy's neck where a red welt the size of a fingernail pulsed. "There's no chance even for the youngest of us," she said. "They're implanting tracking chips so early now. The doctors must have known about the rebellion." She blinked back tears and laid the boy on an empty bottom bunk. As he squirmed, Kat leaned over, kissed him on the forehead, and pulled the curtains closed around the bed, breathing a forlorn sigh. "Sweet dreams, love. I hope the sacred hymns are really true. They are our only hope."

Faye pulled her friend into a warm hug. "I wish we could save your son, Kat." As their embrace tightened, Faye looked over Kat's shoulder at the curtained bunk. Would Kat be willing to go with her? Certainly she wouldn't want to leave her son to die alone.

Pulling back, she nodded at the door a few feet away. "We can try to save Master Joel and Madam Rose's daughter, Kat. I know she's a Noble, but if we help, maybe she'll be able to make a difference."

After wiping her eyes with her apron, Kat touched the red spot on the back of her own neck. "What good would that do? The Nobles have chips same as us. If we run from the gas, we'll only get electrocuted, and I, for one, think that sounds much more painful."

A vision of an escaping slave flashed through Faye's mind, a recent episode she had witnessed herself. The man had been intent on running, despite the warnings. When he struck the invisible barrier, his frame jerked violently as sparks of electricity danced around his eye sockets. He died within seconds, leaving a scorched, smoking body lying on the other side of the palace gate. Faye shivered. Noble or not, Master Joel wasn't cruel like the others. It wasn't his choice to kill runaway slaves. His objections never seemed to matter to the Council of Eight though. Still, one hope remained.

Faye took Kat's hand in hers and whispered, "I recently learned that the Nobles' children don't receive chips until they are five years old."

"I have heard that rumor," Kat said. "If it's true, what difference does it make?"

Faye tugged on Kat's arm and led her to the door, still whispering. "Please help me. Master Joel's daughter is just four. She can evade security."

"What?" Kat set her feet, halting at the door. "Are you talking about kidnapping her? Right out from under Master Joel's nose?"

"It's not a kidnapping." Cold sweat broke out across Faye's skin. The insanity of this plan had never been clearer. But what did it matter? If they failed, they would die anyway. They had nothing to lose. As thoughts of the child she had taken care of for four short years came to mind, a new surge of compassion nearly overwhelmed her. Of course they should try. It would be cruel *not* to try. Monica could live in the Cantral palace. Because of his passion for the opposition, Iain had agreed to take her in as his own. And with news that Cillineese was about to be gassed buzzing through the other city-states by now, he would be waiting at the city's edge in the messenger tunnels when Monica arrived.

"It's Master Joel's plan. No one else knows, but Monica's been so sick so often, hardly anyone realizes he has a child."

"Monica?" Kat's brow furrowed. "I thought her name—"

"We decided to teach her a new name once we took her into hiding." Faye opened the dormitory door, revealing a long, dark, narrow staircase. "Are you coming with me, or not?"

"I can't leave my son. This will never work." Kat wrung her hands together. "Won't she be with her family? How could you get her away without others noticing?"

"I told you; Master Joel knows. He set this up as a last-ditch effort. He should be waiting for me." Faye's wristband beeped loudly, and she checked its digital screen. The signal had come. She stepped down into the staircase and placed her palm on the wall. Low lights sputtered to life at the top of each stair, illuminating dozens of additional steps. "I have to go, with or without you."

"But if I'm not here—"

"Kat . . . " Faye rubbed her hand up and down Kat's arm. "Your son will die whether you're here with him or not. He'll go peacefully in his sleep. If you want to do something for life in the midst of death, come with me. I need your help. I don't think I can get Monica all the way to the wall by myself; the shocks might be brutal."

Kat clenched a handful of her skirt fabric, her knuckles turning white. She stepped onto the first stair, shoulder to shoulder with Faye. "I'll come. As much as I hate to leave him, I don't want to see him die." Glancing back at the curtains enclosing her son's bed, she whispered, "I love you."

Faye reached around Kat and closed the door. Since the stairwell was too narrow for them to descend abreast, Faye walked in front, her hand pressed on the wall, her fingers feeling every groove in the thick stone. She shivered despite the shawl draping her shoulders. Cool air was forever getting trapped in the slave corridors.

"Her room is one floor down from here and through another passage to the right." Faye's words echoed in the narrow space.

Since they stood in an outer wall of the Nobles' palace, they could access any floor from their staircase and not have to descend any ladders to lower levels. Sensing that time was running out, Faye picked up her pace, racing down the stairs and turning into the side passage. She stopped halfway down the hall. A small light-bulb flickered beside a low crack in the wall to her right.

Kat crept up to her side, murmuring, "I'm out-of-bounds even now, you know. This isn't my side of the house." She put a hand on the back of her neck and shivered. "I've already received two warnings." She touched her wristband. "What if someone sees me? The Nobles can knock me out where I stand."

"Everyone will be with their families." Faye knelt by the light and passed her palm over the bulb. The light changed to green for a split second, and a chest-high panel in the wall popped open. She looked at her wristband. Now to tell the computers that Monica needed her. She pushed a button on the band's screen. The girl had been so sickly during her infant and toddler years that the computers were accustomed to the odd hours.

"Everyone's with their families." Kat put a hand on Faye's shoulder. "Just as I should be."

"Go back if you must. I have to save a life." Faye crawled through the opening in the wall, hoping Kat would continue to follow. They were at least a quarter of a mile from the city wall, and she had to get Monica and the paper.

Thickly piled pink carpet enveloped Faye's fingers as she entered the room. Still on hands and knees, she scooted away from the opening to allow Kat space to enter. A large four-poster bed dominated one corner of the suite, dwarfing the small form lying in the center.

Faye rose to her feet and padded to the bed. When she stopped beside the sleeping girl, Kat bumped into her.

"Sorry." Kat shuddered. "The computers don't like me being in here, and I'm not used to this. No Nobles go to the laundry room. Here, someone could come in at any moment."

"And do what? We're all going to die anyway." Faye pursed her lips and shook the little girl snuggled under the blankets. "Monica, wake up, honey."

Monica tugged her blanket over her head. "No."

Faye pulled the top comforter off the bed, leaving just the sheet covering the girl. She tickled Monica and forced herself to laugh. "Come on, you, I need to take you somewhere. You get to meet a friend of mine. Wouldn't you like that?"

"Ah, there you are, Faye." A man's voice rumbled through the room.

Kat jumped, a squeak of surprise escaping her lips. Faye whirled around to face the speaker.

A tall man garbed in dark clothing stood by a door at the other side of the room. He crossed the floor to their side in a few steps. "There's not much time."

Kat grabbed Faye's arm.

Shaking her off, Faye nodded. "I know, Master Joel. I've arranged for someone to meet us at the wall. She'll be taken to Cantral." She looked around Joel's shoulder. "Where is Madam Rose?"

As a shadow fell across his face, he shook his head. "It is best you don't know."

Monica sat up in bed and reached out to her father. "Daddy."

He scooped her up in his arms. "I'm sorry it has to be this way." Joel slipped a tanned muscular hand into his pocket, extracted a folded page, and handed it to Faye, keeping a tight grip on his daughter. "This contains the plans I had hoped to follow if we hadn't been found out. Monica needs to take it out of the city with her. I can only hope your friend will know what to do with it." He swallowed hard. "My brother will be getting his wish. But we may be able to foil him, even after death."

Faye accepted the paper. "Yes sir." She glanced at Kat, who now stood beside her, rigid as a board, her face completely white. "We should go now." She reached for Monica, but the little girl wailed and clung tightly to her father's neck, as if she knew she'd never see him again.

Joel kissed his daughter on the forehead and pried her arms away from his neck.

She kicked and wriggled. "No! No! No!"

"Come on, Monica," Faye whispered. When she plucked Monica out of her father's arms, she squirmed all the more. "We're going to explore the slave tunnels, just like you always wanted to."

Monica relaxed in her maid's arms. "Really?" she said. "You never let me before."

"This is a special, one-time deal." Faye grabbed a blanket from the bed and tucked the paper in its folds. "You have to promise you'll be quiet."

Monica's eyes widened. She nodded fervently, her tousled brown curls falling into her face.

Rumbling shook the room. Faye staggered. Joel caught her elbow and pushed her to the slaves' passage door. "They're closing the dome! The doors will be sealed in moments. You have to go immediately." He shoved Faye through the opening, almost sending her tumbling down the corridor. She caught herself on the wall. Monica's fingernails dug into her neck.

"Faye!" she wailed.

Kat shot through the door. "Come on!" She grabbed Faye's arm and dragged her along.

Dozens of stairs flew by under their feet. Monica whimpered as they jostled down passage after passage, but she didn't say another word.

As they descended into the underground halls, distant screams sounded above their heads. If only they could save more than just this one child.

Faye's lungs burned. Monica kept slipping in her arms. Kat helped adjust the girl's position every few yards. The tunnel floor shook, and bits of dirt fell from the walls and ceiling.

"We must be getting close," Faye said, panting.

They rounded a bend in the passage. A triangular sign protruded from the wall, marking the city limits. Only a little farther—they might just make it! More dirt clods landed and crumbled. A thick metal door protruded from the ceiling, directly behind the warning sign. It descended slowly, the metal already blocking half of the doorway.

Where was Iain? Sweat dripped into Faye's eyes, blurring her vision. He had to be there. If he decided not to show, then not even Monica could be saved. A buzzing pain rattled her skull. Her chip didn't like her being this far out of her normal area. A beep sounded from her wristband. Her foot caught on a clump of dirt. She landed on her side, the force of impact throwing Monica from her arms. Monica unrolled from her blanket and lay crying on the floor.

"Are you all right?" Kat was at Faye's side in an instant.

Pain lanced Faye's chest. "Just get her," she gasped. "Go!"

Kat scooped up the wailing child and took a hard step toward the door. A short, thin man darted out from the other side, ducking under the descending metal plate. He shuddered as he crossed the threshold. Sparks flickered on his shoulders. The small shocks had to be painful, but he pressed on.

"Iain!" Faye yelled. More stabbing pains shot through her chest. She struggled to her knees, still panting.

Iain grabbed Monica from Kat's arms. Inch by inch the door separating them from freedom fell closer to the ground. With a guttural shout, Iain tossed Monica through the foot-tall gap. He dove after her, barely fitting underneath.

Shuffling on her knees, Faye snatched the paper. The door clanged shut, sealing them off from the rest of the world. She stared at the metal plate. The buzzing in the back of her head stopped. The computers no longer cared if they were out-of-bounds. They would soon be dead from the gas.

Kat sank to the floor. More dirt drizzled from the ceiling. "We're stuck. They'll gas us any second." She pulled her knees up to her chest. "I don't want to die, Faye. I haven't done anything wrong."

"I know. It's not your fault."

"They can't do this." Shaking her head, Kat began rocking back and forth. "Why'd you convince me to come? Now my son will die alone, and we didn't even succeed."

Faye smoothed the white page out on the ground. "Monica is safe. We did not fail." She clasped her hands to keep them from shaking. Yes, Monica was safe, but they did fail to get Iain the all-important plans.

Taking off her shawl, Faye whispered, "We can still get the plans to Iain." She wrapped the shawl around the paper. As another shudder rolled through the tunnel, she snatched the boundary sign from the wall and shoved it into the ground, gouging a sizeable hole. She placed the bundle inside and scooped loose dirt over it.

"Iain will know the paper is missing. I'm sure he'll come back to look for it once they start to repopulate the city."

"Long after they've incinerated our corpses," Kat spat out. She rested her head on her knees. "What are they waiting for? They must have sealed the city by now!"

Faye patted the dirt covering the shawl until the site appeared the same as the rest of the floor. Standing, she used the sign's edge to draw a tiny X in the wall at shoulder level to the left of the buried packet. "I pray he finds this. I don't dare leave a bigger mark."

Hissing sounds shot through the walls. More dirt fell from the tunnel sides, exposing metal piping embedded close to the ceiling.

Kat leaped to her feet. She grabbed Faye's shoulder and wailed, "It's happening! It's happening! I don't want to die!"

White steam spewed from minuscule openings in the pipe.

Faye grabbed Monica's discarded blanket and yanked Kat farther down the tunnel, away from the X and the buried bundle. Once they reached a turn, she pulled her friend to the floor and hugged her tightly. "Just think, Kat. We rescued Monica. Perhaps she will be able to help free all the slaves, and no more cities will perish."

The vapor drifted lazily along the tunnel, filling the space above their heads. Faye fought the panic rising in her chest. She had to be brave for Kat during these last moments of their lives.

"But it's too late for us, for our families." Kat shook violently.

Gas clouded Faye's vision. Holding her breath, she blinked back her own tears. Maybe it would be better to stop fighting, to just sink into death's embrace.

"Faye," Kat moaned. "I can't see."

Faye inhaled deeply. Darkness crept into the corners of her eyes. "Neither can I." Fear finally overwhelmed her, and she wept. "Oh, God of our songs, save us now!"

Blindness took over. She struggled for a last breath, but it never came.

CHAPTER 2

FOUR YEARS LATER

Iain shoved his foot into a leather boot. The slave council had no right to say whom Monica had to meet. But they never let a father decide, especially not an adoptive father. If he didn't do what the council dictated, they would take her away and do what they wished. Reporting the secret council to the Nobles wasn't an option.

Iain retrieved a messenger bag from beneath his bed and slung the strap over his head. Grogginess tugged at his eyelids. He shook it off. Why had he been so tired these past few days?

The odor of sweaty bodies filled the room. Some of the slaves slept with their bed curtains open. Even this early in the morning, the heat felt oppressive. The long room hummed with steady breathing. A child's shout broke the drone.

Someone hushed him. "It's only a nightmare."

Curtains parted around other bunks as slaves readied for the day. Two little girls lay asleep on the hardwood floor. Another girl, a blonde in her early teens, shook them awake and said something Iain couldn't hear over the soft murmurings in the room.

A tall man one bunk down yawned and stretched. Iain studied his face, a newcomer transferred just this week. What was his name? Francis?

Iain shook his head. If he could stay in the dorms more than a few minutes every day, he might get a chance to know everyone. Monica always talked about the goings-on of their dorm mates, but he never kept them straight. She knew everyone and everything about them. Emmilah said Monica would often listen to the older women's stories, enraptured by the far-off lands and miracles they spoke of.

The curtain around the upper bunk parted, and a little girl poked her head out. She blinked and rubbed her eyes. "Are you still going to work? Even with the . . ."

Iain smiled at Monica as he snapped on his metal bracelet. "You know I have to." He extended his arms to her. She tumbled out of bed and into his embrace. Iain smoothed her brown curls back from her eyes. "You have to do your chores and pretend today's no different from any other." He set her on the ground and pulled her metal box out from under the bottom bunk. Emmilah usually helped her get ready for the day, but she worked the early shift this morning.

Monica crouched beside the box, picking through the few dingy garments. "I want you to go with me." After selecting a brown dress and knee pads from the pile, Monica stood. "I don't want to go by myself. I don't want things to be different."

Iain knelt and looked her in the eye. "Are you scared?"

Wrapping her arms around herself, she swayed from side to side. "No."

Iain raised an eyebrow.

She turned her head. "Maybe."

He smiled. "Just maybe?"

Rocking on the balls of her feet, she sighed loudly. "I don't want to be *seen*. They're not like us. Maisy says that they know when one of us is in a room and sometimes they spy on us." She squirmed. Her eyes suddenly lit up, and she dropped her dress on the floor. "I forgot to show you!"

"Show me?" Iain asked.

"Yes!" Monica scrambled up her bedpost and crawled into her sleeping quarters.

"I have to go, Monica. I'll be behind schedule." He crossed his arms. Monica wouldn't be ready for any assignment from the council. She was too distractible.

Monica pulled a piece of red paper from a cubbyhole at the head of her bed. "See?" The paper unfolded in her hands and became a row of connected hearts. "Momma helped me make it last night after my lessons. I wanted to show you then, but you didn't get back until really late."

His chip sent a short jolt down his spine. The first warning was always the easiest to handle. He forced a smile. "That's great, honey, but we really do have to get going."

The murmurings of the others grew louder as they prepared to leave for their own assignments.

She folded the paper and jumped into his arms. "It's for you."

Iain set her on her feet. "For me?" Jabbing pains shot through his skull. He winced as he accepted the paper. "Thanks. That's really sweet."

A small boy crawled out of the bunk beside them and dropped to the floor. He jumped up and joined the flow of traffic to the room's exit.

"You're welcome." Monica slipped her dress over her gray camisole and shorts before strapping on her knee pads.

Iain tucked the hearts into his messenger bag. "You'd better get going. I know I need to." He rubbed the nape of his neck, feeling the raised bump covered by short hairs, a constant reminder of his slavery.

"Your chip hurts again?"

"Yes, and the pain's getting worse."

Monica fingered a leather cord around her neck. "Mine is humming, too." She strapped on her own bracelet. "It does it more since I got my new jobs."

Iain yanked the curtains closed around Monica's bed, hiding all the beads and paper decorations she had hung from the ceiling. "Come on."

Monica skipped to the end of the room, weaving through the other slaves who moved about the tight dorm hall. She paused and knelt right in front of a petite woman, blocking her path, and adjusted a slipping knee pad. Iain darted forward and pulled her out of the way.

Turning red, Monica whispered, "Sorry."

Iain gave the woman an apologetic nod. She just shrugged and continued on her way. Every worker looked out for everyone else. There was no time to be mad at a child's mistake.

At the far end of the hall, he snatched their meal packets from the shelf embedded in the wall. Just one breakfast remained in the alcove, with the number *3497198* printed clearly on the top.

Monica pointed at the lone bundle. "Dinner tasted funny, and Allen got sick. He's in the infirmary now."

"Really?" He handed her the package with *61894091* written across the top. "I hope he's okay." He ushered her out the door, following the crowd. "You'll have to eat on the run."

She wolfed down the brown bar of condensed nutrients faster than one would think possible for such a tiny girl. Her thin, short frame made her look more like a sickly five-year-old than her real age.

Shaking his head, Iain guided her down the main staircase. Her chip said she was a slave, but her defined cheekbones and delicate features gave away her Noble heritage. Though the other slaves thought her a risk, they put up with her for the time being. He quickly silenced anyone who grumbled about her presence. But they were right—if she were caught outside the slaves' halls, the Nobles would know she wasn't a regular wall slave as soon as they spotted her.

Ever since he whisked her away from an early death just four years ago, every life in his dorm had hung in the balance. Noble birth couldn't save her then, and it would certainly kill her now.

"Daddy," Monica whimpered, "you're hurting me."

He loosened his hold on her shoulder. "I'm sorry."

They trooped down the stairs after the others. Monica stayed close to her father's side. The crowd thinned as men, women, and children ducked into tiny side halls, entering the walls of the Nobles' rooms, heading for their own work.

Monica stopped beside a dimly lit passage leading deeper into the Nobles' house. Mounted on a hill, a mile-long palace stood in the middle of the drab city. Here, the Nobles could relax above the millions of peasants while slaves skulked through the walls keeping the palace running.

She shivered. "I don't want to meet him by myself. I just want to do my work and go back to the dorm. Then you can read to me. Momma said she found a new book in the trash."

Iain knelt in front of her. "I wish I could go with you, but you have to go alone. If you don't meet this man, we'll . . ." He sighed. How could he make her understand how important she could be to all of the oppressed in the world? "We'll never get to be free. They have more information about the paper. Remember how important it is to find it?"

Her teeth chattered. "I don't care about being free. I want things to be normal. I've looked for the paper enough." Tears filled her eyes. "I don't want to be seen. What if they kill me? I don't want sparks to come out of my eyes." Shuddering, she laid her head on Iain's shoulder.

Pain lanced his brain, but he pushed it away. Comforting Monica was more important right now. He would gladly take a thousand shocks if it would help his little girl.

"They can't get you, Monica." Iain wrapped her in a tight embrace.

She sniffed. "But they spy on us; Maisy said so."

A boy carrying an empty basket trotted by. He raised an eyebrow at the two but said nothing.

Iain nodded at him and waited until he passed. Lowering his voice, he offered a comforting smile. "Don't worry about what Maisy tells you. The Nobles have better things to do than spy on us. They ignore us unless we get in their way. Besides, you aren't like the rest of us, and you should always keep that in mind." He put his hands on her shoulders and held her at arm's length. "They can't get you unless they catch you." He touched her ear lightly. "So be quick to hear, quick to run, and they'll never get you."

She tried not to smile, but a grin broke through. "But . . ." The light fell from her eyes, and tears glittered on her lashes. "Masha wasn't quick enough, was she?"

The pain in Iain's head grew, and another throb, this one of sorrow, pulsed in his heart. He choked. "No, honey. They didn't get Masha. Not like that. She was sick." Gulping, he stood. "Let's go."

Monica wiped her eyes and pointed at the passage on her right. "We're here already. I have to clean a hall before I scrub the Small Dining Room floor." Monica stepped into the narrow corridor. "I'll try to be brave." She looked over her shoulder at him.

He grinned. "That's my girl. Don't worry. Everything will be fine."

She skipped away, disappearing into the darkness.

Iain adjusted his bag strap and jogged down the stairs. The pain in his head eased, and his stomach rumbled, reminding him of his breakfast. He unwrapped the dry food bar and shoved it into his mouth.

The meal stuck to the roof of his mouth, and it took a minute to swallow fully. It tasted strange again today—tangy and sour. Maybe a new cook had been assigned to the slaves' kitchen. At least the bar filled his stomach. No one went hungry, like people did before the Council of Eight came into power over two hundred years ago. The memories of the lean times were kept alive only through the Nobles' stories and history books.

If food supplies grew short and not everyone could be fed, some slaves would be killed, and that would solve the Nobles' problem until the population grew again. After taking a swig from the water bottle in his bag, he dodged past a group of toddlers and their caretaker sitting on the steps. He hustled down the stairs two at a time. If only he could go with Monica to the meeting—but she had to do it without him, as much as he hated the idea. There was no way for him to follow her into the house without getting in trouble.

A blue light blinked on his wristband. He tapped the two-inch monitor in the band's center. Named and numbered coordinates appeared on the screen: *East Tunnel 75, Cantral to Cillineese.* Touching the monitor again, Iain frowned. This wasn't a place he'd ever been assigned before.

The creaking steps led him down to the palace's lower levels and into the underground passages. Dirt walls now surrounded him instead of wooden planks as in the upper stories. They smelled wet and musty, but they were comforting and familiar. The tunnels never betrayed a man like his fellow messengers would.

A woman lugging a laundry basket piled high with rumpled garments passed him on the narrow steps. Though she pressed herself against the wall, her shoulder brushed his. She looked like a ghost wafting up the stairs; her tiny frame seemed to float by, and her thin black hair and pasty white skin only added to the image.

Iain ached to help her with her burden, but that would get them both in trouble. Her assignment must have been unusual already, bringing her so far down the stairs, and she wouldn't want the computer to take any more notice of her.

His chip prodded the back of his head, and he continued on. The trip from the dorm to the messenger tunnels always seemed to take the longest time, even when he had miles to run and hundreds of messages to deliver.

The stairs ended abruptly in front of three closed doors. He opened the one on the left, heading away from the palace.

Iain stopped in front of a steel box embedded in the dirt wall just outside. He pushed the hinged flap and retrieved four foot-long plastic cylinders from the recess. If all went well, perhaps he could get the tubes delivered and reach the coordinates before Monica met the man from the slaves' council. The coordinates were probably a cylinder transfer point. The couriers often had to do relays for messages traveling long distances.

Taking off at a swift jog, he mentally mapped his route. Beetles scurried away from his pounding feet. Bugs were always skittering around the passages. Miles of tunnels zigzagged beneath Cantral to the outlying cities, and he had to keep them memorized. If a messenger were to get lost in the tunnels, it was unlikely he would find his way out again. The maps were outdated, and some of the old passageways had been filled in.

He located the coordinates on his mental image of the labyrinth. East Tunnel 75 was just a quarter mile from the Council Palace, and from there the cylinders had to be taken to Cillineese.

He shuddered. That city was barely getting back on its feet, even with the government's mandatory relocation laws.

Every bit of land must be utilized and cultivated to the maximum, and if a city didn't cooperate, it was wiped out and replaced. The Noble put in charge of running the city-state was supposed to make sure everything went smoothly.

As he ran, Iain replayed Cillineese's extermination in his head. The faces of two terrified slave women came back to him. Half-blinded by pain, he snatched Monica from an untimely death, but he could do nothing to save Faye or her companion.

He shook away the memories. When the Cantral Council decided a city had to go, no one survived—no one according to the official records, that is. Faye hadn't suffered in vain.

Squaring his shoulders, Iain continued his steady pace. His

wristband beeped and his chip vibrated, reminders that he had fallen behind schedule. After a few minutes, he stopped in the middle of the tunnel and rechecked the coordinates. This had to be the place —the coordinates matched. But where was the relay messenger? They always met at an intersection, not the middle of a tunnel.

Soon, another messenger came pelting down the hall. He nodded at Iain but didn't slow his stride. Musty air filled Iain's nose. Drops of water fell from a joint in the piping overhead and splashed into a small puddle on the floor.

Dirt dropped from the packed wall on his right, mixing with the water. He jumped away from the debris. As he scanned the narrow tunnel, pebbles rained from the ceiling. Cantral had no dome, so what could be happening? Was he out-of-bounds? He touched the back of his neck, but his chip stayed quiet, so he must still be on track.

A slab of clay the size of a door swung away from the wall, revealing a narrow passage. A boy stood in the opening. Dark circles surrounded his eyes, and he panted heavily. He beckoned to Iain. "I have to tell you something."

Iain stepped closer. "Who are you?"

"A friend." The boy glanced up and down the tunnel. "Your daughter's in danger if she meets with the slave council's contact." He rubbed his eyes. "The Cantral security team has heard about the slave without a chip."

Iain edged away. It couldn't be a trick, could it? How did this boy get down here? Only the couriers and service slaves traveled these tunnels. He shook his head. "How can you be here? You can't possibly be authorized."

"My father's a trader. I'm allowed within our routes." The boy put a hand to his head. His pallid skin dripped with sweat, despite the cool air trapped in the tunnel. "Our Seen spy turned traitor and lied to our contact in New Reni." He scraped his black hair out of his eyes. "The man your daughter is supposed to meet isn't friends with our council like we thought. He's part of the Cantral security team, and he will kill her."

Iain growled. What if this boy was a liar? Was doubting him worth the risk? Monica could be in trouble. Iain's chip sent a small shock through his system, prodding him to return to his duties. "I have to go. I have more messages to deliver."

"He'll kill her, Iain!" the boy cried. "You have to listen to me! All our plans will fail without her."

Iain raced back down the hall, panic rising in his throat. He had to check on Monica.

He'll kill her. The words echoed through Iain's head with every pounding footfall on the packed clay.

His bag flopped at his side, reminding him of his neglected job. Angry buzzes reverberated through his skull. He pressed a button on his wristband, and the shocks lessened. He could stall the computers for a while by reporting a cave-in, but they would figure out the lie when they sent workers to check the tunnels. He still had to deliver the four cylinders to Cillineese.

Maybe the chip wouldn't kill him for that and for what he was about to do. Reaching the meeting room in time could mean everything.

A man ran past. Iain skidded to a halt and spun around. "Jeco!"

The messenger stopped and trotted back to Iain. "What?" He gritted his teeth. "You're making me late."

Iain snatched the hearts Monica had made for him from his pouch, put them in his pocket, and shoved the bag at Jeco. "Can you run these to the Cillineese depot? I have an emergency." Jeco could be so unpredictable. What if he refused?

Jeco growled and grabbed the satchel. "Whatever it is, you can explain later, but this better not get me in trouble again." He tore down the tunnel and disappeared around a corner.

Iain ran in the opposite direction. The noise in his head changed to a shrill beeping. A yellow light blinked in the corner of the screen on his wristband—the first of a series of warnings before the computers would knock him out.

He bounded up a flight of narrow wooden stairs. The warning would trigger a shock and incapacitate him if he continued too long out-of-bounds. The signal changed to orange as he turned into another passage. The back route would be the safest; the main slaves' stairway would be too crowded.

His shoulders scraped the weathered boards at his sides, a tight fit for a full-grown man. Since only the smallest women and children worked in this part of the palace, minimizing the noise within the hollow walls, the Nobles put up with the whispers and shuffling of feet. To them, slaves were like helpful mice, a tolerable necessity when out of sight, but vile rodents should they ever show themselves.

He squeezed past a ladder bolted to the wall next to one of the higher view ports, a sure sign that children worked hereabout. Since their assignments were kept to the outskirts of the house so they wouldn't get lost among the maze of corridors, the dining room, which lay near the palace's eastern extremity, must be close.

A woman rounded the corner, coming from a side passage. She caught Iain's gaze and froze, her dark eyes wide. "What are you doing here?" she hissed. "You're going to get us all in trouble." She ran back the way she came.

Iain shook off her warning. He had to get Monica out of there. Nothing would happen to the other workers in this area if the two of them could escape without being noticed.

Light filtered into the passage from a metal grate in the wall up ahead. Iain ran to the view port. Monica had described these holes—unfamiliar devices to the messengers. The wall slaves used them to see if it was safe to go into the Nobles' rooms and perform their cleaning duties.

He crouched and peered through the slats. Monica knelt on the dining room's marble floor. She scooted around a heavy chair and under an oak table, dragging a bucket behind her. Brown water sloshed over the sides and splashed on her dress and bare feet. She hummed softly, a tune Emmilah sometimes sang to her.

He sighed. Good, the man hadn't arrived yet.

Gripping a scrub brush in her hands, Monica went to work on one of the floor tiles. The tip of her tongue stuck out as she scrubbed. Her skirt clung to her legs, outlining her knee pads. Iain shook his head. She was so small but did so much, and the computers expected her to get all her chores done no matter what.

Footsteps sounded from far away.

"Monica!" Iain called. This meeting had to be stopped.

Monica jumped up, banging her head on the table. She yelped, dropped the brush, and clutched her head. Groaning, she called, "Who's there?"

Iain grimaced. "It's Daddy," he whispered. "Come here."

She picked up her bucket and scampered to the wall, splashing water all over her clothes. A wooden panel swung open on Iain's right. Monica pushed the bucket through. The dining room door-knob turned, and the door creaked open. Iain slid the bucket out of Monica's way.

She turned and looked over her shoulder. "What's going on? Don't I have to meet our contact?"

"Things have changed." Iain put his hands under her arms, yanked her through, and closed the panel.

"Wait!" someone called.

Monica wriggled away and peered into the view port. "There's a man out there. He looks like a Seen." She tapped his shoulder. "Didn't you want me to talk to him?"

"A Seen?" If this man was really part of the security team, as the boy had said, why was he dressed in a Seen's uniform? Iain nudged Monica. "Scoot over, honey."

"Are you in there?" The person in the dining room paced back and forth, his footsteps echoing in the spacious area. "I haven't much time."

Iain put his eye to the slats. A tall, tanned man in a Seen's black uniform passed by, his hands clasped behind his back. Iain drew away. His head throbbed, and his wristband beeped again. Sweat poured down his face. He couldn't stay conscious much longer. Maybe this was the man Monica was supposed to meet. The council could never gather as a group, and there was little they could tell him about the plans beforehand.

Monica tugged on his sleeve. "Are you okay, Daddy?"

"I can hear you, so please come out," the man in the dining room said. "I need to get back to my duties."

Iain shook his head. He needed to figure this out quickly and keep Monica safe at the same time. "I'll talk to him. You stay here, okay?"

She nodded, her eyes wide. "Okay."

He crawled through the opening and jumped to his feet.

The Seen man stared at him. "Not quite whom I was expecting."

Iain pulled the panel shut. His hands shook. He needed to confirm who this was and quickly, or he would be knocked out before he could get back to the messenger tunnels.

"Are you my contact?" The man looked at the screen on his metal band, his brow wrinkling. "I thought it was someone younger."

A flash of pain brought Iain to his knees, and he grabbed the back of his neck. The computer was giving its final warning.

The man touched his wristband. "This isn't good," he muttered.

The agony subsided little by little until it dissipated completely. Iain shuddered and climbed back to his feet. What kind of Seen had the power to dismiss the computer? "Who are you?"

"My name's Fox." He circled around Iain and pushed on the wall, but it didn't budge. "Present circumstances have me concerned that my meeting has been compromised."

Iain pressed his hands against his sides. Something wasn't right. This person didn't look like any Seen Monica had ever described. He was too tan and stood as though he owned the place.

Fox withdrew a messenger cylinder from a bag at his side. "You're at great risk coming here, a messenger like yourself. Why would you do that?" He scratched his clean-shaven chin. "Unless you were faking pain and recovery, I assume you are not without a chip. Besides, you're much too old."

"I never said I didn't have a chip." Iain leaned toward the wall access. Maybe he could get the slave council's message and return to his duties before anything else happened. He reached for the cylinder. "Is that the message I'm supposed to pick up? My wristband called me here."

"No, this is one I just received. Perhaps your contact has changed. Check again."

Iain glanced at his wristband. "You're right. I'd better leave."

"Stay another moment." Fox popped open one end of the tube and slid out a scroll. "The Seen have been murmuring about a chipless child for some time, and I can only assume the wall slaves have as well."

Iain slid a hand into his pocket and fingered the hearts from Monica. He had to keep her safe. Somehow his chip had been silenced, but there was no telling how long it would stay that way.

"Very interesting news." Fox scanned the page before shoving it back into the container. As he moved his hand, something glittered on his wristband. A diamond? "I need some more information."

A shiver shook Iain's body. Fox had to be a Noble. "You're not a Seen, are you?"

"I never said I was a Seen." Fox smiled, his lips curling up just enough to show white, even teeth. "And you do have a chip. I was able to put off the computers, but they won't listen to me for long. You're a renegade slave who must be dealt with, or so they think."

"You're a Noble." Iain glanced around the room. What was he

supposed to do? Just return to the messenger tunnels and get back to work? Continue a conversation with this man who obviously wasn't who he pretended to be? "I need to go."

"It would be in your best interest to stay, at least for a little while longer." Fox patted his leather shoulder bag. "The more information I can get, the safer you will be. Maybe I can take your cause before the Council of Eight. They are always willing to listen to reason and to the pleas from their people."

Iain gulped. Fox wouldn't let him out of here alive. He was just stalling so he could get more information. The Council of Eight wouldn't really listen to a slave—that was for sure. "What do you want to know?"

"Are the rumors about a chip-less slave true? If so, how can we contact him? It's important that the chip system is fixed. We cannot live without order. The world would soon start to die again." Fox shook his head. "We certainly don't want to lose any lives."

"The system should be done away with completely. There's no way to fix a society that disdains human life." Iain looked Fox in the eye, an action forbidden to all slaves, even the Seen. "The Council would never listen to a slave's word, and they would kill a chip-less person without hesitation."

Fox scowled. "You take liberties with my kindness, messenger. Don't push my limits. According to law, I could have killed you on sight."

Iain lowered his gaze. "I apologize, sir. I have nothing else to say on the matter." Maybe there was a chance he could survive if he handled the situation delicately. Monica needed to get back to her duties, and so did he.

"Good." Fox looked at his wristband again. "Now, answer my questions, and you may yet live. We have good evidence that there is a chip-less slave. The Seen don't get stirred up into spreading rumors over nothing, so you might as well admit it."

Iain shook his head. "Every slave I know has a chip." He studied his worn boots; he couldn't look Fox in the eye again. It was true; every slave he knew did have a chip, though Monica's was not embedded in her skull.

"You traveled to Cillineese on the day of its termination, and you crossed the boundary even though the computer almost terminated you. You must have had some reason to do all that." Fox clenched a fist. "Did you ferry the slave here? Where is he?"

"I didn't bring any chip-less slave here." Keeping his posture relaxed, Iain shrugged. "If there is such a slave, wouldn't he want to stay away from the capital? It seems to me he'd go as far away as he could and live underground. It's what I would want to do."

"I see your point." Fox slapped the messenger tube against his open palm. "Our searches of the slave dorms have come up clean, so we will broaden our horizons and search more cities."

Iain gritted his teeth. The Nobles had searched the dorms? But how did they do that without anyone noticing? His heart skipped a beat. Of course! The past few nights the meals had tasted strange, and he had been so tired. They were drugging the meal bars.

Fox paced back and forth. "We'll continue our searches, and don't worry—we'll find him even without your help. The changes we have planned will make it nearly impossible for him to evade us for much longer." He smirked and slapped Iain on the shoulder. "You've been more helpful than you may realize."

Iain stiffened. Monica always kept her chip on, so she would stay safe from the searches, but what if they physically checked every slave? She had no scar on her neck. "May I return to my duties, sir?"

"Get out of here." Fox waved his hand at the wall. "I have better things to do."

"Thank you, sir." Iain knocked on the wooden panel. When it popped inward, he crawled through the opening.

Monica crouched beside the view port. She stared at him, her green eyes reflecting the bars of light from the view hole. "You're okay?"

He nodded and pushed the door closed. "I'm fine." He hugged her. "Get back to work as soon as he leaves, okay? But be on guard; someone might be watching you."

A beep sounded from the dining room. Iain knelt beside Monica and peeked through the view port. Fox stood in the same spot, his head bowed as he studied his wristband screen. He looked up and stared at the wall, a frown etched in his brow. Iain flinched. Fox couldn't see the view port—it was too well hidden in the wood-work—but his eyes still seemed to bore right through the panel.

Fox sighed deeply and fiddled with his wristband. "This wasn't what I had planned, messenger, but the others have different ideas. They say you've heard too much."

"What does he mean, Daddy?" Monica whispered in Iain's ear. "What's going on?"

"I'm not sure." Iain edged away from the port. What was Fox going to do?

"I'm sorry it has to end this way," Fox called. "I didn't mean for others to be punished, too."

A flash of white-hot pain threw Iain to the floor. He yelled and grabbed the back of his neck.

"Daddy!" Monica screamed, as she clutched his hand. "What's happening?"

Another wave of agony swept over him. "I'm sorry, honey." He squeezed her hand. "I'm so sorry."

She knelt beside him, tears running down her smudged cheeks. "I don't understand."

"Take it off." A shudder ran through him, and his vision grew hazy. "Take off your chip, Monica, now!"

She reached for the cord around her neck. A gasp shook her body, and she doubled over.

"No!" As blackness flooded his vision, he gritted his teeth.

Monica's grip on his hand slackened. She thumped to the floor beside him.

"Monica?" the word barely escaped his lips. His thoughts grew distant. He couldn't concentrate.

Another gasp came from where Monica lay. "It doesn't hurt so much anymore, Daddy. Are you all right?"

He tried to tell his hands to move, but they wouldn't cooperate. Everything went still and cold.

CHAPTER 3

EIGHT YEARS LATER

The itching crawled over her scalp, making her hair feel like a bug-infested jungle. The odor came next, a putrid mix of sweat, dirt, and cleaning fluid. Monica sat up in bed and ran her fingers through her greasy, stringy mop of hair. The clinging residue worked its way onto her hands, making her shudder. She scratched her scalp, but it barely relieved the itching. As always, she couldn't get into the bathing caverns without a chip, and if the council didn't find a new identity for her soon, she'd go crazy.

She plucked an elastic band from behind the bed slats over her head. The occupant above continued to snore, oblivious to Monica's suffering. She tied her matted locks back before pulling the bed curtain open. Swinging her legs over the side of the bed, she kicked her feet, smacking the wood floor. Rubbing her toes against the grain of the boards, she tried to take her mind off how long ago she had last bathed.

Her stomach rumbled. She winced. Hunger pains were almost as common now as being dirty. Was it bad to wish someone would die soon so she could take her place?

The overhead lights flickered on for a second before shutting off once more. Monica sighed. Soon the hustle and bustle of morning preparations would begin, and she would be forced to smell the food the others ate while she had nothing. Even the meal bars were appetizing right now.

Maybe she could beg some crumbs from Maisy, but she had given up a share just the day before. The rations were too closely monitored and each person's calorie intake carefully counted. Maisy needed every bit of her own rations.

A person across the aisle slipped off his bed and crept from the room. In the dim lighting, Monica couldn't make out who it was. He must be headed for the chamber pot in the hall; no one in this dorm could go anywhere else at this hour. Monica scratched her head. At least she didn't need a chip to use the pots. Since they were strategically located in alcoves throughout the halls, guarded by only a curtain, anyone could access them whenever necessary.

The lights turned on. The fluorescent bulbs buzzed loudly. Monica's stomach rolled. The noise always made her shudder, taking her back to days when she had to get up as soon as they turned on and work until they turned off again. Sometimes she fainted and slept on the floor all night. As much as she needed a new assignment, she hoped she would get an easy one this time.

She pulled her feet back onto the mattress and rested her head on her knees. Tuning out her discomfort, she listened while everyone prepared for the day. Now, after a month's practice, she could tell who got out of bed and what they were doing without peeking. A week ago she still had to peek to see if she was right.

A loud thump sounded to her left. That must be Chris, Tris's son. He would be transferred to the fields soon; everybody said so. If a dorm overseer caught sight of him, he'd be declared much too big to stay and work in the house, especially after his most recent growth spurt.

The bed above her own shook, rattling her sleeping quarters.

What was the little boy's name again? He had been reassigned to this dorm only two days ago. Someone brought him in late that night and left him with no possessions other than a piece of paper telling his bed assignment and what part of the house he'd be working in.

She rolled the information around in her head. Ransom. She smiled. Yes, that was his name. Only Maisy had been able to pry it out of him. He wouldn't speak to anyone else.

A burning sensation on her chest ripped Monica out of her thoughts. Wincing, she sat up and rubbed at the irritation. The pain would pass soon; it always did.

Ransom pulled his clothes box out from under their shared bunk and sifted through its contents. He glanced up at her. Monica managed to smile at him. The tops of his ears burned red, and he turned his attention back to his box. He grabbed something from the bottom before shoving it under the bed and scampering toward the door.

Monica sighed and watched the others leave. After the last person disappeared into the stairwell, she stood and wandered over to the meal shelf, a small recess in the wall by the exit.

She rubbed her hand across the smooth, metal surface. Maybe the council would send her a message today. If she could just leave this place and have something to do . . . Even the fruitless searching for the elusive plans, whatever they were, would be better than this. Maybe the council would have a new chip for her, and she could finally get into the bathing caverns and be relieved of this itching.

A tiny piece of paper stuck out of the recess's inner corner. She leaned in to grab the scrap, shifting her weight to her arm.

The metal yielded and sank down an inch. Monica snatched the paper and backed away from the meal area just as the shelf began its descent to the kitchen. A metal door lowered itself over the hole the dumbwaiter left, completely hiding the gap in the wall.

Monica unfolded the paper. In the corner of the scrap, small, neat letters written in ink spelled out *slaves' kitchen* in the Central language. She sighed and shredded the message. At least she knew now that the council wanted her. Sometimes late at night as her stomach growled, she wondered if they even remembered her existence.

She stuffed the paper shreds into her ragged dress pocket. How could she get to the workers' kitchens? And which one did they mean? Every worker knew where the kitchens were—all the meal bars came from there—but no one in this dorm had ever been to them.

The dumbwaiter had already left, and all the doors to the tunnels required identification. Maybe a dorm with a later shift would still have its meal shelf open. She rubbed her scalp. If she missed this meeting, there was no telling when the next would be.

Monica raced out of the dorm room and jogged up a flight of steps to the top floor. Just as she reached the door, a group of people trooped out, making their way down the stairs. Monica dodged past two women and nearly tripped over a small child. As she slipped by, a man scowled at her.

She sneaked to the meal shelf beside the door and watched as the last of the workers retrieved their breakfasts. The smell of the dry meal bars made her stomach rumble again. She pushed away the ache. Maybe she would eat when she met whoever sent the message.

A little boy dashed out last, pulling a shirt on over his head as he ran. Monica closed the door to the dormitory. She scrambled onto the meal shelf just as the door started to descend. Tucking her knees up to her chest, she took a deep breath. The hatch closed, shutting out all light. She exhaled sharply. The dumbwaiter jerked as it sank.

Another shake tossed her to the other side of the metal container. No door protected her from the brick wall. Wind whistled past her face from the opening. As the dumbwaiter reached another dorm level, it rumbled again.

Putting a hand on the side wall, she steadied herself in the middle of the shelf. The darkness seemed to encroach. She rested her head on her knees again. Dim lights always kept the tunnels and dorms lit, even in the early hours of the morning; she never had to be in complete darkness. The council must not have been thinking clearly when they told her to go to the kitchen.

The shelf shuddered to a stop. A door swung open, and Monica tumbled out of the dumbwaiter. A pair of arms caught her, keeping her from hitting the ground. She jerked away, balled her hands into fists, and whirled around.

A short woman stood in front of her, her thin arms folded across her chest, wrinkling her smudged gray dress. She raised one brown eyebrow. "I thought the dumbwaiter sounded more labored today. It shook and creaked like an entire dormitory's worth of meals coming back uneaten." Without another word, she stalked away.

Monica brushed herself off. Was this her contact? Or was she supposed to wait for someone else?

The woman stopped at a steel-covered wall on the opposite side of the room. She turned one of the hundreds of knobs scattered across its surface. Her spidery hands moved around the control panel with lightning speed, turning other knobs and pushing colored buttons.

Monica crept up behind her, her footsteps falling silently on the dirt floor. The woman glanced over her shoulder. She pursed her lips and continued her work, adjusting dials and watching a small monitor near the wall's center. Her shoulder-length hair fell across her eyes.

Monica shifted to the worker's left. "Hello," she whispered.

The woman flinched. "No one's supposed to be down here." She pointed at a chest-high door on the wall to the left. "You can get out that way." She touched something on the video monitor.

"I received a message from here." Monica stared at the screen. Long lines of letters filled the monitor, but they scrolled by too quickly for her to read. "Did you send it?" She looked at the door. A small red light blinked on and off above the knob. "Besides, I can't get out that way unless you open it for me."

"I wasn't the one who sent you the message. I load and unload the meal shelves as directed, that is all." She sighed and gazed at the ceiling. "You need to get out the door if you're trying to meet someone." She turned a dial. "If I open it for you, they'll think I'm trying to get out, and I could get in trouble. I'm only allowed to leave when absolutely necessary. My chip is under close surveillance."

Monica nodded. "I understand, but it's important that I get to where I need to go."

"As important as my life?" The woman's shoulders drooped. "They only put the most troublesome women down here. I've caused problems too many times." She hugged herself and swayed back and forth. "Solitary confinement. No one is supposed to talk to me." The woman stopped her rhythmic motion and dropped her gaze. "I can send you back up the dumbwaiter at lunch time."

Monica sighed. If she didn't get to this meeting, she wouldn't receive her new assignment, and it could be months before she had another chance. Her stomach started to ache again, despite her efforts to ignore the pangs. She could starve to death before that.

She had to convince this woman to open the door for her. "If you didn't put the message in there, then you must have let someone else do it, and they must have been recorded entering the kitchen. You'd have been in trouble for letting someone in."

"There are some allowed in here for supply delivery," the woman snapped. "I let one of the delivery boys put it in there. I wasn't the one who wrote it. You're just going to have to find a way through the door or go back up the dumbwaiter. I'm not going to help any more than that. It's not worth it."

Monica scratched her head. "Are you expecting more deliveries today?"

The woman nodded. "I am. You might be able to sneak out when one arrives." A tear tracked down her cheek. "I don't understand why they're willing to risk so much for you." She slapped a button. The computer beeped loudly. She crouched and arranged her skirt to cover her bare feet and legs. "So much loss of life. And you haven't done anything to shut down the Nobles' system." She hid her face in her hands.

Monica shook her head. She would just have to wait here for a delivery. This worker obviously wasn't going to help. Turning toward the door, Monica tugged on the handle. A buzzer sounded, but the door didn't budge.

"My son died because of you," the woman said.

"What?" Monica whirled around and faced the worker. "When?"

The woman kept her hands over her eyes and rested her elbows on her knees. "When the Nobles killed your father, they also killed everyone in the halls next to the dining room to keep them quiet about something." She rocked back and forth on her heels. "He was so excited to be on a new assignment."

"I'm sorry." Monica turned away. "But that wasn't my fault. I didn't know what was going on." Her heart fluttered. Nausea overwhelmed her. She wasn't more than eight at the time. But she knew something was different that day. She had realized she was going to meet people who would be giving her assignments other than her official jobs, but at the time it was just a foreboding new idea.

Dropping to her knees, Monica watched the woman. Her own head spun with sorrow and guilt. As in every nightmare, her father writhed on the floor beside her in the worker's passage.

She sat and drew her knees to her chest. Her stomach rumbled. A sick, desperate feeling swept over her. "I really didn't know what was going on." Tears filled her eyes. The image of her father's dying moments wouldn't leave. "I couldn't stop it. My father said I would be fine, and I thought *he* would be. There wasn't anything I could do." Gulping in deep breaths, she tried to stop the shaking.

A buzzer sounded. Monica jumped to her feet. She wiped her eyes and crossed her shaking arms over her chest. Her limbs still trembled, and more tears threatened to fall. The alarm went off again.

Monica glanced around the room. "What is that?"

"It means you're in luck." The woman put her hands on the floor and pushed herself up. A joint popped loudly, and she winced. "A delivery is coming in." She wiped the back of her skirt free of dirt. "It's unscheduled. Perhaps a new shipment has arrived." Muttering, she shuffled back to the computer. "Means more work for me."

Monica's eyes burned from crying. She rubbed them, but the grime on her fingers made the pain even worse. Blinking rapidly, she dropped her hands to her sides.

The light above the doorknob turned green, and the door swung open, pushed by the front of a metal cart. A boy held the other end of the trolley piled high with bulging burlap sacks. He dug his toes into the ground, throwing all his weight into his task. Sweat beaded on his pale face and scrawny arms.

Monica grabbed the end holding the door open and tugged the trolley into the room. The door slammed closed just as he stepped from the threshold.

Breathing heavily, he heaved a bag from the top of the pile to the floor. Monica grabbed the next, staggering under its weight. The bag dropped to the ground, and she backed away. Her muscles quivered, and dizziness took over her entire body. She knelt and bowed her head, trying to shake the nausea.

After the boy dropped the third bag, a sack almost as big as himself, he asked, "Are you all right?"

Monica sat up and rubbed her temples. "I haven't eaten in so long. I guess I can't work if I don't eat." She smiled. "I'm sorry I can't help you."

"That's okay!" the boy said. He flexed his tiny arm. "I'm strong, see?" Dirt smudged his pale skin, and his thick brown hair stuck to his forehead. He raised his eyebrows. "Why haven't you eaten, and why are you here? They never assign two to a food-prep room."

The woman put her hands on her hips. "Get back to work, Drake." She scowled and tilted her chin up. "How many new ones this time?"

Drake rolled the last sack to the floor. "Eleven. They're all being assigned to various parts of the house." He turned his too-big wristband around on his arm and looked at the screen. "Two to the top dorm, six to the middle, and three to the lowest."

Monica grabbed the cart and hauled herself up. As she leaned against the handle and took deep breaths, the roaring in her head eased enough for her to speak. "I wasn't assigned here. I need to meet someone."

Drake wiped his hands on his shirt. "Then why would you come here? Only Sophia and slaves assigned to delivery are allowed in, and we don't need to meet you." He squinted. "Wait." His eyes widened, and he took a step back. "You're the chip-less slave, aren't you? My mother used to tell me stories about you."

"Yes." She squared her shoulders. "You know where I'm supposed to go?"

He put a hand on the back of his neck. "No. I wasn't scheduled here until the last minute." Glancing at Sophia, he said, "But you can sneak out of here with me."

Monica let out a long sigh. "Thank you."

Sophia waved her hands at them, shooing them toward the door. "Go on. Leave me to my work. I don't want to get in trouble."

Drake pushed the cart up to the door and gestured to Monica. "I think it'd be best if you rode on the cart. The door doesn't open long enough to get the cart and both of us through."

"All right." Monica climbed on. Her head swimming, she gripped the sides of the trolley tightly.

Drake put his hand on the doorknob, and the light turned green. When he yanked the door open, Monica tightened her hold on the cart's sides and closed her eyes. The wheels bounced on the dirt floor, and the cart jerked forward. The momentum forced her into a tilt to one side, but she stayed in her seat, listening to the kitchen clatter retreat behind her. Then, the door slammed shut, sealing off the sounds.

CHAPTER 4

"You can look now," Drake said.

Monica released her death hold on the cart and opened her eyes. When Drake offered her his hand, she shook her head and climbed down. "Thank you."

"No problem." He grinned. "Anything for the girl who's going to free us all."

Heat rose to Monica's cheeks. "What?"

"That's what my mom used to say." Drake shrugged. He pushed the cart down the tunnel. The wheels squeaked loudly as they bounced along.

Monica jogged to keep up. "I'm not trying to free anyone right now. I just need to find out where to go from here." The itching on her scalp started again with a vengeance. She scratched so fast her fingers grew warm. "I probably smell pretty bad, huh? I can't get into the showers until I get a new chip."

Drake wrinkled his nose. "I hadn't noticed that much." He stopped in the middle of a fork in the tunnel. "There should be a messenger coming this way soon. He might know where you're supposed to go."

"Thank you for your help," Monica called.

He trotted down the left tunnel, pushing his cart ahead. A second later he disappeared into the dimly lit passage.

Footsteps pounded down the right tunnel fork. Monica tensed. This must be the messenger.

A man burst into the main corridor, a small leather bag flopping at his side. He skidded to a halt. "Sorry I'm late." He gasped and bent over, resting his hands on his knees. "I was supposed to meet you at the kitchen, but I didn't get the assignment as planned. I'm not allowed to be here."

"That's okay." Monica relaxed her muscles. At least he had come, and he knew why she was here. "I'm a little late, too. I wasn't sure what to do at first."

The man straightened. "Then our timing is near perfect, but we need to speak quickly; my chip won't let me stay long."

Monica nodded. "I'm listening."

As his breathing calmed, he adjusted his satchel. "I just came from Cillineese. I heard about your new assignment from the head of our council this morning. They've found a new identity for you. You're supposed to go to the west wing's infirmary to pick it up."

"But I don't know how to get to the west wing!" Panic rose in Monica's chest. "I can't even remember ever leaving the east wing. A new identity doesn't do me any good if I can't get to it."

"Calm down. Just take the tunnel I came from, and then the one on the right." Wincing, he shook his head. "I need to go. I hope this new assignment works for you. You obviously need it." The man turned to leave, but a spasm shook his body. He stopped and doubled over.

Monica scampered to his side. "Are you okay?"

"No." Holding up a hand to stop her, he closed his eyes. "Just give me a minute. I'm over a mile away from my assignment."

"Can I help?" She bit her lip. Of course she wanted to get this new assignment as soon as possible, but this man had risked his life to tell her about the chip—the least she could do was make sure he was all right.

He straightened and took a stumbling step down the corridor, one hand pressed on the wall. His body trembled again, but he continued to inch forward.

Monica tiptoed at his side, ready to grab his arm if he fell.

"Just go." He waved her away. "You need your new chip. I can make it back on my own."

"Okay." Monica frowned. If he wouldn't let her help him, what else could she do? She crept down the passage in the direction he had indicated.

The man groaned. Monica looked over her shoulder. He crumpled in a heap on the floor.

She darted to him, knelt at his side, and put a hand on his. "Please, let me help you!"

As he propped himself on his elbows, his arms quivered. "I don't want you to get hurt. You can't do anything for me. Just get out of here."

A shock ran through her fingers. She jerked away. Blue sparks skittered up and down the man's body. As his eyes rolled back in his head, he flopped to the floor. She swallowed a sob and scrambled to her feet. If only she could have helped him!

His body continued to twitch, though he remained silent. Monica grimaced and closed her eyes. The other workers sometimes said prayers over the dead before a team from the furnace came to incinerate the body, but as she tried to recall them, all the words slipped from her mind, like grains of sand in an hourglass.

Tears welling, she knelt again by his body. When the sparks disappeared, she closed his eyelids with a finger. "I'm sorry. I wish it didn't have to be this way."

Sighing, Monica climbed to her feet. There was nothing to do now but continue on to the infirmary. Someone from the furnaces would arrive soon and carry him off. Why did the Nobles have to be so strict, so cruel? They claimed it helped keep order, but was all this death really necessary?

Her father ranted against them while he was alive, and he taught her to fight the system. Everything she did now was for his sake.

She jogged down the path. There wasn't time to be thinking about this. She needed to get her new identity. Maybe she would pass someone who could provide better directions to the infirmary. It wasn't as though there were road signs at each tunnel fork telling her which way to go. The messengers had an easier time knowing where they were, since their chips would zap them if they went even one turn off course. But the same guiding shocks could also kill, if the messengers insisted on staying off the assigned paths.

As she followed the passage, her bare feet made whispering noises on the packed clay. The spacing between the overhead lights widened, leaving long stretches of darkness. As she walked under a clear fixture, the lights flickered off.

Gasping, she put her hand on the wall. The lights would come on again any second. Her fingers clutched a support beam, feeling the grain of wood. At least she had something stable to hold on to.

Something heavy and warm crawled over her foot. Fur brushed her toes. She touched the spot with a hand. Probably just a rat. The lights flashed on again.

She leaned against the wall directly under the brightness. Why did the lights go off? Everything should be kept in perfect order. Someone must be shirking his job.

Monica shuddered and continued on her way. Every time she walked through even the smallest dark patch in the tunnels, it seemed as though the walls were closing in on her. She glanced up and down the passage. The narrow maze of corridors felt like home, but when darkness shrouded them, they became a hideous monster, ready to swallow her—never to be seen again.

She jumped over a puddle in the middle of the floor. Someone once told her that many workers suffered from a phobia and could barely function if they had to leave the dim corridors inside the palace walls for long. A shiver crawled up her spine. The fears were valid. If a worker was caught outside his designated rooms by a Noble, he could be killed on sight.

A tunnel ahead veered to the right while hers kept going straight. Monica stopped at the intersection. Which one did the messenger say to take? They appeared identical with no indication as to which led to the west wing. She pointed at each one, going over in her mind what the messenger had said. Was it the right one? She nodded—that had to be it.

As she shuffled down the passage, her knees quaked, and her stomach growled. Would this journey never end?

Just before the passage took a sharp turn to the left, three doors embedded in the dirt wall came into view, barely visible in the glow of a flickering ceiling light. Running a finger along the metal sign to the right of the leftmost door, she read *West Wing Dorm Stairs*. The middle sign read *West Wing Infirmary*.

The middle doorknob felt cold in her hand. Her thumb fit into a dent in the metal as she twisted the knob. The door swung inward easily, revealing a dim room lined with cots.

Monica crept inside. A woman bent over a bed where a small form lay covered by a thin blanket. Monica passed between two cots and touched her on the shoulder.

The woman jumped and grabbed Monica's wrist. "Who are you? What are you doing here?"

"I was told to come here." The woman's fingernails dug into Monica's skin. She winced. "I didn't mean to startle you."

The woman released her arm. "I'm sorry." She rubbed Monica's wrist between her hands. "Are you ill?"

"No." Monica pulled her arm away. "I'm looking for the next step I'm supposed to take. The council told me to come here."

"Oh. You're the chip-less girl." The woman smiled. "Rueben has been griping about your coming for a day now." Her smile faded. "I only wish . . ."

"Wish what?"

"It's not important now." She brushed a strand of hair from her eyes. "I'm glad we can help you."

"Thank you." Monica looked at the floor. Rueben was griping? Would he be one of the workers who bullied her and only helped if someone did him a favor? Maybe he wouldn't give her the chip unless she ran an errand for him. Her stomach rumbled. Whatever the case, she needed to talk to him. "Where is Rueben?"

"In the corner bed, by the far wall." The woman gestured toward the dark corner where a solitary bed stood by a door.

Monica walked to the bedside. A man lay on the cot, his eyes staring straight up at the ceiling. Wrinkles lined his pockmarked face, and stringy gray hair covered his pillow.

She shivered. Could he be dead? She laid her hand on his blanket. No, his chest was still moving.

Rueben's eyes shifted toward her. Monica flinched.

"I've been waiting for you," he muttered. "About time you made your way here."

Monica knelt on the marred wood floor and steadied her breathing. She couldn't let him know how much he had startled her. "I'm sorry. The messenger was late, and then he . . ." She folded her hands on her knees. This wasn't the time to think about that. "It took me a while to get here."

"I suppose I can't expect any better from someone like you." The man struggled to sit up in the low bed.

"Let me help you." Monica took his hand.

He shook her off and lay back down. "No, never mind." Resting his head on the dirty pillow, he heaved a long sigh. "I wish they would get it over with and kill me. Why make an old man suffer?"

Monica wrinkled her brow. The messenger in the tunnel would gladly have taken this man's place. Who wouldn't want to live? Their lives might be difficult, but what was there after death? The relief promised in hymns sung by old women? Staying alive had always been her primary concern. Her father had told her it was her duty to live so she could find the missing paper and free them. She had always held on to that single purpose every time she lost a chip and faced uncertainty.

"Do you have my assignment?" She tried to make her voice sound monotone to hide the anger and grief welling up inside.

"I do." He clutched a handful of his ragged white shirt in his clawlike fingers. "It's been difficult keeping it alive, too. It will be killed in a few hours if it's not taken to its previous owner's assigned task."

Monica scooted back from the bed and sat on her heels. "Keep it alive?" The scar on her sternum twinged at the memory of being burned by terminated tracking chips. The last time she'd been caught out-of-bounds, the shock had knocked her cold for two days, and she had to wait a month for a new chip to be found. "Is it malfunctioning?"

"No, no. Not malfunctioning." He reached into his shirt and pulled a leather string out from under the stained fabric. A glass vial hung at one end of the cord. The man tapped the cylinder, shaking the piece of metal inside.

Monica leaned forward and took the glass from his hands. She held it up to the flickering ceiling light and peered at the chip. No bigger than a grain of rice, it gleamed in the light. "Are you trying to trick me?"

The man grinned, revealing yellow teeth. "No. Not a trick. That's the new design. Smaller, more efficient, less expensive. Harder to extract and still keep running, too."

"It's so much smaller than all the others." She gripped the vial in her fist. "Whose was this?"

"A luckier slave than I, and it's a good thing I took sick when I did, or you'd never have gotten it." Sighing, he rested his head against the wall. "And now I'm stuck in this infirmary until I kick the bucket or I run out of sick days and I'm forced back to work, well or not."

She draped the cord around her neck and slipped the vial under her dress. "Thank you for helping me. I hope you're better soon."

"I don't," the man grumbled. "I don't want to go back to work. I've worked for sixty years. My time will be up soon anyway."

"Why would you want to give up?" Prickles traveled up and down her legs. Squatting beside the bed must have made them fall asleep. She scratched her head. All the slaves were terminated when they reached sixty-five, but in five years, things might be different. "Five years is a long time."

The man glared at her. "You wouldn't understand." He coughed loudly. "You've never had a chip embedded in your skull, dictating your every move."

Monica bit back a retort. She might not understand how others felt, but none of them could possibly know what she went through, either.

The tingling in her legs forced her to stand, but dizziness threatened to bring her to her knees again. She set her hand on the wall. Blinking, she shook her head and tried to keep her voice steady. "So is there anything special about this chip? You said something about keeping it alive."

"Yes." The man sighed. "To make them more efficient the scientists have managed to get the chip to run off of your own electromagnetic field."

"Electro . . . what?"

Grimacing, he waved a hand. "You wouldn't know what that is, I'm sure. They haven't taught science to any children other than the Nobles for over a hundred years." He pointed at the strap. "Just don't let it get more than a few inches away from your body and you should be fine. Otherwise it will stop working, and we'll have to wait for another person to die so you can have their chip. Who knows? Maybe you'll get mine soon."

Monica clutched her dress, grabbing the vial. "If they haven't taught anyone but the Nobles, then how do *you* know?"

"I was one of the Seen many years ago, tutor to one of their children until I was demoted." He handed her a small scrap of paper. "Here is the previous owner's name and information. She had only a day of sick leave left when she succumbed to her illness. She died yesterday, so if you don't check in to work soon, you'll receive a nasty—"

"I know," Monica said. "Thank you."

Rueben pointed at the door near his bed. "Go that way and be quick about it."

She gripped the paper tightly and nodded at the infirmary nurse who stood near an empty bed. "Thank you for your help."

Tears pooled in the woman's eyes, twinkling in the light. Her lip quivered. "You're welcome. I hope you can use it for a long time. Sasha was such a sweet girl."

Monica rolled the name around in her mind. *Sasha.* Now the chip seemed like something more than a sliver of metal. How could she be happy to receive it? Her survival depended on someone else's tragedy.

She sighed. For the wall workers, that was the way of life. Everyone suffers. Everyone dies.

She stuffed the paper into her pocket and ran out. Little time remained before Sasha would be nothing more than another dead worker, cleared from a computer's memory and forgotten. At least now she wouldn't die in vain.

CHAPTER 5

onica's legs shook as she clambered up a narrow set of stairs. She should have asked for more specific directions, but it had slipped her mind.

She stopped at the top of the first flight. A large doorway revealed a wide, ornate, arched hall leading down the length of the palace's west wing. She looked around. Did she accidentally come out of the workers' halls? She turned to run back to the infirmary.

"You there! Girl!" a woman whispered.

Someone grabbed Monica's dress collar and jerked her to a stop. Monica yanked at the material, relieving the painful pinch.

Her captor turned her around and laid a hand on her shoulder. "What are you doing here?"

Dizziness forced Monica to her knees. "I'm sorry!" As she looked the woman up and down, studying her clean, black dress, her breathing steadied. This woman wasn't a Noble, but she was a Seen, and that was bad enough. "I don't know where I am."

"Ah." The woman helped Monica to her feet. "Were you just transferred here?"

Monica clutched the paper in her pocket. "You could say that. Since Sasha died, they needed a new laborer."

"So the poor girl didn't make it?" The woman shook her head. "Her mother will need to be told if she doesn't know already. They wouldn't even let her stay with her dying child." She walked up the hall, leaving Monica standing on the stairs. "I need to continue my rounds."

She followed the woman through the long marble hall. Was this woman not really a Seen, then? Why would she know about Sasha? The Seen didn't have the same infirmary as the wall workers. "Where am I? Can I get to the dorm stairs from here?"

"This is the hall leading to one of the eight Cantral computers. I'm the guard." The woman twisted her wristband. "I have the authority to kill any unauthorized persons here. And if I don't get you out of here soon, you'll be killed by the automated system. There's a panel nearby leading to the wall slaves' dorm stairs."

Monica sidled away. She couldn't risk losing this identity. Her insides felt raw, as though someone had run her stomach through a cheese grater, a mixture of fear and hunger pains. "Would you show me where it is, please?"

"I'm not a walking directory." The woman nodded at a tall statue of a man reading a book. "The panel is by that. I believe it goes straight to the stairs."

"Thank you." Monica started for the sculpture, then turned. "I'm Monica, by the way."

"Anna." She smiled. "You'd better be on your way before the computer marks you late. I'm surprised you don't feel the effects already."

Monica jogged to the hidden panel and popped it open. She crawled through the space and scrambled up a narrow passage before coming into the wider main stair. She sighed. At least lunch time would arrive soon, and she could take a break.

She passed three doorways and came to a crawl space to her

left just before another stairway led to a higher level in the house. She pulled the paper from her pocket and unrolled it.

The scrap said *Sasha, #71124051, Age eight. West Wing, same assignment as mother.* Monica winced. Just eight years old and now buried in an unmarked grave in the messenger tunnels. She hadn't even stopped working with her mother yet. Monica returned the assignment to her pocket. She couldn't pass as an eight-year-old, but no one in the dorms would be likely to question her.

A young boy scooted out of the crawl space. Cobwebs covered his hair, and a long scrape marked his left arm. He jumped to his feet and dusted himself off.

Monica grimaced. "Is it really that dusty in there?"

"There?" The boy jerked a thumb at the crawl space. "No, lots of people go that way; it's always clean." He sneezed. "I was just in a duct someone's been neglecting." He sneezed again and ran up the stairs, showers of dust raining from his clothes with every step he took.

Monica waved a hand in front of her face, clearing away the clouds of dust. Duct cleaning, one of the dirtiest jobs in the palace. As she imagined the boy crawling through a narrow duct, a haunting memory surfaced. After Iain died, the council swept her away and kept her in hiding for weeks while she recovered from her chip burns. Only recently had they explained the reason. They were waiting for enough time to pass for her pursuer to believe the story they were concocting.

After about a month, they dug a six-year-old girl's body out of the wall where they had kept her after removing her chip. Although not Monica's age, their sizes were a close match. Then a council member dragged the corpse into the ductwork, laid her near a blower fan, and pushed her toward it until the blades chopped into her skull. The resulting wound disguised the chip-removal incision, and they left Monica's old chip next to the body with a cord tied to it.

That very day, a member of the slave council reported an odor coming from the vents, prompting the Nobles to send a duct cleaner to locate the source. The discovery of the body led Fox and his cohorts to believe that the chip-less child had been found, killed as she tried to elude them. Ever since, the hunt for her had ceased, though reports of Fox's lingering suspicions still hung in the air. The slaves had to remain vigilant and keep her survival a secret.

The duct-cleaning boy thumped down the stairs, a wrench in hand.

As he dropped down to enter the crawl space, Monica called, "Excuse me, do you know where Sasha's mother is?"

He pointed his wrench into the opening. "I think she's in one of the dining rooms off this passage."

"Thank you."

He nodded and slipped into the hole.

She took a deep breath. Time to get going. Dropping to all fours, she crept down the passage. The chip resting at the center of her chest stayed calm, but that could just mean she was still on sick leave and not being tracked carefully.

As she advanced, the corridor became narrower. This part of the palace must be older than where she worked before. Workers in the east wing often said they had it better than workers in the other wings. The east wing had been recently renovated, and the halls were now newer and wider with bigger doors into the Nobles' rooms.

Monica ducked under a pull-down ladder leading to an upper story's passageway. A spigot jutted out of the wall a few feet in front of her. Drops of water fell from the spout into a bucket below. She knelt by the faucet and took a drink. Who could tell when she would have another opportunity to quench her thirst?

Footsteps echoed around her. She pinpointed their source—the room on her right. Someone had to be walking in there. If only she knew the people in this wing, she would be able to tell if it was another worker or a Noble.

Rays of light filtered into the workers' passage near an intersection just ahead. It had to be a view port. Monica trotted to the spot and knelt. This could be the dining room. Closing one eye, she pressed her face against the metal slats.

A pale, thin woman sat in a chair in front of a long dining table. Tears coursed down her dirty cheeks, and a sob shook her whole body. She held a small gray disk between two fingers. It slipped from her hand, but a cord around her neck caught the medallion before it fell. She dabbed at her eyes with a corner of her dirty apron.

Monica pulled away and flipped the room viewer shut. Such grief! This must be Sasha's mother.

Monica's fingers brushed against the wall and located the hidden access to the Nobles' room. When she scooted closer to the door, a green light blinked on near her head.

When the door swung out, she crawled through the opening. Latching the door behind her, she squinted at the brightly lit room.

Remnants of rich food had spilled over the edges of the table and soiled the otherwise-gleaming floor. A black can on wheels stood near the table's end, already heaped with plates and cups.

Monica ignored the food. She needed to talk to this woman first. As she walked, her feet barely made any noise on the slick wood. She placed herself a few paces away from the woman, but she didn't seem to notice. She just rose, wiped her eyes, and began stacking plates and scraping food into a second cart full of table scraps.

Could this be someone other than Sasha's mother? The council member of this wing probably had rules just as strict as those of Dristan Allen, the east wing's councilman, so she could be mourning for another reason. Perhaps her husband had been transferred, or her child had fallen ill.

"Ma'am?" Monica whispered.

"What?" The woman swept a large chunk of steak from a plate, scraping the fork along the china surface with a metallic screech.

Monica winced at the sound. "Are you Sasha's mother?"

"Sasha is dead." The woman tossed a plate onto a stack, chipping a piece of the gold edging from the rim.

Monica glanced around. Three sets of double doors reaching the ceiling led out of the dining room. With all the careless noise, someone could come in here at any minute. She grabbed the woman's hand, stopping her from throwing another china plate. "Please, don't!"

"You don't understand." Her shoulders quaking, she dropped the plate on the table and wiped her red-rimmed eyes. "Sasha died yesterday. She was all I had. And they could have saved her."

"I'm so sorry."

The woman screamed at the closed doors. "They could have saved her! But they didn't. It was just the flu, the nurse said." She fell to her knees, her voice now a whisper. "If she had medicine, she'd still be alive."

Kneeling at the woman's side, Monica placed a hand on her shoulder. "Is there anything I can do?"

The woman brushed her away. Her shoulders stiffening, she stood and cleared another plate. "Why are you here anyway?"

"To help you." Monica eyed the food the woman scraped into the bin. Her stomach groaned.

"They only assign children to help with a task like this." The woman yanked the stained tablecloth from the cleared section of the table. "You're too old to be an assistant."

Monica stole to the other side and started stacking dishes. How could she break the news to this woman, that she had assumed Sasha's identity? Every time she received a new chip, she contended with the dead person's relatives, but never a grieving mother. "Don't you want help?"

The woman set her hands on her hips. "This banquet hall seats one hundred fifty people, but it only takes one to clean it, so the Nobles say." She threw her cleaning rag on the table.

"I'm supposed to take over for . . ." Monica gulped. "For Sasha."

The woman's shoulders drooped. "Are they reassigning me, then? You're too old to be my helper."

"No, you're not being reassigned." Monica's stomach churned. How could she explain this? "The computers don't know Sasha's dead. They think that I'm her."

"What?" The woman's eyebrows knit together. "What are you talking about?"

Monica sighed. She might as well tell her. How else would she be able to work with this woman? Would she resent her presence like other workers have? "I don't have a chip of my own."

The woman shook her head. "I have heard rumors of a chip-less child. I often wished it was true, but it's not possible." She pushed a chair up to the table. As she gripped the headrest, her knuckles turned white. "If not for your condition, I'd think you're a spy, but no Noble would allow herself to look like that."

Monica glanced at her filthy brown dress and fingered her stringy, oily hair. It used to be curly, but the dirt and grime weighed it down to bone-straight strands. She grimaced, feeling how filthy she was all over again. "That's part of not having a chip. I can't get into the showers, and the spigots for mop buckets don't let me get enough water."

"All right." The woman rested her arm on the chair, all signs of her tears now gone. "If you don't have a chip, then how are you Sasha's replacement?"

Monica tensed. Could someone really get over such an emotional breakdown so quickly? "I can't let the Nobles find out." Her legs weakening, she put her hands on the table, steadying herself. "They'll kill me."

"They'll kill anyone. We're nothing but dirt to them." The

woman stared into Monica's eyes, a frown creasing her forehead. "You think I would try to talk to a Noble? I'd kill myself first."

Monica searched the room again. "It's a long story, but I'm part of our workers' council. I don't have a chip." She sighed. She could barely recall her escape from Cillineese, only the sensation of being scooped up and tumbling under the closing door. Iain had hugged her tight and whispered something to reassure her, though his exact words didn't survive the years.

"I remember when the rumors about a chip-less slave were rampant." The woman's voice quivered. "Sasha was born around then, when security was tightened so much. They took her from me before I even reached my ninth month, and I didn't see her again until she was nearly two months old." As tears coursed down her cheeks, she set a pair of fingers over her mouth. "So it was your fault that the Nobles upped the security. The rumors are true. I thought you looked like a Noble, but there are so many half Seen, half Noble children, I didn't think much of it."

"It's not my—"

She turned away. "I don't want you working with me. You'll bring me more trouble—though death might be a welcome reprieve—I don't really want to be terminated. I've seen it happen before."

"I'm sorry about Sasha, but I really need this job. I'll starve without it." Monica firmed her voice. "I'm a worker, just like you. I hate what the Nobles do to us, but they do take care of us; there's food for everyone." Her stomach rumbled as if to object.

"I'm a slave," the woman snapped, "so are you. They don't care about us."

Heat crept into Monica's cheeks. She hated the word *slave*. The Nobles gave them all their necessities in exchange for their work. Before the current system was set up hundreds of years ago, the whole world was starving. If she would just follow the rules, she would be able to eat like everyone else. "At least we're fed and clothed."

"I don't have time for useless arguments. There's only about an hour left designated for this room, and the job won't get done if we sit around talking."

Monica snapped to attention. "What do you want me to do?"

The woman pointed at a bin on the table beside a mound of food. "Sort the food to be composted and the food that's to be burned. Anything vegetable or bread goes into the compost."

Monica's stomach rumbled. The food smelled spicy and fresh. In the midst of the debate she had forgotten about the delicacies. The temptation to slip a hunk of bread into her pocket made her fingers twitch.

"Don't even think about it," the woman said, not looking up from her work.

"What?" Monica froze. How could she tell what she was thinking?

"The food. I know you're hungry. I can hear your stomach rumbling from here, but don't eat Nobles' food." The woman cleared the last dish from the long table. "There's a spice in it. It makes you sick if you're not used to eating it. Noble children eat it from birth, so they grow accustomed to it." She fastened a lid on the cart full of food and wheeled it to the wall. "You've lived on a steady diet of meal bars for so long you wouldn't be able to handle it."

Monica sorted the food as quickly as she could. This woman certainly knew how to read her thoughts. Was it something all mothers did? She seemed to remember her mother being able to tell if she had shirked her chores.

"Besides . . ." The woman pulled on an ornate portrait frame. It swung forward to reveal a dumbwaiter. "You'd get fat like the rest of the Nobles and wouldn't be able to fit in the walls anymore."

Monica wiped her fingers on a damp cloth and snapped the lid on the compost bin before pressing a hand to her abdomen. With the fabric clinging to her skin, her hips and ribs protruded. "I don't think that would happen soon."

The woman heaved the food bin onto the dumbwaiter. "I'm Alyssa, by the way."

"Monica." She washed the table in silence. Since a vase of flowers in the table's center had been knocked over and their tiny white petals scattered across the floor, it took a long time to clean everything thoroughly enough to please Alyssa.

Alyssa cleared away the rest of the dishes and the compost and put them in the dumbwaiter, then pushed a button hidden in the carvings on the picture frame. "That's all. Christine takes care of the floors and detail work. We have three bedrooms to clean after lunch."

"All right." Monica handed her the rag. "I really am sorry about Sasha. I know what it's like to lose a family member."

Alyssa opened the wall's access panel. "They say she's in a better place now. The other women keep reminding me of our songs, but I have been doubting them. I just wish I could have been with her and held her hand." As more tears came to her eyes, she crawled into the hole in the wall.

Monica followed and latched the panel behind her. The older women did sing songs about a deity who would help free them. Her mother had told her about him when she was little, but all the stories and prayers the workers whispered among themselves seemed useless.

Once again behind the wall, she rubbed her eyes to adjust to the dimness. When she pulled her hands away, Alyssa was already rounding the corner. Monica started forward but stubbed her toe on the bucket under the spigot. Stifling a yell, she hurried on. She couldn't afford to lose sight of Alyssa. She would get lost for sure.

The passage opened up onto the main stair where Alyssa waited. "Come on, we're going to be late." She scurried up the steps, all signs of her crying gone.

CHAPTER 6

Other women and children popped out of passages lining the stairs and flocked up the main staircase. Monica pressed herself against the wall and tried to keep up with Alyssa.

The flow of people stopped, apparently blocked by something higher up. Maybe someone had fallen.

Standing on tiptoes, Monica peered over the shoulder of the sweaty man in front of her. The smell of his perspiration permeated the crowded stairway. Alyssa stood just a few steps ahead.

Two small boys ran into Alyssa's legs as they tried to squeeze through the crowd. She grabbed their shoulders and steadied them. They darted away, one chasing the other up the steps, ducking under people's elbows.

As the crowd started moving again, Monica fell into step with the others, and Alyssa dropped back and joined her. Monica felt the urge to grab Alyssa's hand. There were so many people around, and she didn't know anyone. "I think there are more people in this wing than in my old one," she whispered. "I don't ever remember it being this crowded."

"Really?" Alyssa led Monica into a dorm on their right. "Dristan is supposed to have more power in the Council than Reynolds. I would have thought he'd have more slaves."

Monica shrugged. "I never pay attention to their politics." She surveyed the room in one quick glance. The usual curtained bunk beds lined the walls, and women and children loitered around the beds, munching on their tasteless meals.

"They're your politics, too." Alyssa handed Monica a meal bar with the number *71124051* printed across the front. "We would get better treatment if a Noble who cared about people were put on the Council of Eight."

"Thank you." Monica took the bar and unwrapped the paper coating. She folded it neatly before slipping it into her pocket.

Alyssa nodded toward the beds. "Come, I'll show you Sasha's bunk." Her shoulders and hands shook, as if she were trying to hold back her emotions.

Monica finished the dense bar in seconds. She licked her fingers, though they lacked any residue. Her stomach stopped growling, but she ached for something more substantial.

She followed Alyssa to the far end of the room. A small girl ran between them with another child in hot pursuit.

"This is it." Alyssa fingered a brown paper flower chain clipped to a bottom bunk's curtain. "She loved flowers."

"The ones I've seen in the Nobles' vases are lovely."

"She used to take some of the discarded houseplants and try to revive them, but it never worked." Tears welled in Alyssa's eyes. "It's so hard thinking about her, knowing she's gone forever."

Get-well cards littered the off-white bedsheets. The drab paper from the meal bars didn't look very cheery, but they had nothing else to make their notes out of. Monica bent to pick one up, but Alyssa scooped them into her arms.

"I want to keep them," she muttered. "Everyone loved Sasha."

Monica nodded and touched the flowers hanging from the curtain. "Will you please leave these?"

"Why do you care?" Alyssa folded the cards into a neat stack. "They're just brown paper."

"I've always liked flowers, and my mother would never let me take any from the Nobles' rooms." She shrugged. Alyssa probably thought she was silly for taking interest in such a childish thing. Double-checking to make sure no one was eavesdropping, she lowered her voice. "I've seen flowers in the ground before. I can still remember their smell and soft petals, but I haven't been outside the palace or tunnels since I came here."

"Fine." Alyssa laid the cards on the top bunk across the aisle. "But once you leave I want them back."

The words *once you leave* echoed in Monica's mind. She hoped to keep this identity for a long time. The workers' council hadn't mentioned any new missions for her. Besides, she had to keep this chip close—there was no way for her to go on missions to Cillineese anymore. "I guess I'll go ahead and take them off now, then." She unclipped bits of metal holding the paper chain to the curtain. "I don't want to risk messing them up."

Alyssa placed the flowers on her bed alongside the cards. "We need to go now." She fiddled with her wristband.

"Where did Sasha's wristband go?" Monica asked. Without a work band she wouldn't know where she was supposed to be.

"The infirmary nurse gave it to me when Sasha got sick. I was supposed to return it for recycling if she . . ." Alyssa ducked into her bed and retrieved the metal bracelet from a cubbyhole, her eyes tear-filled once more. "I suppose you need it."

Monica clipped the gray band over her wrist. The child-sized bracelet clung tightly to her skin. She tapped the touch screen, activating it. A digital map of the west wing zoomed into view, a green dot in the upper corner indicating her position. Words just big enough to read scrolled across the screen: *Family Dorm. Next Assignment — Bedroom #13.*

She smiled at Alyssa. "Thank you. This will be very helpful. The last one I had didn't show nearly as much information."

"They upgraded our system. The Nobles think it will make us work more efficiently." Alyssa headed for the exit, her shoulders tense. "Come on. We have work to do."

***

Her feet dragging with every step, Monica thumped down the stairs, barely able to keep going. She needed a bath badly, though, and if she didn't get it now she would have to wait until tomorrow evening, and she would be just as tired then.

The stairway dimmed, indicating the night shift would start soon. Her wristband read: *11:00 PM — Main Slave Stairs*. Alyssa said the workers could be anywhere in the dorms or bath caverns until midnight, but only those on night shift were allowed down the side halls to the Nobles' rooms. Why would anyone want to go into the rooms while off duty? Who had energy for exploring anyway?

A brown-haired little girl skipped up from behind. She passed Monica in a few bounds, taking the stairs two at a time, her curls bouncing at her neck. She turned and looked at Monica. "Are you okay?" she whispered.

"I will be eventually." Monica smiled. She used to have that much energy, too, when she had three square meals a day. Maybe it would come back now that she could eat again. "Are you heading to the baths?"

"Yep!" She took Monica's hand and gripped her fingers tightly. "You're new, aren't you? I didn't know new people were coming. We haven't gotten anyone new in our dorm lately. Which one are you in? Are there any more people coming?"

"You sure ask a lot of questions," Monica said. Maisy would have liked this girl. She loved taking care of the younger children.

A pang of sorrow stabbed Monica's heart. She probably

wouldn't get to see her best friend for a long time to come. She hadn't even remembered to say good-bye.

"Momma says the same thing." The girl swung their clasped hands back and forth. "So is there anyone else? I like meeting new people."

"No, I think I'm the only one."

The stairs ended at a wood-paneled wall. Monica stopped. Did they miss a turn?

"Are we going the right way?" she asked.

"Yep." The girl dug her fingernails into a crevice in the wood and pulled a hidden door ajar. A green light flashed on above the opening. "It was added on after the palace was built. It confuses all the new people. Sometimes it's fun to trick the new kids."

The door swung out, making them take a step back. A red light passed over them, scanning their chips and bodies, a measure the Nobles installed when they were searching for her years ago and never disabled once they thought she was dead.

Monica followed the girl into the narrow tunnel. They walked single file for a few feet before it widened enough for them to walk side by side again.

"You're sure you're the only new person?" Disappointment laced the girl's words. "There aren't any new kids?"

"I didn't come in a regular shipment with the others. I'm from the east wing." Monica ducked at a low place in the tunnel. "My name is Monica."

"I'm Amber." The girl took Monica's hand again.

When they came to a fork in the tunnel, Amber steered her into the right-hand passage. "I've been lonely ever since Sasha got sick. She was the only one who would play with me. I'm with my mom in another dorm, but we all share the same bath cavern, so I got to see her then. I was hoping some new kids would come this time and be in my dorm."

Monica nodded, only half listening. "What's down the other passage?"

Amber giggled. "We're not allowed down there, of course. That's the men's bath." She pointed ahead into the darkness. "We're almost to ours."

"Ah." Monica's cheeks flushed hot. She definitely didn't want to go near the men's bath again. Two identities ago, she was given an older man's chip, and it had been quite a challenge to sneak in there when no one else was around.

The sound of splashing echoed down the hall, bouncing off the walls.

"The floors are tiled ahead, so it gets kind of slippery." Amber tugged a pair of socks from a pocket in her dress. "I like to bring socks so I don't fall." She paused and pushed her feet into the knitted material.

Monica wiggled her dirt-covered toes. "I don't have anything other than this dress."

"That's okay." Amber skipped up to a sliding door and placed her hand on the wood. "Once winter comes you'll get some warmer clothes. It gets really cold here."

She struggled to push the door open. Monica lent a hand, sliding it easily. The noise of shouting children increased.

Amber grinned at Monica. "This is the only place we can be loud. They never hear us down here." She ran off and joined the other children running around on a bathing pool shore.

Monica clutched the necklace holding her chip and crossed the room to a less-crowded part of the pool. The bathing cavern echoed with voices. A couple of women stared at her as they bathed and whispered among themselves.

Could they possibly know who she was? Her fame seemed to be contained to the east wing. At least none of them would dare report her if they did find out, unless some of the women here were among the Seen. They probably had their own bath, though, like they did in the east wing.

She found a bar of brown soap on a shelf by the wall and waded into the warm spring water. Soapsuds drifted around from other people's baths. Slipping off her dress, she sank into the water up to her chin. She scrubbed her dress with the soap and used it as a washcloth.

The water soaked through all her pores and soothed her tight muscles. She threw her dress on shore and placed the slimy soap beside it, then dove beneath the water's surface. The muscle weakness of moments ago washed away like the spring water that drained into the underground river.

Monica resurfaced near a slowly turning waterwheel that ushered the stream to its exit. Water splashed among its paddles and churned the pool to a foamy froth. Could the river lead outside— maybe to the fields where the farmers labored?

Children played on the shore close to the wheel. A toddler pushed another child toward the wheel and laughed, but one of the women quickly grabbed the offender and smacked her bare backside. Her scolding words echoed through the cavern but were lost among all the indecipherable chatter.

Monica treaded water and floated out to the middle of the pool. She tried to touch the rocky bottom, but her toes couldn't reach. Sticking her chin in the air, she dog-paddled back to shore.

She slipped her soaking dress back on and headed out of the bath cavern, sure everyone was staring at her. Her clothes stuck to her legs and chest, making it uncomfortable to walk, but she didn't have a towel like everyone else did. As she started to climb the stairs back to the dorm, someone tugged on her arm.

"Monica?"

She spun around. A redheaded girl wrapped in a thin towel looked up at her, smiling.

"What?" She gave her a blank stare in return. Why would this stranger know her name?

The girl's smile fell. "It's me, Amber. Where are you going?" She held her dress in one hand and swung it in circles.

"Back to the dorm. I can use my blanket to dry off." Monica crossed her arms and shivered as she climbed the stairs. "Are you done with your bath already?"

"Sure. We have to be quick."

Monica stopped and stared at Amber's almost-dry hair. "Was your hair really that dirty before?"

"Yep." Amber pulled her towel tighter. "My job is kind of dusty. I get to climb through the ductworks and clean them. It's fun, but it makes me cough sometimes." She skipped up the stairs ahead of Monica. "I bet you could have had the towels and stuff of whoever had your bunk last."

"I don't know." Monica's legs ached, though the water had eased the soreness some. "I took Sasha's bed. Her mother is kind of protective of her things."

Amber licked her lips. "Have you talked to her yet?"

"Yes." Monica reached her dorm door. "I worked with her earlier today. She was nice enough."

"Oh. That's good." Amber nodded. "I need to go." She climbed up the stairs to the next floor and turned the corner.

Monica entered her new dorm. Men and women milled about, some helping their children change their clothes, others sliding boxes from under beds. A group of women clustered around Alyssa's bunk, whispering among themselves. Monica hurried past them, crawled into her bed, and pulled the curtains closed. The tension in her muscles eased. As she tugged her dress over her head, it dripped on the bedsheets. Now naked and shivering, she snatched her blanket and wrapped it around her body up to her shoulders.

The voices outside her fabric tent rose and fell in waves. Alyssa's voice peaked above the others. "She's here to replace Sasha. No, she's not part of a new shipment." Someone asked another question, but the words scattered in the hum of conversation.

Monica pushed her dress through the curtain and spread it out on the floor. Lying down, she closed her eyes. Her wristband still pinched her skin, but she left it on. She would need it to wake her up on time in the morning.

As she lay there, she tried to familiarize herself with the noises. No one sounded like the people in her old dorm. The family dorms had men and older boys as well as women and children.

Voices and phrases assaulted her ears. "Did you get to see them?"

Another voice across the room piped up, "Mommy, look!"

A whisper crept across from the other bunk. "I just got another assignment. They better give me extra rations for this heavy lifting."

Monica pulled her pillow out of her cubbyhole and covered her head. The noises faded away, but her keen ears still detected people shuffling around the room. Louder footsteps triggered a twitch, part of the survival reflexes she had developed over the years.

As sleep drifted over her, someone walked up to her bed. Monica sat up straight.

A woman's silhouette showed through the curtains but disappeared from view as the lights dimmed. The floor creaked. Someone knelt beside her bed and laid her head against it. Quiet sobs shook her mattress.

Monica reached to open the curtains but pulled away. If Alyssa was mourning her daughter, she would want to be alone. She didn't seem to be the type to seek comfort from anyone.

Shivers ran down Monica's spine. Wrapping her blanket more tightly around her bare shoulders, she silently lay back down.

Thoughts of her own lost family tumbled into her mind. She experienced Alyssa's sadness from the other side—a child losing her parents. Tears came to her eyes. She didn't just lose her parents. In a way, she lost them twice.

A hiccup forced its way up her throat. If she didn't stop this flood of emotions, she would be crying just as hard as the woman leaning on her bed.

Before her daddy died, he sometimes talked about her first mother and father, the two she could barely remember. Joel and Rose, he said their names were.

Whenever she thought about their names, the scent of a rich perfume came to mind—a faint memory she couldn't quite grasp.

Alyssa coughed, and the crying stopped. As Monica held back sobs of her own, her chest ached. When her mother was taken away to the fields, did she experience such grief? Did all mothers weep with such passion and then swallow their sobs when duty called?

Monica pressed her lips together. She lost her adopted mother and father in the same day, just as she lost her birth parents. Memories of her adoptive parents washed to the forefront of her mind—the silky feel of Emmilah's golden hair between her fingers and the way Iain would pat her on the head when she did a job right.

A tear squeezed through her clenched eyelid and rolled down her cheek. Two slaves risked their lives for one little girl whom they had never met, and they completely accepted her as their own. They even had a chip for her so she could survive in hiding.

As sobs shook her chest, she put her pillow over her face. Only the littlest children cried for no reason. All of this happened so long ago, she should forget it. She couldn't change the past.

Despite her mental protests, the tears kept coming. A girl needed her parents. How wonderful it would be to live with them again.

A cool hand took hold of Monica's warm one. She tensed, the crying startled out of her. Dropping the pillow, she stared at the chapped fingers holding her own. Alyssa must have heard her. Her cheeks flushed hot, and she pulled away, yanking her blankets up to her neck.

"Crying isn't something to be ashamed of, Monica," Alyssa whispered, her voice cracking. "When they told me Sasha was dead, I didn't believe it at first. Today was the first time I let myself cry. Trust me. It helps."

"You lost Sasha only yesterday." Monica sat up and wrapped her blankets around her shoulders. "My parents died years ago." She opened the curtain an inch.

"You never get over the loss of a loved one." The buzzing lights overhead barely illuminated Alyssa's tear-tracked face. "When my husband was transferred, it was as if he were dead. I knew I would never see him again, but . . ." She smiled. "He managed to send me this to let me know he was okay." She reached under her dress collar and pulled out a smooth metal disk. As it rotated on its leather cord, it reflected the light, throwing round flashes of brilliance into Monica's bed. "He was sent to work in the Cillineese furnaces." A sigh caught in her throat. "He didn't even know Sasha got sick."

Monica reached out and took Alyssa's hand again, clasping the medallion between their palms. "I'm sorry."

Alyssa gripped Monica's hand tightly. "You should get some sleep. We have other things to worry about in the morning." She released Monica's fingers and drew the curtain closed. Squeaking floorboards signaled Alyssa's slow return to her own bed.

Monica laid her palm against her cheek. The squeeze from the woman's rough, calloused hand still lingered—firm, yet filled with solace, a mother's comforting touch.

Closing her eyes, Monica drifted toward sleep. Tomorrow held more work, and the Nobles would have no mercy on sleepy slaves.

CHAPTER 7

"Hurry up!" Alyssa crossed the dorm room and headed down the stairs. "Your breakfast is on your bed."

Monica snatched up the bar and squeezed past a child sitting in the aisle between the bunks. Scrambling after Alyssa and wolfing down her meal, she dodged in and out among the other workers making their way to their own assignments.

As she tried to avoid a woman helping a child to his feet, her damp dress twisted around her legs, making her skid.

Alyssa caught her wrist with a strong grip that sent a tingle through Monica's arm.

"Are you all right?" Alyssa asked as she let go.

"Yes. Thank you."

"Be more careful." Alyssa continued, descending deeper beneath ground level.

Monica followed, more slowly this time. The stairway grew dimmer, indicating that not many slaves traveled here for work duty. She tapped her wristband. Digital words floated across the screen: *Same Assignment as Mother — Excess Laundry.*

The stairs came to a dead end at the bath cave entrance. Alyssa turned to the left and pushed on the wall. When a doorway opened, she grabbed Monica and pulled her into a dark room.

Blinking, Monica stumbled and leaned against the back wall.

"Just wait a second," Alyssa said.

The floor shifted. The entire world bounced, then dropped.

Monica shrieked and grabbed Alyssa's arm. "I can't see anything!"

"Just wait!" Alyssa growled. "You're acting like a baby."

Monica's teeth chattered. As the darkness pressed around her on all sides, they continued plunging farther and farther. How much deeper could they go?

The room shuddered to a stop, throwing Monica to the floor. As a door opened in front of them, light flooded the room.

Alyssa helped Monica to her feet, making tsking noises with her tongue. "You act like you've never been in an elevator before."

"We don't have any in the east wing," Monica muttered. She tried to keep her voice from shaking. "We have dumbwaiters, but they're tiny, and I've only been in one once. I wasn't expecting the floor to move!"

Alyssa shook her head. "It's too far of a walk for the laundry to be brought up by stairs. The Nobles are cruel, but they are usually efficient, at least when it comes to their food and clothing."

When they stepped out of the elevator, the door closed behind them. In this new passage, bright lights shone from the ceiling all the way to a glass door at the end. Fog completely covered the glass, and beads of condensation rolled down the length of the pane.

Alyssa marched forward. "There's a meeting going on this week. All the head rulers of the city-states are gathering here for their yearly assembly."

"They should all just mind their own business and stay in their own cities."

Alyssa pushed the door open, and they stepped into a room

filled with clouds of white steam. "And you should pay more attention to the city you live in." She shut the door. "There are a lot of things people should do but don't."

A woman bent over a pool of boiling water. She pushed at floating bundles of clothes with a long wooden paddle.

"Nastya?" Alyssa called.

Nastya looked up and laid the paddle on the pool's raised stone edge. Droplets of steam covered her hair and face. She wiped her forehead with the back of her hand, but sweat continued pouring. "Alyssa? What are you doing here?" Her voice sounded weary and worn, as if all the life had been washed away like the dirt from the laundry.

"We're your backup." Sweat beaded on Alyssa's upper lip.

"I have Camry and Shannon here and Shannon's kid." Nastya picked up her paddle and stirred the clothing in the pool. "I don't need any more help."

"The other city-state council members started arriving yesterday. Didn't you get more laundry?"

Nastya nodded. "I noticed. Just wasn't sure if the trend would continue." Pushing wayward strands of gray hair from her eyes, she snorted. "They never tell us what's going on—just to get everything done."

"Typical." Alyssa picked up a paddle leaning against the whitewashed wall. "What can I do?"

Nastya waved at the cloud of steam behind her. "There's a vat that needs to be filled back there. When the water starts boiling, call me. Keep the coals hot."

"Right." Alyssa disappeared into the steam.

Monica stared at her feet. Only one person would need to do that job. Did Nastya even realize she was here?

A small girl staggered out of the whiteness, swaying back and forth as she carried a pile of blue clothes stacked to her chin. She stepped on the cuff of a trailing sleeve and pitched forward, falling flat on her face. The clothes flew everywhere and scattered across the floor. She scrambled to her feet and darted every which way, snatching up the pieces of clothing.

"Careless girl!" Nastya aimed a kick at the girl, but she dodged. "You're lucky those are still dirty. If they weren't, you'd have to clean them all again yourself."

The girl made a face at Nastya's back and finished picking up the laundry.

"I know what you're doing, child." Nastya growled. "Being impudent doesn't help anything."

Monica cleared her throat. Her tongue cleaved to the roof of her mouth. How could anyone stand to work in this environment?

"Why are you here?" Nastya poked the end of the paddle at Monica, tapping her in the stomach. Red water dripped down the front of Monica's dress.

"I … I came with Alyssa," she said, taking a step back. "I'm supposed to be working here, too."

Nastya turned on her heel and faced the pool once more. "Fine. Go on. Follow the useless child over there. She'll show you how to sort the laundry."

The girl ran to the far side of the room and dumped her load in a pool of boiling water that Alyssa now stirred. The girl then skipped back to Nastya's side and tugged on Monica's hand. "Come on. We have to hurry or Nastya gets even snappier." She led the way to a table that ran the length of the room. Clothes had fallen from the wooden surface and lay stacked high on the floor. Square holes gaped in the ceiling above the table, a red sock hanging from one of the openings.

The girl clambered up onto the waist-high table and snatched the offending garment. "Here's where we sort everything." She sat on the edge and dangled her feet over the side. "I'm Sam, by the way. What's your name?"

"Monica." She poked a chest-high stack of clothes with her foot. "You guys do all of this?"

"We do all of the west wing laundry. Even yours." Sam jumped down, dragged a wicker basket out from under a pile, and dumped the dirty clothes. "If you find something red, put it in here." She tossed the sock into the basket.

"How long did it take to accumulate?"

"About half of yesterday and today." Grinning, Sam held up a blue dress shirt. "This wouldn't go in the basket." She tossed it to the side and started digging through the piles with fervor. Rich, embroidered clothing flew behind her, and when she tossed a shirt over her shoulder, sequins scattered.

"So Nastya thought I'd need help learning this?" Monica crouched by a pile that came up to her head and yanked on a red robe buried in the middle.

"She's mean." A bundle of rumpled clothing fell through one of the holes, and Sam ducked out of the way. "This is the most fun job, though. Everything else is really hot."

Monica wiped sweat from her forehead. The droplets kept forming and rolling down her cheeks and nose. At this rate, she'd be dehydrated in just a few minutes. Sighing, she tugged the robe the rest of the way out. "This isn't really hot?" she asked under her breath.

"Nope, and it smells nice in here, too." Sam tossed an armload of red garments into the basket. "My mom and Camry are working in the other room on our laundry. And that *really* smells bad."

Monica fingered a hole in the robe's sleeve. As she slid her hand through, stitches pulled away from the fabric, and the sleeve fell off. She widened her eyes and dropped the robe. "Will I get in trouble for that?"

Sam slid out from a pile of clothing. A white shirt stayed on her head, making a floppy hat. She snatched the robe and read a small tag sewn in its seam. "No." She pointed at a strange symbol on the tag. "If it's under a certain value it doesn't get repaired. We can even keep some of the garments if we want."

"They throw away something like this just for a missing sleeve?" Monica rubbed the silk, then slid the sleeve on. As the slippery fabric caressed her skin, the hairs on her arm stood on end. "What does that symbol mean, anyway?" She leaned forward to get a closer look. "My father taught me to read, but I don't recognize that."

"We use them in the laundry." Sam bundled up the robe and threw it across the room. The garment landed in a heap beside one of the stone washing pools. "I only know the pricing ones."

Nastya shouted from across the room, "Get back to work, girls. We're behind as it is!"

Sam lowered her voice. "Nastya knows every single one of them. People's names and everything."

Monica sorted clothing more rapidly, separating other colors into their own piles. "Why'd you throw the robe away? I thought you said we could keep it."

Raising an eyebrow, Sam laughed. "You want to keep that? No one would wear it!"

"Why not?"

"Because. It's red. Too noticeable for a wall slave to wear." As another pile of clothes fell down a chute, Sam ducked under the table. "And it's long-sleeved. Too hot for us laundry workers."

A large jacket smacked Monica in the face. Yanking it off, she exclaimed, "How many clothes do these people wear in a day?"

"A half dozen outfits or so." Sam snatched the jacket from Monica and turned it over in her hands. She fingered a large stain on the lapel and poked a finger through a hole above a front pocket. "We can keep this one, though." She held up the long brown jacket in front of Monica's stained, rumpled dress. "You want it? It looks like it'd go down to your knees."

"Don't you want it?" Monica went back to her sorting.

"No. It's too big for me. Besides, I have as many clothes as I want." Sam folded it up and tucked it farther under the table. "Since you're a new transfer you must need some new clothes, right?"

Nastya appeared beside them, a huge paddle in her hand. "Do I need to separate you two?"

"No ma'am!" Sam grinned from her place under the table. "We're working our little tails off." She giggled and hid behind a pile of clothing.

"Worthless child," Nastya muttered.

Monica bowed her head and separated colors even faster than before.

"Is there a problem?" Alyssa walked up beside Nastya, hands on her hips and breathing heavily.

Nastya glared at Monica, then shook her head. "I think they'll be fine now. Sam tries to distract the new people from their work. She needs more discipline."

"I see." Alyssa shot a sharp look at Monica. "The faster the work is caught up, the sooner we go to another assignment."

Monica pursed her lips. If she kept quiet maybe they would leave. The heat made her head swim, and while Sam's chatter was a welcome distraction, she needed to keep about her work.

When she looked up again, the two women were gone. She glanced at the jacket. It could come in handy in these winter months. The walls were sometimes so cold the mop water froze in the buckets, but right now it was hard to think about anything other than the roasting temperatures in the wash room.

CHAPTER 8

"**N**ow you know what real work is," Alyssa said as she guided Monica into the elevator.

Monica groaned. Her shoulders throbbed. Her fingers twitched and cramped around the jacket. Her dress stuck to her frame like a second skin.

The elevator door slid shut, sealing off the light. The darkness stung her eyes and made her shiver, but she ached too badly to react. "Are we done for the day now?" Monica moaned.

As the door swung open into the upper floor, new light streamed in. Alyssa snorted and dragged Monica by her arm. "It's time for you to stop being babied. All your months without work have made you soft."

"I'm not soft," Monica growled. Her parched throat stinging, she immediately regretted her retort.

Alyssa stopped next to a water spout at a passage intersection. She filled one of two dippers hanging on the faucet and drank.

Monica cupped the other dipper in her hands and guzzled the

cool water. It soothed her throat and coated her thirsty tongue, spilling down her chin to her already-soaked clothes and mixing with sweat and laundry room condensation.

Pushing the ladle away, she gasped for breath. "Do they get used to working in there?"

Alyssa dipped herself another drink. "I assume so." She pulled at her dress collar, peeling the wet fabric away from her skin. "I definitely don't relish doing all this again tomorrow."

"Tomorrow?" Monica dropped the jacket, leaned against the wall, and slid to the floor. "And we still have more to do today?" She covered her face with her hands. "How do you know this will be our assignment tomorrow?"

Alyssa picked up the jacket and held it up to the light. "So you found something new to wear?"

Monica wanted to snatch it back, but she let her hands rest at her sides. "Yes." She licked her lips. "How do you know about tomorrow's assignment?"

"Because the computer prefers to assign the same people to the same jobs, and the other Nobles will still be here tomorrow morning." She tossed the jacket onto Monica's knees and offered her a hand up. "The slave council will probably want to see you this evening, if you can manage to get back to the east wing."

Monica took her hand and scrambled to her feet. Her head swam, and her vision grew fuzzy. "How do you know?"

"Just a guess."

Monica laid a hand on her forehead. Blood throbbed through her veins, magnifying every beat of her heart. "It doesn't matter. This chip won't let me go, and I can't take it off."

"You can't? Why not?" Alyssa looked at her wristband. "Explain on the way to lunch." She pushed Monica up the stairs. "Hurry."

Her head still aching, Monica picked up her pace. Maybe some food would help.

"So what's this about Sasha's chip?" Alyssa jogged alongside. She kept an easy stride and breathed normally as they clopped up the stairs.

Gulping, Monica paused. "It's a new design, apparently. Newer than any of the others I've had, anyway." Her head started spinning, so she continued, her breath coming in short gasps.

"What good are you, then, if this chip makes you just like us?" Alyssa hurried on, leaving Monica alone in the passage.

Monica shook her head. What good *was* she? Maybe the slave council could tell her, but she had to find a way to get to them first. This chip had provided food and a bath, but it also sealed her in a new kind of prison.

The vial resting on her chest vibrated, reminding her of the schedule she had to keep. If she arrived late for lunch she wouldn't get anything until dinner.

When she reached the dorm, the other women and children were already gathered, eating their meager meals. Alyssa mingled in the middle of a crowd of women. Her eyes looked puffy, as if she had been crying again.

Monica picked up the sole remaining meal packet on the dumbwaiter. She ate at her bed, resting on its edge. Nearby, some children played a card game with pieces of meal wrappers. They made wagers with small crumbs from their meal bars until a woman scolded them.

One of the children scooped up the crumbs and stuffed them into his pocket, then dashed out of the room, chased by two other little boys.

Monica shook her head. How could anyone gamble away food? Ever since she lost her first chip, she had known hunger for weeks at a time. The council would find her a new chip, but then they would hear a rumor about where the paper from Joel lay and send her off on another unsuccessful search for it, killing her chip when she stepped out of the previous owner's bounds. Then she would need a new chip again. The never-ending cycle was maddening but crucial. The paper had to be found, and no one else could freely look for it.

The boys ran back into the room, two holding the third captive. They marched him up to a man sitting on a bunk and started whispering fervently.

Monica rested her chin on her hand and watched the scene. Should she bother to get to know the others this time? She tried so hard in the last dorm but left them after less than a month. Still, she might stay here longer. It would be good to make new friends.

She fiddled with the vial hanging from her neck. If she didn't get any more paper-search assignments, she could be here until a regular rotation, and that would be a year or two from now.

At a corner of the room, two girls about Monica's age conversed. They glanced at her, then looked away. Monica crumpled the meal wrapper and tossed it into her cubbyhole along with her new jacket. Maybe no one would want to be friends with her. She didn't really blend in. With this chip, she had to stick close to Alyssa, as if she were Alyssa's child. No one would understand her situation.

The other workers started filing out of the room, their chatter dying down. As soon as the workers passed over the door's threshold, they fell completely silent.

When the last person left, Monica joined Alyssa at the exit. "Do you know everyone here?"

Alyssa nodded. "They're the closest thing to family I have. All the women were like Sasha's aunts, and the children were her cousins."

"That must have been wonderful for her."

Smiling, Alyssa nodded. "Sometimes Sasha and the other children would sneak out of the dorm at night as long as they could stand the warnings from the computers. It was sort of a badge of honor if you could last the longest." She clenched her hands into fists. "Sometimes

I regret how many times I scolded her for risking it. The computers are hesitant to kill someone that young. She was fine."

"You were just trying to be a good mother. I'm sure she knew that."

Alyssa stared at Monica for a moment, a tear brimming. "We need to go."

Monica felt like she should comfort this grieving mother in some way, but what could she do? Alyssa resented her for taking Sasha's chip. The poor girl was probably secretly buried in a tunnel floor now, off the record and unrecorded, just so Monica could take her place. She pressed her hands against her sides. Trying to comfort Alyssa probably wouldn't help.

"I thought of a way for you to get to the east wing." Alyssa's words rose barely above a whisper.

Monica turned to her. "Really?" She stumbled on a stair.

Alyssa grabbed her arm. "If I didn't know better, I'd think you'd never been in the slaves' passages before."

"You really thought of something?" Monica regained her footing and shook off Alyssa's hand. "We can't risk much. The chip dies if it can't feed off my electro . . . something or other."

"Electromagnetic field."

"Right." When they turned into a side passage, Monica barely noticed. "If it gets too far away from my body, it'll shut down and we can't get it started again."

"I was thinking I could probably keep it for you." Alyssa stopped at a ladder in the narrow hall. She started climbing the rungs, her voice now muffled. "Since it's a child's chip, it's supposed to be with me all the time anyway."

Monica climbed the ladder after her. Alyssa's skirt flared out, revealing tight shorts underneath. Monica looked down at her own dress and tucked the fabric between her knees as she climbed. Maybe if she went to the laundry room again she could get a pair of discarded shorts to go along with the underwear she had found.

Alyssa disappeared through a hole in the ceiling. She reached down and offered a hand up. Monica grabbed it and pulled herself through to the next level.

"Isn't there another way to get up here?" Monica said as she scooted away from the hole in the floor.

Alyssa slid a wooden trapdoor over the opening and tapped it down tight. "Not to this particular level." She stood, her stomach almost touching the wall, and sidestepped down the passage.

Monica fit her hips between the walls and walked normally. Lack of food provided at least this benefit.

"You might get stuck ahead if you walk like that." Alyssa knit her brow. "This is one of the original levels of the palace. It was actually changed later to help us move about even this much."

When she came to a wall support, Monica sucked in her stomach to wriggle by. "Where are we going?" She let out her breath with the words, making a whooshing noise.

"You'll see soon enough."

Monica rolled her eyes. Another wait-and-see answer. The worker's council was the same way. They seemed to forget she existed at times, as if they could put her on a shelf and bring her down again whenever they needed her. These tasks assigned by her chip took up her time when she could be doing something important. Even fruitless searches for the paper were better than this. Every job she did for the Nobles kept them in power and her in slavery that much longer.

Sometimes, though, the searches proved to be dangerous. On two occasions, her chips died because of boundary transgressions and reported her location. Once, when a furnace room crew arrived to fetch her body for incineration, she barely convinced them not to tell the authorities.

Shuddering, Monica blocked out the discontented thoughts. The other workers probably never had these ponderings. She should try to be normal.

"Thinking deep thoughts?" Alyssa asked as she continued her strange shuffle.

"Not really." Monica eyed her. Why did Alyssa suddenly care about what she was thinking? "I just don't like doing these tasks when I know there's so much more I could be doing for the workers' council."

"It has to be done. You're not exempt."

"I know." Monica hung her head. "I'm sorry."

Alyssa slid into a hallway intersection. The passage perpendicular to theirs widened enough so they could walk side by side.

Breathing more easily now, Monica set her hands on her hips. "So where now?"

"Up this hall. Fortunately it's not far. I don't much like being in this level." She marched onward. "The walls are thinner here, so you need to be quiet."

Monica crept behind, stepping lightly on the wood floor. If these Nobles wanted to get more work out of them, they should let them come out in the open, in the light, not having to worry about being seen or heard by those they served.

The Nobles always argued in the law books that being silent and living in the walls kept the slaves in their place and allowed the Nobles to stay on task. Monica wiped a strand of hair from her eyes. *But we're the ones who are doing all the work.*

Alyssa quickened her pace, forcing Monica to hurry. Her feet slapped against the floorboards, making quiet pattering noises. Let the Nobles think they were hearing rats. They deserved to be disturbed sometimes.

Alyssa stooped in front of a crawl panel with a pull handle at one side. She closed an eye and peered through a thumb-sized, glass-covered hole in the wood.

Crouching beside her, Monica whispered, "What are you looking at?"

"Just checking if the coast is clear." Alyssa gave her a skeptical glance. "Surely you peeked into the rooms when you were on your own assignments."

"Yes, of course!" Monica hissed. "But what kind of view port is that? It's nothing like the others I've seen."

Alyssa shook her hair over her shoulder and slid the panel to the side. "I told you this part is old."

After Alyssa crawled through, Monica followed on hands and knees, focusing on the dim form in front. Why such a condescending reply? She just hadn't seen this before; was there something wrong with that?

They came out into a spacious bedroom. An unmade canopy bed took up the left half, and a lush green carpet covered the floor. Monica stood and wiggled her toes in the softness. "Someone has a nice room." She bounced on the balls of her feet.

"Yes. Now come help make the bed." Alyssa sneaked across the room, passing her hand over a large dresser as she walked by. Rubbing her fingers together, she shook her head. "We're going to have to dust, too."

"Okay." Monica ran up to the bed and, resisting the urge to fling herself on the downy mattress, began tugging at the sheets. Splaying her hands over the crisp, white fabric, she sighed. "Wouldn't it be great to live in a room like this?"

Alyssa yanked a pillowcase off of a pillow. "Not if it meant being a Noble." She threw the case at Monica.

"Hey!" Monica snatched it out of the air. "What—"

"Put it in the laundry chute."

Monica spun on her heel and spied a lamp on a bedside table. She pulled on the lamp's chain, sending a soft glow through the cream-colored shade. A painting depicting a group of dogs chasing a furry red animal hung on the wall above the table.

"Where is the chute?" She held up the pillowcase. "I don't see it."

"Haven't you cleaned a bedroom before?" Alyssa rounded the bed, another case in her hand.

Monica shook her head. "I'm usually given dining rooms and parlors."

Alyssa tapped the wall just below the painting, and a foot-high panel popped open, almost hitting the lamp. "Here, I'll do it." She grabbed the pillowcase from Monica and threw it and hers into the chute. "If you think you can manage it, get new ones from the bottom drawer in the dresser across the room."

Monica scurried to the dresser and yanked open the drawer. Talk about mood swings. One minute this woman was caring, and the next she was being meaner than a bat.

"Monica!" someone hissed.

Monica turned, trying to find the source of the voice.

A woman leaned in the bedroom's doorway. Wearing the black dress uniform of the female Seen workers, she beckoned to Monica.

Alyssa stormed up to the woman, hands on her hips. "What's one of the Seen doing here? Come to gloat over the lowly wall slaves?"

"No." The woman frowned. "I need to give Monica a message."

Alyssa put her arm around Monica's shoulders. "She's new to this wing. How do you know about her?"

"Stop it." Monica slid away from Alyssa. "Let her talk."

CHAPTER 9

"**M**onica." The woman eased into the room and shut the door behind her. "The slave council was able to get a message to me through one of their channels. They have a new lead. They said you would understand what that means."

Monica looked at Alyssa and whispered, "They want me to go back to Cillineese."

The woman nodded, also whispering. "And it's urgent. The council thinks the Nobles might have been able to hear the most recent meeting." Her gaze darted around the room. "They're becoming more aware of us. The rumors about a chip-less girl are resurfacing. You must come at once."

Alyssa pushed Monica toward the woman. "Then go."

Monica snatched the necklace from around her neck and laid it in Alyssa's hands. "Take this, please."

"Just know that if you go, you'll put me behind schedule. I can't finish all the bedrooms and other assignments in time without help." Alyssa draped the chip around her own neck, then went back to work on the bed. "Get out of here. Go rescue the slaves."

The woman took Monica's hand and led her out of the room. They entered a long hall with an arched ceiling. Chandeliers lit the way down the passage, illuminating the gleaming wood floors and ornate paintings.

"We have to be careful," she whispered. "If a Noble catches you here, we're both dead." She broke into a jog, still clutching Monica's hand. "They should all be on lower floors right now, but they could come back to their bedrooms."

"Why can't we go through the workers' halls?" Monica pointed at a wall. "I could be in there, completely safe from being seen."

"Because they're so narrow up here. Didn't you notice?" The woman yanked Monica into a side hall and down a flight of stairs. "Once we get to the next floor, I can get you into the slaves' halls, and you can find other people to let you through the doors requiring chips."

The woman sneaked into the hallway, pressed herself against the wall, and peered around a corner.

Monica followed suit. An archway on the same wall opened into a living room where a dozen men sat in lounge chairs, talking and laughing among themselves. She shoved Monica past the opening and then followed, sashaying by the door.

The woman smiled and nodded to the men. As soon as she slipped by, she took Monica's hand again and broke into a run.

Monica's heart pounded in her chest. For a split second, it seemed as if the woman was going to push her in front of the Nobles and tell them everything. "You're able to walk around in front of them like that?"

"The privilege of being a Seen. It has its disadvantages, too." The woman darted into an empty room, pulling Monica. She knelt by a long couch in the ornate living room and touched one of the gold-colored walls, springing a door open. "Come on. I have to get back to my own work. I have more freedom than most, but I don't have much access to the slaves' halls." She placed her hand flat on the wall. "Take this passage to the stairs and go to the infirmary. The nurse speaks with injured messengers frequently, and she can give you directions from there."

Monica slid into the opening. "Thanks."

She ran down the hall. The hurried trip through the rooms made her head spin. She had heard that the Seen walked around the Nobles all the time, but witnessing it for herself seemed surreal, and coming so close to the Nobles had disoriented her.

Just a few steps ahead, the main workers' stair opened up, and she sprinted the rest of the way. It wasn't very far to the infirmary from here.

***

Monica stopped in the infirmary just long enough to talk to the nurse before dashing up the passage to the east wing. The thought of going back to the city of her birth parents' deaths churned her stomach, but she pressed on, turning up the staircase to the east wing's main workers' stair.

She passed a teenage girl in the tunnel before skidding to a stop. "Maisy?"

The girl turned, gaping. "Monica! I thought you got transferred. I thought I'd never see you again."

Monica hugged Maisy tightly. "I'm sorry I didn't say good-bye!"

"Well, you're back now!" Maisy returned Monica's embrace. As she pulled away, the brow above her gray eyes wrinkled. "Did your other assignment not work out, then?" She played with a lock of her frizzy brown hair, twisting it between two fingers. "Maybe you can get another assignment here."

"Do you have somewhere to be?" Monica asked, touching Maisy's shoulder. "Or can you stay awhile and talk?"

"I'd love to, but I really have to go." She hugged Monica again and dashed off.

Monica grimaced. If only she had more time to spend with her friend. If it weren't for Maisy, she would probably have died while waiting for a new identity.

As she began to run again, her legs ached. She dug her toes into the floor and added a burst of speed, hurtling down the path. Someone would be waiting for her in Cillineese or on the way. A messenger approached from the opposite direction. She caught the runner's eye, but he continued without acknowledging her presence.

The tunnel went on and on, forcing her to slow her pace. Dizziness washed through her head, but she shook it off. *Go rescue the slaves.* The words echoed in her mind. Alyssa made it sound like the day was just around the corner, but all these silly assignments the council sent her on seemed to be of no use. They didn't really know where the piece of paper was. They kept sending her to different places to look, and the searches always proved fruitless. The council knew that the page held information about the Cillineese computers, but exactly what that information might be remained a mystery.

During the long journey, more runners passed by, but none paid her any more mind than the first. Her breath shortening to shallow gasps, she pounded to a halt. A steel door blocked further progress. Why was it shut? The underground doors to the other cities usually stayed open, so the workers could travel unhindered from one place to another. Was Cillineese under close watch again?

She sank to the floor. The cold seeped through her clothes. Now what? As her heart continued a rapid thump, the overhead light dimmed.

The sudden change raised a shudder. What if the light went out? Could she find her way back? And how long should she wait? Maybe this door had been closed and sealed permanently, and experienced travelers knew about another route.

She closed her eyes. She could wait for a while. What choice did she have? If this was really still the way to Cillineese, retracing her steps would be foolish. Someone would come along and tell her what to do—someone had to come.

***

Monica's joints ached with cold. With every minute she stayed on the floor, the pain increased. How long had she been waiting? Three hours? Four?

She clambered to her feet and stepped away from the door. Would a messenger come through soon? What if no one from Cillineese had any personal messages to send out to Cantral today?

Shaking her head, she clenched her fists. That was impossible, of course. The Nobles of the city-states were always sending confidential messages to Cantral. After all, it was the center of the world.

As the seconds ticked by, she drummed her fingers on the door. After a few minutes, her wristband beeped wildly. She cupped her hand around the glowing monitor and squinted at the screen.

Words scrolled across in quick succession. *Twenty Minutes Behind — Wrong Room — Switch Immediately.*

Monica gulped. Had Alyssa gotten behind in her work? Did she really need her help that much for those rooms? Maybe this journey to Cillineese should have been put off.

The door rumbled up into a ceiling pocket. A man ambled through, a full messenger bag at his side. Pausing, he glanced both ways before nodding at Monica, his expression anxious.

She stepped over to the Cillineese side and stood face-to-face with him, the door's former position now between them. "Am I supposed to meet you?"

"Go to your old bedroom. There—" The door slammed against the ground before he could say another word.

"Wait a minute! I don't even know where that is." She slapped the smooth metal surface. Why did everyone assume she remembered everything from her past? She barely remembered her previous life at all, let alone the location of her bedroom.

She kicked at the floor, loosening some dirt. Her watch beeped again. She unclipped the band and slipped it into her pocket. There was nothing she could do for Alyssa right now.

She squinted in the dim light, unable to see the end of the tunnel. In the distance, another messenger jogged her way.

When he arrived, he raised an eyebrow as he placed his palm on the door to the Cantral messenger tunnels and waited for it to lift into the ceiling.

"Stop, please!" she called. "Which way to the dorms?"

The man looked from left to right before answering. "Up the passage, to the right, up the stairs all the way, and to the right again." He disappeared into the tunnel, and the door clanked shut behind him.

Smiling, Monica began a slow jog. He probably didn't get many requests for those directions. Everyone who lived here already knew how to get anywhere in the palace. Her aching feet pounded the floor once more, carrying her on.

When she reached the stairs, she stopped at their base. What good would it do to go to the dorms? No one would know where her room was. Every original resident of Cillineese was dead and had been dead for twelve years. There was no one to ask. If only that messenger had had time to give her more information, but of course the timers on the doors wouldn't allow them to stay open that long.

As she climbed the stairs, her knees protested. Even if no one could tell her, she could check all the bedrooms off of the main workers' stairwell. Maybe something inside one of the rooms would provide a clue.

Memories of stairs flying by raced through her mind. A woman had carried her tightly in her arms while traversing these steps. Whispered words floated through her ears, as though the walls spoke the captions to her memories. *They're closing the dome! You have to go immediately.* The man's haunting voice sounded so clear, as if he followed her up the stairs.

Monica turned and looked over her shoulder. No one followed. A shudder racked her whole body. Could the voice from the past have been her birth father's?

As she continued up the stairs, more voices entered her mind, two women this time, though their words were indecipherable.

Two young girls holding a bucket between them thumped down the steps, interrupting the voices. They stopped in their tracks and stared at her. "Who are you?" They spoke in unison.

Monica stared back at them, now noting their identical features—the same brown eyes and straight blonde hair, as well as matching narrow faces and gray cotton dresses. She rubbed her eyes before replying. "I'm Monica. I'm looking for someone."

The girl on the left giggled. "You're not seeing double."

"Nope." The girl on the right shook her head. "Who are you looking for, anyway? You're not from around here."

"I'm looking for someone who's supposed to meet me." She bit her lip. Could these girls be trusted? Who ever heard of slaves having twins before? She'd seen twins in some Nobles' family portraits, but never anywhere else.

"Meet you?" the girl on the left said. "Are you being transferred here?"

Monica shuddered. Returning briefly to Cillineese with all these resurfacing memories was bad enough, but to be transferred here, to the palace where she once lived as a Noble, would be even worse. "No, I just need to talk to someone, and then I have to go back to Cantral." And she hoped she could find out what was wrong with Alyssa.

"Oh!" the girl on the right exclaimed. "You're from the capital? I've always wanted to go there. Momma says it's so pretty and the gardens are really big and full of fruit trees."

"They might be, but you'd probably never get to see them." Monica took a step back. "How does your mother know that? We're all kept inside. There are specialized gardens, but wall slaves never work them. And once you're sent outside, you never get reassigned."

"Momma used to be a Seen before she was transferred here," the girl said, tilting her nose into the air.

The other girl nudged her. "Tali, you're not supposed to say."

"She's not going to tell anyone." Tali glared at her sister.

"No," Monica said, "I won't tell anyone, but how did your mother—"

They both gasped at the same time. Their eyes widened, and they galloped down the stairs, nearly knocking Monica over.

"We're late." Tali yelled over her shoulder. "Bye!"

Monica stared after them. Obviously they weren't her contacts. She climbed the stairs slowly, peering into each view port she came across. The rooms all had fine furnishings and lavish decorations, though they were void of any people. Crawl spaces and passages went off the stairs here and there and branched away farther into the palace, but traveling down one of them could get her desperately lost.

Footsteps sounded from a passage behind her. She whirled around. A young boy trotted down the stairs in the opposite direction.

"Wait!" Monica ran after him.

The boy stopped, smiling as she drew closer. "Oh! There you are. I waited in your old room as long as I could. I was afraid I would have to tell Graff I wasn't able to find you."

Monica sighed in relief. "Graff? How did you know where—" She shook her head. "Never mind. I assume you're the one I'm supposed to meet."

"Yes." The boy looked her up and down, his eyes narrowing. "The way they talked about you, I thought you'd be an adult."

She shrugged. "Sorry, I can't really help my age. Besides, kids are less noticeable than adults." Her wristband buzzed in her pocket, vibrating against her leg. "What is it you're supposed to tell me? I need to get back to Cantral."

His gaze strayed to her pocket before returning to her face. "You know they're looking for a paper, right?"

She nodded. "But I've searched for it so many other times. We've been looking for years."

"I can fill you in." He rubbed the back of his head. "Can you walk with me while I explain?"

"Yes." She followed him down the stairs.

"All right. I just have to get on track to my next assignment." He turned down a side corridor. "When you were sneaked out of here, your nurse tried to give Iain a paper for the slave council, but he never got it." He stopped abruptly and knelt beside an access panel.

Monica almost fell on top of him. She slapped her hand against the wall to stay upright. "Yeah," she grunted. "My dad drilled the page's importance into me every time I was sent to look for it."

"Shh." He set a finger to his lips and opened the panel. After crawling through the hole, he held the door for Monica. "They have a new lead on where it's hidden. I'll tell you more in a minute."

They entered a long hallway with huge chandeliers hanging at even intervals. The tile floors shone brightly in their light. Monica stared at the golden fixtures. The Nobles said that the world was over-populated and everything had to be controlled or even more people would die. They talked about how the waters and land must be cultivated so not even an inch would be wasted, yet they lived like this. She wiggled her fingers, feeling the rough calluses in her palms. Sometimes she needed to be reminded of why she wanted to risk her life to get rid of this system. Witnessing their hypocrisy was enough.

"Monica?" The boy waved a hand in front of her face.

She jumped to her feet. "Sorry, my mind wandered for a second."

"I'll say it did; you looked really angry, too." He scampered across the hall and knelt by a tall pillar abutting the wall. When he tapped on its base, a square section swung open. "Anyway," he said, lowering his voice to a whisper, "the council has a new idea where to look. Some of the messengers have been working on it as much as they can." He reached up into the pillar, his arm disappearing inside all the way to his shoulder.

"What do you mean they've been working on it?"

"Just a minute." The boy stuck his tongue out as he strained to grab something in the opening.

"Do you need help?"

He shook his head. "I don't know how it got wedged up in here so far." He yanked out a handful of cloths and a can of polish. "The council thinks your maid must have hidden it somewhere on her way from your bedroom to the boundary wall." The boy put the can and rags on the floor and shinnied up the pillar, gripping the marble with his knees and feet. He called over his shoulder, "The messengers have been searching as much as they can, but they're not allowed to loiter around the door to Cantral at all." When he reached the middle of the pillar, he untied a rope attached to a hooked piece of metal embedded in the wall.

"So my death-defying trip to the attic to search through my father's old desk was a waste of my time?"

"Huh?" He looked over his shoulder at her, the rope gripped tightly in one hand. "What did you say?"

"Never mind." Monica put her hands on her hips. What was this kid doing, anyway? "So I'm supposed to search by the door?"

As the boy let the rope slide through his hands, a chandelier inched its way to the floor. He grunted as it descended, his skinny arms bulging. When the dangling crystals touched the tiles with a soft clink, he tied off the excess rope and slid down the pillar. "Yep. There's about ten feet of space in front of the door that the messengers can't hang around long enough to look at carefully."

"It's a tunnel with no hiding places. Wouldn't it only take a moment?"

"No." He rubbed the reddened sides of his knees. "They think she buried it."

"They want me to dig up the tunnel floor?" Monica's eyes widened. There was no telling if the paper would be hidden there at all. It might have been swept up and destroyed when the sweepers went through Cillineese twelve years ago, burning all the corpses of the gassing victims.

"Just ten feet of it." The boy started polishing the ornate metalwork in the chandelier, swiping the cloth over the gold-plated swirls. "Like I said, they already had some of us combing the stairs and landings, all the way up to within several feet of the gate, but we can't be thorough that close to the door."

Monica watched the boy's small fingers weave in and out of the metalwork's tight corners. "Is there anything else I should know before I start digging up the tunnel?"

"Just be thorough." He grinned before adding, "If it's in the floor, it shouldn't be very deep, or it could be in a wall. If she had time to hide it well, it won't be easy to spot." He slid beneath the chandelier and began polishing the underside.

"Thank you. I'd better get going." Monica backed toward the exit panel. "What's your name?"

"Sean." He rolled out from under the chandelier. "And you're welcome. Maybe I'll get something out of it, too, if you manage to find the paper." He crawled back under the fixture and scrubbed at the metal with a vengeance.

"Thanks again, Sean." She scooted through the opening and back into the workers' hall, closing the door behind her. Her stomach rumbled, reminding her how long ago lunch had been. If she could find the buried paper quickly, maybe she could make it back in time for dinner.

CHAPTER 10

Monica trotted down the stairs and ran through the tunnel toward the door to Cantral. Her feet and muscles no longer ached, and she felt lighter on her toes. This could be a turning point in her service for the workers' council. If she found this paper and they shut down the computers, then she wouldn't have to run errands anymore. Everyone would be free to do as they pleased, and she could finally have a normal life.

Glaring at the dirty floor, she ran on. A normal life? It would never happen. Even if the Cillineese computers were shut down, there were still dozens of others, and Cantral had its own monster computer that would have to be dismantled.

She gripped her hands into fists. The council would always need her. She would never be free. They wouldn't be able to find another chip-less puppet to order around. Since the powers-that-be now implanted chips in slaves and Nobles alike at birth, only she could get around the Nobles' security. Tears came to her eyes as she ran. Since she needed a chip to survive, they would pull her marionette strings for years to come.

Her feet slowed. She could just go back to Cantral and forget this mission, but that wasn't a realistic option. Even if the council didn't deserve her cooperation, the children needed help. She couldn't abandon them. Not now. Not ever.

When she reached the metal door leading out of Cillineese, she counted off ten feet from the exit. She spun on her heel and searched the area. Maybe there was something she could use to dig.

A rock lay on the floor near the door, probably dislodged by the frequent opening and closing of the metal slab. She grabbed it, then knelt in the middle of the hall.

With Alyssa holding her chip, no computer could halt her efforts with a shock, and with messengers opening the door now and then, escape back to Cantral lay within reach.

Sitting on her heels, she scratched the surface with the jagged rock. Years of pounding had compressed the floor into packed clay, making it tough to penetrate. Once she loosened an inch or two in a small square, she sifted through the reddish chunks. Finding nothing, she slid closer to the door and tried again, repeating the scratching and sifting in each square. After what seemed like an hour, she had advanced only a foot toward the door.

Her hands and knees ached. Hunger again stabbed her stomach. Even though the computers had no way to stop her, soon her own body would.

Monica stood and stretched. Wiggling her fingers, she walked back and forth from the door to her digging spot. She leaned against a support beam. If only she could see better, maybe she could find a clue somewhere.

The light overhead cast gloomy shadows into the passage corners. She studied the red dirt wall. The workers' council said that when they took chips from the recently dead, they sometimes hid the bodies in the walls. What if she were to come across a skeleton entombed in the clay? She put a finger on the dirt. Of course, no one could linger long enough in this area to bury someone, so she had nothing to fear.

Dirt crumbled away from around her fingernail. Squinting at the area, she cocked her head. A shallow groove marred the wall's surface. It meandered down one inch and then back up, creating a *V*. She brushed more dirt away until two more grooves appeared, making the *V* into an *X*. Was this some symbol left from long ago? Did her nurse sit here and carve the letter into the wall as she waited to die?

Monica sat back down, staring at the once-even floor, looking for any hint that there might be something under the dirt. The letter must mean something. She had to be close.

As she dug into the earth, her fingers twinged. Cillineese's original inhabitants had all been killed twelve years ago. Their bodies were ashes, their lives but memories, yet someone had left that mark for a reason.

Her fingers touched something fibrous. A strand of purple yarn protruded from the soil, a stark contrast to the reddish clay. She chipped at the dirt around the string and uncovered what looked like a crumbling scarf. As she touched the strands of yarn, they crackled, and bits of dirt fell away from the fibers.

Could this be it? No worker would lose her scarf and let it be buried. It must have been put here intentionally. She moved the garment from its grave, laid it on the ground, and began unwrapping the layers. Scraps of paper rested inside, none more than two inches square.

She touched one of the larger pieces with her fingertip, turning it over to reveal neat handwriting on the other side. The script flowed across the piece, ending abruptly at a tear. She tried to read the words, but they weren't in the language of Cantral.

Monica's breaths came in short gasps. She'd finally found it! During all those other missions, she had been looking in the wrong places. Why hadn't they thought of this before? The workers' council had always sent her to more remote locations, places her birth father might have hidden the page, when she should have been looking here all along. Of course Faye had hidden the paper here when she couldn't get it to Iain. She had even left a mark on the wall, hoping someone would find it and know what it meant.

Monica wrapped the paper back in its shroud, blinking at the revelation. The name just popped into her head. Faye was her nurse when she was a child. She smiled to herself. The name and memories of her rescuers had faded over time, and now she had one of them back.

As the gritty dirt rubbed against her tender fingertips, she frowned. What now? Go back and ask Sean what she was supposed to do once she found the paper? Had they expected her to find it? She had never found anything before, so this might be another one of the council's stabs in the dark. Maybe they hadn't planned the next step at all.

She swiped all the loose dirt back into place with her feet and tamped it down. Holding the scarf out in front of her, she walked back to the Cillineese Nobles' palace. The paper bits crackled every time she jarred them, making her wince. Would they ever be able to put the pieces together?

After climbing the stairs, she crept to the hall where she had left Sean. A red light blinked above the access panel, and the door wouldn't budge. She peered through the view port slats. Sean clung to a pillar with his knees like one of the monkeys painted on the Noble children's walls. He tugged on a rope, his pinched face red and sweaty. The chandelier on the floor inched off the ground, creaking and groaning as it rose. Panting heavily, he slid down the pillar a foot. He yelped but held on to the rope.

Monica pushed on the panel again, but it moved no more than before. She needed to get in there and help him! That chandelier weighed ten times as much as he did. She tapped the red light, silently begging it to change to green, but it pulsed as red as ever.

Sean grunted. Monica checked the view port again. After heaving the chandelier a foot off the ground, he gained some slack in the rope and tied it off on the metal hook. He slid down the pillar and lay on the floor, his chest rising and falling rapidly.

While keeping an eye on Sean, she pounded on the panel. He leaped to his feet, his gaze darting back and forth across the room. He swayed and almost fell.

"Sean," Monica whispered. "Sean, it's Monica. Please let me in!"

Laying a hand on his head, he stumbled to the door. The light changed to green. After Monica pushed the panel open, Sean stared at her face-to-face.

"You're back. Did you find it?" He wiped sweat from his brow. "I can't stay long. I gotta finish my work. I'm a little behind schedule."

Monica held out the scarf. "It's in pieces, but I did find it." She looked over Sean's shoulder at the dangling chandelier. "Do you need help with that?"

"I guess so." Sean backed out of the opening and knelt on the floor. "I usually do them all by myself, but I can't seem to get this last one up." He tugged on his shirt collar, flapping the damp fabric. "I think the air system is broken. It's not usually this hot."

She crawled into the hall and closed the panel. The room didn't feel any warmer than usual, but she hadn't been working as hard as he had, and the tunnels were much cooler than the palace anyway.

Sean stumbled over to the pillar and patted the surface. "Have you ever climbed one of these before? It's not very easy."

Monica laid the scarf down and put her hand on the smooth, cool surface. Craning her neck, she peered at the top of the pillar where it reached the ceiling. "It must be at least thirty feet high," she whispered.

"Yep." The boy shifted in place. "But you only have to go half-way up." He looked down the long hall. "We'd better hurry. The council will want to see you, and a Noble might come here soon."

Monica placed her hands on the sides of the pillar and clenched her bare toes against the cool rock surface. She flexed her muscles. This might not be as easy as it looked. Gripping with her knees, she inched her way up.

"You sure you want to do this?" Sean shuffled in place. "I'm not so tired anymore. I can give it another try."

"I'm sure." Grunting, Monica pulled herself up even farther. Her knees scraped on the surface, and her fingertips ached with each inch of progress.

The metal spike penetrating the pillar glistened in the light just a foot above her head. If she reached out, she could probably touch it with her fingers, but that could mean losing her grip.

"Are you okay?" Sean called. "Maybe I should do it."

Monica gritted her teeth and hauled herself the rest of the way. She grasped the spike with both hands. "I got it!" She turned her head and looked down at Sean but immediately regretted the action. Nausea rolled in her stomach. She was so high. If she fell, she'd certainly break something, and that would be the end of her career completing dangerous missions.

"Okay." Sean sounded nervous now. "Just unwrap the rope and pull on it, but keep a good grip with your knees or you'll fall."

Monica wanted to turn to see what he was doing, but it would only make her dizzy again. "I will." Strengthening her hold with her knees, she started unwinding the thick rope. Her thighs and calves complained. Her muscles quivered. Finally, the rope came off the hook. The chandelier's weight jerked on her arms, almost pulling her from the column.

Gasping, she yanked back, throwing as much muscle as she could into the effort. The chandelier slipped a notch, but as she gained control, it inched its way back up.

"That's good!" Sean cried. "Now pull hand over hand. You can use the hook as leverage if you need to."

She tugged on the rope as instructed and heaved the chande-lier toward the ceiling. Fibers bit into the palms of her hands. She labored for breath. How could such a small boy stand doing this so many times?

When the swinging chandelier approached the ceiling, she wrapped the rope around the hook. "Is that right?" she called down to Sean.

"Looks like it."

Monica tied the rope in place and shinnied down the pillar. She collapsed in a heap at the bottom. Laughing, she tried to get to her feet, but her legs felt no firmer than the jelly she sometimes scraped from the Nobles' table. "That's some job you have there."

"Yeah." Sean took her arm and steadied her, though he stood only as high as her elbow. "They allotted me plenty of time to finish when I first started, so I was able to take all day to clean them. Sometimes I had to climb all the way to the top to make sure a Noble didn't see me, though." He grinned at her. "If you thought it made you dizzy just halfway up, you should try going to the top sometime."

Monica's stomach rolled again at the thought. "How'd you know I was dizzy?"

"By the way you were swaying back and forth when you looked down at me." Sean tugged on her arm. "Come on, I need to get to my next job, and I need to find Renin."

"Renin? I've never met him before." After picking up the scarf, Monica slid through the workers' access panel and into the narrow hallway. She scooted down the floor, making room for Sean to climb through.

When he shut the door behind him, the light above the panel flashed red. "He doesn't ever leave Cillineese. He's actually pretty close to being transferred outside." Sean shuddered. "I've heard that field slaves have to work in the sun all day in blazing hot weather. The air is even hotter than the furnaces in the lowest level of the palace."

Monica climbed to her feet and dusted off her dress, the scarf cradled in one arm. "How do you know all this?"

"I worked in the furnace rooms with my dad for a while, but I got transferred out of there after . . ." He blushed. "After I fainted from the heat too many times." He squeezed between Monica and the wall and led the way to the main corridor. "Then I got this job. My dad was afraid I'd get sent outside to the fields."

Monica imagined a steaming furnace and sweaty, shirtless men working around it. To make this strong little boy faint, the heat must have been terrible. Besides her recent laundry experience, the hottest she had ever felt was during long summer nights in the dorms when everyone kept their bed curtains open. Those evenings made her sweat and feel a little uncomfortable but never faint.

Voices issued from an open view port. She lowered her own voice as they scurried past. "Does your dad still work there?"

"I heard that he works on the north side of the palace, but I never see him anymore." His shoulders drooped. "I think my mom's still there, too."

Monica descended the stairs behind him, wishing she could see his expression. Did he miss them? How long ago had he last seen them? The Cillineese Nobles were said to be kinder than the Eight of Cantral, so why would they take such a young boy from his family?

"I miss my parents," Monica whispered. "My mother was sent to the fields when I was eight. I remember her singing me to sleep at bedtime. Her voice was so soft and soothing. I don't think I've slept as well ever since."

"Just hug a wadded towel at night. That's what I do. It's not warm, but it's better than nothing." Sean trotted down more steps and entered the chilly, dirt-floor tunnels under the palace. "Renin works hauling supplies from outside down to the Nobles' kitchens."

"Oh." As they crept deeper into the ground, chills shook Monica's body. "He gets to go outside?"

"Sometimes." Sean pulled farther ahead, now barely visible in the dimness. His voice echoed back to her. "There's a gate that separates the tunnels from the outside, and usually the stuff just gets passed through, and he doesn't go out unless there's a big shipment or something."

Monica sighed. How she wished she could venture into the outside world. Sometimes it seemed that the breeze tickled her skin, and the sun warmed her face, but they were just distant memories, and maybe even figments of her imagination. Iain had said that her father had kept her hidden from sight most of the time. He might never have taken her out into the gardens. She rubbed a hand up and down her arm. The chill in this tunnel seemed worse than ever.

Sean stopped. Monica sidled up to him and peered ahead, but the passage looked just like the tunnel behind them. "What's wrong?"

Putting a hand at the back of his head, Sean grimaced. "This is the very edge of my boundary. I'll get knocked out if I go much farther." He smiled through his pained expression. "Sorry, but you'll have to go on by yourself."

"Don't worry about me. Just tell me which way to go."

He stepped behind her and pointed. "It's really simple. Renin works between the gate farther ahead and the one leading outside. He's told some of us kids stories, so that's how I know. Anyway, just go to the end of this tunnel, turn right, and you'll see a barred gate. You might pass some other workers, but they won't bother you."

"Okay." Turning toward him, Monica licked her lips. "You'd better get back before you're in even more trouble."

"Yeah." Sean saluted her and grinned. "I've always wanted to do that." Adding a wave, he trotted away.

Monica shook her head and continued, following the boy's instructions. After a few minutes, her drab surroundings started blurring together. The support beams, the dirt floor, and the walls all looked the same. Had she gone too far? Or not far enough? Sean had said to turn at the end of the tunnel, but the passage never seemed to end.

Of course the supplies came from the farms—tracts of land situated far from the Cillineese palace—so it made sense that she had to walk a long way, but doubts still lingered. As far as the farms were, they still lay inside the city's walls. Since Sean knew the way only from stories that might have been designed for entertainment, maybe trusting them didn't make sense. Yet, what choice did she have? If she went back, who would tell her what to do?

Still cradling the scarf, Monica caressed the brittle material. At this point, marching onward seemed to be the only option.

CHAPTER 11

The tunnel ended at a dirt wall. Monica halted. What happened? There was supposed to be a turn. She touched the wall on the right, but the dirt didn't budge. Pounding with a fist, she shouted, "Open up!"

Pebbles rained down from the ceiling, but the wall stayed upright and unmoved. Monica sank to the floor. As she suspected, Sean was wrong. The stories must have been untrue, just embellished tales for the children.

Something bumped her thigh. She jumped to her feet. A head-high section of the wall on the right swung out, hinged on a support beam.

A man stood on the other side, an eyebrow raised. "What are you doing here?"

"Are you who I'm looking for?" Monica blurted. She eyed the man up and down. He wore a tight, sleeveless shirt and knee-length pants.

The man scowled at her. "Could be. Are you Monica?"

"I am." With the scarf still cradled in one hand, she set the other on her hip.

He motioned for her to come inside. When she complied, he shut the door.

"How do they do that?" She pointed at the seamless wall where the door had been. "How can they get the dirt to stay in that shape?"

"It's not important." As the man jogged down the hall, he called, "Come on. I have to get back to work. You're lucky I was close enough to hear you yell."

Monica ran after him, taking two steps for every one of his. As they continued, her legs cramped, forcing her to halt. Bending over, she massaged a calf muscle. The pain was worse than awful.

The man hurried back and shook her shoulder. "Come on, little girl, surely you can run farther than this!"

She brushed his hand off. "Not at your speed!"

He grabbed her wrist and jerked her along. "If you were in as much pain as I am standing here, then perhaps you'd understand."

As they galloped, she tried to wrench her arm away, but his fingers held fast. "Can't I catch up to you later?"

"No," he growled. He hardly sounded winded at all.

Monica's foot caught in a divot. She plunged forward, but the man yanked her to her feet.

She coughed as she spoke. "Can we . . . please . . . slow down?"

He gave no answer. He just kept running. She willed her feet to move in time with his, but he was too fast. Every several steps, she stumbled, forcing him to jerk her up and drag her until her feet again caught up with the pace. With the ceiling lights getting dimmer and farther apart, the spaces between them became like black pits, too dark to see the floor under her feet and the scowling face of the man who dragged her ever onward.

After what seemed like more than a mile, an iron-barred gate appeared in the distance. The man slowed to a fast jog but kept a hold on Monica's wrist. "I will probably have to carry you through the gate. It stays open for only a second."

Monica nodded. "All right." It wasn't really all right, but what choice did she have? At least it would be better than running at top speed.

When they reached the barrier, he swept her up and cradled her like a baby. She folded her arms over the scarf and hugged it close, defying the urge to struggle.

A light above the gate turned green. The bars swung open just enough for the man to pass through before slamming closed again.

When he came to a stop, he set Monica on her feet. "All right. Now that I'm back in my area, what did you find?"

Monica dusted herself off, glad to have her feet on the ground. She glanced around the room—another tunnel, its opposite end blocked by a solid door. If this man decided he wanted to steal the scarf, there'd be no one to stop him. Even if not, she couldn't give it to just anyone. "First you have to confirm who you are."

He held out his wristband. When he pushed a button on the side, his ID number *3498372* flashed across the screen. "My name is Renin. I'm the one who talked to Sean. Satisfied?"

She nodded and handed him the scarf. "I found it buried in the floor in the tunnel heading for Cantral. The paper's inside."

Renin carefully pushed the scarf into a large pocket in his shorts. "I assume it's not intact."

She shook her head. "And I couldn't read the words. It wasn't written in the Cantral language."

He walked to the other end of the corridor. "I'll be able to find someone to read it after it's put back together."

Monica hurried to catch up. "I didn't recognize the writing." As she drew near, she pointed at the purple yarn sticking out of his pocket. "It's in pretty bad shape. Do you really think you'll be able to put it together?"

"I know a Seen who works in the Nobles' library. I think I can get him to do it." He stopped in front of the metal barrier. "And it's probably written in Old Cillineese, the language they had before the termination."

"Old Cillineese? No one's ever mentioned that to me before."

"All the current residents of Cillineese are from the northeast part of the world, from Bacha, including me. The new language is a mix of Bachan and Old Cillineese. Only the scholars bother to learn the old language." Crossing his arms over his chest, he glared at the door. "This delivery is late. It's going to mess up my schedule."

"No one speaks it at all?" A lump formed in her throat. The Nobles were wiping out her entire past.

"Maybe a few slaves here and there who were transferred from Cillineese before it was gassed, but they're so spread out it's probably useless to them. Who knows? Maybe they've all forgotten it."

"Shouldn't I take it to the library for you?" She rubbed her hand up and down her arm, sloughing off loose dirt. "And how am I going to get back to Cantral?"

He put his hand over his pocket. "You probably could take it for me." He looked her in the eye. "If you could find your way to the Cillineese library."

"I don't know where it is, but if you'll give me directions—"

"It might be better to send you through this door to the outside. One of the delivery workers will help you get into the palace and give you directions to the library from there."

"Outside?" Monica bit her lip, trying to hide her excitement. Yet, fear mixed into her emotions. What if she couldn't get into the palace without being seen? "Why can't I go back the way I came?"

"Opening the hidden door requires a chip, and I can't risk going that far from my station again. The computers are only so forgiving before they decide to shock me. No one else uses it until the night shift. You could go that way, if you wanted to sit there until midnight." He withdrew the scarf from his pocket and handed it to her, the scraps of paper still enclosed within its folds. "Whichever way you choose to get to the library, you'll need to give it to Simon the book mender. It would be a month before I could get it there myself."

A rumbling sounded, and the door shook. Renin tensed. "Here we go. You'd better make your decision. The way you came or outside?"

Monica again cradled the scarf in her hands. If she went outside, she could see trees and grass and the sky again, but she might have trouble getting back inside. What if she never got another chance? If she stayed, she would have to sit in the dark for hours by herself, but she would be safe, and maybe she would get the page to Simon more quickly.

The door opened, disappearing into the ceiling. On the other side, a man stood by a wheeled cart full of burlap sacks.

"Too late." Renin picked her up and tossed her through the opening. As she held tightly to the scarf, she flew into the other man's arms. He kicked the cart, making it shoot through to Renin.

"Ask for directions from any slave," Renin called as he caught the cart. "Don't trust any Seen."

The door fell shut.

Monica wriggled to the ground and checked the scarf. Nothing had fallen out. Turning, she nodded at the man. "Thank you."

He backed away. "Where did you come from? It's not every day Renin throws a girl through the door."

"I, uh . . ." Monica pushed the scarf into her pocket. ". . . I came from the passage back there, of course." She stared at the man's skin. Holding her hand out, she compared her porcelain complexion to his brown tones.

The man laughed. "That's what happens to someone who goes outside." He clapped a hand on her shoulder. "I suppose it doesn't matter if you don't tell me why you're here. The computers will track you down eventually."

Monica stepped back. This man acted like he saw stray workers in this passage all the time, but it couldn't be a common occurrence. Any lost worker would be quickly knocked out by his chip.

"They won't find me, and I need to get somewhere." She studied the man's wild brown hair and deep-set eyes. "Where are we?"

He motioned for her to follow. "Come on then, lass." He trudged up the tunnel's slope, not seeming to notice the steep incline.

Monica scrambled after him, the uphill walk making her calves hurt once again.

"We are in the Cillineese supply tunnel." He stopped and tapped a flickering light in the ceiling. "Come on, little thing, you can stay lit."

The light blinked off.

"Agh," the man growled. "Just be impertinent, then." He unscrewed the glass dome covering the light and handed it to Monica. "Hold this."

The hot glass stung her hands. She gritted her teeth, held her skirt out like a bag, and placed the globe inside. "Where do I go from here?"

The man fished in a bag at his side and pulled out a tiny bulb. He replaced the burned-out light in the ceiling and took the dome from Monica. "You still haven't told me who you are." He fixed the glass back into place.

Monica blew on her stinging fingertips. "I don't know who you are, either."

The man crushed the tiny lightbulb between his fingers, making it crumble into dust. "And I'm surprised you haven't felt any effects from being out of your boundaries." He scattered the dust around the floor.

"I don't have any normal boundaries like everyone else." Monica squinted in the dimness, trying to read his face. "Why hasn't the light come back on?"

"What are you, some kind of Noble child thinking you're on an adventure?" The man tapped on the globe, and light flooded their patch of tunnel. He glared down at her, deep lines creasing his cheeks and forehead. "But Renin wouldn't have helped you if you were."

Monica returned his hard stare. She held the look for a few seconds but couldn't help blinking in the light. "I'm on my way to the library. I need to talk to someone there." She rubbed her hands together, and the burning sensation disappeared. "I'm trying to help all of us. I'm a worker just like you."

"Really now?" He tramped up the tunnel, leaving her behind.

"Does this tunnel lead outside?" she called after him.

When he didn't answer, she ran to catch up.

He looked over his shoulder. "You don't look like a slave."

She reached him and trotted alongside, barely keeping up. "What does a slave look like?"

"Someone who doesn't look like you."

She rolled her eyes. This conversation wasn't getting anywhere. "Does this path lead outside? Renin said it did, but last time I followed someone's directions I got a little lost."

"It does." The man stopped and stared at Monica.

She returned the look. When he didn't break his gaze, she crossed her arms over her chest and glared. There was no way she could get away from here without being let out, so she was stuck dealing with this odd fellow. "What?" she snapped. "Why are you looking at me like that?"

"You sure you're not a Noble?" He raised an eyebrow.

"If I were able to live with the Nobles, there's no way you'd find me down here, and I wouldn't be dressed like I am." Monica lifted her chin. "Don't you have a shipment to get or anything? I'd really like to get out of here."

"It doesn't come in for another fifteen minutes." He broke eye contact and tapped on his wristband. "It's a big one. I should be able to get you through."

"Thanks." Monica relaxed and followed the man to the end of the tunnel where a metal door blocked the way out. "I'm Monica, by the way."

"I think I've heard of you, the chip-less girl." The man rested his back against a wall. "My name's Sham."

"Sham?" Monica squinted at him. "That's a stra—"

"It's my name. Do you have a problem with it?"

"No, no problem."

He closed his eyes and sighed loudly. "Fifteen minutes seems like a long time right now."

"Sorry. I didn't exactly choose to be here." Monica sat cross-legged on the floor. "Where have you heard of me? The workers' council has kind of tried to keep everything quiet outside of Cantral."

"They haven't done a very good job then." Sham grunted. "I've heard murmurings about some sort of slave who's supposed to break the Nobles' control. Those started years ago, whisperings about a girl named Monica. They had died down for a while, but they started again recently." He glared at her. "So far, your reputation hasn't made it any easier for the others. They get their chips at birth now, and our security is even tighter. Instead of getting broken, their control's been getting worse every year."

"How is security tighter?"

He pointed at the door. "All of the access doors used to be kept open going from city to city and to the outside, but nowadays they're kept sealed. Cantral suspects Cillineese is the root of the problem. There's talk about wiping it out permanently and just using this area for fields."

Monica dug her thumbnail into the floor's dark clay, chipping out a small dent. "I'm sorry."

"Sorry is an easy excuse. You're old enough to have done something by now."

She clenched a handful of dirt. "But it's not my fault. I didn't ask for this job." She let the clumps of soil fall to the floor. "If I don't do what the workers' council says, they won't help me when I need a new chip, and I'll starve."

"None of us asked to be a slave." As Sham looked her in the eye, his expression softened. "I suppose I'm the one who should apologize. You're here now, and you're doing what you're supposed to do. If you and our council can free us, then it's worth putting up with the tighter measures. As soon as that door opens, we'll send you where you need to go."

CHAPTER 12

Monica pulled her knees to her chest and stared at the door, studying the minuscule scratches on the surface. Her stomach growled. Two meals were not enough to make up for all those she had missed.

She drummed her fingers on the dirt floor. This was turning into a very long fifteen minutes.

"It's almost time," Sham said. "Have a little patience."

She pressed a hand against her stomach, making the bracelet in her pocket shift. She plucked it out and touched the screen. *Reassigned — See Dorm Leader* scrolled across in letters that appeared brighter than usual in the dim tunnel. At least she hadn't lost this chip. If she had, it would have been a new how-quickly-Monica-lost-her-chip record.

She slipped the wristband on, ignoring the painful pinch. Back at Cantral, Alyssa continued helping her dead daughter's replacement, even risking her own safety. And for what gain? A bare hope that this strange girl might stumble her way into aiding the slaves?

"I hope she's okay," Monica whispered.

Sham squinted at her. "You hope who's okay?"

"Someone who was helping me in Cantral." She stared at the words as they continued scrolling across her screen. "I think she got in trouble while I was gone."

"I see." He glared at her, one eyebrow raised again. "You're not going to get me in trouble, are you?"

"I hope not." Monica covered the screen with her hand, hiding the words from view, though they stayed in her mind's eye. "I don't try to get anyone in trouble. The computers are just too smart to trick sometimes."

Sham nodded. "I know what you mean. That's why I never try."

As they sat in silence, Monica's legs started to grow numb. She shivered. Goose bumps rose on her arms. Was it getting colder?

She stood and dusted off the back of her dress. "Do you just sit here in the dark, doing nothing for hours between deliveries?"

"What would you suggest I do?" He scratched his head, rumpling his dirty brown hair. "Tell stories to the walls?"

"I don't know." She shrugged. Sitting here all day would drive her crazy, she was sure of that. What was the purpose of this job other than to feed the fat Nobles' bellies? No, she definitely couldn't stand for this, but Sham had no choice.

"I can't read, and there's no one to talk to." He coughed. "Before today, that is. I'm content with it. I'm thankful it's not field work."

The door rumbled.

"Finally." Sham beckoned to Monica. "Come on. Stick close."

She rushed to his side and pressed herself as close as she could to his arm without touching him.

The metal door rose slowly from the floor, shaking loose dirt from the ceiling as steel ground against steel.

Monica sneezed and covered her face. Sham grabbed her

shoulder and pushed her forward. She stumbled, but he caught her before she could fall. She sneezed again and rubbed her eyes, trying to adjust to the darkness as the dust cleared.

Sham released his death grip on her shoulder. "Sorry about that." He pointed at the closed door behind them. "It only stays open for a moment, and you froze up."

She nodded. "I didn't mean to."

"I didn't think you'd want to be left behind." He meandered up the dark tunnel. "Doing nothing but sitting there until midnight."

Monica picked up her pace, but with his form so dim, she didn't want to collide with him. "Why is it so dark?"

Sham stopped, withdrew something from his bag, and shook it. A round object appeared, glowing green and yellow, brighter with every passing second. "They don't bother lighting the outer tunnels. At one time, all we needed was daylight, but now they keep the doors closed." He tossed the glowing light to Monica.

She caught the ball and held it high. "Thanks." The ball illuminated the tunnel floor and ceiling in a small circle around her body, a stark contrast to the darkness ahead, a black void as far as she could see.

"It's late evening now anyway, and it's winter," Sham said. "The sun goes down early in the day, so even if the doors were open, they wouldn't help much. That's why I carry these around."

A sigh caught in Monica's throat. She had so wanted to see the sunlight. Now being outside would hardly seem any different than staying inside the Nobles' walls in the artificial light. "Where does this tunnel lead?"

Sham trooped on ahead. "Into the back delivery road of the palace, where the traders bring supplies. There's a delivery coming in for the Nobles' and slaves' kitchens."

"Can I get to the library from there?" She trotted behind him, jumping over woody branches jutting out of the wall. "And where are all these plant things coming from?"

"One question at a time, child." He took a sharp turn in the passage. "Yes, you should be able to get to the library."

He kicked at one of the branches. It snapped back and whipped Monica's ankles. Yelping, she dropped to her knees and examined the lacerations in the light of her glowing ball. Dirt flecked the bleeding cuts, and pain burned across the area.

Sham crouched beside her and held out his hand. "Sorry about that." He hauled her to her feet. "These roots are from the trees planted over the tunnels that aren't underneath buildings."

"That explains why I've never dealt with them before." Wincing, she held the ball up again.

Sham pointed ahead. "We're almost to the exit. You'll be able to feel the grass between your toes soon."

Monica stood on tiptoes and held the light higher, but the tunnel seemed as dark as ever.

"I'm falling behind schedule," Sham said as he lengthened his stride, "so hurry up."

Monica ran, grimacing with every step. Blood still dripped down her ankles, but not as quickly as before.

The tunnel ended abruptly at a metal door. "Here we are." Sham pushed up a bar on the door and shoved it open. Sticking his head outside, he looked in both directions. "Where is he?"

Monica inched by him. A cool breeze rippled past, caressing her cheeks and swirling her skirt around her legs. She closed her eyes and breathed deeply. The spicy scent of salt water and greenery met her nose. She inhaled again, taking in the smells that were so different from those in the dank, musty workers' halls.

She spun in a circle. Although the sphere of light barely illuminated the space five feet in front of her, the pale flicker revealed grass poking through the surrounding stones.

"Hurry up and get out of here," Sham said. "Taylor's late. I'm going to be under surveillance if he doesn't show up soon, and you don't need to be around."

"Where do I go? I have no idea where the library is." She looked at the path as it forked in all directions. "I don't know where anything in Cillineese is."

Sham pointed into the darkness. "Go that way. There's a high wall, and a gate is a few hundred feet down from here, hidden in the stonework. The child who opens the access panel should let you in. He can give you more information."

Monica nodded and gave him a thumbs-up. "Got it. Thanks."

Sham waved her off. "Don't use those silly Noble children's gestures with me. Get out of here before you get us both in trouble."

Wheels crunched on gravel.

Monica jumped and ran in the direction Sham had pointed. A sharp rock dug into her foot. She bit her lip and kept running, more pebbles cutting her bare toes.

Moonlight illuminated a wall just ahead, jutting into the dark sky. Smooth bricks lined the top of the stones at intervals, rising higher than the rest of the wall. As she sneaked along the base of the wall, footsteps sounded in the distance.

Monica froze. Where were they coming from? She gulped and held her breath. If a field overseer saw her now, she would be in deep trouble. The curfew applied to all workers. Even without a chip they might be able to see her, and the Nobles had other ways to kill workers besides chip termination.

The steps passed right by her head. She leaped away from the wall, her heart pounding. The noise stopped.

Whispers reached her ears, two voices.

She strained to listen and took a step forward. Where were the voices coming from?

"Is someone out there?" a female asked.

"I'm not sure." The second voice sounded younger than the first, maybe a boy's.

"There shouldn't be."

Monica gulped. "Who's there?" she called in a whisper. She

took another step forward, putting her ear on the wall. Were the people inside?

"There *is* someone," the boy said.

"Then let them in!"

"But what if it's—"

Monica pounded on the wall. "Let me in, please!" The rough surface scratched her fists. "I have to get in."

A door hidden in the stone swung open, throwing her backwards. Her head slammed against the ground, and the ball of light flew from her grip.

Something grabbed her feet. Fingers wrapped around her ankles, squeezing the stinging wounds. She kicked at her captor.

"Stop it!" someone hissed. "I'm trying to help you."

Every instinct screamed at her to run and get away, but she resisted their demands. This was a wall worker. He would help her. She relaxed and allowed herself to be jerked through the doorway.

The door closed without a sound. "You okay?"

Monica held her hands out in front of her face, but even her fingers were invisible in the darkness. She sighed. She had wanted to keep the ball, but there was no way she'd risk going back out there again. "I lost it."

"Lost what?" A hand touched Monica's shoulder.

She jerked away, slamming her arm into a solid object. Grunting, she grabbed her elbow. "Nothing really important."

"Who are you?" the speaker whispered, sounding like the boy. "You have some explaining to do. I can't open the palace wall for just anyone, but I didn't want you to get in trouble."

"I'm looking for the library. I need to talk to Simon." Monica shivered. The darkness seemed to be closing in on her. As her elbow still throbbed, she focused on the pain. She had to forget about the nothingness around her.

"That's in the middle of the palace," he said. "It's hard to get to if you don't know the way, and you still haven't told me who you are."

Shivers overtook Monica's body. "Can we get some light in here?"

"I'd rather not." He touched her arm. "I'm used to the darkness. I can see you okay."

"I can't see, and I don't like that."

"Hold on."

An orb in the ceiling started to glow, the orange brilliance seeping into the farthest reaches of the passage.

Monica's pupils ached as they tried to adjust. She willed herself to keep her eyes open.

A small boy crouched in front of her. He set a hand near his face, covering the right side. "So who are you?"

"My name's Monica. I'm on an errand." Her shoulders relaxed, and her shivers stopped. She put a hand on the passage's stone wall. "I really need to get to the library, but I don't know the way."

The boy kept his hand close to his face. "That's kind of unusual. Don't you errand runners usually hand your messages off to someone? I wasn't told about anyone coming."

"Yeah, it is unusual." Monica touched the scarf in her pocket. "But I have to be the one to do it, and I need to get back quickly." She glanced at the band on her arm. It still read the same message as before. If the chip had been changed from child worker to solo jobs, then someone other than Alyssa must be keeping the chip alive, but why would Sasha's status change so suddenly?

The boy frowned. "Maybe Myra was right. I shouldn't have let you in. You should get out of here before you get me in trouble."

She stared at him. Was he just afraid of the computers noticing him? They wouldn't give him such a sensitive job if he had been in much trouble lately. "Trust me, as soon as you show me the way to the library, I'm leaving."

"Okay." The boy nodded and jerked his thumb behind him.

"Just follow that wall. It goes straight around the palace until it connects to the building where the moat starts." He sat down on the cobblestone floor, his hand still pressed to his cheek. "There's a stairway there. Take that all the way up to the dorms. They're on the top floor. Someone can direct you from there."

"Thanks." Monica squeezed past him, heading in the direction he pointed.

"Hurry up, so I can turn off the light."

Monica jogged down the corridor. The orange glow behind her diminished with every step. She picked up her pace, pumping her legs as fast as she could. The path seemed to go on and on. When a stone wall and adjacent staircase appeared just ahead, the light turned off.

Groaning, she slowed. Why couldn't he just leave the light on? She shuffled her feet along the floor until her toes tapped against the base of the stairs.

"I told Rod he shouldn't let you in." The voice came from the blackness in front of her.

Monica's heart thumped. "Who's there?"

"Myra," the voice said. "I heard everything you said to Rod, and I'm not satisfied."

Gritting her teeth, Monica tried to calm her breathing, but it still came fast and furious. "Does it matter? I really need to go."

"It matters to me. You could get us into trouble."

"Not if nobody sees me. I'm a wall slave. I would never report anyone." She gripped the scarf in her pocket. "Can I go now?"

"I'm not stopping you."

Bending over, Monica felt her way up the first two stairs, touching the smooth boards with her hands before putting her feet down. "I can't see you."

"They don't let us light the back stairs unless we have to." Myra's voice faded into the distance. "Don't worry about getting lost. I'll make sure the others watch you."

"Thank you." Monica crawled up the stairs, trying not to think about the blackness pressing in on her, but shivers soon crept up her spine and shook her shoulders.

Why would the Nobles keep the lights off here? Was it mostly unused? If so, why would they station someone there just to open the door?

She started counting steps. A dozen went by in a moment. She strained her ears, trying to hear any indication of other workers moving about, but picked up nothing. Myra must have gone into an unseen side passage, or she moved more quietly than a mouse.

On the fiftieth stair, a splinter dug into Monica's hand. As the sting raced up her palm, she gritted her teeth and moved on. Her eyes began to ache from the total darkness. She blinked rapidly, but they still burned.

Footsteps clattered down the wooden planks. Monica stopped and called out, "Wait! Don't run over me." She covered her head with her hands.

A calloused foot nudged her arm. "Who's there?" The toes brushed her again. "What are you doing here?"

"I'm on my way to the library." She shoved the foot away and backed down a step. "Rod told me to come this way."

"Rod did?" The speaker breathed a long sigh. "The boy's been a little strange ever since his accident, but if he let you through maybe you're all right. Who are you?"

"Monica. I'm on an errand of sorts." She felt her way up two more stairs. "Can you tell me how to get to the library?"

"Of sorts?" A glowing ball lit up the speaker's hand.

Monica narrowed her eyes, but the change of light still stung. "Yes, of sorts."

A tall, thin woman stood on the next step above. As she held a glistening orb over her head, it illuminated her dark brown hair and pasty skin. The woman's pale brow wrinkled. "You're not from my dorm."

"No." Monica stood and put her hand on the cool wall. "I'm from Cantral."

"Then why are you here? These stairs aren't used much even by us."

Monica tried to squeeze past her, but the woman shifted to the side and blocked her path. Monica crossed her arms. "I really need to get by. I have to get back to Cantral as soon as I can." She tapped her wristband. "Someone there will be in trouble because of me, and the longer I stay here, the more trouble I'll be in, too."

The woman moved over and shooed Monica by. "Then get going, but you'd better not stir anything up." She handed her the ball. "Everyone here is still under surveillance." Setting a hand on the back of her head, the woman closed her eyes. "You would think it's been long enough."

Monica cupped the sphere and held it close to her chest. "Thank you. I hope things get better for you soon."

"Your words won't help us," the woman said, "but maybe you will bring us relief at a later time."

Monica turned and faced her. "What do you mean?"

The woman looked her in the eye, their gazes level, though Monica stood two steps above her. "I won't keep you any longer." She winced. "And I must go. Hurry off on your mission *of sorts*. Continue up the stairs and go to your left until you find someone else to direct you."

Monica nodded and scampered away. Pinching the ball tightly, she placed her free hand on each stair, steadying her climb. As the light cast its brilliance, shadows danced in and out of side passages, looking like dark ghosts ready to grab her and end this upward journey. The Nobles would love to do just that, yet so many slaves were willing to help her, despite the risks. How could she live up to their expectations? She was just one girl who couldn't even conquer her fear of the dark.

CHAPTER 13

When the stairs ended, Monica bounced onto the narrow landing at the top and turned right into a dorm. A floorboard in the long room creaked. She jumped at the sound and, softening her footfalls, held the glowing ball high.

Across the room, a set of bed curtains swirled, as though a breeze wafted through. Monica shivered. Since it was early in the night, no one should be in here. Everyone worked later than this.

The curtain moved again. She tiptoed across the room, grabbed a bedpost, and yanked the curtain open. Chips of carved wood stirred in the draft, mixing with pieces of paper, all hanging from bits of string tied to the bed slats.

Monica touched a smooth star. Memories of her own decorations from childhood awoke in her mind. Her father sometimes found shells in the messenger tunnels, some with bright colors and odd curves and textures. She had the best decorations of any of the other children.

"What are you doing?"

Monica yanked the curtain closed and whirled around.

A small girl stared up at her and pointed at the bed. "That one's mine." She eyed Monica up and down and lifted her chin higher. "Are you a new transfer?"

"I'm sorry. I didn't know." Monica patted the curtain's thin fabric and straightened the wrinkles. "And no, I'm not a new transfer. I'm just passing through."

The girl smiled and nodded. "Good. Because there's no extra beds." She wrinkled her nose. "And I'm not sharing mine. I just got it."

"I see." Monica pointed at a door just a few feet away. "Is that the way to the main hall?"

"Yes." The girl reached up and touched Monica's elbow. "I could take you to the top of the steps, if you'd like."

"Thank you." Monica followed the girl down the room and into the workers' main stair.

"I'm assigned to cleaning the dorms today," the girl whispered. "So I can't go any farther."

"Again, thank you." Monica stepped onto the first stair, and lights embedded in the boards' edges lit up all the way down the first flight.

"You're welcome." The girl leaned against the door frame. "Where are you headed, anyway, if you're not a transfer? I know most all the rules now, and people don't travel around much without a reason."

"I'm trying to get to the library." Monica shrugged. "It's sort of a secret assignment." She looked into the girl's dark brown eyes. "Can you keep my secret?"

The girl glanced at the floor and wiggled her bare toes. "Maybe." She met Monica's gaze again. "I'll do better this time, and I won't tell anyone at all."

"This time? Have you told secrets before?"

"A few." Grinning, she raised her hands, palms up. "But since you didn't tell me yours, I won't be able to tell anyone else."

"No, I guess not." Monica handed her the glowing ball. She wouldn't need it in the main halls. "Would you like to keep this?"

"Oh!" The girl cradled it in her hands and stroked the smooth glassy surface. "What do I have to do to get it?"

"Don't let anyone know I was here, and tell me where the library is."

"My brother worked there once!" The girl tucked the ball into her dress pocket. "It's up about as far as you can go. Every time you come to stairs, you have to go up. He always complained about the stairs." She stuck out her bottom lip. "But he got transferred."

"So just up?" Monica asked. "There's no up from here, though. I thought this was as high as we could go."

"You have to go down the stairs first, and then there's a hall and another stair to go down. Take the right passage, then go up and up." The girl spun on her bare heel. "It used to be that way; it should still be the same." She stopped and put a finger to her chin. "I think they did some reno—renovations?" She nodded to herself. "Yeah, renovations sometime, so it might have changed."

Monica trotted down the steps, glancing back. "Thanks."

The girl waved. "Thank *you* for the ball! I'll keep your secret."

***

Monica climbed the last step. The stairs ended at a solid wooden panel. A solitary light dangled overhead, illuminating the space.

As she tugged on a panel, bits of dirt fell away from the doorjamb. She ran her hands over the rough wood. There wasn't a security system on this door, so why wasn't it letting her in?

She dug her fingers into the loose soil in the cracks and yanked on the door. It flew open, and she fell on the landing. Light poured into the hall, washing over her entire body.

After brushing herself off, Monica crawled through the opening onto the polished library floor and sneaked behind a ceiling-high bookshelf near the wall. A long aisle of shelves stretched out in front of her. More carved wooden bookcases formed lines up and down the room.

Monica peered around the corner of her shelf. A tall, gangly boy dressed in the uniform of the Seen—trim black pants and long-sleeved shirt—stood in the next aisle, a yellowed volume clutched to his chest.

He stared at her. "Who are you? How did you get in here?"

"Through the workers' panel." She walked to his side and pointed at the still-open doorway.

"But that's been closed for years." The boy chewed on a finger-nail. "We don't need help from the wall slaves."

A crackly voice spoke from the other room, "Who's out there, Nat?"

"Some wall slave found her way in here," Nat shouted over his shoulder.

Monica crossed her arms and glanced from left to right, but saw no one else between the bookcases. "I came here to meet Simon."

Nat rolled his eyes. "I see." He shoved the book onto a shelf, grabbed her elbow, and led her to the end of the room. "Simon! She says she's here to talk to you."

They strode through a looming arch into a sitting room. A wrinkled man hunched over a desk with a dozen lamps lighting the surface. Pursing his lips, he threaded a large needle with a thin strand of leather.

Monica jogged across the room's colorful rug and skirted a leather chair near the desk. She drew the scarf from her pocket. "Simon?"

The man scratched his white hair. He stitched together some ink-dotted pages before looking up. "What do you want?"

"Renin sent me." Monica put the scarf on the desk, covering some papers scattered across the top. "He said you could take care of this."

"I haven't seen Renin in years." Simon brushed the bundle to the side, sliding it next to one of the metal lamps.

Monica snatched the scarf and held it close. "This is important."

She unwrapped the yarn packaging, revealing bits of paper, and wispered, "The workers' council needs this put together and translated."

Simon shoved back his chair, scraping wood against wood. "I suppose I have time . . . if it's that important." He took the scarf and laid it out on the table. A pair of glasses appeared in his hand, as if out of nowhere. He put them on and began fingering the brittle pieces of paper.

"Thank you." Monica heaved a long sigh. Now she had to go see what was happening to her chip.

He looked up at her, his glasses magnifying his brown eyes. "You're welcome. It is a real pain and a cramp in my schedule. Unless . . ." He cast his gaze on Nat. "Unless someone picks up the slack and stops messing up my books." He pulled a round piece of glass from a drawer. "I might have a certain young man demoted and get a new assistant."

Nat glared at Monica, grabbed an armload of books, and shuffled out of the room.

Monica flinched. Would he blame her for Simon's threat? He was a Seen, and there was no telling what they would do. "You wouldn't really do that, would you?"

"Don't put it past me." Simon placed the glass on the paper scraps, magnifying them. "Now get out of here. I'll contact the council when this is finished."

"Thank you very much, Simon." Monica ran back to the workers' opening and glanced at Nat. He frowned at her, dropped his pile of books on the floor, and stormed away.

Monica shivered and ducked into the passage. Renin had told her not to trust the Seen, but he had also said she should talk to Simon, and he was a Seen. Should she have waited until Nat had left to speak to the librarian? She sighed and jogged down the stairs. There was nothing she could do about it now.

CHAPTER 14

After running through the dim tunnel for more than a mile, Monica hugged her aching ribs. She had to be getting close to Cantral by now. One way or another, she'd have to rest soon, either when she arrived or else somewhere between the two cities.

A steel wall popped into view. She skidded to a stop just inches before impact. Plopping on the ground, she gulped in huge swallows of air. Her knees quivered, and her lungs burned.

Groaning, she lay on the dirt floor. How could she have forgotten the blockade? There was no telling when someone would come to open it. Closing her eyes, she stretched out across the tunnel. The tips of her toes pressed against one wall, and her fingers touched the other.

Sleep overcame her in moments.

It seemed as if mere seconds passed when someone nudged her ribs. "Hey, what are you doing out of your dorm?"

Monica rolled onto her stomach and leaped to her feet. "I'm trying to get back to Cantral." She rubbed the sleep from her eyes. "Can you open the door for me?"

"Why don't you open it yourself?" The speaker held up a light ball, and his image became clear. A tall man in a beige messenger uniform stood in front of her, a scowl etched on his clean-shaven face.

"I can't." She tapped the metal door with her knuckle. "But you have to open it, right? So it won't make any difference to you if I go through with you."

The man checked his wristband. "I suppose. But you'll only be getting yourself in trouble." He looked at her again. "Are you Monica?"

She nodded. How did he know her? He didn't look familiar.

"Were you successful? Did Sean deliver my message?"

She widened her eyes and nodded again. "Are you Graff? Sean mentioned you."

"Yes, I am." He pressed his palm against the door, and the metal slid into the ceiling. Grabbing Monica's wrist, he yanked her through before it had a chance to close.

Metal met dirt in a loud clunk.

Monica wriggled her wrist from Graff's hold. "Thanks."

He shrugged. "Just returning the favor. Hopefully, the paper will be of use." He ran off toward Cantral, his lanky form shrinking in the tunnel's dim light.

Monica raced after him, but with her shorter legs, still stiff and aching, she fell farther and farther back. Soon, he turned into a side tunnel and disappeared.

Slowing her pace, she continued on alone until she reached the door to Cantral's east wing's work tunnel. The light above the metal slab glowed a steady red.

Leaning her forehead against the cool door, she sighed. More waiting. If only she had a chip from one of the Council of Eight, then this whole mission would be over in no time, and life could be good for everyone. But that was useless thinking. If a Noble on the council died, everyone would know, and his chip wouldn't work anymore.

Drowsiness tugged at her eyelids. She slid to the floor and laid her head on the dirt. Maybe she could catch up on her sleep. She had never stayed up all night before.

As she closed her eyes, her stomach rumbled. Clenching her fists, she willed the pain away. She had ignored the nagging for this long. She could wait a little while longer. There would be food for her back at the dorm if no one had eaten her dinner.

"Hey."

Monica blinked her eyes open and sat up.

Drake peered over a cart full of empty burlap bags. His brown hair stuck out in all directions, and he panted as if he had just been running. "What are you doing here?"

Smiling, Monica crawled to her feet. He would certainly help her. "Drake, I need to get in."

He pushed the cart up to the door. "You're okay! I was worried you wouldn't find who you were looking for."

Monica sighed loudly. The events of that morning seemed so long ago. "I found him. A lot has happened since then, too."

"I don't have time for explanations." Drake set his dirty bare feet on the edge of the cart's lowest shelf, bouncing as he spoke. "I have to get going. My delivery route is very important, you know. No one gets to eat if I don't make my deliveries, and people get cranky with no food."

"Can you get me through, then? Like you did from the kitchen?"

Drake jumped down and nodded. "Sure." He shoved the cart at Monica. "But you get to push this time!" He climbed onto the sacks and sat cross-legged. "And I get to ride. I've been pushing this thing for hours."

Monica hid a smile. "I think I can do that."

Gripping the front edge, Drake grinned at Monica over his shoulder. "Get ready."

He put his palm against the door. The room shook, and the door slid into the ceiling. Monica shoved the trolley and leaped onto the bottom shelf's edge. As she rode it through the opening, Drake raised his hands above his head and yelled.

Monica laughed at his antics. It was good to see someone have fun for a change. When the door closed, she dug her heels into the ground and pulled the cart to a stop.

Drake hopped off and took the cart back. "Thanks for the ride. I have to get going."

"You're welcome." Monica waved as he ran away. "And thank you."

After dashing through the halls, she raced through the infirmary. An old nurse yelled at her as she passed. "Slow down, child!"

Monica tried to slow her pace as she entered the main stairway but tripped on the steps. Her hands smacked the wood, and her knees landed with a thump.

"Watch out." A black-haired boy helped her to her feet.

"Thanks." Her palms and knees stung.

Other slaves bypassed them, traveling up and down the passage. With yawns and stretches, they appeared to have recently rolled out of bed.

Fatigue washed over Monica's limbs. "Has the morning shift started already?"

The boy rubbed the back of his head, ruffling his hair. "Yeah. It started just a few minutes ago."

"I won't keep you." She scrambled up the stairs and ran into her dorm room.

As she walked up to the alcove, the meal shelf started to lower. She grabbed the meal bar with Sasha's number across the top and choked it down between gasps for breath.

Her mouth grew drier with every bite. Cupping her hands, she collected water from a spout beside the door. The quick drink soothed her throat, settling the dusty crumbs that coated her tongue.

She meandered to her bed and opened the curtain. As she sat

on the flat mattress, exhaustion weighed her down. If someone had news about her chip and Alyssa, they would have to find her themselves. She couldn't stay awake much longer.

Just as she settled on the rock-hard pillow, something squeaked. Monica shot up, slamming her head on the upper bunk. She rubbed her forehead and threw her pillow to the floor. A metal cage sat at the head of her bed, a brown rat staring at her through the tiny bars.

"What in the world?" When she picked up the cage, a wrinkled sheet of paper attached to the bottom rose with it.

Setting the cage back on the mattress, she pulled the page away and read the scratchy letters scrawled from margin to margin.

Your chip was upgraded to child solo worker. We have been able to keep your chip active with this animal. By the time you get back here, you'll be behind schedule. Your wristband will tell you where to go next. Someone will contact you next time we need you.

Monica shredded the message before peering at the rat. A leather string held her chip to its neck. She opened the tiny latch at the top of the cage, then reached in and grabbed the rat. It squealed and snapped at her fingers. She worked at the knot with her free hand, deftly dodging the teeth.

As soon as the chip fell into her grasp, she dropped the rat back into the cage and fastened the latch. She tied the string around her neck and let the vial fall into place on her chest. Rubbing the burn scar where the past chips had fried her skin, she sighed. Time to work on the monotonous tasks, serving the self-righteous Nobles. But where had Alyssa gone? The wristband's warnings had indicated that she had gotten in trouble, but there was no one here to ask.

Her wristband vibrated and beeped. Finding Alyssa would have to wait. Monica slid the cage into her cubbyhole at the head of her bed. Something clinked against the cage. Whatever it was would have to wait, too. She was already behind.

She dashed out of the dorm and galloped down the steps. Text scrolled across her wristband screen: *West Library — Dusting — Five Minutes Late.*

As her chip tried to send warning signals to her brain, heat coursed across her skin. She clutched the hot glass and held it away from the sensitive scar. Not only was she late, she had no idea where the west wing library was.

She danced around a cluster of children sitting on the steps. A girl, a few years older than the rest, called to her, "You're late, aren't you?"

Monica stopped. "Yes, can you tell me where the library is?"

Holding a baby on her lap, the girl nodded. "It's down the stairs, past a passage on your right, and take the next passage you come to." The baby gurgled and reached his skinny arms out to Monica.

She stepped away. "And after that?"

The girl jiggled the baby boy on her knee. "It's a little fuzzy. I only went twice with my mother before getting assigned to these guys." She gestured at the five toddlers sitting around her. Each child gazed at her with adoration, and a little boy wrapped his arms around her leg. She smiled and ruffled his hair.

Monica's vial heated up again. She tried to smile at the girl, but urgency and pain kept her face tense. "Maybe I can find someone else to help me when I get to the second passage."

"I doubt it." The girl freed a strand of her black hair from the baby's grip. "I think it's to the left, down four more passages, and up a ladder. Then you should be there."

"Thank you." Monica dashed off. The directions were better than nothing, even if vague.

"No problem," the girl yelled.

Monica followed the directions and came to the ladder in moments. Her chip cooled off. She let the glass cylinder fall back to her chest and tucked it under her dress. The ladder bolted to the wall began at eye level and rose to a trapdoor in the ceiling. Pausing to tuck her skirt between her knees, she took a deep breath.

She gripped the first rung within reach and pulled herself off the ground. Her feet making contact with the wall's smooth wood, she inhaled sharply and climbed hand over hand.

Monica shoved the trapdoor, swinging it open with a dull thud. After crawling through the ceiling, she rolled out of the hole and jumped to her feet. Slick, buffed wood caressed the bottoms of her toes.

Crouching, she did a quick three-sixty scan of the room. Bookshelves lined the circular expanse, surrounding fat leather chairs and end tables that held sparkling lamps.

Panic closed Monica's throat. Who would put the slaves' access in the middle of the floor, so out in the open like this? She stepped back into the hole and stood on a lower rung, now eye-level with the floor.

Nothing stirred in the plush surroundings. Monica crept back onto the shining hardwood floor and kicked the trapdoor into place.

She ran across the room, her feet making no noise. If the library was set up like all the other rooms she had ever cleaned, then a concealed panel would be hiding the cleaning materials nearby. Reaching a bare spot on the wall between bookcases, she pushed. A waist-high door clicked open. She peeked into the child-sized hole. A dozen bottles of unlabeled liquids, jugs of white polishing cream, clean rags, and odd-looking tools lay inside.

More dust cloths hung from hooks in the back corner. She lifted one from a rusty metal peg and grabbed the handle of a brown plastic container, almost as big as the baby in the girl's lap. This job needed to be done as quickly as possible. There would be nowhere to hide if a Noble came in.

After lugging the container out, she unscrewed the two-fist-sized lid, revealing thick white cream that rose halfway to the top. She dipped the thin cloth inside and scooped up a dollop.

She turned to the first shelf and started polishing the wooden planks, working the cream into the grain. As she used rag after rag and took every book from the shelves and dusted every bookcase and leather binding, minutes turned into hours. Her neck and back ached from the bending and reaching. Muscles in her calves burned as she stooped and gathered the last pile of books.

Shoving the final tome back with the others, she let out a long sigh. This job was supposed to have gone to a little eight-year-old, suddenly torn from working with her mother. Monica put her hands on her hips and stared at the shelves that reached to the ceiling. Even with the rolling ladder attached to the cases, an eight-year-old would have trouble reaching every crevice.

She shook her head. There would have been no way she could have done this at that age. How could the Nobles expect a little girl to do this task?

After replacing her supplies, she climbed down the trapdoor hole and headed back to the dorm. Her chip and bracelet stayed quiet during her journey.

As she entered the main stairway, other workers crowded around. The men dripped with sweat from their heavy labors. Women's eyelids drooped as they climbed the stairs, their bodies worn from long hours of cleaning.

Monica squeezed around them, weaving through the weary masses. As she climbed, her fatigue drifted away. She hurried up the steps and retrieved her lunch from the pyramid of meals stacked on the dumbwaiter.

After she reached her bed, she drew the curtains around her. She sat cross-legged and pulled the cage from her storage cupboard. The rat hissed at her, its back bowed and its teeth bared.

A round piece of metal was wedged between two of the cage's bars. Monica set the cage on the bed before plucking the disk free and turning it over. How did that get there? Fingering the leather cord that protruded from a hole bored in the disk's top, she rotated the metal circle, a medallion maybe. It looked familiar for some reason. Her stomach rumbled, reminding her how long ago breakfast had been.

She put the necklace on the bed and unwrapped her six-inch nutrient bar. A piece broke and fell on the stained sheets. The rat pushed its tiny claws through the bars, trying to snatch up the crumb.

Flicking the piece into the rat's cage, Monica chewed off a piece of her own. As other workers walked around the dorm, her bunk's footboard curtain wavered. Quiet conversations melded together in a garbled murmur. A child's giggle rose above the rest of the mutterings.

Monica watched the rat consume the crumb, standing on his back legs and turning the piece around with his front paws. She smiled. The rodent might be a bit smelly and dirty, but he definitely looked cute.

She shoved down the rest of her meal before putting the rat back in the cubbyhole. Patting the bars, she nodded at the cage. Whoever made it did a pretty good job. "Now behave." She rolled her eyes. "Like you could get out of there. And I'm talking to a rat."

She picked the medallion back up, but the vial on her chest started to feel warm against her skin. Further examination would have to wait. She tucked the leather cord into one of the bed slats of the bunk above hers so the metal hung a foot over her mattress.

Noises in the room died down, and the slaves started shuffling out. Monica lifted the vial. She tapped the glass, moving the tiny flake of metal on the inside. In some ways, the chip was her salvation, a way to fill her stomach, a provider of bed and bath. In other ways, it was a symbol of oppression, a tracking bloodhound, the bearer of a whip. Could there be a way to provide without including torture?

Shrill beeps vibrated her wristband. She tucked the vial under her dress and groaned. This was going to be a long day.

CHAPTER 15

Monica's back ached as she lay on her bunk. Burning pain rippled through her shoulders and arms. Groaning, she pulled her blanket over her dirty face, too sore and tired to wade through the crowds to the baths.

As her eyes drooped, a blend of sounds reached her ears. The rat skittered around his cage, weary whispers flittered across the room, and feet shuffled toward the door as tired slaves headed for the underground bath.

She tried to separate the voices, hoping to learn the different workers and families, but they all blurred as she drifted toward sleep.

"Hey." Someone jabbed her shoulder.

Monica jerked away. She rolled off the bed and thudded to the floor, striking her elbow.

"Sorry." A small boy peered down at her from her bunk.

Monica jumped to her feet, holding her elbow. "What are you trying to do?"

The boy sat on the edge of her bed, the curtain falling over his shoulders and head. "I'm supposed to tell you something." He swung his legs back and forth, thumping his heels on the bed's sideboard. "My name's Fargo."

"Maybe you could have just talked to me instead of scaring me so badly, Fargo." She squinted at the dark outlines of the bunks. The lights were turned low for the night, so she must have slept for a little while.

"Sorry." Fargo jumped off the bed. "I'm supposed to tell you that you're supposed to go to the library."

"Who told you that? It's past curfew." Monica glanced at the other beds and lowered her voice. "And which library?"

"The one here in the west wing. Trip, someone from another dorm, told me. He stopped me on the stairs." Fargo yawned and rubbed his eyes. "He gave me some of his dinner so I'd give you the message." He shrugged. "Anyway, I told you. I'm going back to sleep."

"Wait!" She climbed back onto her bed. "Do you know Alyssa? I think something happened to her."

"Yeah, I know her." He pointed at something behind her. "You have her picture of Sasha right there. Where did you get it?"

"It was here when I got back from an assignment." She grabbed the cord and brought the medallion into view. "How did you know it was there?"

"I could see it. It's kind of shiny."

"Are you sure it's hers?"

"As sure as I can be." His brow furrowed. "Everyone knows she never takes it off."

Monica gripped the leather so hard her hand hurt. If Alyssa never took it off, then . . . No. She shook her head. Alyssa had to be okay.

"Are you all right?"

"Sure. I'm fine." She held Alyssa's treasure close. Someone

had to protect it for her until she returned. "I'll think about what Trip told you."

He nodded, his gaze sliding to the medallion again. "Okay." He scampered into the darkness.

Monica lay down, her head again on the pillow. How did Alyssa's necklace get here? Did whoever leave the rat bring it as well? She held the metal up to the light, studying the engraving. What did Fargo mean—a picture of Sasha? Only Nobles had portraits.

The threadlike outline meandered around the disk's surface, creating the image of a little girl's face. Monica tilted the disk so that the light danced across the girl's short hair and narrow features. The artist could catch only so much detail in a simple outline, but the girl's eyes stared back at her with a hauntingly empty expression.

Monica ran a finger over the etching. This was Alyssa's last connection with her husband and daughter. She wouldn't leave it here unless . . . Monica clenched the disk in her hand, letting the edge cut into her palm. They killed her. The Nobles had killed Alyssa. *And it was my fault.* If not for the latest mission to Cillineese, Alyssa wouldn't have fallen behind, and she would be safe right now.

Tears pooled in Monica's eyes. She slipped Alyssa's necklace around her neck and let the medallion fall next to her chip. If only the slaves' council could figure out that paper. They could save all the slaves. No one else would have to die under the cruel thumb of the Nobles' Council, whether from overwork or lack of medicine.

And it was her responsibility to go, both then and now, to not let anyone else down. Her father often talked about how she was saved for a reason, and she needed to take it seriously. Although she hadn't seen her parents since her father was killed and her mother dragged off to the fields, she couldn't keep their words and memories away. Now Alyssa was added to those memories, to the people who had counted on her.

Sliding off the bed, she untied her chip's cord. The computers would notice if she went out of the dorm at this hour. She caught the rat and, running her fingers across his furry body in the dark, secured the tie around its neck.

She yanked her bed curtains closed. The room seemed to hum with the regular breathing of the other workers. Grabbing one bed-post after another, she made her way through the darkness.

Monica retraced the path she had traveled early that morning. The main stair lights were dimmed for the night shift, but she could still discern the outline of each step and the side passages. She passed only one other slave on her way, and the woman shot her a strange look. When Monica offered a weak smile, the woman turned away and broke into a run.

As she climbed the ladder to the trapdoor, shivers ran down her spine. What could this meeting be for? She had given Simon the paper, so the council couldn't need her again so soon.

She slammed her forearm into the wood above her head. The door shuddered and slid off the hole. As before, she stood on a rung that allowed her a floor-level view. Scanning the room, she climbed out of the opening, squinting at every dark corner. Tiny lights glowed in small recesses in the bookcases, illuminating the book covers.

A shadowy form rested in one of the armchairs in the center of the circular room. A side table lamp revealed his dark hair and spindly slave's frame.

Monica crawled on hands and knees to the chair and knelt behind the high leather back. Reaching around, she prodded the man's elbow. "You wanted to talk to me?"

He leaped from his seat and grabbed the lamp, stretching the cord and almost ripping the plug from the floor. He whirled around and raised it high. "Who's there?"

"It's just me." Monica raised her hands and stood behind the table. "Are you Trip?"

"Yes." He exhaled in a relieved sort of way. "Yes, I am Trip."

"Didn't you ask for me to come?"

"Yes, I did."

She nodded at the lamp. "Well, if I had been a Noble, you'd be dead now for threatening me."

Fumbling with the lamp, Trip gulped. "Sorry. I'm just a little jumpy. I . . ." He slapped the back of his neck.

Monica stepped away. "Maybe we should head back to the main stairs."

"The Nobles in the west wing don't come into the library." Trip glanced around the room. "Reynolds cares about books the least out of the entire Council of Eight. He only has them for show."

"I meant to help you." She tapped the back of her neck. "You know, ease the pain?"

Trip shook his head. "No, we need to stay here."

"Why?" Monica circled the sitting area and sank into one of the slippery chairs.

"Because the computers can't reach us up here on the highest level as well as they can in the lower sections. They're underground." He twitched. His hands trembled, and his eyes rolled back in his head.

Monica jumped up. She caught him as he fell, but his weight brought her crashing to the floor. "Apparently," she said, grunting, "they can still reach us pretty well." She wriggled out from under him. Jabbing his chest with a finger, she spoke in a sharp whisper. "Come on, wake up. What were you going to tell me?"

She hooked her arms under his and tried to drag him onto a chair. He slipped away and thumped back to the floor, his head smacking the wooden planks.

"Sorry." She adjusted her grip under his arms and walked backwards, dragging him toward the trapdoor. Someone would be coming to check on the report of a wayward slave soon. Why couldn't the slave council just let her meet him in the halls? Sometimes their thinking made no sense.

Trip's head tipped back, his mouth hanging open. His stale breath struck her in the face. She coughed and kept going, inching along.

Her sweaty bare feet adhered to the floor, helping her get a solid grip on the boards. Trip moaned, but his eyes stayed closed, his breaths uneven.

When her heel touched the edge of the hole, she let Trip's shoulders fall. Crouching beside him, she sighed. "Come on, you have to wake up. I can't carry you down the ladder."

She pried his eyelid open. His eye looked glassy—unseeing. She sat back and rocked on her heels. "Trip, you really need to get up, or I'm leaving. No use us both getting caught."

He moaned again, still unresponsive.

Monica looked around the circular room. No footsteps sounded yet, but the Nobles would surely send a Seen to check out the situation.

Pushing his arms against the floor, Trip rolled onto his stomach.

Monica tapped his back. "Are you waking up?"

Nodding, Trip crawled to the trapdoor. "The paper isn't done. They're working on it now, but they're having trouble with piecing it together and translating it." He eased himself into the hole, a look of relief washing over his face. His chip must have backed off its torment, giving him incentive to keep going.

"Let me guess." Monica sank to a sitting position and buried her face in her hands. "They want me to find something or other for them, and they don't know where it is exactly, and they want me to risk my life to find it."

"Yes." Trip inched down the ladder. "I think I'm going to faint again if I don't go." He gulped. "They want you to go back to Cillineese and help look for some old book."

Monica jumped to her feet. "What?" She kicked the trapdoor. Her toes throbbed, but she stomped the floor despite the pain.

"They can't be serious. I've been working for them for years now, and I just got off an assignment, and I can't lose this chip. Why can't Simon find the stupid book? He's the librarian!"

Trip flinched. "Hey, don't yell at me. Samuel was the guy who told me. Take it up with him. He lives in the east wing." He slid down the ladder and called up to her. "I delivered the message, so I'm leaving now."

"I'm not going to go find Samuel. If he wants to talk to me, he should come himself." Monica slammed the door shut. She sat on the floor and curled her knees up to her chest. Why were they demanding so much of her? Of course she had to do what only a chip-less slave could do, but now they wanted her to risk her assignment to find something almost anyone could search for. She had become the council's personal slave.

She pounded the floor with a fist. If they kept risking her life for menial tasks, they wouldn't have a chip-less girl when it counted. They were being careless and lazy.

Quiet footsteps whispered around the room—someone sneaking through the hall. Monica unfolded herself and dug her fingernails into the small cracks outlining the trapdoor. She tugged on the hatch, but it didn't budge.

She sat back on her heels. It must have wedged when she slammed it closed.

The footfalls drew closer.

She kicked at the door, but it stayed put.

They drew closer still.

She ran to a chair and crouched beside the arm. A bookcase swung away from the wall. Two books fell and clattered on the floor. A girl about her own age slipped out from behind the shelves. The dim light from the bookcase illuminated her straight-line black dress and pale face. Purple bruises drew a circle around one dark eye.

Monica squatted beside the chair, her eyes level with the arm.

The girl let the bookcase swing closed. A latch on the inside clicked loudly, holding the door in place. She crept across the room, her feet making barely any noise. "Is anyone in here?" She touched a blank spot on the wall. Lights flickered to life all around the room.

Monica dove for cover and closed her eyes, squeezing herself into a tight ball. If she stayed low and still, the girl wouldn't see her.

"Is someone here?" The girl's sliding steps continued around the room until she stopped on the opposite side. "I'm already in trouble," she said with a moan. "If I can't give a report, I could be demoted."

Monica opened her eyes. The girl stood a few steps past the trapdoor, her head tipped up. Looking at the ceiling, she called out, "So, is there anyone here, or are the computers being stupid again?"

Monica licked her dry lips. If the girl looked down, she would see her. There was no way she wouldn't.

The girl turned. Her eyes met Monica's. They both gasped.

"So there *is* someone here." She fumbled with her loose wrist-band. "Who are you?"

"Wait!" Monica crawled to her feet, her legs shaking. "Don't!"

The girl froze. The bruise on her face glowed with drying tears. "I have to." Her hands trembled as she pushed a button on her watch. "I'm this close to being demoted. I have to report you."

"You can't." Monica edged toward the disguised trapdoor, closing in on the girl.

The girl gulped and backed against a shelf, her fingers poised over her wristband screen. "Stay where you are."

Monica gripped the edge of the trapdoor and tried to pull it open, but the boards again stayed put. "Really, you can't report me." She pointed at the girl's wrist. "It can't see me. See for yourself."

The girl unclipped the band and held it close to her face. She shook the metal casing. "What's wrong with it?"

"Nothing." Monica yanked at the door again. It popped free from the frame and smacked against the floor.

"What should I tell them?" As tears poured down the girl's face, she fumbled with her wristband and clipped it back on her arm. "I've had to report computer errors twice this week. I don't want to have to do it again. They won't believe me."

Monica jumped onto the first rung and started down the ladder. "Just tell them I ran off before your band could get a reading."

The girl shook her head. "I don't know if that will work." She peered down at Monica. "Can't you just give me your number? I could report it manually."

Monica stopped and gaped at her. "You can't be serious."

The girl stared at her, her eyes wide.

"Okay." Monica bowed her head. "I guess you are." She rested her forehead against the wooden rung. "If you report it like I told you to, you might get demoted, right?"

"Right."

"It's just *might*, and it's only a demotion. They'll try to *kill* me. But I won't die. I'll just starve to death."

The girl shook her head. "They wouldn't really try to kill you, would they?"

"Where have you been your whole life?" Monica growled. "Of course they would."

"I worked in the children's nursery." She pushed her hair away from the bruise on her face. "Until I got reassigned two weeks ago. I hate my new assignment."

Monica clambered up the ladder and sat on the edge of the hole. "You must have been pretty sheltered." She picked at a splinter lodged in her hand. "Didn't you hang out with the other Seen?"

The girl wiped her eyes. "No, I had to stay in the nursery, except when I ran errands for the children. I slept in an alcove hidden in the wall." She sat beside Monica. "I was just moved to one of the

Seen dorms, though. Now I have to run errands for anyone who wants me to, and I wait on tables."

Monica dug at the piece of wood, though she couldn't feel it. This girl obviously needed someone to talk to, but why now? "Okay. I'm sorry for your troubles, but I could tell you about some people who are a lot worse off. It's much worse being a wall slave than a Seen." She sighed. "I'm going to go now, okay?"

"Sorry." The girl hugged herself. "I just never get to talk to anyone, and when you started talking to me, I just couldn't stop. I used to talk to my sister, before we got assigned to different places years ago."

Monica groaned and lay back on the floor. "Don't you need to be somewhere?"

"They give me extra time if I need it." She shrugged. "The computers know I'm on a pretty loose leash."

"It's still a leash, loose or not."

She nodded sadly. "After not being able to report you, they'll probably put up more restrictions . . . if they don't demote me. Third strike, you know?"

"No, actually." Monica sat up. "What's third strike?"

The girl's eyes brightened. "It's something the kids played. A game, with a ball. And there were these things called strikes, which were bad, and if you had three of them you were out." She smiled. "I was always out, but they never told me all the rules, so it was a little hard to play."

"Oh." Monica poked at the splinter again. "We're not allowed to play with balls in the dorms or in the walls. They make too much noise."

The girl's smile fell. "Oh." She drew her knees up to her chin. "My name is Opal, by the way."

Monica looked around the room. The lights started to dim, casting a pall of darkness over all the furniture. Should she tell this girl her name? She sounded nice enough, but Renin told her not to trust Seen. "I'd better go."

"Well, it was nice to meet you." Opal touched the back of her neck. "Under the circumstances . . ."

"Same here. You're nicer than most."

The girl stood and offered a hand. "I guess I won't see you again."

Monica took her hand and pulled herself to her feet. "Yeah. Guess not." She hoped she would never meet another Seen again. They almost always meant trouble.

"I'll tell them you got away," Opal said. "I'll just have to hope they don't demote me."

"And hope you don't get three strikes."

"Right." Her head dipping lower, she frowned. "What about you?"

Monica set a foot on a ladder rung again. "What about me?"

"Aren't you in pain?" Opal asked.

"I'm not in pain. Not from my chip, at least."

"If you weren't supposed to be here, the computers wouldn't have alerted us, but I don't understand why you didn't show up on my wristband."

"I really can't explain. I have to go." Monica continued down the rungs. "Bye." She closed the trapdoor.

"Bye." Opal's voice came through muffled.

Monica scrambled to the floor and hurried toward her dorm. She needed to catch as much sleep as she could before this next mission. As she ran, Opal's face came to mind, the bruised face of bitter affliction. Even the Seen bowed under the brutal hand of the Nobles. The suffering seemed to get worse all the time. What could it mean? Were they worried about something, tightening their fist in order to keep control?

Sighing, she entered the dorm and tiptoed toward her bunk, listening to the buzz of sleep all around. If she had anything to do with it, the days of brutalized slaves would soon come to an end.

CHAPTER 16

"**M**onica?" The voice came through the curtain. Monica rolled to her side and pulled the blankets over her head. Couldn't they just leave her alone? She had only been asleep for a few moments—at least that was what it felt like. Her eyelids sagged, and she started to drift off again.

"Monica? Are you awake?" A draft wafted over her bed.

"Hey!" Monica sat bolt upright.

Fargo peered in at her through a gap in the curtains. He reached out and poked her arm. "I guess that's a yes?"

Monica scooted against the headboard. "What do you want?"

"Didn't you get the message?" He climbed onto her bed and sat by her feet. "You're supposed to go."

"If you knew what I was supposed to do, then why didn't you just tell me?" Monica hugged her pillow. "You could have saved me a lot of trouble."

Fargo shook his head. "I didn't know anything except you were supposed to meet Trip at the library and then you'd be leaving." He pointed at the dark recess behind her head. "When you go, can I have your rat?"

Twisting her body, Monica checked the cage. The rat's glowing yellow eyes stared at her. "How'd you know about him?"

"I heard him squeaking earlier." Fargo got up on his knees and looked over her shoulder. "He's cute."

Monica arranged her blankets around her legs. "Shouldn't you be sleeping? You have to work."

"There's still a couple hours left before morning." He held out his hands. "So can I have him? It'd be fun to put him in the deliveries for the Nobles."

"In that case, definitely not." Monica pulled the cage from the cubbyhole. "If you did that, they'd kill you."

"Nah, they'd just think it sneaked in for the food. Rats get in things all the time." Fargo dropped his hands back in his lap. "So you're going to take him with you?"

"No. But I can't let you have him, either."

His expression drooped. "Well, did you talk to Trip, or didn't you?"

"I talked to him."

"Then why were you sleeping? He told me you were going to Cillineese. They're expecting you."

"Expecting me?" She shook her head. "For a secret mission, it seems like a lot of people know about it."

"It's the only way." He fingered the bunk's curtains. "We can't move around like you can, so we have to relay information. Trip can't come into this dorm, and he didn't want to tell me the details of the plan for some reason, something about not wanting to mention someone's name to too many people."

The person in the bed above rolled over, making the bunk sway.

Fargo glanced up at the slats above their heads. "Is he going to wake up?"

"If he's not already, I'm sure he will if you don't be quiet." Monica leaned forward and whispered into his ear. "Listen, I know I have to go back to Cillineese, but if I don't get some sleep . . ." She pinched the skin on her bony arm. "And something more to eat, I'll never make it."

"But if you leave now, could you be back before dawn? You'd be done and still get breakfast."

Monica shook her head. "Even if I could, you forgot about sleep. I'd have to get right to work."

"Oh." He lowered his head. "Right."

"And besides, what they're asking me to do might take a while. I have no idea when I'd be able to come back." She pulled the blanket over her head. "Can you just leave me alone now?"

"Okay. Okay." The sound of sliding curtains penetrated the blanket, then all fell silent.

Monica shut her eyes and tried to go back to sleep, but the drowsiness that tugged at her just minutes ago had fled, replaced by Fargo's persistent nagging. The kid was probably right. The sooner she got this mission done, the better it would be for all.

Whispers flittered through the room. Apparently, other people couldn't sleep, either. Monica sat up, sighing. Maybe she should go to the east wing and talk to Samuel. That way, she could learn more about the mission before leaving for Cillineese. He would be in his dorm. She could find him and get back before morning. At least she wouldn't have to go all the way to Cillineese tonight.

Monica peered into the rat's cage. After checking the knot holding the vial to the rat's back, she placed the cage in the middle of the bed and crawled out of the curtained space.

"Thank you."

Monica looked up. Fargo stared down at her from the top bunk beside her bed.

"Go to sleep," she hissed.

He grinned and ducked back into his bed.

She shook her head. Fargo just wouldn't give up. At least one person was happy about this.

She crept from the room and down the main stairs. As she trotted to the infirmary, the lights remained dim. Every time she entered a dark alcove, shivers tried to cripple her, but she warded them off. The sooner she found Samuel, the sooner she could go back to bed.

She sneaked to the infirmary door. Gripping the tarnished knob, she took a deep breath and turned the metal handle. The door swung open, groaning loudly.

A woman sitting on one of the beds jumped to her feet. "Who's there? Is someone sick?"

Monica slipped into the room and snapped the door shut. "I'm just passing through."

"I remember you." The woman nodded and sat back down. "You're the girl who took Sasha's chip. Where are you going now?"

Monica crossed the room in a few strides and paused at the next door. "Not to be rude, but it's not any of your business."

"You are being rude, child, and you shouldn't treat your elders that way. You owe me a lot." The woman folded her hands in her lap and closed her eyes. "But be on your way, then; I'm sure you have important places to go."

"I'm just in a hurry, so I don't want to explain." Monica turned the doorknob. "But why do I owe you?"

Tears squeezed out from the woman's closed eyes. "Who do you think got that chip for you? Who do you think had to dig it from the poor girl's skull just moments after she died?" The woman wiped her bony cheeks with the back of her hand. "I took care of Sasha for almost a week, being there when her mother couldn't be, and she still died."

Monica rubbed the scar on her chest where so many chips had burned her. Her own suffering was minimal compared to what slaves like Sasha went through. "I'm sorry for being rude.

I shouldn't have been." She opened the door, slipped into the east wing, and pushed the door shut. Leaning back, she closed her eyes. "I wish Sasha had lived," she whispered to herself. "I want it all to be different, but I didn't have anything to do with her death."

Sighing, she looked at the stairwell ahead, another climb, another stranger to meet, another dangerous mission laid at the feet of a girl who didn't ask for this responsibility. But what could she do but ascend? No one else could.

***

Monica trudged up a flight of stairs. Each step provided a reminder of how long it had been since she slept. She rubbed her eyes. The dorms couldn't be far now. After twelve years of running through the Nobles' walls and heeding the computers' beck and call, every inch of the east wing was etched into her memory, but weariness made everything seem cloudy.

She turned into the first dorm and slumped to her knees. Two rows of beds stretched out in front of her. The workers' breathing stirred the air around the room, providing a background hum. Faded gray curtains around each bed fluttered in and out as if they had breath of their own.

Monica let out a quiet groan. How was she ever going to find Samuel? There were still two other dorms besides this one. She couldn't check every bed, could she? Shaking her head, she climbed to her feet. There had to be another way.

She skulked to the first set of bunks. "Samuel?" she whispered.

"There's no Samuel here," someone muttered. "Go away. People are trying to sleep."

"Sorry." Monica continued to the other end of the dorm and tried again but received a similar answer.

The second dorm ended with the same results—more grumbling of sleeping inhabitants and no Samuel.

Monica clambered up the last steps to the final dorm just as the overhead lights flickered on. She crept inside and stationed herself near the door. Curtains surrounding the beds opened all around the room. Men, women, and children crawled out of their bunks. Children whispered among themselves while they dug through their clothes boxes. Some of the younger women traded gossip with each other, but the older adults kept quiet.

Monica crouched next to the meal tray already stacked high with the slaves' breakfasts. If Samuel was in this dorm, he would have to pass by. If he didn't hurry up, she might not make it back to the west wing in time for her own meal.

A few children rushed past, running to their work. They chattered as they galloped down the stairs. An older woman gave chase, futilely trying to shush them. Two teenage girls passed by, dark bags under their eyes. One girl raised an eyebrow at Monica but continued into the stairway without a word.

A man approached the dumbwaiter. His skin hung loose, and he staggered as he walked.

Monica jumped to her feet. "Are you all right?"

He waved her away. "I'll be fine." His voice cracked. He swayed and caught hold of the meal shelf.

Monica grabbed his arm. "Are you sure you're okay?"

"Yes, I'm fine." His shaking hand scooped up his breakfast bar.

"Let me help you." Monica took the package from him and ripped open the wrapper. "Here." She handed it back.

He stuffed it into his mouth. Monica guided him from the dumbwaiter, out of everyone's way. Two men grumbled about the man's slow shuffling. Monica glared at them but said nothing.

The man patted her hand. "It's all right. They don't bother me."

"Are you new here?" Monica helped him sit on an empty bunk. "I don't remember you. I used to live in this dorm until a few days ago."

The man coughed. "Then what are you doing back?" He wiped some crumbs from his mouth and licked them from his hand.

Monica's stomach rumbled. Breakfast was certainly out of the question now; by the time she returned, someone else would have taken it, thinking something had happened to her.

"I'm looking for a man." Her wristband beeped and vibrated. Maybe she would just get a warning and return before her chip died completely. "Do you know a Samuel? I couldn't find him in the other dorms."

"I'm Samuel." He looked her up and down, his forehead wrinkling. "I suppose you're Monica? You're supposed to be in Cillineese."

"To get a book, but then I want to come back." Monica sighed. "What about my new chip? I don't want to lose it already. Let me stay in Cantral."

"No. That won't do." Samuel pushed himself to his feet. "These old joints don't work very well anymore. I'm going to have to pass my job on soon."

Monica followed him to the door. "Why do you want me to stay in Cillineese?"

"Because we need your help there more than here now. Our council has decided that we can make better use of you in Cillineese." Samuel pressed his hand against the wall and started down the stairs, easing onto each plank, his knees popping with every step.

"Better use of me?" Monica growled. "You guys can't just use me like I'm some sort of machine. If you have an assignment that only a chip-less slave can do to stop the Nobles, then fine, but don't risk my life to do things a lazy librarian can do for himself. I want to stay alive. I want to keep this job. You can't just give me a new chip and then take it away again a few days later for no good reason."

"Girl, without us, you would never get a chip. We don't enjoy finding dying slaves so you can take their identity." He stopped, his breaths coming heavily. "Perhaps you'd like us to stop having anything to do with you."

Monica bowed her head. If they cut her off, she would eventually die of starvation, a much more terrible fate than being electrocuted in an instant. It would take weeks for her to die. She put her hand on her chest where her scar rested under her dress. Twinges of past pain seared the tissue, but she brushed them away.

"I didn't think so." Samuel continued his slow progress down the stairs. "I wish they had ramps for people like me. I suppose the stairs are to weed out all the old men."

"So that's it, then?" Monica asked. "I'm just supposed to go to Cillineese, no more questions asked? Just to find a book?"

"That's correct." Samuel turned into a corridor on the right. "You need to talk to Simon. He'll know more about what you're supposed to do."

Monica stopped in the passage doorway. "You guys seem able to get messages to each other without my help. Why don't *you* tell me more about the book?" Her wristband beeped and shook, making her hand tremble.

"We do send messages to each other easily, but I know very little about the book. As I said, talk to Simon." Samuel moved on into the dim hall. "Don't worry about your old chip, but I'd take that rat if I were you . . . if it's not dead yet."

Monica punched the wall. Why did the council treat her this way? Getting pushed around by the Nobles was bad enough, but slaves should know better. They should realize what getting jerked by a leash feels like.

He was right, though; she might need the rat, and it would be difficult to catch another. The chip's electric impulses would cause only minor pain to someone receiving warnings, but it could probably kill a small rodent. She galloped down the stairs. Maybe it was already too late.

CHAPTER 17

Monica ran all the way to the west wing. Her feet pounding the wood floors, she flew up the stairs and into the dorm. The empty room echoed her footfalls. She ripped open the curtain around her bed. It tore from its hangings and fell to the ground. The rat lay at the bottom of the cage, its legs twitching.

"Sorry." Monica unfastened the latch. As her hands fumbled with the metal bar, drool slid from the rat's jaws. She flipped the lid open and untied the leather strap from around the rodent's shoulders and neck. "I didn't think about you getting hurt when I put it on."

She held the vial by the string, keeping the hot glass away from her palm. "Now I'm supposed to give this thing up and go back to the place of my nightmares." She dropped the vial into her dress pocket. "And I'm talking to a rat again." She closed the cage, retrieved her jacket from the cubbyhole, and pulled it on. The morning messengers would still be going from city to city, and she should be able to find one who would let her through the Cillineese gate.

She darted to the meal shelf, the rat cage in hand, but the door was already closed and her breakfast gone. Kneeling at the water spigot, she set the rat's cage on the floor. The rodent lay on the bars, a whisker twitching.

Monica turned on the water. A slow stream trickled out and fell into a drain in the floor. She cupped her hands and took a quick drink before sprinkling the rat. It crawled slowly to its feet, staring at her.

"Good. You're alive." She clutched the cage to her chest and ran down the stairs toward the messenger tunnels. Her wristband beeped shrilly with every step.

Just as she reached the bottom of the stairs, a delivery boy came through the access door. She rushed forward and squeezed past him through the narrowing entrance.

"Hey!" the boy yelled. "What are you doing?"

She slipped on the floor and dropped the cage. The rat squealed as the container hit the floor, and she face-planted in the dirt. Dust and clay ground into her teeth.

She scrambled back up. Coughing, she spat out blood-tinged dirt. Grit still covered her tongue and clogged her throat. She pounded a fist against her chest, hacking violently. After choking out a wad of mud, she wiped her mouth, picked the cage back up, and stumbled along the tunnel.

"That was great." She coughed and spat again. Maybe she should have waited for another messenger, but most of them would be dispersed all along the main tunnels now. She might not see another runner in this out-of-the-way corridor for hours.

The rat snapped at her hands again.

"Hey!" She held the cage at a distance. "Stop that. I'm sorry about falling, but I couldn't help it, and you didn't even get any dirt in your mouth."

The rat stared at her.

Monica spat yet again. Her tongue felt thick in her throat. She skulked down the tunnel, looking in every crevice for a water faucet. Where did the messengers get their water? Her father used to keep a bottle in his bag. He had to have refilled it somewhere.

She came to an intersection of tunnels. Three other passages met hers, a metal message box embedded in a wall of each one with a red light flashing above it. She set the cage down and knocked on the first box. The panel cover echoed with each smack of her knuckles.

If the door was locked, there had to be messages inside. And if there were messages, then a courier would be along soon to pick them up. A hissing sound snaked through the cracks in the panel. Something clunked inside the box, maybe another message arriving. Monica bent over and set her ear close to the slick metal. The noise came again.

"What are you doing?" a man yelled, his voice echoing from farther down the tunnel.

She jumped away and snatched up the cage. "Nothing. I was waiting for someone."

The man strode up to the box and put his hand on the panel. "You're not supposed to be down here. Women and girls are never allowed in these tunnels."

"I'm going to Cillineese." Monica licked her dry lips. "Do you know where I can get some water?"

"Transfers always go in groups and on the vehicles." He retrieved three plastic cylinders from the box and tucked them into his bag. "So what are you doing here?"

"I told you; I'm going to Cillineese."

"With a rat? And on foot?" The man brushed his shaggy brown hair from his eyes. "I have some water, but you can't have it until you tell me more."

"Fine." She sighed. "Samuel told me to go to Cillineese, so I'm going. The rat's kind of a pet."

"I don't know who Samuel is, but here." The man tossed her a brown plastic bottle.

She caught it with one hand, the rat's cage balanced in the other. "Thanks."

"You can walk with me to Cillineese." He closed his bag and patted the leather. "These messages are low priority, so I don't have to hurry."

She tucked the cage under her arm and popped the bottle's lid open. Water trickled into her mouth, washing the dirt from her teeth and down her throat. Coughing, she capped the bottle and threw it back to the man. "I'm Monica."

He slung it into his bag. "Kraft."

He started off at a slow jog. "Can you keep up?"

"I think so." Monica ran alongside at his pace. She'd rather go by herself and avoid all the questions, but he would be able to get her through the Cillineese barrier, and that was definitely worth the inconvenience.

"So what's your story, kid?" His voice shook as he jogged, making his words seem to bounce.

"It's a little involved." The rat squealed with her every step as it slid around its floor. She tried to steady it, but even her softest footfalls shook the cage.

"Okay, just start off with why you're bothering with that creature. If you want a pet, any of the delivery boys could get you a new one in Cillineese, but all they do is eat your food." Kraft slowed to a walk and nodded at the cage. "You want me to put that in my bag?"

Monica handed the cage to him. He shoved it into his pouch, creating a bulge in the leather, stretching the seams. "Thanks." As they accelerated again, she concentrated on keeping up the pace. "Let's just say that he's trained to do something for me."

"Okay, that'll do." Kraft kept his eyes straight ahead. "Now tell me why you're down here alone."

"I have a new assignment, I guess you could say." Monica's heart thumped hard in her chest. It was a new assignment, just not the kind this guy would think it was. But she couldn't tell him what was really happening, could she?

"You guess I could say?" Kraft raised an eyebrow and looked at her, not shortening his stride or missing a step. "Why don't you tell me straight out?"

Monica felt a blush creeping up her neck and cheeks. "I've been telling a lot of people recently, and it's not safe."

"Who am I going to tell?" Kraft looked ahead again, staring into the dimly lit tunnel. "Your secret's safe with me. Besides, I'm doing you a favor, letting you travel with me. Some cave monster might get you if you were here by yourself." He laughed, but the soft chuckle sounded choked. He pressed his face into his elbow and coughed loudly, his footfalls slowing. "I'm getting too old for all this running."

"Well, to answer your question, you could tell the Nobles. You talk to them all the time, and there are no monsters in the tunnels." As Kraft again coughed violently, Monica frowned. "Are you okay?"

He stopped and braced his hands on his knees. "I avoid the Nobles as much as possible." He glared at her. "You house slaves don't have much to do with us messengers, but we don't relish our jobs any more than you do." Another fit of coughing shook his body.

Monica shrugged. "I like to work. It's better than doing nothing." She tapped his bag. "Are you sure you're okay? I could carry it for you."

"We're almost to Cillineese." Kraft straightened and rubbed the back of his head. "We'd better hurry up." He broke into a run, as if unaffected by his coughing spell.

Monica darted after him. Her toes dug into the dirt, but her shorter strides barely kept up with Kraft's. As she drew up to his side, a scowl etched his features, probably because of the pain from his chip.

"Here we are." Kraft's words came in short gasps as he pounded to a halt in front of the huge steel door blocking the way to the

Cillineese tunnels. He wrenched the rat's cage from his bag and handed it to Monica. "There you go."

She held the cage close. "Thank you."

Kraft put his hand on the door. The steel slid upward, inching into the ceiling's metal pocket. He ushered Monica through the widening gap. "Quick—it closes pretty fast."

She stumbled forward. Kraft jogged through after her, his big boots just missing her feet as he shoved her farther into the tunnel. The door slid closed, catching the corner of Kraft's bag between the metal and the wall. "Great." He yanked on the satchel, and the corner tore away, leaving a chunk of leather in the crack.

Monica pressed herself against the wall, a hand on her chest. "That was close."

One of the message cylinders slid through the hole in Kraft's bag. He caught the tube in one hand. "Perfect. Now I need a new bag. This will put me even further behind." He tapped the message box embedded in the wall and, after the door opened, dumped two of the cylinders inside. Glancing at Monica, he pulled the bag's strap over his head and bundled it into one hand. "Don't you have somewhere to be?"

"First you interrogate me," Monica muttered, "then you try to get rid of me."

"Just trying to keep you out of trouble." Kraft handed his bag to her. "Could you put this in a laundry chute for me? There's one on the way to the dorms."

"Fine." Monica folded the bag under her arm. "Do you know where the library is from here?"

"No, I don't."

She shifted the cage in her arms, keeping her fingers clear of the rat's teeth. "Last time I went to that library . . ." She stopped. There was no reason to tell this man about her previous journey. He was nosy enough already. "I guess I can find my own way."

Kraft gripped his last message tube. "One of the house slaves will be able to help you. They know every inch of the palace. I stick to the tunnels." He pointed at the open tunnel in front of them. "Just follow that and take the stairs up to the dorms. It's almost a quarter mile to the stairs."

Monica nodded. "Okay. Thanks for helping me."

"Sure." Kraft ran down the tunnel, again coughing.

Monica walked toward the dorm stairs, her legs feeling rubbery. Time to figure out why in the world the slaves' council wanted her to find this book and what it had to do with the all-important paper.

CHAPTER 18

The tunnel looked the same as all the others—walls and ceilings of packed dirt and wooden beams supporting the weight of the earth above, extending far into the darkness.

She trudged along, dragging her feet over clay. After a few minutes, a sharp jolt stabbed her thigh. Crying out, she fell to the ground, dropping the rat's cage and Kraft's bag. She clawed at her pocket, and ripped it from the seam. Her wristband and vial tumbled out. As pain lanced through her skin, she clamped her hands on her thigh and groaned. The chip's vial rolled on the floor, and her wristband's screen blinked off.

She sat on the hard ground and pulled her skirt hem up. A red welt pulsed a few inches below her hip. Shaking her head, she climbed back to her feet and kicked the white-hot vial into the tunnel wall. The computers must have given up on getting her back in bounds and terminated her.

She ripped away a section of her dress's hem. As she tied the cloth around the wound, the pain grew. "Cursed thing." She pounded the wall with a fist, tears welling in her eyes. If she hadn't been so careless, this wouldn't have happened. Forgetting about the chip was stupid.

Arcs of electricity leaped between the wristband and vial, illuminating the tunnel floor and walls. Pressing a hand against the wrapped burn, she picked up the cage and bag and scurried away, her leg aching from the shock. If the chip had stayed in her pocket any longer, those electric jolts could have paralyzed her.

The journey to the dorms stretched on and on. Every step reminded her of the jolt, and climbing the stairs to the dorms only increased the pain. When she placed her weight on each step, the board lit up, as if telling the world of her agony.

At the top of the first set of stairs, a small girl lay on the landing, her head cradled in her arms. Water covered the floor around her, and her skimpy dress clung to her thin frame.

Monica knelt beside her and nudged her shoulder. "Hey, are you okay?"

A cough racked the girl's body. She opened her eyes. "I'm fine." She crawled to a sitting position and set a hand on her forehead. "Don't tell anyone I was sleeping. Please?" Coughing again, she picked up a scrub brush that lay beside her. "I don't want to go to the infirmary." She scrubbed vigorously at the smooth boards.

"You should go to the infirmary. The rest would be good for you." Monica massaged her burn. Once when she was much younger, she had to go to the infirmary after a chip had given her a particularly nasty shock. The nurse tried to be nice, but the dark room had been frightening, and her parents weren't allowed to see her.

Monica set the rat's cage on the floor. "Can you tell me how to get to the library from here?"

"I've never been to the library." The girl dropped the brush into a bucket. "My aunt worked there for a while, but no one goes there anymore." She leaned her head against the wall. "I want to go back to sleep."

"Just stay awake a minute more, okay?" Monica put a hand on

the girl's shoulder. "Can you tell me which way your aunt used to go? Maybe you can point me in the right direction."

The girl closed her eyes. "It's near the middle of the palace. I think." She tapped the wall. "You just have to head away from here. It will take a while . . ." Her head drooped against her shoulder, and her breathing slowed.

Monica felt the girl's pasty forehead—hot and sweaty—then slid her wristband all the way up to her thin shoulder and tapped a button on the screen. A list of options scrolled across the monitor—*Delayed*, *Trouble*, and *Sick*. She selected the last in the line and chose *Pick up* from a new list.

Brushing the damp hair from around the girl's closed eyes, Monica said, "I'm sorry, but you're too sick to stay here. I had to call them."

The girl moaned. "I don't want to go."

Monica helped her lie back down. "You'll get to rest. You won't have to work. You can sleep all day long."

"My grandpa never came back." The girl's eyes opened wide. A glassy film covered the dark brown orbs. "I never got to see him again."

"Don't worry." Monica held the girl's hand. "I'll stay with you until the nurse comes. She'll take good care of you."

Two girls galloped down the stairs.

"Watch out!" Monica yelled.

The girls skidded to a halt. They plopped down on the steps and stared at Monica. "It's you again."

Monica nodded at the twins. "Yeah, I'm back. Why are you in such a hurry?"

The girl on the left, Tali, spoke up, "We like to run, and we're on an errand for someone." She pointed at the sick child. "Is Margo okay?"

Monica shook her head. "No, she's sick."

Tali shrugged. "Nanci will take care of her." She stood and

took her sister's arm and tugged her past Margo. "We're going to be late, Jas."

Jas followed her sister down the stairs, calling over her shoulder, "Feel better soon, Margo."

Monica squeezed Margo's hand. "Tali is right; Nanci will take care of you."

Margo's shoulders quaked. Tears seeped through her clenched eyelids. She gripped Monica's hand so hard, her knuckles turned white, her skin hot to the touch.

"It's okay. Nanci should be here soon." Monica's heart raced. Oftentimes an older person would get sick, but the children were usually healthy. She dipped her fingers into the bucket of water and let some droplets fall on Margo's forehead.

Quiet footfalls whispered through the staircase. A woman appeared at Monica's side, as if from nowhere.

Monica glanced up at the wrinkled, stooped woman. "You're here. Thank goodness."

Nanci smiled, revealing crooked, yellowing teeth. "Yes, of course." She tapped her wristband. "The sick call, and I answer." Her cracked fingernails clicked on the rusted watch screen.

"She's really sick." Monica scooped up the feather-light girl. "Can you help her? I know they don't give you medicine, but you can still help her, right?"

"Of course." Nanci extended her sticklike arms. "Just give her to me, and I'll take her to the infirmary right away."

"Are you able to carry her?" Monica asked. "I mean—I could carry her for you." She would be even later meeting Simon, but helping Margo was more important.

"It would certainly be nice, but there's no use offering something you can't deliver, so just give her to me."

Monica shook her head. "But I can. I'm mostly free."

Nanci's brow knit together. "That doesn't make sense, but my arthritis is mighty fierce today, so I'd be appreciative of the help."

"Glad to. I'm going to be here for a while, so I might as well get to know the area."

Margo wrapped her feverish arms around Monica's neck. "Don't leave me."

Nanci smiled. "That settles it, then." She waved Monica down a side tunnel. "Once you drop her off at the infirmary, I can tell you where to go from there for your next assignment."

"Thank you." Smiling, she nodded toward the rat and the bag. "Could you carry those for me?"

***

Monica tramped up the last set of stairs to the library, her leg still twinging, though no longer a real bother. The steps ended at a chest-high wooden door. Black caulking sealed the edges all around and covered the handle and latch.

She poked the caulk. Some of it stuck under her fingernail, and she wiped it on her dress. Nanci had said the library was sealed off from the house slaves, so this was no surprise, and the entrance Monica used during the previous visit had also been jammed.

Putting her ear to the door, she pressed herself against the wood, trying to hear anything stirring on the other side. Papers rustled somewhere in the room. Shuffling footsteps scraped across the smooth floor, perhaps an older person or an exhausted worker. Maybe Simon was in there.

Monica set the caged rat on the ground before knocking on the door. "Is there someone there? Can you let me in?"

The footsteps drew closer. "Who's there?" the voice came through muffled.

Monica pushed on the solid wood, but it didn't budge. "I'm looking for Simon. I was here yesterday."

"Oh, yes, you," Simon said. "The girl who brought me that impossible paper." The sound of fingernails on wood penetrated the wall. "I don't know if this door will open, actually. Haven't used it in years, but you do need to come in. I need a new assistant. Just a moment."

Monica sat on her heels. "Okay."

The door shuddered. Bits of black caulk flew from the frame. The pieces fell on Monica's lap and littered the floor.

Monica scooted back. "What are you doing?"

"Trying to get the door open. What do you think?" He grunted, and the door shook again. "I'm too old for this. You try."

Monica set her shoulder against the thick door. Bracing her feet, she threw her weight into it. The boards groaned. More bits of hardened black resin fell to the ground.

As she slammed into the door again and again, her shoulder throbbed. After several heaves, something cracked. Splinters pierced her dress, digging into her skin.

When she backed away, a shaft of light poured through a fist-sized hole in the door. Simon's face appeared in the gap. "That was a bit drastic. Now I'll have to get it repaired."

Monica rubbed her shoulder. "I'm okay. Don't worry about me."

"I wasn't worried about you."

"I guessed that." She frowned at the tiny hole. "This doesn't help me get through."

Simon's wrinkled face disappeared. "Just a moment. I'll look for a pry bar of some kind." His voice sounded far away.

"I'll just wait here, then." Monica slid her neckband to the side and picked some splinters from her shoulder. Flecks of blood oozed around the tiny wounds. Wincing, she rolled her shoulder back and forth, loosening the muscles and joint until the pain started to ease.

She looked again at the hole. Where was Simon going to find a pry bar in the library anyway? He had said something about needing a new assistant. Did he really do something to Nat like he threatened?

Simon reappeared, a rusty hooked bar in his hands. He passed it through. "Try this, but don't make the hole any bigger. It'll be hard enough to hide as it is."

"I'll do my best." After sliding the cage out of the way, she took the bar and jabbed it between the door and its frame. As the caulk pulled away, the frame's wood shrieked and splintered, and the bar's claw gouged out a chunk of the door. Gritting her teeth and bracing herself, she threw her whole body into the next effort. The door ripped away from the frame in one piece, bringing the hinges with it.

The momentum threw Monica to the floor, the pry bar clanking at one side and the door landing with a thud at the other. As dust and debris rained on her body, she held her arms in front of her face.

Simon's stooped figure appeared in the opening. He waved a hand through the cloud of dust. "You really knocked it away, didn't you?"

Monica jumped back to her feet, coughing through her reply. "Sorry about that."

The rat sneezed.

"I think your friend doesn't approve." Simon nudged the cage with his shoe. "Of the dust or his imprisonment."

Monica wiped grit from her eyes and picked up the cage, then pushed past Simon into the well-lit library. Her lungs clearing, she breathed more easily.

Simon followed her, pry bar in hand. "You're very trouble-some, young lady."

"Troublesome?" Monica wiped dirt off her dress. She shook her head, and a rain of pebbles and splinters fell from her hair. "Prying it was your idea."

"You're the one who wanted to come in." Simon shuffled to a bookshelf lying on its back in the middle of the room and laid the pry bar on the floor. "Come help me with this."

Monica put the rat down and scurried to his side. She glanced around the room. A whole row of shelves had fallen over, and papers lay scattered everywhere. "What happened?"

"A minor disaster. After we block the hole, I will explain."

She picked up one end of the shelf. As Simon helped her lift, his skinny arms bulged under his black uniform. When the shelf reached an upright position, now towering over Monica's head, its wooden legs rocked back and forth. Bracing the side with a hand, she steadied it until the wobbling stopped.

At her feet, piles of worn books littered the floor where they had toppled from the shelves. Dust bunnies sailed through the disturbed air. She picked up a book and brushed off its faded green jacket. White flowing script covered the front—George Orwell, *Nineteen Eighty-Four*, a novel.

After flipping through the book's brittle yellow pages, she handed it to Simon. "You certainly have a big mess to clean up."

"Be careful." Simon snatched the volume. He stroked the spine and settled the novel on the shelf. "This is hundreds of years old, a first edition. We don't have many from this time period." He scratched his head. "Lots of book burnings when things started to fall apart, but men like me managed to save some." Stooping, he began sorting and stacking the jumble of tomes. "If that stupid boy hadn't been so clumsy, I wouldn't be in this mess."

"Is he okay?" Monica crouched beside Simon. Her leg throbbed, reminding her why she was here. "I was told you wanted me for something. Did you finish the paper I gave you?"

"Those bits of shredded tree fiber? Hardly worth calling paper." He shoved more books back into place. "The writing is so faded. Who would bury paper anyway? It's not good for it."

"So you didn't finish?" Monica's heart sank. Why would the council tell her to come if Simon hadn't even finished restoring the note?

"No, I didn't finish. That's why I need you here. You certainly took your time arriving, too." Simon cradled a book that had been pressed between the shelf and the floor. He ran his gnarled fingers over the torn, threadbare cover. "*Ben Hur*. What a masterpiece.

And torn by a clumsy mistake." He set the novel on a table at his side. "Fortunately, he can't do it again. And once I repair Mr. Hur, it will be just like it was before."

Monica picked up another torn book, *Dead Souls* by Nikolai Gogol. She handed it to Simon. "Did Nat get reassigned?"

"In a manner of speaking." Simon shoved the book onto the shelf. "Gogol never finished writing that one." He stood and stretched. "This is too hard on an old man's back." He shuffled to a folding chair beside one of the overturned bookcases and sat down. "Nat reassigned himself."

Monica raised an eyebrow. A self-reassignment? That would be new. She continued stacking books, reading the title of each one, names she had never seen before. Only a few of the slaves could read, and they were never given any books. Her father taught both her and her mother how to read using the papers and notes her mother brought to the dorm when she cleaned the Noble children's schoolrooms. "Can Seen reassign themselves?"

"No, of course not. No one but the computers can reassign people." Simon sat back in his chair and closed his eyes. "Nat decided to use the shelves in this room as dominoes, probably by accident, but he was crushed by one, so he won't ever get to tell us."

A wave of dizziness made her sway in place. "He's dead?"

"Sure is. That's why I need you, a new assistant. It's hard to find even a Seen who can read. Being a Noble, I assumed you could."

Monica imagined the toppling shelves. Poor Nat. How could a boy so thin accidentally knock one of these huge cases over? He must have been terrified when it came crashing down.

Simon dug into his pocket and pulled out a tiny glass cylinder and wristband. "You'll be happy to know that I saved his chip for you. They told me how to get it out properly and care for it. You'd think something so small wouldn't be so difficult."

Monica gulped. Just yesterday Nat had been alive and well.

She had seen slaves killed by the Nobles for being out-of-bounds, but she never heard of someone dying because of an accident.

Simon rose to his feet and handed Monica the vial and band. "You're welcome. It was a nasty business, and it was difficult getting the infirmary nurse to agree to help me."

Monica clenched the vial in her fist. "You're so hard-hearted. Maybe she just doesn't like you."

"I care not who likes me or hates me. I will shed no tears."

"How can you not be sad about Nat? He was so young."

"Easy." Simon shrugged. "He was a nuisance, and he often messed up books. I don't like anyone who ruins these treasures, and I don't have the patience to deal with children. You're much older, so I hope you do better."

Monica jumped to her feet, glaring at him. "I'm here only until the council has another assignment for me. I hope they make it fast, too." She tied the vial around her neck with the short leather strap that had been strung through a hole in the cylinder. "And I'll have to hide every time a Noble comes in here, you know. I'm not a boy, and I'm not dressed like a Seen. Nat might have been bigger than me, but he was a lot younger, like you said." She touched her worn dress. "And you can see for yourself that I'm not really a Noble."

"Those are all simple problems." Simon grinned, showing all his crooked teeth. "I'll get the laundry to send us a spare dress, and if a Noble sees you, they'll assume the computers made a mistake. It happens."

She fastened the chain-link wristband around her wrist. "They'll buy that a girl has been registered as a boy for sixteen years?"

"Perhaps, but only children and the more scholarly relatives visit. The governor never comes up here. He has little interest in books." Simon scurried to his desk in the adjoining room and rifled through some papers in a drawer.

Monica ran after him. "What are you doing?"

"Sending a message to the laundry, of course." He scribbled a quick note on a page and shoved it into a courier's tube, which he deposited in a hole in the floor. "There you are. Someone should be up here in a few minutes. I told them it was urgent."

"So what do we do now?"

"We?" He shuffled around some papers on the desk. "I'll be working on that terrible paper you gave me." Some pages slipped to the floor, but he ignored them. "You can finish picking up those books."

"Is there anything I can do to help you with the page?"

"As a matter of fact, there is." He handed her a thin yellow book. "You were called here to find a book. Look around for one like this, a diary written in Old Cillineese. I need at least one. More would be better. You see, in order to understand what is written on the paper, I need more examples of the language. If I can translate parts of the diary, I should be able to translate the paper." Waving her away, he slid on a spindly pair of glasses. "Go on now. I'm busy."

She clutched the book tightly in one hand. "Fine."

Gritting her teeth, she stomped into the other room. After sliding the rat's cage near one of the overturned cases, she sat with her back to the case's side and flipped through the book.

Handwritten, flowing script filled each page. The alphabet was familiar, the same one they used in Cantral, but the words they created made no sense. A printed date appeared at the top of each page, beginning with January 1, 2852, on the first and ending with May 15, 2857, on the last.

She touched the final date. Whoever wrote this had started just months before she was born and ended a week before Cillineese's termination. She slid the book into her pocket and started sorting through others. She had to find more Old Cillineese. For now, nothing else mattered.   •

CHAPTER 19

Monica wiped the sweat from her eyes. Four bookshelves standing, just one left to put up. A grimy handkerchief kept her hair tied back from her face, but some strands escaped and stuck to her damp forehead.

She sat next to a pile of books waiting to go in their proper places. Her back and legs ached from lifting the shelves to their feet. Simon had insisted she do the work alone, complaining that his limbs were too weak and feeble for such a task.

Monica rubbed her sore thigh. He hadn't asked how *she* felt about the job. She was tired, too. He certainly showed he had enough strength earlier when moving the first shelf.

She nudged a stack of books with a bare foot. Most of the volumes sorted easily into categories, but she had some set aside to ask Simon about. He claimed he was too busy to help her at the moment.

In the other room, he sat at his desk, scribbling furiously with a fountain pen. Whenever he lifted the point from the paper, drops of ink sprayed this way and that. As he tried to piece the paper together, his mutterings floated by, nothing more than indistinct gibberish.

Monica's dress stuck to her body, and, as she sat still, the room seemed to get hotter. She peeled off her jacket and let it drop to the floor. As soon as it landed, the rat pulled a sleeve into its cage.

Monica yanked it away. "Don't do that! I might need it later."

"Why are you keeping that thing around, anyway?" Simon yelled from his workstation. "Rodents chew my books. I set traps for them. They are a nice side dish to go with the meal bars."

Monica grimaced. "That's disgusting. You don't really eat rats, do you?"

Simon placed his pen on the desk and leaned back in his chair. "Yes, of course. They're very tasty, not disgusting at all. It'd be wasteful just to dispose of them."

A soft scratching noise sounded at the library's double doors. Monica froze. "I need to hide."

"No, of course not." Simon rose to his feet. "Just a minute," he shouted.

She glanced at the gaping opening in the wall. "What about the hole?"

"Nothing to worry about."

Monica gulped. Was he trying to get her in trouble? She crept up behind him, ready to dart if a Noble or Seen waited at the entry.

Simon pulled the door open. A sweaty little boy stood at the threshold, holding out a brown paper package bound with twine. "We got a message, sir, down in the laundry." He wiped sweat from his eyes with his ragged sleeve. "You said you needed this."

"Yes, I did, and that was an hour ago. What took you so long?"

The boy's gaze darted all around the room. "I can't get in the library directly; all the passages are sealed off. I had to come out another access door down the hall, but no one caught me." He handed the package to Simon. "Do you need anything else?"

Simon tugged at the fibrous twine. "No, no. Nothing else."

The boy darted away, his feet slipping out from under him in his frantic dash. He fell on the floor and bounced back up, as if he were attached to puppet strings.

"The east passage from the infirmary isn't sealed anymore!" Simon yelled after him. "But that doesn't mean you wall slaves can come poking in here whenever you want to."

He slammed the door shut and threw the package at Monica. "Something decent for you to wear."

Monica caught the bundle. "What I'm wearing is decent." When she untied the string, a soft black dress tumbled out of the wrappings.

"I would call your dress a rag. It doesn't fall into the *nice* category at all. This new one, however, is definitely nice." Simon took the paper and twine from her, crumpling them into a wad. He tossed them over his shoulder, and they landed in a wire basket by his desk.

Monica stroked the silky fabric. He was right. Compared to this dress, her current garment was a rag. Her fingertips left dusty marks on the shoulders and long sleeves. "Where do Seen bathe? I don't want to get my new dress dirty."

"We have a bathroom attached to our dormitories." He rolled his eyes upward, as if imagining his living quarters. "Unfortunately, you'll have to wait until night duty to shower. You're stuck here until then. I'm afraid Nat was on probation, so you won't be able to push any boundaries when you're wearing his chip."

"Thanks for the warning." Monica sighed. "So you're saying since this is a guy's chip, I'll have to use the men's bathroom now."

"Of course." Simon shuffled to his desk, sat down heavily in his chair, and picked up his pen. "The computers don't look kindly upon males sneaking into the ladies' facilities."

As the memory of her recent shock surfaced, she massaged her thigh. The last time she had a male's chip, she had to be very careful when bathing. Maybe the Seen bathrooms were different, though. They had a lot more privileges than did the slaves in the walls.

When Monica entered Simon's room, he held out his hand. "Do you have that journal I gave you earlier? I need it back."

"It's right here." She dropped the book on the desk. "Are you close to translating any of the page?"

"It's possible." He traced his finger over some words near the end of the journal. "Your name is in here. Did you know that?"

Monica peered over his hand. Amidst the jumble of unrecognizable words, her name appeared twice on the page. "No, I didn't. Is this from someone in my family?"

"I thought you would have noticed your own name. After the middle of the book, it's on almost every page." Simon picked up his glasses. "It could easily be from one of your family members, probably your mother."

Monica gasped. "My mother?"

He glared at her. "If you had found more books in this language, this would take a lot less time." His glasses magnified his dark brown eyes, making his beady stare even more piercing.

"I'll get back to searching. I still have at least one shelf to go. The first one was full of fiction almost a thousand years old. And I couldn't even read all of the titles. They weren't Old Cillineese, though."

"Leave the last shelf for now." Simon pulled a magnifying glass from a drawer, along with a roll of book mender's tape. "There's a shelf across from the toppled ones. It has more recent books on it. I've searched the upper half already."

Just as she turned to leave, he continued. "And put that dress on. I already have enough messes in here. If someone comes in to use the library, there will be too many questions to answer without you hanging around here looking like a wall slave." He ripped off a piece of tape and joined two bits of paper with it. "Now go on."

Monica nodded, ran to the shelf, and hid behind the long row. She unfastened the two buttons on the back of her dress and changed into the new garment as fast as she could. The silky material fell only to her knees, and the long sleeves stopped half an inch from her wrists. "Simon?" She stepped out from behind the bookcase, smoothing the plain-cut bodice. "I don't think it fits right." She wiggled her bare toes. "And don't Seen wear shoes?"

"You are very ungrateful," Simon said, his head still bowed over his work. "I'll find you some shoes later. I don't think Nat's will fit you. The dress will have to do."

Monica sighed. "Fine." She threw the old dress on the floor next to her jacket, then pulled over one of the rolling ladders attached to the shelves. As she climbed, her toes gripped the rungs, steadying her. Books of all sizes and colors filled the middle shelf, each spine bearing the book's title. Different languages covered them, and they seemed to be in no particular order.

"Simon?" Monica called, "Don't you have any sort of shelving system for these books?" She picked up one written with a strange-looking alphabet. Long strokes made up different shapes. Some looked like pictures, but others just appeared to be random, skewed forms. "I can't even read most of these."

"Of course I have a system. I just can't remember it." Simon snorted. "Why can't you read other languages? You're a Noble."

Monica slid the book back and ran her finger down the spines of five more. None appeared to be written in Old Cillineese. "I don't know who gave you that idea. I'm a wall slave."

"It's obvious. I see Nobles every day. You're definitely a Noble. Your face is too refined to even be half Seen, half Noble. However, the slave council trusts you, so you must be safe to talk to." He turned in his chair and looked at her. "Your heritage is puzzling, but that's of little matter."

Monica climbed down the ladder and sat on the floor. "The council trusts me? They order me around like they *own* me."

"Quiet down!" Simon growled. "Someone's coming."

The door creaked open. A little girl crept into the room. Her head barely reached the pull ring embedded in the wood. She leaned her back against the door and threw her weight into closing it.

"Simon? I finished the novels you picked out for me." She dragged an embroidered bag to Simon's desk, her shoulders bowed by the weight.

Simon pushed back his chair. "Already, Audrey? That was faster than ever." He took the bag from her and piled the books onto his desk. "Is your tutor pleased with your translations this time?"

"Yes." She wiped her forehead with the back of her long-sleeved blue dress. "But he says I need to work on my French." She did a three-sixty, spinning on her heel. Her skirt flared as she turned, showing off the gold embroidery around the hem. "What happened to everything?"

"Oh, just an accident." Simon waved at the books scattered across the floor and frowned at Monica. "I had to get a new assistant."

Audrey stared at Monica, her eyes widening.

Monica matched the girl's gaze. As Audrey continued to stare, Monica raised an eyebrow and shrugged. What was with this girl? She acted like she had never met a Seen before.

Audrey blinked and looked back at Simon. "Why'd Nat have to go?"

Simon rolled a wooden cart piled with aged novels up to her. "He caused too much trouble. Monica is much better behaved." He selected two large tomes and laid them in Audrey's arms. The top of the books touched her chin. "Here you are. *Les Miserables*, in French. You're very fortunate to have that. Most of the copies were lost, but your father found one and had a print made just for this library."

She wrinkled her nose. "They're huge."

"But fascinating." He tapped the book on top. "And this one, *Under the Sea*. A more recent work by one of the Nobles of a lesser city in the arctic ice houses. I chose that one because of your fascination with seals. This copy was translated for Cantral's library, as required by law. I thought you might like it as a break from all the dead languages."

"Thank you." Audrey lifted her chin and sneezed. "How long have these been sitting here?"

"A month or two." Simon held out the girl's bag, and she slid the novels inside. "I have several others set aside, but they will wait." He nodded toward Monica. "My assistant and I have a translation project at the moment." Glaring at Monica, he snarled, "Get back to work!"

Monica shuddered. She'd been watching them so intently that she forgot about her search. She rose to her feet and scanned the books. The titles swirled before her eyes. If her father hadn't rebelled, could she have been like this girl? She had just started her formal education when her nurse whisked her away from death.

While Simon puttered about nearby, she finished going through another two shelves. In the final row, some books lay across the tops of the others, squeezed into the last inch of space. Rising to tiptoes, she picked up one that lay across the top. The words across the spine seemed familiar. Letters from the Cantral alphabet formed words she couldn't read. As she tried to place the memories, she whispered, "Simon?"

He peered around the shelf, his hands on a cart piled high with books. "What is it? I have another two students coming soon. I need to find selections for them."

"Is this one in Old Cillineese?" She handed him the tattered book. "The words sort of look like the diary."

"Really?" Simon opened the brittle pages and caressed the faded words. "Excellent!"

"So it's what we're looking for?" She bounced on her toes. "Can you translate it?"

Simon pushed the cart into her grasp. "Yes, of course. This is a children's story, written by a renowned author. He lived in the eastern continent that was once Europe. The stories have been popular for over a hundred years." Simon's smile grew. "I have at least three other copies of this in various languages. It will be simple to translate it to Cantral."

Monica gripped the trolley's edge. "That's great! When do you think you can have it done?"

"Patience!" Simon stared at her. "I haven't finished piecing together the note yet. I have other duties to perform first."

"I know. I just thought this was more important."

He pointed a shaking finger at her. "You do realize that if the authorities find out about this project we will both be killed. And they would consider terminating Cillineese again." He limped to his desk, the book tucked under his arm. "I can't believe I'm doing this. My curiosity is just too much for me. There are books that talk about cats being killed for having too much curiosity. I wonder where I could get a cat." He sat down, still muttering to himself. "But then I would have to share the rats with it."

"If you're so worried about it, why did you tell Audrey about the translation?"

"A secret project makes people curious. The more open I am, the fewer probing noses we'll see."

"I suppose you're right." Monica sighed. "Didn't you say you had some other people coming?"

"Yes, yes." Simon's voice carried across the room. His fingers busily shuffled the scraps of paper around as he spoke. "The governor's nephews are visiting from Gilnel. Their father is a lesser Noble there. Apparently, he thinks they will receive a better education here in Cillineese. Why anyone would send his children to a city under such a tight watch is beyond my grasp."

Monica rolled her eyes. This guy sure could talk if you got him started. "I guess Nobles can do what they please."

"They can't do just anything," Simon said. "The Nobles have

to ask for transfers from the highest council, of course. Naturally, the biggest city-states get special privileges. Easier to control that way."

She wheeled the cart forward an inch. "What do you want me to do with this?"

He attached two more pieces together with tape and held the joined scraps up to the magnifying glass. "Put it in front of that disgraceful hole, but clean up the debris first. Toss the rubble inside the tunnel. Someone will come along to collect it."

"What do you want me to do with all these books? I don't know your shelving system."

Simon didn't answer. He didn't even bother to turn his head.

Sighing again, Monica rolled the trolley to the gaping hole in the wall. Bits of caulking, wood, and dust covered the floor in a three-foot radius. She picked up a wood shard and stared at its sharp point. This could take a while.

CHAPTER 20

Monica pushed the last book onto its proper shelf. Now that this job was done, maybe Simon would give her something more interesting to do. Her hands folded behind her, she walked toward his desk where he still sat, bent over his work. "How is it going?"

"There are a few pieces missing." Simon leaned back in his chair. He rubbed his eyes, pushing his glasses up onto his forehead. "They must have crumbled while they were buried in the tunnel. I have managed to reassemble most of it." Holding up a new sheet of paper, he yawned. "I have some of the readable bits translated, but our shift has ended."

Monica drooped her shoulders. "You're quitting?"

"Of course not." Simon shuffled his papers and slid them into a folder. "I'm just done for the night. I'm an old man, and I need my rest. If I get sick and go to the infirmary, you would have to go to the north wing of Cantral or even Restrin to find someone who could do the same job as I. Restrin is over a hundred miles away. I doubt you would like making that journey outside."

"Maybe I would. You never know."

"No, you wouldn't." He tucked the folder under his arm. "It would be especially difficult for you, since you're agoraphobic."

As she silently tried to repeat the strange word, he stared over the tops of his glasses. "At least, I assume you are; all the other wall slaves are, but with your early Noble upbringing, perhaps not." Stroking his chin, Simon ambled toward the door. "Even Audrey noticed."

"Audrey noticed what?" Heat rose into Monica's cheeks. "And no, I don't want you to get sick, but I don't know what agora . . . whatever you said, means."

"Excellent. Being sick is most inconvenient. You shouldn't wish it on anyone." Simon opened the door and gestured for her to go first. "Audrey noticed your striking resemblance. You look very much like Audrey and her sister. Your features give you away. Don't you ever look in a mirror?"

Monica bundled the rat cage, her jacket, and old dress into her arms. "No, we didn't have any mirrors. No one really cares how they look." She stepped into the marble-floored hallway. "I don't know where we're going."

Simon snapped the door shut and jammed a thick gold key into the lock. "I've been here since right after the termination. I could get to my dorm with my eyes closed. Fortunately for you, Nat was in the same dorm as I. Otherwise you'd be on your own. The other dorm is not nearly as nice as ours, and it's on the other side of the palace."

"Oh." Monica tugged the hem of her old dress out of the rat's paws. "Our dorms aren't like that. They're always the same. One isn't nicer than another."

Simon ushered her down the spacious corridor, past suits of armor and elaborate paintings. "Don't speak about that out here. Your dorms are the same as mine. Don't forget; you're a Seen."

Monica gazed at the elaborate mural etched across the ceiling. Shivers crawled up and down her spine. This space was so huge. Though the ornate carved walls hid the movements of the slaves inside, the faintest rustling of their footsteps passed through as they went about their work.

Out in this expansive hall, the walls were far from pressing on her shoulders, and there were no pipes or air ducts to crawl around.

Monica hugged her bundle close. "I might be a Seen officially, but I sure don't feel like one."

"That's all right. Just act like one, and you will be fine." As Simon guided her down a side passage, he lowered his voice. "Whisper in the halls. We are allowed to be around the Nobles, but they want us to be as quiet as possible."

They passed under gold light fixtures slightly smaller than those in the main hall and paintings less colorful. As they walked into an even narrower corridor, Monica tensed. Where were the Seen dorms, anyway? "I've only met a few Seen in my entire life. I don't know how you act."

"Faye was Seen. She took care of you your first four years. Act like your nurse, and you'll be fine." Simon raised a finger. "Except for the last part, since she ended up dead."

Monica sighed. "I don't remember her very well, so that doesn't help."

He tugged on a thick rope dangling beside floor-to-ceiling velvet curtains. "Stand back, please."

As she retreated a few steps, a staircase unfolded from the ceiling until the bottom step hung a foot above the floor. Two rope railings led to a small hole at the top. Light shone from the entrance and into the hallway.

Monica craned her neck to see inside, but no one appeared through the opening. "I didn't know there was anything above our dorms."

"Of course not. We're kept in the attic section. None of the wall slaves' tunnels reach us." Simon prodded her in the back. "Hurry up. We're out-of-bounds now. Past curfew."

Monica tucked her bundle under one arm and grabbed a rope railing. "This doesn't look very sturdy."

Simon poked her again. "Twenty people use this every morning and evening. It is quite sturdy. Now climb before you cause me any more pain."

"All right." She placed one foot on the first board. The step shook under her weight and swayed back and forth. Simon jabbed her between the shoulder blades, forcing her up the stairs.

As she entered the hole carved in the ceiling, she ducked to avoid the frame. A cool breeze blew her hair into her eyes. She shook it away and stepped into the attic room.

Fans hanging from the ceiling stirred the air. Ten beds lined the sides of the rooms. The standard curtains surrounded each bed, though they were bright and embroidered, not the usual drab colors. The lights in the fans' fixtures blinked once.

Simon popped through the hole and folded the ladder up before covering the opening with a board. A small boy unrolled a blue and gold rug, hiding the trapdoor.

"Thank you, Alfred." Simon ruffled the boy's hair.

Alfred grinned. "You're welcome. You're late." He pointed at Monica. "Is she Nat's replacement?"

"Yes, but don't point." Simon pushed the boy's hand down. "I've told you before; it's rude."

Monica nodded. "Yeah, I'm here to replace him."

Simon set his file folder on top of Monica's bundle. "Keep this, and don't lose it."

"What's that?" Alfred stood on his tiptoes.

"It's none of your business." Simon ushered him away. "Your mother put me in charge of you before she was transferred, and I won't let you put yourself in danger."

The boy climbed into a bed in the corner. "Danger?" He bounced on the bed. "Are you in some sort of plot? Libraries are always significant in those stories you read me."

"That's because I make most of those up." Simon snapped the curtains closed. "Now go to sleep. You'll be sorry in the morning if you don't."

"Fine," Alfred groaned.

Simon shuffled back to Monica, an almost-normal smile on his face. "All right then. Nat's bed is on the other side of the room."

The lights flickered again. "Where is everyone else?"

"In bed already, of course." Simon pulled the curtains from around the last bed on the left. Meal bar wrappers covered the bedding. The sheets lay wadded in the corner of the mattress, and papers were stuffed in the cubbyhole.

Monica wrinkled her nose. Tragic death or not, Nat was a slob.

She placed her load on the bed. "What am I supposed to do with his trash?"

"Throw it away." Simon shrugged his stooped shoulders. "There's a garbage chute inside the bathroom."

"Quiet down!" the occupant of the next bed growled.

"Sorry." Scooping up an armful of papers, Monica whispered, "Where is the bathroom?"

Simon pointed at the blank wall at the end of the room. "Two doors are hidden there. The men's bathroom will open on the left when you press on it. As we discussed, it reads your chip."

"As we discussed," she muttered under her breath.

Simon frowned. "If you continue displaying such ungrateful—"

"Ungrateful!" she hissed. "I once had to go two months without a bath because of this same problem."

Simon wrinkled his nose. "Then I would not want to be around you after two months."

"No. You wouldn't." Monica shuddered at the memory. "Actually, it only took two days before the others started complaining."

"There won't be anyone in there. Sensible Seen are in bed

by now. In a way, our life is more stressful than that of the wall slaves."

Bending her brow, she looked at the wall. "As long as you're sure."

"The longer you stay out here talking, the more you risk waking them up." He grinned his crooked smile and saluted her. "I'm going to bed now, so you needn't worry about me intruding, either."

Monica carried the wadded papers to the wall and pressed her shoulder against the boards. A low beep sounded. The boards separated from the wall in a door shape, rising into the ceiling. A red light flashed, scanning her body. As soon as she stepped into the sparkling clean bathroom, the door slid closed behind her.

She walked across the room, eyeing the fixtures. Ten toilets lined the wall to her left, and showers stood to her right, both surrounded by shiny tiles. The white porcelain glittered under the buzzing lightbulbs overhead. When she reached the far end of the room, Monica yanked open one of the garbage receptacles next to a sink and stuffed the papers inside. When the metal door clanked shut, smoke poured through the cracks and drifted into a vent by the sink.

"Yuck." Monica waved a hand in front of her face, clearing the smoke. She trudged back to the bed and dragged the rest of the papers and her sheets into the bathroom.

As she pushed the papers into the bin, she caught a glimpse of herself in the minuscule mirror above the sink. She froze. The garbage door slammed.

She leaned over the sink, peering at the unfamiliar face. Did she really look like a Noble?

She ripped off her head covering, revealing grease-coated hair. Dirt smudged her nose and face. Sweat tracked lines through the dust covering her pasty white cheeks. She touched her small dimpled chin. Did Audrey's look like this? Her delicately pointed nose matched Audrey's, and her dark green eyes were the same shade.

She covered the mirror with a hand and turned away. Were the similarities really there? Or had Simon planted the idea in her head?

She crept away from the mirror and hung one of the bedsheets over the entrance of a shower alcove, using bars of soap to weigh the upper corners down on the head-high wall. She undressed and showered as quickly as she could. The door stayed closed and the bedroom silent.

As she pulled her dress over her head, the material stuck to her wet skin. Vents above the showers blasted cool air into the room, sending water droplets splattering across her makeshift curtain. When she pulled it down, the bars of soap tumbled to the floor with the sheet, breaking against the tile.

She piled all the bars back onto the shelf. The sheet had soaked up a puddle by the shower, exposing blotchy stains throughout. As she grabbed it up, she tried to avoid the mysterious spots. The smell of musty socks clogged her nose.

At a hole in the ground next to the entry door, black tiles formed the word *Laundry*. She dumped the sheets in the chute, then set her ear against the door and tried to pinpoint sounds in the other room. Her dress still clinging to her legs and arms, she tugged at the fabric as she listened. The fans whirred softly, and the curtains rustled in the breeze. Someone snored, but the room stayed quiet otherwise.

She pushed against the door. When it rose into the ceiling, she peered into the sleeping quarters. Since the coast was clear, she darted out and dove onto her bed. She sat cross-legged on the bare, stained mattress. The rat stared at her from its cage. Its whiskers drooped, and its eyes shone in the dimming overhead lights.

Monica's stomach rumbled. She picked up the cage and her old clothing. "I didn't get dinner, either, little guy. I don't know how it works for the Seen. I didn't see a meal shelf." She put the cage in the cubbyhole and untied Alyssa's medallion from her neck. After pushing it into the jacket pocket, she shoved the clothing beneath her pillow. If the wrappers Nat had left were any indication, then the Seen ate the same food as the wall slaves.

She yanked her curtains closed and lay down. The lights turned off with a final flicker. Cold water on her arms and legs slowly dried off. Shivering, and with the smell of dirty feet in her nose, Monica fell asleep.

CHAPTER 21

The curtains sprang open around Monica. Light flooded her bed. "What do you want, Simon?" Clenching her eyelids closed, she reached to pull the sheet over her head before remembering she had none.

"It's me, Alfred, not Simon. Simon already went to work."

Sitting up, she rubbed her eyes. The small boy crouched on the side of her bed, his toes clutching the sideboard, holding him in place. He gripped a curtain in one hand. "You slept in too late. He even got his secret folder from you, and you didn't budge an inch."

"He did?" Monica scratched her head. Her thick curls hung every which way. She tugged on one of the frizzy ringlets. They certainly didn't like being slept on wet. Her head pounded, and shivers crept up her arms. The rest of her body didn't appreciate the cold night, either. "Is everyone else gone, too?"

The boy grinned. "Yep, you slept in really late. If you don't get to the library soon, you'll be in trouble." He glanced around the bed. "What happened to your sheets? And your shoes and socks?" His eyes bugged out. "Is that a rat?"

Monica put a hand to her forehead. "Do you always ask so many questions?" She combed her fingers through her hair. "I'd be happy for some new sheets if you could tell me where to get some. The old ones were too dirty to keep."

"We get new ones once a week. A wall slave brings us new laundry every time. That's not until tomorrow." Alfred jumped off the bed and straightened his black button-up suit coat. "I have some extra socks, though, if you'd like them. Just to borrow, of course." He jumped down and ran off.

"Thanks." Monica finished combing her hair with her fingers, then tied it back with the black head scarf she wore yesterday.

Alfred reappeared next to her bed, a long pair of black socks dangling from one hand. He tossed them to her. "They might be too small at first, but they're a little stretchy."

Monica tugged the socks on. "I appreciate it. It does seem to be getting colder." Her stomach rumbled, reminding her once again of her lack of food. "Where do you go for your meals?"

He plucked a half-eaten meal bar from his pocket. "They're delivered to our assignments. Yours is waiting in the library." He broke off a piece. "Can I give some to your rat?"

"If you want to." Monica slid the cage from the cubby and set it on the bed.

Alfred held the piece out to the rat. "What's his name?"

Monica rolled up the rug covering the trapdoor. "He doesn't have one."

"Can I take care of him while you're gone?" Alfred picked up the cage. "It doesn't take me long to clean up the bathrooms and stuff."

Monica dug her fingers into the crevice at the top of the board and lifted it, revealing the ladder tucked in the space beneath. A second trapdoor under the ladder kept it in place. "Sure. You can name him, too, if you want. Just don't let him loose." She tapped the ladder. "How do you get this open?"

"I'll do it." Alfred put the cage down and ran to her side. He slid on his sock-covered feet, almost tumbling into the hole. Monica caught his sleeve and pulled him back. After another slide, he landed on his rear end. Laughing, he climbed to his knees. "Oops."

"Are you all right?"

"Sure, I'm fine." He tugged at something under the floorboards. "This switch gets stuck sometimes." A click sounded, and the lower trapdoor fell open. Alfred kicked the top of the ladder, sending it clacking downward as it unfolded. "There you go. I'll open it again when you're back in the evening, just like last night."

Monica lowered her feet onto the first rung. "Thank you."

"You're welcome." Alfred peered down at her. "You're quite late, though. I would suggest running."

"Thanks again." She scurried down the ladder. Her chip stayed quiet the whole time. Why wasn't it scolding her for being late? As she ran to the library, her feet slipped and slid on the marble tile. Remembering each turn from the night before, she arrived in moments.

The door stood open a crack. An angry voice poured through the gap. Her shoulders tensing, Monica pressed herself against the wall.

"When I come into my own library," a man shouted, "I expect it to be neat and orderly! It looks like something exploded in here. What do you do all day? Read the gossip message tubes? When I come here next time, this library must be in order, unless you want to be transferred back to Trentin. My children cannot learn in this environment."

A tall man stormed through the door, slamming it behind him. As he stalked down the hallway, a long white coat swirled around him, and his shoes squeaked on the floor.

Monica kept herself completely still until he turned the corner. As soon as he disappeared, she eased the door open and slipped into the library. Her breathing rattled in her chest. If he had looked back for even a second, he would have seen her out in the open.

"Ah, there you are." Simon stood at his desk. He shuffled some papers, his glasses askew on his nose. "It's a good thing I had the foresight to request half a sick day for you. You didn't even flinch when I sent the request from your wristband."

"Thank you." Monica crept to his side and straightened a stack of fallen books. "Are you all right? Who was that?"

"Master Gerald, the ruling governor of Cillineese. You met his daughter Audrey yesterday." Simon adjusted his glasses. "Send me back to Trentin?" he muttered. "You wouldn't be able to find another librarian who could take care of this collection, Master Gerald, certainly not."

He moved some papers around and tossed Monica a meal bar. "Here is your breakfast. I saved it for you."

She ripped it open and chomped down on the tough collection of stale grains and nuts.

"I would suggest not eating the entire thing. It was designed with Nat's calorie intake in mind. It would be too much for you since you're smaller." He smiled in spite of his harried appearance. "If you ate many of those, you would soon get fat, and then you would be in real trouble."

Monica smirked and finished the last bite. "I think I'll be okay. I missed most of my meals for weeks."

Simon shrugged. "When you go back to the walls you might think otherwise."

A chilly breeze blew through the hole in the wall in the other room. Monica stuffed the wrapper into her pocket and pulled her sleeves farther down her arms. "What do you want me to do?"

He handed her a bent, metal messenger tube. "Fill out this request for someone to come in for repairs. We don't have any Seen carpenters anymore. Gerald thought it an unnecessary expense to keep the extra mouths around—more people to feed, you know."

She took the cylinder and picked up a blank request form from a pile in a tray on Simon's desk. "I've never filled one of these out before. Can't you just send one to the repairman's wristband?"

"No, no, neither of our wristbands can send commands. Our ranks aren't high enough. This has to be approved first, of course, but it won't take too much time." Simon extended a fountain pen, then drew it back. "You can write, can't you?"

Monica rolled her eyes and held her hand out. "Yes, I can write. At least well enough for the messengers to read. My father even taught me their shorthand."

"Really?" Simon's eyes brightened. "Excellent. Your education isn't totally lacking. We can work on your language skills later." He dropped the pen into her hand. "You write up that request, and I will get back to work on this paper." Opening the file folder, he smiled. "Despite Master Gerald's dire warnings, I doubt he'll be back here to check on the library for some months."

Monica scanned the page. Boxes lined the side of the paper asking what was being requested and the urgency. As she wrote, the shorthand her father had taught her flooded back to mind, allowing her to fill out the form in seconds. She blew on the ink before rolling it up and stuffing the scroll into the tube.

"This one looks different than the others I've seen." She flipped the door on the top of the cylinder and latched it closed.

"Our library is not fitted with the latest technology." Simon held a magnifying glass near his eye and lowered his face close to the desk surface, his nose just a fraction of an inch from the paper scraps. "We have to make do with the older messenger tubes. The couriers often complain about them."

Monica held out the tube. "What do I do with it now?"

Simon straightened his back and stretched. "Put it in the hole." He pointed at a round opening in the floor. "It drops down to the basement work tunnels near the furnaces."

Monica released the cylinder into the hole and watched it zip down the tube. As the breeze continued, she shivered and rubbed her arms. "I wish they would stoke the fire. It's kind of chilly in here, don't you think?"

"It is the cold season." Simon pinched a tiny scrap and peered at it through his magnifying glass. "I've heard that inside the walls it is even colder. You should be used to this."

"I'm not. We all hate the cold." She leaned over the desk and watched him work. His spindly fingers moved the yellowed scraps into various positions, trying out every spot they could go. Two corners of the pages were reconstructed, and the words scrawled across their faces were dim and washed out.

Simon's hands paused above his work area. "Must you hover? You could go brush up on your reading or do something useful. Why don't you go alphabetize one of the shelves? I can't concentrate with you hanging over me."

Monica backed away from the desk. "Sorry, I just want to know what it says. I know it's about the computers, but I've risked so much to get it, and now that it's here I can't even read it yet."

"You won't learn what it says until I get it put back together and translated. It might take me a few days." Simon sighed loudly. "I requested you to come here to replace Nat. I miscalculated how soon I would need you beyond finding the book, but there's still plenty of work for you to do here."

"Oh." Monica frowned. "It seems so futile, working for the Nobles, when . . ." She gestured at the desk. "We're working on this."

Simon put down his magnifying glass and stared at her. "Do you want to die, girl?" He glanced around the room. "The library is considered a safe place to talk, but if someone heard you, we would both be killed." His Adam's apple bobbed as he gulped for air. "You might be able to speak freely in the walls, but Seen will turn each other in for favors."

She put a hand on the desk. "Why would they do that? We're

all in this together." Lowering her voice, she continued. "Aren't they just as interested in these plans as the wall slaves?"

"Most of them are content with their lives." Simon scribbled something on a piece of paper. "I, for one, would like to be on my own schedule. The traders and peasants have it much better."

"But—"

"No buts." He wiped his forehead with a handkerchief. "You are not good for my heart, girl. You startle me at the most inconvenient times. If you're too distracted to alphabetize, why don't you go read a book while you wait for the repairman?"

"All right." Monica crossed her arms and trudged to the nearest bookshelf, her legs quaking. How could one Seen betray another to their oppressors?

She picked up a book and flipped through the pages, but her mind wandered. The slaves in the walls would never do such a thing, would they?

Shoving the book back in place, she shrugged. Who could tell? They might if they were given the chance. Yet, what chance would ever come their way? No slave would dare come close enough to a Noble to betray someone. The risk of dying was too great.

She picked out a second book. The back cover said it was about great machinery from 2017. Pictures on the inside depicted huge, metal machines, some set in fields, others in large cities full of sky-high buildings.

She slammed the book closed. What was the point of looking at these ancient hunks of metal? As far as she knew, the farmers of this age weren't using this kind of equipment, anyway. The book talked about gasoline. What was gasoline?

"Simon?" She held up the book. "What's the use of reading books that are almost a thousand years old?"

Simon looked up, his brow furrowed. "Disturbing me every moment is just as bad as hovering, Monica." He exhaled loudly.

"But it is necessary to learn from history. Children have been asking your question for years. You need to learn history so you can learn from others' mistakes. That book you're holding, for instance, tells how foolish we were for relying on oil."

She slid it back onto the shelf. "How did you know what book I had?"

A soft knock sounded at the door. Monica whirled around, her back to the shelf. Who could that be? The Nobles wouldn't knock.

Simon glared at her. "You look like you've seen a ghost. There's nothing to be scared of. It's probably the workman we ordered. Go answer the door, and be quick about it."

Monica dashed to the entrance, sliding to a stop just inches in front of it. She tugged the door open.

A skinny, trembling boy stood on the other side. He clutched a toolbox in one hand, his knuckles white. "You sent for a repairman?" He gulped and looked over his shoulder.

Monica stepped out of the way. "Yes, I said it was for a wall repair, though. Didn't you bring any supplies?"

The boy glanced behind him again. "Can I please come in? Someone might see me." Sweat drenched his threadbare shirt. "I can't bring supplies until I know what I need."

Monica put a hand on his shoulder and pulled him in. "Don't worry, no one's going to see you. I know how you feel."

He shook his head, shaggy brown hair falling in his eyes. "Sorry, but I don't think Seen can really understand." He glanced around. "Where is the hole?"

Monica closed the door and pointed toward the room adjoining the sitting area. "It's over there, by all the bookshelves."

"Thank you." The boy kept his eyes on the floor. "I— I'm sorry I talked back; please don't report me." He darted across the room, the toolbox bouncing at his side.

She followed him. "I wouldn't report you. I'm on your side."

The boy pushed the book cart out of the way and knelt at the hole. "I don't know what you mean," he whispered as he pulled out a measuring tape. "Last time I spoke out of turn to a Seen, I got punished, and I don't want it to happen again."

"Don't worry." Monica knelt beside him. "I won't report you."

"Monica," Simon called, "stop bothering the boy. You have work to do, and so does he. Don't fraternize with the wall slaves." He pointed a withered finger at the boy. "And you make sure you seal up the other access panels again. I know at least one other has come loose."

"Yes sir," the boy squeaked.

"Do you still want me to alphabetize?" Monica rose to her feet and stomped over to his desk. "Isn't there something I could do that would be more important?"

"Not really." Simon held up a half sheet of paper. "I have this part done now. It certainly took me long enough."

"You've done a lot since yesterday." Monica reached for the paper.

Simon pulled it away. "Of course I have. I was working on it while you slept the morning away. I haven't started copying it yet, though, so it will be a while until I have a translation."

Monica tapped the diary beside his pile of tools. "Do you think you'll translate this soon?"

"No, I've decided not to." Simon put the paper down. "I have other library duties, and this will take enough of my time."

"It could be important." Monica started to pick it up, but Simon slid it out of her reach. "Not important enough to bother with now."

"You're the one who said history was important. It could be valuable. We could learn things about Cillineese no one else would know otherwise."

"I thought you didn't care about history." Simon picked up his magnifying glass again.

"I don't care about other people's history. At least not if it's hundreds of years old. But this is mine." She snatched up the diary before Simon could react. "I only remember my adoptive mother. I want to know about my real mother."

Simon glowered at her. "Then you translate it, if you're so eager." He raised the glass to his eye.

"I can't translate. I don't know anything about languages." She hugged the diary. "I can only read the simplest books."

"Then give it back," Simon muttered. "If you can't translate it or read it, it's no use to you."

"Sir?" The boy crept up to the desk. "I finished filling out the list of necessary supplies." He held out a sheet to Simon. The paper shook in his hand. "Would—would you mind if I stayed here while I wait for the delivery? It's a little far to the nearest access."

Simon snatched the paper from the boy and stuffed it into a courier tube before dropping it into the messenger hole. "Yes, yes." He waved him away. "I won't get any work done if you two keep bothering me so much. Just stay out of my sight."

Monica eased the journal behind her. Maybe Simon wouldn't notice.

"And put that journal where you found it." Simon jabbed a finger at Monica. "I don't want you to lose it."

"Fine." Monica placed it on the desk. "But I want it translated."

He lifted an eyebrow. "It seems that the former wall slave has suddenly become rather demanding."

She altered to an entreating tone. "Then could you help me tonight after work?"

"That will not happen. I am an old man, and I need my rest." Simon gripped the chair arms and stared at the puzzle, as if to will the pieces together. "Now go out there and pretend to be in charge. It seems that's all you want to do anyway."

CHAPTER 22

M onica crossed her arms and plopped into a leather chair in the sitting room. The young repairman crept behind her. He crouched on the floor by a coffee table, his head turning as he glanced around the room. Beads of sweat trickled down his forehead, though a chill draft stirred the air.

"Is he always so grouchy?" he whispered.

"As long as I've known him." Monica rested her chin on her fist. If the diary mentioned her name that often, it must have belonged to her mother. She had to know what it said. Translating it would be difficult, though. Simon was right about her lack of education. There was no way she could do this on her own.

The boy's stare shook her out of her thoughts.

"What is it?" she asked. "Why are you staring?"

Sitting cross-legged on the floral rug, the boy looked at the floor. "I didn't mean to stare. I'm sorry."

"That's okay." Monica climbed to her feet. "When will the delivery get here?"

"It'll take a while. They have to bring them through the walls and . . ." He stopped and smiled. "I guess you don't really care why. But it'll take them some time."

A hissing noise shot through the room. Monica flinched. The boy sprang up and started for the hole in the wall.

Simon cackled. "You two are truly phobic." He pointed at the boy. "Stay where you are."

The boy's muscles tensed. "What was that?"

"Just a messenger tube coming in." Simon held up a plastic tube. "I have a request for a book delivery." He tossed it to Monica.

She snatched it out of the air and opened the cylinder's top. "Why don't they come get it themselves?"

"Child, you are going to get yourself in real trouble one day."

She unrolled the parchment. "*Renegades, Microchips and Their Circuitry*, and *Biochemistry*." She squinted at the list. "There's certainly a variety, and where and who is Amelia?"

"Amelia is Audrey's older sister." Simon eased out of his seat and stretched. "Since you are so woefully ignorant of my shelving system, I'll help you find those books." He shuffled to the bookshelf next to his desk. "I have some volumes set apart for the children. They often reserve them ahead of time, but I do not know where *Biochemistry* is." Pulling a thick blue book off the shelf, he shook his head. "Why would she want it anyway? It's outdated."

Monica set the tube on the desk. "So I have to deliver the books to her?"

Simon handed her the book and selected another from the row. "Yes, you were given clearance when the tube came. You'll be expected soon."

As she held the book in her outstretched arms, Simon placed another atop it.

Her arms shook, though the books weren't heavy. "You want me to walk out in the open?"

"Yes, of course."

"How far is it to her room?"

Simon ducked behind a bookshelf. "I don't know exactly, but it is among the Nobles' bedrooms. This side is the offices and meeting rooms." He tugged out a book and blew a thick layer of dust from its tattered surface. "The bedrooms are on the other side. You will have to walk a long way, I know that. My assistants have always run my errands." He slapped the last book on her stack. "There. I'll get you a bag and supervise the repair work. Don't worry."

Dust from the top book blew into her eyes. She sneezed and shook her head. "I wasn't worried about that, but I can't walk out in those halls, Simon." She glanced at the boy. He sat on the floor, chewing his fingernails.

She bent close to Simon, lowering her voice. "I had trouble walking here from the dorm. I can't walk in front of all those Nobles as if I own the place."

Simon threw a canvas shoulder bag at her. "Then take lessons from your rat and creep through the halls. You can ask other Seen for more exact directions." He sat at his desk and glared at her while twirling his pen between his fingers. "Now get out of here."

Monica slid the books into the tote. "If I don't make it back in a few hours, assume I got lost, killed, or scared back into the walls."

She slung the shoulder strap over her head, stormed out the door, and slammed it behind her. She froze in front of the threshold. The hall stretched out as far as she could see. Doors and corridors branched off of the main, vaulted hallway. Chandeliers glittered with light, and ceiling fans stirred the air around the golden cages, making them swing gently in the breeze.

Monica's heart thumped in her throat. She edged to the wall and kept her shoulder pressed against the polished wood as she walked. The floor's white and black marble tile swirled, and the grains in the wood twisted. She shook her head and crept silently down the hall.

Although she had noticed the room's vastness when Simon was

with her, the dizziness wasn't so bad. The floors and walls had stayed still then.

She passed room after room. Golden numbers adorned each mahogany door, starting at 500 and going down one by one. Buzzing voices skittered through the cracks under the doors, the deep rumbling of men mentioning Cillineese in the midst of dread warnings peppered with oaths. Every time she crept by one of these rooms, her heart skipped a beat, but she couldn't turn back, not now.

She trotted down three steps and paused at a balcony that swept out to her left above the lower level, an expanse of polished tile far below. Two staircases, one on each side of the balcony, angled down to the tiles in elegant curves, their marble railings and red carpets giving them a rich, pompous air.

She ran across the uncarpeted edge of the back of the balcony then up three steps to the hall leading off the other end. The cold stone sent shivers through her sock-covered feet. From the alcoves in the wall, houseplants slapped her legs with their long leaves. She moved away from them while still trying to keep off the plush carpet. Shoe impressions marred the red pile, trekking back and forth through the hall. The polished wooden doors now bore names instead of numbers.

The swirling gold letters on the first door read *Francine*. She passed four more rooms and four more names before arriving at the last door on the left. Carved into the wood, vines and flowers formed the name *Amelia*, painted in gold. Beyond this door, a spiral staircase descended into depths unknown.

Making ready to knock, Monica closed her eyes. Behind this door lived a Noble child who'd been pampered and catered to her entire life. How would she react to being disturbed?

Monica tapped the wood with a white knuckle. After a few moments, the door swung open. A petite woman in Seen apparel clutched the doorknob. Strands of gray hair hung loose from her bun.

When her eyes met Monica's, her brow shot up. "Yes, what is it?"

Monica hoisted the shoulder bag higher. "I . . . I have some books from the library for Amelia."

"*Miss* Amelia?" The woman looked over her shoulder. "Show some respect, young lady." She stepped into the hallway and closed the door. "We did not ask for any books. She can't have them."

The knob turned, and the door creaked. The woman pivoted on her heel. "Miss Amelia? What are you doing?" She tapped the door open.

A pale girl leaned on a pair of spindly crutches in the room's entrance hall. Plastic tubes protruded from her nose and wrapped around her face, leading to a backpack. She squinted. "Who are you? Do you have my books?" The girl's curly brown hair fell across her brow, almost covering her eyes.

Monica gulped. Simon might have a point about their similar appearances.

"Miss Amelia, you're supposed to rest." The woman put a hand on the girl's shoulder and guided her to a four-poster canopy bed that dominated one corner of the room.

"I want to keep up my studies, Laney." As Laney lifted Amelia into the ruffle-covered bed, she dropped her crutches, and her body went limp.

Monica crept into the room and stood in the entrance hall. Laney tucked the corners of the fluffy quilts around Amelia's legs and arms.

Amelia tugged an arm out from under the blanket and beckoned to Monica. "I'd like my books now. Did Simon find everything?"

"Yes . . ." Monica glanced at Laney before adding, "Miss." She stole silently across the thick area rug. "Simon found all three books."

"Put them there, please." Amelia pointed at a nightstand covered with pill bottles and glass jars of liquid. "Laney, could you clear those?" Her breath rattled in her throat.

"Miss, you really must relax." Laney plumped the girl's pillows. "Your father is very worried about your health."

"If he were, he'd come to see me." Her face growing pale, Amelia lay back on her pillows and closed her eyes. "I haven't seen him in weeks."

Monica cleared a spot among the bottles and began stacking the books.

Laney smiled, though it seemed forced. "You know he's busy. He has to go to Cantral twice a week on top of his other duties."

"When I'm dead, I hope he regrets not seeing me." She held out her hand to Laney. "It's time for the pink one."

Monica put the third book on the table and backed away.

"Miss Amelia, you will get better." Laney unscrewed the cap from a bottle and shook a pinhead-sized pill into the girl's hand. "You have all the best medicines and doctors."

Amelia swallowed the pill in one gulp before sitting back up. "Please tell Simon thank you. I'd like you to pick them up in a week."

Monica nodded and sneaked out of the room, Laney at her heels. As soon as they had both exited and the latch had clicked, Laney turned on Monica. "You should not have come. She is not to be excited or out of bed. What were you thinking?"

Monica folded her bag into a tight wad. "I didn't know about her condition. Simon told me to deliver them. I was just following his orders."

"No excuses. Simon should have known. If her father finds out about the books, you will both be in trouble. Don't be surprised if you're both transferred."

"I would have gotten in trouble if I didn't deliver them, so what was I supposed to do?"

Laney froze. "Someone's coming. Get back to the library where you belong."

Gritting her teeth, Monica bowed her head and stalked away, her fingers clenching the bag. Why hadn't she heard someone coming first? As a wall slave she should be more atuned to the signs. If she came across a Noble in the hall by herself she would probably panic and give herself away.

Footsteps padded across the carpet ahead. She ducked into an alcove and waited. After the footsteps passed, she skulked along the marble floors until she made her way back to the library.

"It's about time." Simon still sat at his desk. "I assume you made the delivery successfully."

Monica slapped the bag on a pile of books. "You didn't tell me she was so sick. I got chewed out by her nurse. You could have warned me."

"She is sick, isn't she?" Simon scratched his head. "Yes, Audrey did mention that a few months ago. I remember now. Some disease they thought they'd eradicated."

"How could you forget something like that?" Monica sat in an armchair. "She looks like she could die at any minute."

"Perhaps." Simon tapped his papers. "I finished reconstructing the document. Doesn't that make you happy?" He held up a courier tube. "I need you to write a message for me in that awful messenger shorthand." A smile spread across his wrinkled face. "If she's as sick as you say, this could be a real development."

"I'm still mad at you, and I don't see how her being sick changes our situation at all." Monica took the tube and tapped it against her other hand. "What do you need me to write?"

"You are being silly. You shouldn't be mad; there's little reason to be." He handed her a blank piece of paper and an order form. "We're out of spare LEDs for the shelf lights."

Monica held the papers out. "You don't need me for something as simple as that."

Simon took off his glasses and rubbed his eyes. "Do I need to spell everything out for you?" He pointed at the reconstructed paper. "I just finished putting it together. Our messenger for this area is a contact, so he needs to be told."

"Is that safe?" Monica grabbed a pen and began scribbling down the order. "What if he's sick and there's a substitute?"

"Almost all couriers are on our side, and those who aren't won't risk reporting us." He tapped his chin. "We will still put it in code, of course. Nothing too complex. Our couriers are clever at getting places and sneaking around, but they're none too good with word games."

Monica finished the LED order. "So what should I put?"

"I really do have to spell everything out for you." Simon massaged his temples. "The library received a new puzzle. We completed a portion, but it has more pieces than expected. The children have a missing piece for Cantral."

Monica wrote it down in the messengers' shorthand. "They're going to know what this means."

"That's the point. We just don't want it to be blatantly obvious."

She rolled the two pieces of paper into a scroll and slid them into the messenger's tube. "What did you mean about the children having a puzzle piece?" She put the cylinder down and planted her elbows on the desk, resting her chin in her hands.

"So you *didn't* know what that meant." Simon picked up her discarded pen. "Too cocky too soon." He put the pen in a navy mug with gold edging. "You're going back to Cantral."

Shaking her head, she took a step back from the desk. "I just got here a day ago. You can't get rid of me that quickly. I don't have an identity in Cantral."

"You will soon, if Amelia is as sick as you say." He rubbed his hands together. "This will be perfect. And I'm the one who thought of it. The council will certainly reward me when these plans go through."

Monica stiffened and snatched up the tube. "Which council? What are you planning?"

"Our council, silly girl. Not the Noble council." Simon pushed back his chair. "You should think better of me. I got that very chip you're wearing now. You wouldn't believe how hard it was to dispose of Nat's body without anyone knowing."

Monica looked at her feet. Thinking about Nat brought a surge of nausea. She had to change the subject. "I'm sorry I doubted you. You've done a lot for me. What do you have in mind?"

"Amelia will be sent to Cantral because her father is Tristan Allen's cousin, the east wing's high councilman. They have the best doctors. You will be following her."

Monica hugged the cylinder close. "Why do *I* have to go, too? I'm not saying I like Cillineese, but I don't have anything to go back to in Cantral. I only have one friend and no identity."

"Like I said, you will soon." He tugged the message from her and poked it through a hole in the corner of his desk. The air whistled around the cylinder as the note plummeted to the tunnels below.

"How can you know if they have a chip for me? I've been with you almost the whole time."

"Between sleeping half the day and taking eons to deliver the books, I should say not."

Monica crossed her arms over her chest. "I don't appreciate being pushed around."

"I would think you'd be used to it by now." Simon slipped the reconstructed page into its file along with the journal and children's book. "I have official business to attend to now. I've spent too much time on this already."

"You're not going to work on the translation?" Monica relaxed her defensive posture. "But you're so close, and you said it wouldn't take very long."

"Not today." Simon slid the folder into a file drawer. "I need to finish cleaning up that shelving mess and find a few books that were ordered to be put aside. I'm a librarian, not your personal slave."

Monica gritted her teeth. Of course he wasn't her slave, but this was important. He needed to see the big picture. The sooner he could get this done, the sooner the workers' council could figure out how to shut down the computers, if that's really what the paper talked about.

"While you're deep in thought . . ." Simon pushed himself from his chair. "That boy should be done with the wall by now, if he hasn't been lazing around."

"He's still here?" Monica peered around a bookcase.

The boy knelt by the wall, holding scraps of dark polished wood up to the patched hole.

"You didn't tell me he was still here," Monica hissed. "You said we have to be careful saying stuff around others, and you go spouting off about plans with him able to hear everything."

Simon shrugged and shuffled into the other room. "He's too scared to say anything to anyone."

"You tell me to be more trusting, but I think you're too trusting."

Simon tapped the boy on the head. "Status report, Trace. When will you be finished?"

The boy flinched and almost dropped a piece of wood. "I don't know yet, sir, but it shouldn't be too much longer." He fitted another piece into the wooden jigsaw. "I sealed up both holes, and I just have to finish the new paneling."

"You need to be done within the hour. The children will be here soon."

Trace bowed his head. "Yes sir, I know. I'll be done before then, for sure." He shoved the board into position, and the dark wood popped into place with the others.

Monica glanced between man and boy. How odd that so many people knew such secret plans. It seemed that the slightest misplaced whisper could make everything crumble. Yet, what could she do but follow along? She was the chip-less puppet, and everyone else held her strings.

CHAPTER 23

Simon walked to a bookshelf in the corner. "Monica, come here, please."

Her muscles tense, she stalked over to him. He pulled her to his side and leaned close to her ear. "I have the idea all planned out." He rubbed his hands together. "When they move Amelia to Cantral, you will find where she is, and when she dies, you will take her place." He handed her a book from the very top shelf. "Hold this."

The leather binding and creamy yellow pages felt heavy in her hands. "That's ridiculous. I could never pass for Amelia. They'd tell us apart in a second, and all the council plans will be useless without me."

"Because of the potential contagion, only the Seen maid will be with her until she recovers, though, in this case she will not recover. She will die, and you'll take her place. Then you will emerge as Amelia, miraculously healed." His eyes scanned her face. "You definitely look enough like her so that no one in Cantral will question you. Children's appearances often change after a long illness." He handed her a second book.

Monica shook her head. "There's no way I'm taking that girl's place. This is your idea, not our council's, and there is no way I could pass as a Noble. I barely made it to Amelia's room and back without having a heart attack."

"I'm sure the council will approve of my plan." Simon unfolded a crumpled piece of paper from his pocket. "The other titles are elsewhere." He ushered her through the lines of shelves to a bookcase in another corner, far away from Trace's work. "Besides, you're forgetting something. You won't be pretending to be a Noble." He took down two more volumes. "You *are* a Noble, and don't worry, it will come back to you quickly. You already have the superiority and the huffy attitude down perfectly."

Monica's face flushed hot. "I still don't think it's a good idea. You'll have to get our council's go-ahead before I do anything."

Simon gave her another three books, stacking them to her chin. "You are a very insubordinate young lady. Of course I must talk to them first. I don't have any contacts in Cantral myself. You'd be in a real fix without their support."

Monica craned her neck to talk over the precarious column swaying in her arms. "I know. I've been subjected to their displeasure before. I've been without a chip for months at a time."

"As you're so fond of reminding me." Simon pointed at the sitting room. "Back to my desk. These need to be put on that cart."

"All right, all right." The books pressed against her waist and chest, making it difficult to breathe. She staggered to the empty wooden cart and dumped them in a heap.

"Be careful with those!" Simon rushed over and straightened the jumbled mess. "Some of these are valuable and cannot be replaced."

Monica backed up, holding her hands out in front of her. "Sorry, but they were about to fall anyway."

Trace crept up beside them. "Excuse me, Mister Simon."

Simon stopped his frantic rearranging and glared at the boy. "Yes, what is it?"

He clutched his supply bag's thick shoulder strap. Pieces of wood and metal stuck through the opening, and a measuring tape dangled out of a hole in the bottom. "I'll be heading back now, unless you need something else."

"No, nothing else," Simon grunted. "And the library was completely quiet while you were here, do you understand?"

The boy's head shot up, his eyes wide as he nodded vigorously. "Yes sir, I didn't hear anything. You and your assistant were working the whole time."

"Good boy." Simon pointed. "Now go away."

Trace darted for the exit. In his mad dash, his bare feet slid on the polished boards. The door slammed behind him, and his footsteps faded away.

Monica crossed her arms. Simon shouldn't order the poor kid around like that, but Trace seemed to expect that sort of treatment. Before meeting Simon, Seen had appeared to be bossy and commanding. And Simon certainly adhered to that standard, but not as frighteningly as before.

After Simon straightened the last book, he plopped himself into the desk chair and leaned against the slatted back. "What has you so deep in thought?"

"I wasn't really deep in thought." Monica sighed. He could never understand how she felt. He had been a Seen all his life while she had to try to be a Noble, a wall slave, and a Seen all in one lifetime.

"Then you were frowning for no reason." He closed his eyes. "Or perhaps you're angry with me, though I can't imagine why."

She glared at him, saying nothing.

He tapped his desktop. "Open the bottom left drawer. Our lunch is in there."

Monica yanked the drawer open. At least he had dropped the subject. If he had kept pressing her, she'd have explained her mood and not with the kindest of words.

Two meal bars rolled around the drawer, their wrappers crinkling against an assortment of pens and pencils. As she lifted their lunches, dust bunnies the size of her fingers clung to the brown paper.

"How long have these things been in here?" She brushed the dust into a wastebasket by the desk. The numbers across the tops of the bars read *3291100* and *71128752*. She held them out to Simon. "Which one is mine? You never told me what Nat's number was."

"I am thirty-two, ninety-one, one hundred." Simon took the bar from her. His fingers made quick work of the wrapper, shredding it into little pieces. "The older a person, the lower his or her number. The computers have a system for numbering us, but I don't know what it is exactly." He chomped his bar down in a few quick bites.

Monica ate half of her own and stuck the other half in her pocket. Her stomach still felt heavy from breakfast that morning. It wasn't used to so much food. Nat definitely had a higher calorie allotment than she did, just as Simon had warned.

A messenger canister shot up through the hole in Simon's desk, rocketing two feet in the air. He snatched it before it started to fall.

"Finally. I was hoping they would get back to me quickly. Our Cillineese council has become quite active since your arrival." He twisted the top open and slid out a note. The crumpled paper had the odd curling hash marks of the messengers' code scribbled across the top. A package of fingernail-sized lightbulbs tumbled out after the page. He scooped them up and handed Monica the note. "They know I can't read that gobbledygook."

"You did have me write to them with it, so I guess they figured you learned." She smoothed out the creases and ran her finger over each letter. "It says that the head has received your message and knows the situation. I'm supposed to stay here until it's figured out."

"Shred it," Simon growled. "He'll change his mind once he hears my plan, that's for sure. I just need to find a safe way to tell him."

Monica held up her hands. "I am not running any more daring missions for anybody unless it's authorized. They want me to stay here until this is all translated, and that's what I'm doing."

Simon dumped the LED bulbs from their packaging. "My plan might mean you get to go back to Cantral sooner, you know."

"Yeah, and then take a dead Noble's identity, and there's no telling when she'll actually die." She crossed her arms again. "I might end up starving for another month."

Simon scooped the lights into his palm and heaved himself out of his chair. "If I send in another complaint about Nat to the computers, his chip will be terminated, and you will be without an identity anyway. I would feel little remorse."

Monica balled her hands into fists. He really didn't care about anything but his silly plan. "What do you want me to do?"

"So you agree?"

Monica shook her head. "But you're not giving me a choice, so I might as well listen."

"That is reasonable of you." Simon made his way to one of the bookcases next to Trace's patch job. "You will leave Nat's chip with your rat and meet with the council leader to tell him my plan."

Holding her hands up again, Monica backed away, laughing nervously. "Oh, no. I can't do that. There's just no way."

"Is that so? Give me one good reason."

"For one thing, I don't know who the leader is. I've only met one or two of the council, and I would have no idea where to find them again."

"Really?" Simon slipped the bulbs into his pocket and unclipped two brass hooks on the sides of one of the shelves. "With everything they tell you to do, I thought you would be in communication with them all the time."

"They always send me messages, just like they do for you."

Simon dug his finger into a crack on top of the shelf in front of the row of books. He slid out a four-inch section of thin paneling, revealing a space underneath chiseled into the shelf. Wires and lightbulbs coursed through the space and disappeared into tiny holes bored into the shelf's sides. He handed her the thin board that had covered the space. "Hold this."

She inserted a finger into one of the board's lightbulb holes and twirled it. "So do you have another plan? Or do I get to stay here until you finish?"

"I'll think of something." He unscrewed three lightbulbs and replaced them with new ones. The old bulbs crumbled to dust between his fingertips, the same way Sham's had disintegrated in the tunnel.

When Monica handed him the board, he popped it into place. They performed the same operation for five more shelves around the room. Simon tested the new lights on each shelf before moving on.

"Fortunately, we only have to replace them once every fifteen years or so. These bulbs have been here since before the last termination. They could tell some interesting stories, I'm sure." Simon let the dust from the last dead bulb fall to the floor.

The library doors swung open and banged against the wall. Two teenage boys tramped into the room, their hands stuffed in their pockets. Each wore an identical bag slung over his shoulder.

Monica pressed herself against the bookcase, her legs stiff.

Simon handed her the last five LEDs. "There's just one other shelf to do. It's in the back of the room, away from the boys, so don't worry. I need to go take care of their requests now."

She rolled her fingers around the bulbs and whispered, "Okay."

Clasping his hands together, Simon scurried over to the boys. "Well, young sirs, I assume you're here for your assigned reading material?"

Monica ducked into the back aisle and crept to the shelf Simon had indicated. He would probably come up with yet another new plan by evening, and she needed to think of new excuses to avoid the assignment. She couldn't lose this chip, too. And since getting a new one meant waiting for a poor, sick girl to die, any excuse would do.

CHAPTER 24

"Hello, Alfred." Monica poked her head through the dormitory floor.

He nodded. "You're out late again."

She sighed. "Yes, Simon's a real slave driver."

Simon snorted and pushed her up the last step. "You should be grateful for the work at all." When both had climbed to their feet on the dormitory level, he yanked the ladder closed behind them. "Alfred, it's your bedtime."

"All right." Alfred sighed. "Monica, I named your rat Vinnie. I hope that's okay."

Monica smiled. "Yes, thank you."

He grinned and dove into his bed, pulling the curtains closed behind him.

"Don't encourage his foolish behavior," Simon snapped as he kicked the area rug over the ladder's trapdoor. "Now, are you ready to hear my new plan?"

"Not really." Monica untied her head scarf and shook the dust from the black fabric. "But I'll listen. I'm not saying I'll do it."

"You'll do what is necessary to survive." Simon glanced at the beds before lowering his voice. "I think our council leader is in Cillineese at this moment. There certainly have been rumblings about his presence, and security is tighter, though the Nobles don't know what they're guarding against. They're just as scared as some of us."

Monica gave him a skeptical stare. "You *think* he's in Cillineese."

"And I *think* you're impudent." He nodded at the curtained canopy beds. "Listen to the restlessness. Everyone feels it. Cillineese is under heavy watch again. It hasn't been like this since eight years ago when the rumors about you were so widespread. Some of the Nobles are getting jittery. It could be why Master Gerald was in such a foul mood this morning. He just got back from a meeting in Cantral of all the city-state leaders."

"Yeah, I had to help with their laundry." She shook her head. "Of course the Nobles are jittery. I'd be jittery too if I were stuck here."

"You *are* stuck here, unless you carry out my plan."

As she studied his somber expression, the lights dimmed, as if verifying his mood. "Well, you're right about one thing. If they decided we're too out-of-line we'd be terminated in the middle of the night, and I wouldn't be able to get out. The doors are already closed."

"You and millions of others living here. There are four million in Cillineese alone, not counting us slaves. Stop and think about someone other than yourself for once, girl."

Monica sighed and nodded. "Yes, them, too, but they have no chance no matter what. At least I could get out if the doors were open."

"Exactly why your participation is crucial. Your importance as the chip-less slave is immeasurable."

Feeling a chill coming on, she rubbed her hands up and down her arms. "If I'm so important, I can't understand why they're risking me like this. If termination is possible, then why does the council want me to stay?" She glanced around the quiet room. "Are we really that closely under watch? Should we be talking out in the open like this?"

"The dorms are not monitored by the Nobles. The computers just make sure we're in the right place." He put a hand on her shoulder and pushed her to the wall concealing the bathrooms. "But you're right; the others might hear us."

Monica's back pressed against the panel, and the wood lifted. She stumbled into the cold room, her feet slipping on the wet floor. She grabbed the edge of a sink and stayed upright.

When Simon stepped inside, the door closed behind him. "That's better. No one will overhear us."

Chilly water soaked Monica's socks, sending shivers up her legs. She hugged herself and glared at Simon. "I could have fallen."

"But you didn't, so all is well."

"As if you really cared." She turned on her heel, surveying the room. Puddles dotted the once-clean tiles, and dirty towels lay on the sinks and over the shower walls. The soap bars, once stacked in a neat pile, were now scattered, some in the sinks, others in the showers.

"What happened here?" Monica peeled off her dripping socks and hung them on the edge of a sink.

"Alfred cleans this bathroom every other day." Simon picked up a bar of soap and put it on a shelf. "Some of us are sloppier than others."

Monica wrinkled her nose. The place reeked with body odor. "All right, now that we're here, what did you want to tell me?" She kept one eye trained on the door. If anyone came through, she would have a lot of explaining to do.

"As I said, our leader is here in Cillineese. This, I'm rather sure of." He nodded and muttered something to himself before continuing. "You can leave your chip with the rat and go to the furnace tunnels. The air ducts lead to them. We had a new shipment of furnace slaves recently, and I believe the leader is among them."

"You're going to send me down to the furnaces just because you think the head council member will be there?" Monica laughed. "You've got to be kidding me. I could be seen or get lost, and then I'd be in real trouble. And the slaves might report me."

"The furnace slaves hate the Nobles more than any other slaves, wall or Seen. The flames fuel their anger." Simon picked up a bar of wet soap, letting it squeeze through his fingers as he tightened his grip. "Their tempers get shorter and shorter in the winter. They should be willing to help you squeeze the power from the Nobles' grimy hands."

Monica's eyes widened. "Well, if you put it that way . . ." She took a step back. "But I still don't know how to get there, and what if the Council of Eight finds out? We'll be dead before we know what hit us."

"That's why the translation is so important, and why you need to go back to Cantral." Simon threw the soap into the trash bin. "I've translated tiny bits of the words as I put them back together. Your father knew where the Cillineese computers are and had an idea how to shut them down."

"You mean Joel, right?" Monica's cheeks felt hot. When she thought of her father, Iain always came to mind. She couldn't even remember what her birth parents looked like.

"Of course Master Joel." Simon snorted. "Who else? Iain would know nothing about Cillineese, let alone the computers." He washed his hands and dried them on one of the towels that lay crumpled in the next sink. "You will need to tell our council this so they can prepare their next move, and they *must* consider my plan. Where they go from here could be rather dangerous for all of us."

"It's already dangerous." Monica sidled up to the exit. "I'm posing as a Seen, and if someone looks into that too much, they'll learn the truth. Nat's record is bad to start with, so I'm already on a tight lead."

"You'll be fine for now. You will go to the furnaces and talk to the men there and see what they know. You can be back by morning with no problem. The Cillineese palace is large, but not even a quarter of Cantral's size. You should have no trouble."

Monica's shoulders touched the door but not forcefully enough to open it. "I don't know how to get to the furnaces. I've never been anywhere near the furnaces here or in Cantral. And what if the men there won't help me?"

Simon tapped an air vent halfway up the wall. "Just follow the ducts down, and you will get there eventually. Don't worry about them. Of course they'll help."

The metal grill covered a small hole. Monica lifted the grate and set it on the ground, then stuck her head through the opening. "I don't think I can fit in here."

"Of course you can." Simon knelt and clasped his hands in a cradle. "I'll boost you."

Monica stared at him. "What if I get stuck? There's no way I can turn around and come back!"

"Stop making excuses." Simon held his hands out farther. "Get in there and keep going down. You'll reach the furnace level eventually. Tell the first council member you come to of our plans."

"You're crazy." Monica untied her chip and draped the strap over his head before stepping into his cupped hands. "It's not that easy to tell who's on the council!"

Simon boosted her into the metal tunnel. "You'll be fine. You have to do this. Remember, I can report Nat again, and then you would be without food, so don't give up halfway through."

"You're a very mean man." Growling, Monica planted her elbows on the slick metal surface. "I might not be able to find my way back once I get there."

"Then come out on the first floor and use the main passage-ways. Everyone will be in bed by thcn." Simon's voice faded away.

Still growling under her breath, Monica used her elbows and forearms to inch forward. Her legs dragged behind her, almost use-less in the small confines. Whenever she passed across a joint, her knees scraped against the bolts holding the sections together.

Just a few feet in, the tunnel opened into three passages—one veering to the left, another veering to the right, and the third con-tinuing straight ahead. She shimmied down the straight path. Time seemed to tick by in slow motion, and the tunnel seemed to have no end.

Sweat poured down her forehead, neck, and arms. Dirt from the blowing hot air caked her skin and clogged her nose. Finally, she came to a duct that shot straight down. As she lowered herself into the metal tube feet first, her heart thudded loudly in her chest. Certainly someone in one of the rooms would hear it pounding and wake up.

She planted her bare feet on the sides and her back against the wall and scooted down. The inches went by one by one with only the passing bolts digging into her spine providing any sensation of progress.

As she traveled away from the bathroom, the tunnel grew darker. The steel gray walls faded to black. Sweat slickened her fingers and toes, making them slide.

She plunged a foot, then stalled. A sharp pain jabbed her back, probably a bolt that kept her from falling the rest of the way. A whimper escaped her lips. If she faltered now, she'd drop to the basement and break her neck. Then weeks later some duct cleaner would find her broken, rotting corpse, just as they found the poor slave girl the council member used to fake her death.

Gasping, she coughed violently. Dusty air circulated through the shaft, mercilessly stinging her eyes and whipping her hair into her face. Retreating was impossible, and popping out into a random Noble's room was out of the question. Continuing downward remained the only option.

After what seemed like hours, her feet hit the bottom of the air shaft. Crawling again, she eased into the side passage and scooted up to a dust-covered grate in the floor.

She peered into the vent. The holes in the metal grating allowed only a view of the concrete floor below. She unscrewed the tiny fasteners in the frame, and the grate fell from the hooks. She shot her hand out, grabbed it in midair, and drew it slowly into the duct, letting out a hissing exhale of relief.

After setting the grate to the side, she clutched the opening's sharp edge and lowered herself toward the concrete floor until her feet dangled a few feet above the ground. The metal dug into her palms, forcing her to let go. She landed in a crouch, then glanced around.

Thin aluminum cots stood here and there in the long, tunnellike room. The ductwork encircled the area and jutted into the ceiling in random places. Cobwebs hung from the dark corners. Embedded in the wall every few feet, finger-sized lightbulbs cast eerie shadows into the farthest points of the sleeping chamber.

Monica tiptoed toward the door at one end of the room while keeping an eye on a door at the other. Nothing stirred. All the ragged blankets covering the cots lay still.

She gripped the tarnished doorknob with sweaty fingers as she pressed her ear to the door. The clanking of metal on metal came through the thick wood slab, along with a roaring noise that almost drowned out low, humming voices echoing through the chamber—furnace slaves—hardened, angry men who likely wouldn't take kindly to a Seen intruder. This wasn't going to be easy.

CHAPTER 25

Monica turned the knob and opened the door an inch. Hot steam flooded into the room. The shadowy forms of men darted around inside the fog, shouting to one another above a growling, raging river that flowed from right to left through the room's center.

More pipes jutted out from the walls and pierced the high concrete ceiling. Fans attached to ceiling ducts whirred around and around, the blades moving in a blur.

As she leaned her head through the gap, the steam cleared from around a few distinct figures. Some little boys squatted at the water's edge, each holding a wand-like device with flashing lights. On the river's far side, a rusting barrel that reached to the ceiling took up half the shore. Orange light shone through a red grate at its center. A man stood on either side of the grate, each with a giant shovel.

One stood by a pile of black rocky chunks that rose as high as his shoulders and covered the rest of his side of the shore. Every few seconds, more chunks fell to the pile from a hole in the ceiling, and, as if working in rhythm with the dropping chunks, he heaved a shovelful through the grate, stoking a roaring fire inside the barrel.

With every heave, thick black dust flew through the air and swirled with the motions.

Clear tubes protruded from the barrel's sides, making it look like a fire-breathing machine with skinny arms. Some tubes funneled water from the river to the machine, while others fed it into the ductwork and ceiling. At each end of the room, waterwheels churned the river into a foaming froth.

One of the boys got up from the long riverbank and ran toward the door, clutching his wand-like instrument. His eyes focused on a point in the wall to Monica's left.

She pulled back toward the cots.

The boy shouted, "Hey, what are you doing here?"

Monica slammed the door and ran to the other side of the room. She fell against the opposite door and tried to turn the knob, but it didn't budge. It had to be a programmed door, one that needed a chip to open.

The sound of wet feet slapping concrete reverberated through the room. The boy ran toward her. He pumped his skinny arms, and his bare feet smacked the floor. He wore only a pair of ragged shorts, and the outline of his ribs showed through his pale skin.

He stopped a few feet in front of her and rested his hands on his knees. Gasping for breath, he managed to speak. "Why are you here?"

She tried to turn the knob again, but it remained unmoved. "A Seen sent me to find someone. He has a message for him."

The boy wiped sweat from his eyes. "Who are you looking for? I can try to help, but I need to get back to work." He glanced over his shoulder. "And it won't be good if the others find you down here." As he straightened, his breathing slowed. "They don't like Seen." A large scar on his cheek moved as he spoke.

Monica looked down at her dress. "It would take too long to explain. I'm looking for someone who knows about a translation and a puzzle. I don't know his name, but my Seen friend thinks he was transferred here recently."

The boy crossed his arms over his bare chest. "I'm one of the new transfers. I was a Seen in Gahlan, but I got demoted." He looked back toward the furnace room. "There were three men with me in the tunnel carriage. One got sent to the mines. The other two are down here."

"That's great. Do you know them at all?"

The boy shrugged. "They work the waterwheels and the ducts, keeping everything going. Just like I have to now." He looked over his shoulder again, his cheek twitching.

Monica bounced on her toes. "So do you know them or don't you?"

"One is my friend's father. The other keeps to himself and has a bad record, but that's all I know." The boy squinted at her, scanning her from head to toe. "You're not really a Seen, are you?"

A shrill whistle blasted through the room.

The boy jumped. "You have to go. Our shift will be done soon. They'll be back, and then you'll be in trouble."

Monica glanced at both doors. "But I don't know how to get out."

"The same way you got in!" He looked around the room. "Where *did* you come in?"

She pointed at the hole in the duct above their heads. "I can't reach it, and I came from an upper story; I couldn't climb back up again."

The boy studied the duct, his eyes narrowing to slits. "What are you really doing here?"

Monica gritted her teeth. Should she trust him? Simon said Seen betrayed each other, but he wouldn't have the opportunity, and he wasn't really a Seen anymore. She tried the door again, but it didn't open. If she wanted to get out of here unscathed, she

.d have to trust him. "I sneaked in here to try to talk to our ncil leader. He has plans for something we're working on, and I need to talk to him."

The boy's brow wrinkled. He glanced around the room and smirked. "All right then. I can help you." He grabbed a cot and dragged it toward her. As its metal feet screeched against the concrete, Monica cringed. The noise was bound to be noticed by someone.

As soon as he placed the cot beneath the hole, he beckoned to her frantically. "Come on, I'll boost you back up. These ducts go to the first floor rooms. You can get back to wherever you're going from there."

Monica jumped onto the cot. The boy joined her, cupped his hands, and, when she stepped into them, boosted her toward the duct. Gripping the sharp metal with her fingertips, she swung her legs, trying to gain enough momentum to aid her climb.

"Watch it!" the boy called from below.

Grunting, Monica pulled herself up the rest of the way, bumping her head inside the duct before managing a low crawling position with her feet at the edge of the hole. She yelled back at the boy. "You'll ask around for me, right?" Her voice echoed through the metal pipe.

"Yes, I can. Something about a puzzle. Where can I get a message to you?"

Monica squirmed back over the hole, careful to place her feet on the other edge before shifting her weight until her arms supported her head and chest over the opening. "I work in the library. You can send a message up to us. Make sure to address it to Simon. We just had repairs done there this morning, so no one will question it."

"Great. I'll do that." He jumped down from the cot. "The library is easy to remember. I'll ask about the puzzle."

A door banged open. The growling voices of overworked men filled the room.

"What are you doing, kid?" someone shouted. "Are you trying to get us in more trouble? Put my bed back where it belongs."

Shrugging, the boy picked up one end of the cot. "You're the troublemaker, Jasper. I didn't do anything wrong."

Monica replaced the grate, lunged forward, and scampered down the ductwork. They probably wouldn't be able to follow her through such a small hole, but it would be best if they didn't see her at all.

After several feet, she slowed her pace. The tight confines folded in around her once again, and her back pressed against the ceiling, bringing her comfort and a sense of security.

The ductwork continued on in a seemingly endless tube. Bolts scraped her hands and knees, rubbing them raw. The light from the furnace men's dorm faded behind her. As darkness drew closer on all sides, a lump formed in her throat. The black emptiness of the slave tunnels had always been troubling, but at least nothing there would bring harm. Here, something could sneak up from the front or the back without warning.

Her knees banged against the floor and echoed in the tiny space, sounding like a stampede of rats running across the metal surface. Shivers chattered her teeth, adding to the noise.

As she continued, she recalled her past adventures. Being moved from dorm to dorm, meeting hundreds of new people, there was little she hadn't seen. She gritted her teeth and forced the chattering away. She had been sent on errands in the middle of the night, searching attics and prying up loose stairs. A Noble had almost caught her more than once, and she had survived. Her father had been killed in front of her, and yet life went on. She blinked away tears. If she could get through all those other trials, this bit of darkness wasn't about to stop her.

The duct turned sharply to the right. At the end of the new tunnel, a grate let light in through its tiny square holes. She scurried to it. Poking her fingertips through the holes, she tried to force the door open. The metal shuddered, but latches on the outside kept it in place.

She shook the grate again. One latch shifted a tiny bit. She scooted forward on her elbows. Pressing the side of her face against the grate, she tried to peer into the room. If someone was sleeping on the other side of this wall, she certainly didn't want to make a lot of noise.

An empty hall stretched out to the left and right. Suits of armor and ornate tapestries lined the marble walls, and thick, long rugs covered the floor.

Monica pushed a finger through one of the holes and tried to flip an upper latch open. Her pinky touched the very tip of the metal switch. Sticking her tongue out, she squinted. Just another fraction of an inch and she could get it open. The metal rubbed against her skin . . . not quite enough.

Finally, her finger made full contact, and the latch flipped open. Smiling to herself, she poked at the switch at the other top corner, one of three more latches holding the grate in place. As she wiggled her finger around, the grate wobbled back and forth. When the second latch popped free, the entire grate tipped out. Her finger stayed curled, keeping the metal from banging on the floor.

She lowered the vent, the bottom two latches acting as hinges. After crawling out, she snapped the grate closed behind her and rose to her feet. Sucking on her raw pinky finger, she crept down the hall.

The corridor went on and on both behind and in front. As she looked around the vast expanse, her head swam. Either way could be right or wrong. A stairway leading to the dorm level would help.

Her sooty, sore feet welcomed the soft rug beneath her toes. As she sneaked down the hall, closed doors stood at attention every dozen feet or so. She tried opening a few, but none of the knobs would budge.

At last, a spiral staircase came into view. She scampered up the wooden, carpet-covered steps and entered a familiar row of bedrooms. On her right stood Amelia's door, and on her left one that read *Daniel*. She sprinted down the corridor, past the balcony, and up the hall full of business rooms, finally reaching the area underneath the Seens' dorm.

She tugged the thick cord beside the curtains. The trapdoor high in the ceiling stayed in place. As she craned her neck to stare at the boards, her muscles protested. Why didn't the doors move? Weren't they automatic? Or did Alfred really operate the hatch every time someone pulled the rope?

Bouncing on the balls of her feet, she glanced around the narrow hall. Cold air sent shivers down her arms and legs. Her bare feet ached where her skin touched the chilly marble. If only she had a pair of socks and shoes.

Hugging herself, she swayed back and forth. Her jacket was in the dorm as well. Clenching her teeth, she tried to stop shivering. If she were still in the walls, it would be much worse. They had little insulation, and during some winters her toes turned so blue, it seemed that they might fall off.

She yanked on the rope again. Just up the flight of rickety stairs was a bed and curtains to keep her warm. Her socks might be dry now, too.

The trapdoor remained closed. She gripped the cord with trembling hands and gave it an extra hard tug, then tucked her arms close to her body. Simon should be waiting up for her. He was the one who was so excited about this mission. Of course, he would be disappointed with the results, but leaving a message was her only option. The boy seemed trustworthy enough, and he saved her from the other slaves, that is, if they really didn't like Seen as much as he said.

Her eyelids drooping again, she sank to the floor. Why wasn't he coming? She sat cross-legged and massaged her dirty toes with her stiff, numb fingers. Soot marked her exposed calves and forearms. The same black powder probably covered her hair. A shower would be nice, even if the water was cold.

She pulled her knees up to her chest, rested her head, and closed her eyes. Someone would have to come down eventually. Maybe she could get upstairs and wash before Simon conjured another crazy plan. As the chill settled deep in her skin, sleep overcame her aching body.

CHAPTER 26

A sharp finger prodded Monica's arm. "What are you doing here, girl?"

She snapped her eyes open and jumped up, bumping her head on something solid. As pain roared through her skull, she covered her scalp with her hands and plopped back to the floor.

"Ow!" the other person squealed. "What was that for?"

Monica looked up, still rubbing her head. A short woman in a Seen uniform stood over her, a hand on her nose.

"I'm sorry." Monica climbed to her feet. "You startled me."

Pinching her nose, the woman shook her head. "Just be quiet."

Monica pulled a hand away from her hair. Grimy soot now covered her once-white palm. "I'm sorry."

"Sorry doesn't ease the pain." The woman rolled her green eyes. "You really got me."

Monica grimaced. If this woman was one of the untrustworthy Seen, every plan could be ruined.

The woman let go of her reddened nose. "What are you doing down here this early?"

Monica looked down at her dirty dress hem. "I got locked out last night. No one let me in when I pulled the cord."

"So you were the one ringing the bell at one in the morning?" The woman laughed. "I thought it was Matthew or Daniel playing tricks on us, as usual."

Monica sighed. If the two boys regularly rang the bell at night, no wonder no one let her in, but Simon should have at least checked to see if she was back. "They're Master Gerald's nephews, aren't they?"

"Yes, they are." The woman set her hands on her narrow hips. "I haven't laid eyes on a Seen child so filthy in years. Where do you work, anyway?"

"I work with Simon in the library." Monica looked the woman in the eye. She wasn't about to reveal where she had been, not if she could help it.

The woman nodded. "I remember now. Simon's last assistant got killed. Makes sense that working with him would get you into a mess." She brushed a lock of matted hair from Monica's shoulder, raising a cloud of black dust. "I don't know what you would be doing to get yourself this dirty, though. I suggest getting cleaned up before anyone else sees you."

"I will." Monica looked up. The stairs to the Seen dorm hung unfolded, suspended from the ceiling by their rope handrails. "I need to get going. Simon gets grouchy if I'm late."

"If he's the one who kept you out late working, he should understand."

"Not likely."

"I can't stay to chat. My charge will be wondering where her breakfast is." The woman scurried down the hall and turned toward the bedrooms.

Monica ran up the ladder and into the dorm. Two women sat on the edge of a bed, whispering to each other. Monica grimaced. They would certainly notice if she went into the men's bathroom.

The women stopped talking and stared at her. After glancing around in search of Simon, she smiled at them and crept to her bed. As soon as she pulled her curtains closed, they started chattering again. Their whispers were mostly indistinct, but a few short sentences filtered through. "And there's another one. Whether Nobles or Seen, these teenagers have no shame, cavorting in plain sight now. The elder Nobles should put a stop to them, but they're often as bad as the younger. Just last week I heard . . ."

Monica shook her head. They had no idea what she was doing, and it was all to benefit them and the wall slaves. She could have died in the air vents, and no one would have cared.

Sitting cross-legged, she massaged her still-numb feet. Her legs and back ached from sleeping in a crouch all night long.

The rat squeaked at her. She smiled at the furry beast. "At least someone is starting to appreciate me." She reached into the cage and untied the vial from its back. "There you go, Vinnie." As she fastened the leather cord around her neck, she whispered, "I have some of my dinner left over. You can have it." She retrieved the bar from her dress pocket and unwrapped it. Soot covered the surface as well as her hands and fingers, but the rat wouldn't care.

Vinnie snatched the morsel and turned it around and around in his tiny paws. She sighed. Now she was talking to a rat yet again. If those women heard, more gossip would fly. Didn't the Seen women have anything better to do? The sooner they left for their jobs, the sooner she could take a shower. She gave the rest of the meal bar to Vinnie. He chewed it down quickly, coughing every few bites.

"Sorry," she whispered, "I can't get to the water yet."

The curtains ripped open. Monica yelped and grabbed Vinnie's cage.

Simon stood outside her bed, one hand on the bed frame. "Well?"

Monica put Vinnie's cage down and glared at Simon. "You scared me half to death!"

Simon shrugged. His thinning white hair stood on end, and dried spit speckled his chin. "Did you find him?"

She inched away. "No, but I left a message with someone in the furnace room. He said he'd contact us through the message tubes."

"Terrible idea." Simon rubbed his chin. Flecks of the white spittle drizzled to the floor. "Someone might intercept it."

Monica wrinkled her nose. "You did the same thing yesterday. How is it a bad idea now?"

"I did?" He shook his head. "Yes, I suppose I did, but mine was cryptic. Perhaps it will work out anyway." He scratched his head and stared at her. "You're filthy."

"Glad you noticed."

"Well, get washed. We need to work."

She raised an eyebrow. Was he always this messed up in the mornings? "Are you okay, Simon?"

"Yes, of course. I just need a quick shower and I'll be fine. Translation work to be done." He shuffled away.

Monica pulled her curtains closed and lay down. He definitely wasn't acting himself, but what could she do about it? She couldn't even get cleaned up until the others left.

Closing her eyes, she relaxed on the still-bare mattress. More of the Seen moved around the dorm now. Their voices blended together to make a low buzzing noise, like the sound she heard every day of her life in the wall dorms. She picked apart the different speakers. Two men grumbled about their duties, serving food and carrying heavy loads around the house. A woman scolded a child about his messy appearance, demanding he cut his hair before he was demoted for slovenliness. Monica smiled. They sounded just like the wall slaves now.

Vinnie tugged on her hair.

She forced open her eyes and shoved the cage away. Rubbing her temple, she glared at the rat. The wall slaves and Seen were the same for now, but as soon as the Seen climbed down that ladder to the rooms below, they were completely different, not only in the way they thought of themselves, but how they treated others.

Monica touched the vial dangling from her neck. She had to act just like them if she wanted to survive.

The voices faded down the stairs. Someone laughed loudly and was quickly shushed by another Seen. Monica poked her head out from the bed curtains. The trapdoor slammed closed over the folded stairs.

Alfred knelt by the door and rolled out the rug. His eyes met hers, and he jumped to his feet. "What are you doing here?"

She climbed out of bed and glanced around the room. The spacious canopy beds all stood empty, their curtains drawn away from the mattresses. "I was waiting for everyone to leave."

"Why?" Alfred cocked his head to one side. "You'll be late again."

Monica ran a hand across her filthy dress. "I need to get cleaned up." She glanced at the bathroom door. "And I didn't want to wash until everyone had left. It's a complicated situation."

Alfred sauntered to a bed and ripped the sheets from the thin mattress. "Whatever it is, I don't want to be in your shoes. Simon's been acting weird lately, and he won't be happy when you're late."

"I noticed this morning he didn't look good."

"I did, too." Alfred bundled the fabric into a ball and tossed it into the middle of the room. "But he's not the only weird one, if you know what I mean. I've never met anyone who has to shower alone."

Monica edged toward the bathrooms. "I might as well tell you." Her cheeks heated up. There was no way to avoid revealing the truth. "My chip is . . ." How should she put it? "*Different* than it should be for me, and it's registered as a guy's, so it won't let me in the girls' bathroom, and I have to use the men's."

Alfred stripped another bed and shrugged. "That's happened before. I see why you waited. That could be awkward." He grinned. "Don't worry, though. I'll stay out here."

"Thanks for understanding." Monica tugged on her dress sleeve. "Where can I get a change of clothes?"

"We got a new set today. They should be in your cubbyhole." Alfred pointed at her bed. "They must do things really differently where you're from, huh?"

"Yeah, sort of." She kept the details to herself. They never got a change of clothes in the Central wall dorms. They were given the laundry castoffs and traded and bartered among themselves for clothing that fit.

Monica dug into her cubbyhole and pulled out a pair of black pants and a long-sleeved button-up shirt. Of course they would still be sending up Nat's clothing. Since the laundry slaves thought he was still alive, they had no idea why Simon had asked for the dress. "They got it wrong." Monica held up the much-too-big garments. "They gave me a boy's clothes."

Alfred shrugged. "I guess you'll have to wear them. You work in the library; it's not like anyone goes there except the kids. At least, that's what Simon tells me. You'll be fine."

"Except they're way too big," Monica grumbled. As she walked to the bathroom, the chip heated up a small patch of skin on her chest. She rushed through her shower, working all the grime and soot off in minutes.

After drying off with a towel from a stack on a shelf, she slid her clothes on and rolled up the pant legs and sleeve cuffs. Even after tucking them up, the hems of her pants encircled her heels. She marched in place for a second. The slick fabric rubbed together, making a swishing noise. The waistband barely clung to her hips, threatening to slide off at any second.

She gripped the waistband in one hand and shuffled out of the bathroom, careful not to trip on a hem. Her legs seemed to swim in the roomy fabric tubes. She reached her bed and pulled the belt out of the jacket she had taken from the Central laundry room. After threading it through the belt loops, she cinched up the waistband.

Alfred added another set of sheets to the growing pile. "It doesn't look too bad."

"I hope you're right." Monica scampered to the trapdoor and lowered the ladder, copying the movements Alfred had shown her the morning before. "Could you give Vinnie some water for me, please?"

"Sure." Alfred saluted as she ran down the steps. "He'll be fine."

Monica shook her head. What a weird kid. At least he understood what was going on and didn't threaten to report her all the time, like some people she knew. With the chip heating up again, she skipped down the hall to the library, keeping one hand on her waistband. The belt helped, but the pants still slid around with every step.

As she swung the library door open, Simon greeted her. "There you are. Finally. I thought your chip had done you in."

"No." Monica poked her head in and glanced around. "I'm fine."

Simon reclined at his desk, tapping his now-clean chin with a pen and drumming papers with a thumb. Throughout the library, the bookshelves all stood in neat rows with no one browsing the books. Besides the noises Simon made, the room was quiet.

Monica crept inside and closed the door without a sound. "Sorry I'm late. I had to wait for the bathroom."

Simon beckoned to her. "Come, come. I think I've made a breakthrough. I was having trouble with this word here, but I finally cracked it, and the rest has flowed easily. I only have one paragraph to go. It's quite amazing."

"Really?" Monica peered over the desk at two pieces of paper—the old, taped-up piece with its unintelligible words, and a new, crisp page with Simon's precise handwriting. "Something more about the computers?"

"Yes, exactly!" Simon tapped his finger on the page. "This describes how the computers can be shut down. Your father figured it all out. It's amazing. I didn't know they could be turned off at all."

Monica felt the blood drain from her head. She braced herself on the desk corner. "But no one knows where the computers *are* in Cillineese. They would be heavily guarded anyway."

"Not if no one knows where they are—there's no reason to guard them." Simon laughed. "The less fuss is made over them, the less people take notice. They're out of sight and out of mind." He wrote another word on his work in progress. "The Central computers are talked about often to remind us of their power, but the city-states' computers are the ones that receive the dome commands. If we turn them off, Cantral cannot tell the dome to close."

Monica shook her head. "They'd kill anyone who got close to the computers. Since Cillineese has control over all of its own chips, it'd be easy to keep people away."

"Exactly!" Simon jabbed a finger into her shoulder. "They can't kill you through your chip. Just take it off."

"But, guards or not, the doors will certainly be locked. I can't open them without a chip." Monica scowled at him. "Your plans are good only for the first half. You never think of the details. You never finish what you start."

He averted his eyes. "I'm sure I have no idea what you're talking about."

"Don't play games, Simon. Like last night. I didn't find the leader, and now you seem to have forgotten all about the plan to replace Amelia. And I almost died in those vents!" She rubbed her shoulder. It still ached from the climb, and Simon poking it didn't help.

"The Cillineese computers are just a drop in the bucket in the scheme of things. The plan with Amelia is still relevant." Simon returned her gaze, now frowning. "Who did you tell to look for the leader anyway?"

"A boy who had been transferred down there recently. He said he was a Seen before."

Simon's shoulders tensed. "He'd just been demoted? And you told him our plans?"

"No, I just told him I needed to talk to someone about a puzzle." She raised an eyebrow. "What's your problem? You said I should be more trusting. I was giving it a shot."

"A shot in the dark, and you certainly missed." Simon clutched his head. "This is very bad."

Monica glared at him eye to eye. "It would be really nice if you would just tell me what you're thinking, stop changing your mind so much, and be a lot clearer. Things would be much better if you did!"

He put his pen down and laid his head on the papers. "Recently demoted Seen children have the most volatile emotions." The corner of a page rattled as he spoke. "They report people left and right, not sure of their new station. He won't realize yet that he can't be put back in place. Once demoted, you stay there the rest of your life. He will be trying to regain favor."

"He'll report me?" Monica gulped. "I thought it would be safe. You said the workmen down there were trustworthy."

"Yes, he'll report you! Don't be so dense. I just explained that he would." Simon clenched his eyes shut. "I hope you had the sense not to tell him about me."

"I don't think I mentioned you." Monica's face burned. Was she remembering correctly? It certainly wasn't the whole story. Lowering her voice to a whisper, she added, "I did tell him I worked in the library, though."

He snapped his head up. "You what?"

"I told him I worked in the—"

"I heard you!" Simon snatched up his pen. "I need to get back to work. They could come down on us at any moment. We need to be ready."

Monica climbed up and sat on the back of an armchair. "There is a chance he will just do what I asked, isn't there?"

"Perhaps." Simon's pen slowed, and his breathing calmed.

"Did he seem agitated in any way? Did you speak to any of the other workers?"

"No." Monica studied her bare feet. The mottled purple toes reminded her of how cold the floor was and of the promised socks and shoes Simon had never delivered. "He said they didn't like Seen."

"He wanted to keep you away from the others."

"Why?"

He threw his pen to the desk. "Think, child! To get credit for reporting you himself!"

She lowered her head again. "I guess that's possible."

"Not possible. A near certainty." Simon sighed. "I wish I could have gone instead, but, of course, I could not." Coughing, he picked up his pen and continued writing. "I believe I'm getting ill, child. Not to mention old."

Monica rubbed one of her feet with the toes of the other. A tingly, needling sensation shot through to her ankle. Of course he was getting sick. Any older person would get sick in this icebox of a library. "So what are you going to do?"

"Work frantically on this translation. You'll have to be prepared to leave at any moment."

She unrolled her hems and let them cover her feet. "I'm ready. It's not like I own anything."

"Yes, you do," Simon said, not looking up from his paper. "You'll want to take your rat and that jacket you've been carrying around with you. If you have to leave in a hurry, the council won't learn your whereabouts or status for a while, and it certainly gets chilly without blankets or a bed."

"Will the chip let me go back to the dorm?" She tugged at the leather cord around her neck. "It was getting hot earlier."

"Just leave it with me. Alfred will let you up; he's a good boy." Simon held his hand out, still scribbling furiously with the other.

Monica untied the cord and dropped the vial into his hand.

"Thank you. I'll get Vinnie and be right back. I don't want anyone to see me in this outfit, that's for sure."

"It is quite shocking to see a girl in pants. Quite unladylike, but I can't risk drawing more attention to ourselves by getting you another dress." Simon tucked the vial into his shirt pocket next to a protruding pen. "Now, hurry up."

"They're way too big to hurry." Monica rolled the hems back up over her frozen ankles and ran out of the room. When she reached the cord, she tugged it as hard as she could. Glancing over her shoulder, she took a deep breath. Simon was probably overreacting. He tended to get into a frenzy sometimes and didn't know what he was talking about. By the time she returned to the library, he would probably have changed his mind about the entire thing.

CHAPTER 27

As soon as Alfred dropped the ladder, Monica scampered into the dorm.

"Back already?" Alfred sat in the middle of a towering pile of sheets and blankets. One sheet covered his head, and the others engulfed his body.

"Temporarily." Monica plucked Alyssa's medallion from the jacket pocket and hung the leather cord around her neck, leaving the garment where it lay. Despite what Simon said about the cold, if she needed to run, she wouldn't want to be hindered by the jacket, but the medallion was too important to leave behind. "What are you doing?"

"Checking to see if any of the sheets are worn or torn." Alfred held a threadbare blanket up to the light. "They get sent to the wall slaves if they are."

"Figures." She retrieved Vinnie from her bed.

He nodded at the cage in her arms. "I took care of Vinnie already. Where are you going with him?"

"To the library. I want him with me for now." She headed down the stairs. "Thanks for giving him water."

"Doesn't your chip hurt?" Alfred called. "Being away from the library?"

"No, I'm fine." Monica descended to the hallway below before he could ask any more questions. No one other than Simon needed to know about her chip—the fewer people who knew, the better. She hustled back to the library and set Vinnie's cage on a corner of Simon's desk, far away from any papers or pens.

"That was quick." Simon looked up from his work.

Monica nodded. Would he forget why she had left and send her back again? "I just got the rat, like you said."

He picked up the chip's vial from the corner of the desk and held it out to her. "Here you are."

She snatched it from his hand, her heart thumping wildly. "I saw you put it in your pocket. Why did you take it out?"

"I withdrew a pen, and the cord came out with it. I was just about to pick it up again when you barged back in."

"How long has it been sitting there? You know it has to be kept close to your body!"

Simon twiddled his thumbs. "Not too long. Only a moment. It will be fine."

"It had better be." She tied it in place and sat on the back of the plush chair, waiting for her heart to settle. Leaving the chip on the desk probably wasn't enough to hurt it. "Have you figured out any more?"

"Another few lines." He scratched his head and made a mark in the margin. "Go occupy yourself with something useful."

She kicked her heels against the back of the chair. "What do you want me to do?" The library was all in order now, and she had dusted everything twice yesterday. Did Simon just sit around in his spare time?

"Read a book. Work on learning a new language. You're in a library; you'll never run out of things to do here. Just don't bother me." He waved her away but froze midwave. "On second thought, I need you to look for a map of the Cillineese Palace. As you said before, we don't actually know where the computers are."

"And I don't know where you keep the maps." Monica hopped off the chair and crossed her arms, tucking her chilly fingers beneath them. The slaves in the walls rarely had use for maps. When a new transfer came, though, the older slaves often had to tell him where to go or sketch out quick routes on meal wrappers.

Simon's glasses slid down his nose. He pushed them up and glanced around the circular room. "They should be in here somewhere."

She rolled her eyes. "I figured that." She shuffled to the other side of the room, trying to keep her feet covered with the cuffs of her pants. The first bookshelf reached the ceiling, and stacks of books of every color filled its shelves.

She stuck one finger out of the shirt's long sleeves and placed it on the first row of spines, reading each one as she sidestepped. Her finger skidded over the coarse fabrics, smooth papers, and glossy words. She continued through two shelves of floor-to-ceiling volumes, using the rolling ladders whenever she had to scan the higher tomes.

The third shelf held volumes taller and thinner than the others. She picked one with slick, shiny pages. Lines crisscrossed the papers—blue, red, orange, and every other color of the rainbow. A box in the paper's lower right corner told what each mark meant.

"Simon?" Monica held up the book. "This looks sort of like a map to me." She flipped through the pages once more. "But a lot more complicated than any I've seen, that's for sure."

Simon looked up. "Oh, yes, you're right. That's where they are. What you are holding is called an atlas."

"And which one is for Cillineese?" She squinted at the words scrawled across the page. Some were in Cantral, but many were written in another language. "Is this the current language of Cillineese?" She pointed at the tiny script.

"I can't see it from here," Simon growled. "I can't possibly know if it's of Cillineese unless you bring it over for me to look at."

"Sorry." Monica hopped off the ladder and carried the tall book to his desk. "I've only heard people speak the language of Cantral while I've been here. Why is that?"

"The new Cillineese is too difficult for most people, and Cantral is the language of the court, so that's all anybody really has to know." He placed the atlas over his papers and flipped it open. "The wall slaves here all know Cantral, as mandated, and they prefer it. The new Cillineese will soon become a dead language, too, if the Noble children neglect their books."

"Oh." Monica shrugged. It didn't matter much. Other than a few phrases she had picked up from transfers, she knew only the Cantral language.

"If we all had just one language, the world would get on much better." Simon flipped through a couple of pages. "But it would be much less interesting." He paused on one page and shook his head. "No, no, these are Cillineese trade routes and who's allowed where and when." He shoved the atlas away. "We need one of the palace. It will look like an actual building, but massive."

Monica heaved the book into her arms and shuffled back to the shelf. "I'll keep looking." She perused five more books of maps before finding one that looked promising enough to show to Simon. This book's pages had yellowed, and brown streaks stained every one, as if it had been left under a fountain of water.

When she brought it over to him, he laid its battered pages down as if they would crumple under his touch. "Excellent. This appears to be very old, and that's good in this case." He rubbed his hands together and sat back in his seat. "The trade routes and such must be kept updated at all times. This map is too old to be of use to study those routes, but the palace rarely changes, so it will be fine for our purposes." Turning a delicate page, his brow knitted. "When the city was repopulated, there were some Seen dorms added. The wall slaves and Seen used to room together, but it was much too crowded."

"So these will work?" Monica leaned in close to the weatherworn page. The ink smeared in places where the water had reached, making some parts of the script unreadable.

Simon set his magnifying glass over the words. "Yes, they will be fine. These might even be the originals. I don't know why I didn't put them in a case. They need to be preserved. Of course, they didn't receive such damage under *my* care. Of that I'm certain." He gingerly unfolded a corner of the page, expanding the map. "Aha!" He pointed at a blue blob in the lower corner. "Here is the library. So this must be the palace's second story."

"That gives us a good starting point, right?" Monica pulled a chair up to Simon's side and sat down cross-legged. "Will the computers be marked?"

"I highly doubt it." Simon turned to the previous page. "This must be the first floor. If they follow the same protocol as Cantral, then the computers are underground, somewhere they can get constant hydroelectric power."

She straightened in her seat. "There's a river flowing through the furnace room. That's hydroelectric power, right?" She winced. Maybe she was wrong and spoke too soon.

His eyebrows shot up. "Yes, it is. With your sketchy education, I wasn't sure you would know what that meant."

Monica exhaled. Someone had mentioned water power a long time ago, and she had been curious enough to convince Iain to explain it to her.

Simon turned through four more pages to the back of the book. Roach droppings and dead silverfish fell from the binding.

He wiped them into a wastebasket. "Apparently, you didn't

clean the library as thoroughly as you thought." He brushed his hand clean on his pant leg. "The computers should be underground and near the river."

"What are you doing, Simon?" Audrey peered at them over the desk, her eyes just reaching the top.

Monica shot off her chair. What had Audrey heard?

Simon flinched. His glasses fell on the desk. "Audrey, I didn't realize you were coming today. Don't you have lessons with your tutor?"

"What are you looking at?" Audrey walked around the desk corner and climbed onto the arm of Simon's chair. "Is this one of the antiques you're always talking about?"

Simon set the tiny girl in his lap. "Yes, it is." He picked up his glasses. "The blueprints of this very palace. We could probably find your room in here, if you'd like."

Monica gaped at him. What was he doing? He had already told Audrey too much the other day when he talked about the translations. She probably heard everything about the computers, too.

"Really?" Audrey put her hands on the desk and looked down at the page. "I don't recognize these rooms; they're all blurry!"

"That's because that's where the servants live. Lots of nasty rats down there." Simon turned the pages until they reached the map of the second story.

Monica glanced at Vinnie. Audrey probably hadn't noticed him yet, but moving his cage now would surely draw her attention to the beady-eyed rodent, frightening her. Why wouldn't she just leave and let them get back to their plans?

Tilting her head to one side, Audrey squinted. "What are the words here? I don't recognize them!" She clenched a fist over the page. "I know the elementary words from every language in use and the primary dead languages. What is this?"

"Old Cillineese, my dear, the language of the Nobles who lived here before your family." Simon patted her dark brown curls. "Much before your time, but I'm sure your tutors covered it."

Audrey dodged his hand. "Yes, I suppose Francis didn't think it was important to study."

Monica edged away from the table and from the image of the life she was supposed to have lived. If her birth father had obeyed the rules, she would be in this library as a Noble now. Someone else would be the librarian, and she might have a little sister just like Audrey. Her cousins might live with her as well.

She inhaled sharply. This girl could be her cousin, or maybe her second cousin. All the Nobles were at least distantly related. Simon had mentioned a relationship earlier, but it hadn't hit so hard before.

Audrey pointed at a room in the upper part of the map. "I think these are the bedrooms. Mine is next to Amelia's." She tapped the page. "I think that's it. It's all smudged, and it just says bedroom number twenty."

"It most likely is." Simon's finger followed hers over the diagram. He set the magnifying glass to the side and helped Audrey to the floor. "Now what was it you came in here for, Miss Audrey?"

She tapped her chin. "Amelia is going to Cantral in two days, and I want to do something for her since I can't go, but I can't think of anything she can do but read, so I wanted your help."

"Is she now?" Simon closed the book of maps and held it out to Monica while continuing to address Audrey. "We could put together a collection of short stories for her. She enjoys the faerie tales."

Monica took the heavy book. Did he want her to keep searching the maps on her own? She carried it to the small table between the lounge chairs.

While Simon kept talking to Audrey as he led her to a row of short bookcases, Monica laid out the pages and unfolded the basement map. Brown watermarks covered some of the outlying tunnels leading away from the palace, but most of the black ink had survived in readable form. Familiar letters spelled out words in another language here and there, enough like Cantral to allow guesses as to their meaning.

Two large rooms took up much of the basement blueprints—one labeled *Furnace Room* and the other *Dormitories and Storage*. Tunnels and passages carved in and out and this way and that across the map, some labeled *River* and others *Messenger*. Some passages remained unmarked, and large blank spaces dotted the area.

Monica shook her head. Trying to make sense of this would take forever, and they didn't have that much time. Any of these unlabeled places might just be dirt walls supporting the palace above, or one could be the secret room she was looking for. And if the mapmakers drew these long ago, there could be new rooms constructed since that time, and one of them could house the computers.

Sighing, she looked at Simon, still chatting with Audrey. Sometimes his sense of priorities spun way out of whack. He had said himself that someone could come down on them soon. Why would he be so careless now?

CHAPTER 28

Monica folded her legs underneath her and continued poring over the map pages. Although some labels were decipherable, a few seemed beyond recognition.

"Simon? I don't understand this." She looked over her shoulder, but he was nowhere to be seen. "Great." She rested her hands on her knees and stared at the book. Maybe something important would jump out eventually.

She kept her gaze trained on the page, her eyes roving over every line and ink stain until it seemed that the details had burned into her memory.

After what seemed like half an hour, Simon sidled up to her table. "Making headway?"

Audrey stood beside him with an armload of papers and books. "She's still working on that?"

"Yes, it's important to our history." He guided her to the door. "Don't forget to ask your nurse about the scissors and glue. She will definitely be able to help you."

"Thank you. She wanted to come with me, but I told her I could come by myself." While Simon held the door, Audrey shuffled out of the room.

As soon as she cleared the doorway, Simon snapped the door closed. "I thought she would never leave." He returned to Monica's side and took a seat in one of the fat leather chairs. "Now then, have you made any headway?"

"Not really." She pulled the table closer to the chairs. "I don't know old Cillineese, and the lines aren't very clear. I can't tell which is a room and what's dirt."

"Yes, it is very confusing." Simon dug his glasses from his shirt pocket and put them on. He placed the crumbling book in his lap, letting the pages unfold over the arms of the chair. "Here's the furnace room," he said as he traced the lines with a finger, "and the river, the dormitory, and the messenger tunnels. Those are all clear enough."

"I got that part." She circled the chair and looked over his shoulder at the faded page. "I went into the dormitory last night, and I saw the furnace room through a doorway there. There was another door on the opposite side of the dorm, but it was locked."

He pointed at the dorm's outline. "I suppose you were right here. There's a messenger tunnel that leads to a door, probably that locked one you mentioned, and an open chamber beside it that's not labeled. The chamber is a good place to start." He pointed at his desk. "Be a good girl and fetch me my pen and paper."

Monica ran to the desk and scurried back with the items.

He laid the paper on top of the book and sketched the blueprints onto the new sheet. "We'll need to mark this up, and I do not want to write in this book."

"Someone should make a new copy."

"Cantral is certain to have one in its archives." Simon shrugged. "Whenever a city is terminated, all the bodies must be disposed of. It takes a while to search all the rooms. They have the maps to help with the process."

Monica shuddered. She closed her eyes, imagining the dark halls of Cillineese after the termination twelve years ago. The cleanup crews probably wore headlamps and gas masks, sneaking through the barely opened doors into the city. They likely found messengers sprawled out in the tunnels, bodies lying in their beds, and slave women clutching their children to their chests even as they lay dead.

The feeling of strong arms around her shoulders pierced her thoughts. They carried her at breakneck speed down a passage. Someone cried loudly. A sharp chill ran down her spine.

She opened her eyes and shook away the images. Letting those distant memories take over might raise jitters that would make it impossible to complete this new plan. She rubbed a hand up and down one arm.

"Here we are." Simon held up the paper, now covered with a tracing of the original map. "A section of the basement. You'll have to go duct diving again tonight."

She took the paper and turned it around and around. The furnace room and dormitory covered most of the page. The passage that led away from the locked door at one end of the dorm and the unlabeled space reached the edges of the paper.

"I hardly got any sleep last night." Monica handed it back to him. "Can I rest first? Besides, the door was locked. I won't be able to get in this time, either."

"Don't make excuses." Rising from his chair, Simon closed the book and put it back on its shelf. "Just climb through the ducts until you find the right room. The computer room has to have air vents of its own, or the equipment would overheat."

"That doesn't seem very secure to me. There are workers who clean the ducts. Someone could easily sabotage the computers."

Simon folded up the new map and handed it to her. "None of the duct workers could get close. If one dropped out of the ducts into the room, he'd be executed immediately. They stay in the ducts where they're safe. The computers are rumored to have a field around them that causes any chip within five feet of it to be terminated, killing anyone who penetrates the field."

"The Nobles couldn't see a problem with that?" Monica stuffed the paper into her pocket. "Anyone who came along without a chip could get at them and ruin the whole system."

"As far as they can see, it is impossible for anyone not to have a chip." Simon snorted and walked back to his desk. "They're not that dense. The original Nobles who initiated the system made it impossible for someone to escape being chipped, and the chips can't be removed without killing a person. Believe me, there are people who've tried. It is not a pretty sight."

Monica grimaced. Taking the chip from someone who had just died was bad enough, but when they were still alive? How would anyone stand such pain? "But I beat the system, so it's obviously possible."

"You're the first person since the system was initiated two hundred years ago. I would say it has worked rather well." He poked her shoulder. "You're one of a kind."

She jerked away from his hand.

Simon smiled. "Besides, you're technically dead. No one should have been able to escape a city's termination. You were the right age at the right time, and you had a nurse willing to endure the pain of going out-of-bounds to save you."

"I know that." She folded her arms over her chest. "I don't remember much at all, but it's started to come back to me recently. I can see Faye more clearly now than ever." When her nurse's dark brown eyes and thin face came again to her mind's eye, Monica brushed them away.

Simon raised a finger. "Remembering her isn't necessary, only what she did, and you can repay her by making sure Cillineese can never be terminated again."

Long, striding steps clopped behind the door.

Monica froze. "Are you expecting someone?"

"Quick," Simon hissed, "go hide in the bookshelves. Be ready to run."

She grabbed Vinnie's cage and dashed into the maze of shelves. As she hunkered down behind a case, she sucked in short, fast gulps, trying to keep them quiet. She peered over the top of a row of novels, allowing a view into the other room.

The library door banged open, smashing against the wall and knocking some books from a shelf. Master Gerald stood in the doorway, his feet spread wide apart, one hand on the door. His brow knitted, and his eyes flashed. "Simon, what is the meaning of this?" He brandished a full sheet of paper in his other hand as he strode into the room, his boots banging against the wood floor.

Simon's mouth dropped open. "Ma . . . Master Gerald. I . . . I don't know what you mean."

Monica clenched her fists so hard her knuckles ached. What could Gerald possibly want?

"This, right here." Gerald slammed the paper on the desk. "I have a report here that you and your library assistant are talking of rebellion."

Simon's hands shook as he picked up the paper. "Sir, that is what it says, but who would report such a lie? I have been work-ing for you for twelve years in Cillineese and with your family in Trentin for thirty years before the transfer." He bowed his head. "I am sorry you would think such things of me."

"It isn't what I think that matters right now, Simon." As Gerald paced the floor, his cape swirled around him. "We are under tight surveillance already. If Cantral hears about this, we won't be given the benefit of the doubt." He stopped and looked Simon in the eye. "Do you want Audrey and Amelia to die?"

Simon shook his head and sighed. "No, Master Gerald, I do not."

"Amelia has already been moved to Cantral ahead of schedule, but they will be checking all the reports. If we are under suspicion, the High Council might not allow her to receive the attention she needs." Gerald set his fists on his hips and looked at the floor. "If she is denied treatment, I will blame you and your assistant."

"I understand. If the report were true, your conclusion would be reasonable. But the report—"

"Of course it's reasonable." Gerald turned on his heel, his eyes scanning the room. "Where is your assistant?" He glanced at an ornate gold wristband clinging to his forearm. "Is he here? I can't pick him up on my monitor."

Monica gulped. She drew the chip's cylinder out from under her dress. The rice-sized piece wobbled back and forth in the glass. What was wrong with it? Why didn't it tell Gerald she was here?

Simon licked his lips. He glanced at the bookcase and caught Monica's eye. Nodding, he beckoned for her to come out. "Come here please . . . Marie."

Monica blinked. Marie? She left Vinnie's cage between two encyclopedias and stepped into the open. Apparently, Simon was trying to hide her identity. He said he wouldn't betray her. So far, he had told her the truth, but what could he be thinking now?

She crept into the main room, her arms and legs trembling. Gerald stared at her. She flinched under his heavy gaze.

He looked at his wristband again and pushed a button on the side. "Simon, what is this? I still don't see her."

"Allow me to check." Simon grabbed Monica's arm and leaned close to the base of her skull, whispering, "Run to the dorms if I give the word." When he straightened, he focused again on Gerald. "Her chip appears to be active."

Gerald looked Monica up and down, his frown deepening. "Your assistant is supposed to be a boy, eight years old. What's going on?"

"A malfunction perhaps, sir?" Simon raised his hands in the air. "Marie has had trouble with her chip calling her a boy on scanners many times before, as you may tell from her clothing. Her chip must be faulty. It seems clear to me that whoever filed this report didn't even know that my assistant was really a girl, proving that this is likely a spurious claim."

Gerald gritted his teeth. "You had better not be hiding something from me, Simon. As much as you have been my friend, I would not hesitate to terminate you if it would save my family."

Monica slid her arm from Simon's grip and looked around Gerald's elbow. The door was still wide open, but could she get to the dorms and have Alfred lower the ladder before Gerald could catch up? She was fast from all her years of running stairs, but was she as fast as a grown man?

"Yes, Master Gerald, I understand." Simon handed Monica the sheet of paper. "Girl, do you know anything about this?"

She pinched the paper, trembling as she drew it close. With a quick glance, she tried to read Simon's expression, but his face remained a blank slate.

The page had neat rows of information boxes running down each side. Questions like, *Identification Number of Person Being Reported, Area Reported, Date,* and *Priority Level* filled the white sheet. *Library* had been written in the space for *Area Reported* and Simon's and Nat's numbers filled the box labeled *Problem Slaves.* What did Simon want her to say? He knew she was the cause of this. The boy in the furnace room must have reported her, just as Simon had predicted.

"Well?" Gerald snatched the paper from her. "You had better come up with an explanation quickly, girl, or you will be demoted to the fields this instant."

Monica clasped her hands behind her back. Should she lie and save herself? Telling him the truth was out of the question. He would kill Simon right there if she told him about the plot.

She bit her lip. "I do know who reported me."

"You do?" Gerald folded the paper. "That boy should never have been anywhere near you. He risked everything to get this to

me, however, so he must have had a good reason to suspect you."
Gerald checked his wrist again. "And you could easily have been
near him. My wristband is still not picking up your chip's signal."

Monica shrank away from him. Why was he being so calm?
"It was active all morning, sir." She gulped. "You can check the
room's log."

"I will." Gerald stared at his wristband for a moment before
shaking his head. "Yes, I see the problem." He clicked a few more
buttons, then looked Monica in the eye. "According to this, you
died an hour ago."

CHAPTER 29

"**W**hat?" Monica's heart skipped a beat. An hour ago? That was when Simon left the chip on the desk. "How could my chip have died?"

"Simon?" Gerald ground out the name. "Chips cannot die. They have a life span of seventy-five years, and no one has lived that long in two centuries. How do you explain this phenomenon?"

Simon shuffled around the desk and folded up some papers while shifting others aimlessly. "Master, I have never heard of such a thing before, either." He pulled a book from a drawer and leafed through the pages. "The chips are supposed to last ten years longer than their owners. This girl is only sixteen. I have my doubts any-one would dare try to remove or deactivate a chip again since the last demonstration." His hands shook as he brought the book and papers around to the desk's front.

Gerald grimaced. "I was in attendance, as was every other Noble." He kept his gaze trained on Monica.

Trembling, she focused on the floor. When would he drop the

subject and let them get back to their plans? He had decided not to punish them, hadn't he?

"Girl," Gerald said, his voice softer now, "where are your parents?"

Monica risked another look. His gaze burned into hers, demanding she tell the truth, but which parents did he mean? Could he possibly know her secret?

Shuddering, she whispered, "They're dead. They died eight years ago."

"Really?" Gerald's eyes narrowed. "I don't think you're telling me the truth. You look very familiar, very much like my own daughters."

"My parents lived in the walls, sir." Monica blinked. Iain and Emmilah were the only parents she remembered. They took her in and died for it. "My father was a messenger, and my mother worked as a maid until she was sent to the fields."

"And did either of them have any resemblance to the Noble class?" Gerald snatched the book from Simon. "What are you getting these out for?"

"It's documentation on chip malfunctions, sir."

As Gerald thumbed through the pages, Simon slipped Monica the translation. She tucked it into her pocket with the map.

Gerald snapped the book shut. "What do you have there?"

She held her hands up, showing empty palms. "Nothing, sir."

He grabbed her wrist. "My brother was killed when Cillineese was terminated twelve years ago. I was one of the few people who knew his wife had a child."

Monica clenched her teeth and wiped her face of all emotion.

"I wondered why they kept it from the public at the time. She was put into the Cillineese records at birth, as is customary, but had yet to be assigned a chip." He shifted his grip to the back of her neck and probed her skin with his fingers. "I assumed the girl died with my brother."

As he pressed his thumb against Monica's skull, pain shot down her spine, but she held her tongue.

"It seems clear now that I assumed incorrectly, as did every other Noble." Releasing her neck and grabbing her wrist again, he smiled, but it didn't show in his eyes. "Whatever you were planning, it's over now . . . Sierra."

Monica blinked. The name seemed so familiar. Why would he call her that?

"I see by your expression you have forgotten your birth name, but a simple test will determine whether or not you're really my niece."

She shot a look at Simon, but he stood with his head bowed and hands clasped behind his back. "Simon?" she squeaked.

"Simon," Gerald continued, "I understand why you wanted to protect this girl. If, however, you will now renounce her and deny all these plans, then you will be allowed to live. You will be restricted to your dorm, but you will be alive." He grabbed Monica's other wrist. She struggled, but he held firm.

Simon nodded. "Yes, Master, I understand. I will do as you say."

"Very good." He spun her toward the door. "Niece or not, I must turn you in. This report was sent to Cantral, and if I do not bring someone forward to blame, the Council of Eight will terminate our city, killing millions, including myself and Audrey." He pulled her along. "Don't worry. I'm sure your execution will be mostly painless."

Monica planted her feet on the floor, but he jerked her forward. "Come on, Sierra, we haven't much time. I must report to Cantral before they grow tired of waiting and close the dome."

The map in her pocket brushed against her thigh. If only he would let her try the plan. None of this would matter. They would all be safe, and no one would die. "Please, sir, let me explain!"

"The time for explanations has passed. The system works. I would not have anyone compromise it." He yanked her into the hall. "Tristan Allen will soon die, and if I turn you over, the first person to escape the system, I should be up for promotion to his council seat."

"Promotion? You're treating me like this to get a promotion?"

"This isn't just for me." Setting tight fingers around her neck, he pushed her forward. "My daughters would live in the Cantral palace, never having to worry about termination again. Do you think I would give that up just to spare one girl's life?"

As his grip tightened, she gasped for breath. She should have listened to Simon and been more prepared to run, but even he had betrayed her in the end, saving his own life over procuring the slaves' freedom.

"What do we have here? Your plans?" He plucked the papers from her pocket. "I have no time to read these now. The dome will close in an hour if I don't contact them. Fortunately, Amelia left moments ago without a problem." He marched her down the corridor. "We'll look over the plans on our way to Cantral."

As they left the Seen dormitory corridor behind, her head swam. Just an hour to live. Since she was chip-less, the Cantral authorities would execute her on the spot. She would never take Amelia's place. The computers would remain intact, and the system would go on for another two hundred years. Millions of slaves would continue suffering day after day, all because she had failed them.

After they passed four more corridors, Gerald's grip relaxed. She breathed deeply, but the air seemed to burn in her lungs. They turned left onto the balcony where huge windows in the ceiling flooded the chamber with light. Gerald marched her down one of the sweeping staircases toward the first floor.

Monica's pant hems fell over her feet. She tripped on the slick black fabric and fell away from Gerald's grasp. Crying out, she tumbled down the stairs. Her cheek slammed against a step, and she slid the rest of the way down. Waves of pain racking her skull, she sat on the lowest step and braced her elbows on her knees.

Gerald's hand gripped her shoulder. "Are you all right?"

Tears sprang to Monica's eyes. She tried to hold back the sobs, but they squeezed through her clenched lips. The tears dripped from her chin to the red carpet below. Their salty trails stung her cheeks where the stair had torn her skin.

"Are you going to be able to stand?"

She kept her head low. "Why do you care? You're taking me to be executed."

He leaned over her, one arm draped on the railing. "It would be terrible if you were to arrive dead. I wouldn't be able to prove that you never had a chip. Perhaps they will think it was removed." His fingers brushed her hair from the back of her neck. "I see no scar, though, so keeping you alive might not be necessary."

The gentle touch sent shivers down her spine. More tears flowed. How could this man touch her and speak to her as gently as a father while discussing her death? He cared nothing for her, his brother's daughter.

Monica eyed the pages in his hand. She wouldn't let him take her so easily. Simon had given up on her, but he had told her what to do. *Run.*

She snatched the papers and leaped up, slamming her head into his nose. He cried out and covered his face with his hands, yelling obscenities. She clambered up the stairs. The hem of her pants fell over her feet, making her trip twice before reaching the top.

She turned toward the library and took off in a mad dash, stuffing the papers back into her pocket as she ran. The pant hems caught her feet twice more, but she stayed upright. Her head throbbed. "Alfred!" she screamed as she glanced back. "Alfred!"

Gerald pounded after her, closing the gap. He held a hand to his face, pinching his bleeding nose.

She skidded into the dorm hall. Alfred peered down at her from the open trapdoor. "What's the matter?"

The ladder hung from the ceiling half unfolded. She leaped for the lowest rung. Her fingertips slapped the wood but slipped away. "Send it the rest of the way! Hurry!"

"What's going on?" He lowered another section. "Where's Simon?"

"No time!" Monica caught the first rung and pulled herself up. Her arms quivering, she reached the next step and clambered up the rest of the way.

As the last section unfolded, Gerald swept into the hall.

"Master Gerald?" Alfred squealed. "Monica, what did you do?"

Monica grabbed Alfred's hand and raced to the bathroom. "Hurry, please hurry." She pressed Alfred's hand to the door. As it slowly rose toward the ceiling, the folding ladder groaned and creaked.

"He's coming!" Alfred pulled away, ran back to the beds, and dove into a curtained shelter.

As the doorway continued to grow, Monica ducked through the gap.

"Stop, girl!" Gerald bellowed.

She hoisted herself onto a sink counter, slid into the vent opening, and shimmied into the duct. The turn was just ahead. Safety lay only seconds away.

A hand grabbed her ankle. She screamed and lunged for the turn. Her fingers caught the side tunnel's edges. As Gerald pulled, the sheet metal dug into her knuckles. She squirmed and kicked to drive her body forward, but his tug kept her in place. Sweat mingled with her tears, burning the cuts on her face and hands. She gasped for breath. He jerked back savagely, but she held on. Darkness spotted her vision, and the duct seemed to grow dimmer.

"I don't want to have to kill you, Sierra, but I will if it comes down to it." Gerald panted loudly as he pulled on her foot again. "We haven't much time. Your struggle will kill millions!"

Monica closed her eyes and gritted her teeth. She squeezed her other leg up to her chest, forcing her back against the duct ceiling. What he said was true, but if he let her go, she could save them. The plans had to work.

Her knee under her chest pressed her body into a wedge. She loosened her fingers' death hold. Gerald yanked again. Her ankle popped, and pain shot up her leg, but she didn't budge.

Gerald re-gripped her ankle. She unfolded her other leg and kicked at his hand. His fingers cracked. Screaming, he released her, propelling her farther into the tunnel. She army crawled out of his reach to the downturn in the shaft.

He shouted after her. "I'll send another slave in there to flush you out, girl. I'll find you, wherever you're going! You won't get us killed."

Monica lowered herself into the shaft leading to the furnace room. As she scooted down the ducts, pain ripped through her ankle. "I won't get us killed," she yelled back at him. *I'm going to save us.*

CHAPTER 30

The duct's cool metal slid past foot by foot. Monica repeated her tactics from the night before, scooting down with her back to the wall. Blood coated her knuckles and fingers. Air blew through the tunnel, drying her sweat and sending chills over her skin despite her long sleeves.

Only an hour left—only an hour. As she slid faster down the tunnel, she gritted her teeth. Friction warmed her back and toes. After almost a minute, she smacked into the shaft below.

"Finally." She glanced up, but only the dim outline of the duct's edge reached her eyes. Whether or not Gerald followed up on his threat, she had to move quickly.

She tore the dead wristband from her arm and snapped the chip's cord from around her neck, but it snagged on the medallion's strap. After untangling the snarl, she threw the chip and wristband farther into the ducts. Both were useless now.

She dug in her pocket and pulled out the map, then scooted to the grate over the furnace room dorm. The grate allowed just enough light into the duct to illuminate the map's faint lines.

"I wish I had more to go on." She laid the paper on the metal, allowing light to shine through the back. She touched the outline of the furnace room and the dormitory. If she continued straight ahead, she should reach the messenger tunnel and the unidentified room.

She tucked the pages away and crawled onward. The ducts might not go in a straight line for very long, but at least the vents into the dormitory gave her enough light to see pretty far.

The tube took a sharp upward turn. She ducked her head and planted her elbows on the floor, now a squishy metallic substance that swayed as she crawled. Soon, the path turned downward, changing back to the slippery metal ducts.

Just ahead, a grate in the floor let in a glow. Monica scurried to it and pressed her cheek against the perforated surface. A tiny light shone from below, revealing the dirt walls and floors of a messengers' passage.

Rising again to hands and knees, she continued on. There had to be a tunnel leading to the right, to the mysterious room. She crawled twenty more paces, counting each slap of her hand on cold metal. The temperature dropped with every step. Her knuckles and knees ached. Her limbs stiffened, and numbness crept into her fingers. After five more slaps, two ducts veered away to each side of the main path.

She turned to the right and crawled through the new passage. As the path narrowed, her shoulders touched the sides. She squeezed herself farther into the ducts.

Something clicked. The sound of whirring fans filled her ears. The duct floor shivered beneath her touch.

Wind whipped dust over her from back to front, forcing her to close her eyes. She slid across the slick metal floor, as if the wind pulled her along with it. The clatter grew louder. Wind tugged at her clothes and pulled on Alyssa's medallion, stretching the leather cord as if trying to rip it away.

The whirring thundered in her ears. Could the computers be ahead? Simon had said they needed a cooling system, but what caused such a powerful suction and all that noise? Whatever it was, it couldn't be safe. She would have to find another path.

The cord slipped from around her neck and shot forward. She reached out and snatched the medallion. A thunk interrupted the whir. Slicing pain ripped down her fingers.

She yanked back her hand. A scream tore through her throat. Something thumped to the floor. Warm liquid flowed down her palm, across the rescued medallion, and trickled to her wrist.

She backed out of the passage and sat in the intersection. She held her hand up, but the light was too dim to see anything. Her breath choked her. She gulped and pressed her hand against her chest. The liquid seeped through her shirt. Her middle and pointer fingers ached as though they'd been bitten.

She crawled back to the messengers' tunnel grate and held her hand above the opening. A gasp caught in her throat. Blood dripped to the floor below, hitting the dirt without a sound. She bit her lip. The nail and top of her pointer finger had been sliced away, but her middle finger's first knuckle had been cut clean off. The sliced appendages still clasped Alyssa's necklace, the sticky cord now wrapped around the medallion.

Blood flowed freely from the wounds. A bit of bone peeked out of the carnage that was once her middle finger. She whimpered at the sight. The light filtering through the mesh grate painted a bright crisscross pattern on the wounds.

She tore at her pant cuff, trying to rip away some fabric, but the cloth held firm. One hand couldn't get enough of a grip to tear the solid material. She tried grasping it with her wounded hand's pinky and thumb, but pain shooting through her arm paralyzed her fingers.

Groaning, she crawled back the way she had come. Maybe something in the furnace room dorm could help. She held her hand against her chest and limped along.

She stumbled through the crinkly material uphill and then downhill. Her left arm ached from supporting her body by itself. The air grew warmer. Her fingers thawed, and the pain flared. Gritting her teeth, she kicked at the grate to the furnace dorm.

The clang of metal as it hit the floor jarred her nerves, but everything in the room below stayed still. She rested her elbows on the edge of the hole and lowered herself. Her legs swung through empty air. The pressure on her shoulders and biceps made her bite back a scream.

Arms wrapped around her knees. She kicked, but her captor's grip held firm.

"Let me go!" She tried to pull herself back into the duct.

"Where do you think you're going?" a man growled.

He yanked her from the opening. The metal edge ripped her sleeves and the skin on her forearms. She crumpled to the floor, hugging herself and gritting her teeth as she tried to keep back tears.

A toe nudged her shoulder. "Are you alive?"

Monica gripped her hand close to her body. Blood oozed to the floor from her arms and fingers, darkening the concrete. Her head throbbed.

"You're breathing, anyway." The speaker ripped a piece of fabric. The sound reverberated through the room. "You got yourself into some scrape or other." He tugged her arm away from her chest and plucked the metal disk from her hand. "You're making the cuts worse by holding onto that." He wrapped the soft material around her hands and fingers.

Monica locked her gaze on the hairy hands winding the bandage. As she tried to turn her neck, her muscles ached.

"Hold still. I didn't mean to drop you like that. You squirmed too much." The man spoke soothingly as he wrapped each forearm in white gauzy material. He cut away the remaining shreds of her sleeves with a knife. "Almost done."

As he finished the bandage job, a soothing sensation covered her forearms. He touched her hair. "I see a lump on your head. Can you move your neck at all?"

She blinked and turned her head from side to side. As she sat up, her vision grew fuzzy, and she swayed in place.

The man set a hand behind her shoulders and helped her lean forward. "Whoa, take it easy."

She rubbed her eyes. Her vision clearing, she looked up at him. "Who are you?"

He combed his fingers through his closely cropped brown hair. His smooth brow wrinkled. "I was wondering the same thing about you, Missy. I'm the one who belongs down here. Girls don't work these areas."

Monica wiggled her gauze-covered fingers, her middle one now shorter than the two next to it. She cringed at the sight. There must have been a fan inside the ducts, blocking her way to the computer rooms. No wonder duct-cleaning slaves had never found the computers. They'd get killed before they could reach the room.

The medic bent down and snatched the medallion from the ground. Wiping off the bloody surface, he handed it to her. "You were clutching that pretty tightly."

"Thank you." She turned the metal in a circle. Half of the medallion had been torn away, leaving a jagged edge cutting through the girl's face. Monica pushed the necklace into her pocket with a sigh. She should have taken better care of it. Alyssa wouldn't want anything to happen to it.

"You know." The medic interrupted her thoughts. "I used to make tokens like that one. Pity it got torn." He picked up a roll of gauze, a pair of scissors, a pill bottle, and a tube of ointment from the cot and stuffed them and his knife into a satchel. "You need to tell me what you were up to. The others will be back soon, and I assure you, you don't want to be here when they arrive."

Monica nodded. She did owe him an answer. He had just saved

her. "I was heading for a room off of the messenger tunnels, but there was a fan in the ducts, and it sliced my fingers."

"I guessed that part." He bundled all his supplies into a bag and slung it over his shoulder. "Do you clean the ducts, then?"

"No." Monica glanced around the room. A small form lay on one rickety cot, but all the others stood empty, just as they were when she visited last night. "I was looking for something. We're in danger."

"Danger? What kind of danger?"

Monica ran the perils through her mind. The dome could close within the hour. Master Gerald had been in a panic. He might send someone down after her, maybe even Alfred.

She leaped to her feet. "I need to hurry." A wave of blackness crashed over her, making her stumble.

The man caught her hand. "You lost quite a bit of blood back there. I wouldn't be in a hurry, if I were you." He guided her to a bed and sat her down. "Now tell me why you're here and what this danger business is all about, and I'll let you get on your way. Otherwise, I'll have to report you."

Her brow wrinkled. Who was this man? He had medical supplies and was in the furnace room. That didn't make sense. Only infirmary workers had supplies for the slaves, and only the barest of bandages, no soothing ointments or pills.

"Last time I told someone what I was doing, it almost got me killed, and it's going to get us killed, too, if you don't let me go." She crossed her arms, careful not to jar her fingers. "And I've already been reported, so it's useless to do it again." She nodded at his bag. "Who are you, anyway?"

"Medic for the furnace workers. The Nobles like to keep them healthier than most." He touched her forehead and the side of her face, his fingers calloused but gentle. "You banged your head hard somewhere along the road. Do you need something for that?"

She jerked away and glared. "My pant hems tripped me up. I fell down the stairs."

The man pulled his knife out again. "I could cut those shorter if you'd like."

"Okay." She needed to hurry up, and the extra-long pants kept tripping her. "Listen, I really need to go now. I have to find a way into the messenger tunnels. If I don't, we're all going to die." She licked her lips and tried to keep her face calm and serious. He had to believe her and let her go.

"Well, if we're going to die soon . . ." The man hacked six inches of fabric off her pant hems and tucked the scraps into his bag. "You might as well tell me your plan so I can help. We're going to die if I don't, right?"

She stood, fists clenched. "Don't make fun of me. It's true. The dome is going to close if I don't find a way to the computers."

"I guessed the dome might close." The man crossed the floor to the figure lying in the cot. "Someone was foolish enough to report a suspicious person."

She crept to his side, glancing at the door to the furnace room with every other step. "What happened?"

The man pulled back a thin blanket, revealing the boy from the night before. Red welts and gashes covered his face and neck. His eyes rolled up into his head, and his lips parted. A short gasp escaped his throat.

Monica gagged and stumbled back.

The man caught her under the shoulders. "It's not that bad; he'll most likely live." He sat her on the bed next to the boy's. "Snap out of it. You have some city saving to do, remember?"

She rubbed her head and nodded. "Yes, I know. What happened to him?"

"The other workers don't like turncoats." The man shrugged. "This boy was recently demoted, and he thought he could win favor by reporting their every misstep. They didn't appreciate it. Apparently, he took it too far last night. I'm not sure what happened. They were rather closed-lipped."

"I was here last night. He pretended to help me." She drew her knees up to her chest and hugged her legs. "But he betrayed me, and that's why we're in this mess."

"I see." The man sat beside her. "This boy reported you."

"I shouldn't have trusted him."

He nodded. "According to the rules, reporting you was his right, but I doubt he knew what trouble it would get him into. Everyone has been on edge about security lately. I am curious, however, as to how you can be here at all. Not even the Nobles are allowed down here. Just us workmen."

She stared at him. Why would this man open up so quickly and talk to her as if she were a normal person and not out-of-place? "I can explain everything, but . . ." She glanced at the boy on the cot.

"Don't worry about him. He won't be reporting anyone anytime soon." The man folded his arms over his chest and looked at her expectantly. "Start talking."

CHAPTER 31

Monica pulled out the map and gingerly unfolded the paper with her bandaged fingers. Whatever he had put on the bandages had numbed the pain, allowing her to open the map with little trouble. "Simon—he's the librarian—Simon and I came up with a plan to shut down the domes so Cantral can't kill us."

The man took the paper and glanced over it. "Blueprints for this half of the underground system. I have the whole thing memorized from my messenger days. Why is this important? There's nothing in these passages that could stop the computer protocols from being sent from Cantral. They've tried to block the signals before, but it's all hardwired, and no one knows where the computers in the city-states are located."

"Simon and I . . ." She frowned. Simon had helped her, but his betrayal stung. No use mentioning him again. "I think I know where they are."

The man's eyebrows shot up. "Really?"

"Yes, really." Monica held out her hands for the paper. "I was trying to get there through the ducts, but the fan was in the way."

He handed the page back. "They're close by, then? Near the tunnel right by the dormitory?"

She tucked the paper away and watched him for a minute more. For a second he seemed too eager. Someone with a job she had never heard of and so willing to help—it didn't make sense.

"I still make you nervous?" He looked her in the eye and shrugged. "I can't help that I'm so friendly. I've always been this way. It's one reason I got demoted from being a messenger. They didn't like how chatty I was."

She broke eye contact and picked at the blanket. "Yeah, I do think the computer room is close. There should be a river flowing through it, too, or near enough so the computers can get power directly from it. Simon . . ." She cleared her throat. "I was told that they run on hydroelectric power, so they need the river."

"And the river runs right through here!" The man clapped his hands. "Right through the next room, anyway. This is excellent."

"But the room is obviously going to be sealed off from the tunnel, and we don't have time to dig or anything, and the ducts have the fans blocking them. I don't know how to turn them off, and I don't want to be chopped to pieces." Her hand twinging, she pulled it close to her chest.

"Yes, I can understand that." He dug through his bag. "I put some ointment on your bandages to stop the pain, but I have some pills if you'd like." He held out a plastic packet containing a single yellow tablet.

She reached for the package, one eyebrow raised. "What's this for?"

"Medicine . . . to stop the pain later on." He set it in her uninjured palm.

She brought it close and raised it to the light. "I thought that was just for Nobles. They never give the wall slaves medicine."

"The furnace men have special privileges when it comes to this kind of thing. The Nobles want them healthy so there's a lower turnover rate."

"Turnover rate?" Monica popped the pill from the plastic. "Are you sure this is safe? My fingers don't really hurt right now. Maybe I don't need it."

"Once the shock goes away, trust me, you'll need it." He retrieved a water bottle from his satchel and handed it to her. "Here, take it and then we gotta get going."

She held the pill out in front of her. He had been helpful so far. The bandages stopped the bleeding and warded off the pain. She swallowed the pill with a quick swig of water. If he had wanted to hurt her, he would have done it already. "Where are we going? You didn't mention a plan."

"I don't really have one yet. Besides, this is your project." He winked at her and pointed at his wristband. "But the men are on their lunch break soon, and they will not be pleased to find a visitor in here, especially after being reported last night."

She handed him the bottle and followed him to the furnace room door, her heart rate rising again. "If they won't want to see me, why are we going *toward* them? Shouldn't we go through the messenger door?"

"I don't have access to the messenger tunnels right now, and the furnace room is the last place they'd want to be once they're on break. They're all thinking about their lunches." He positioned her behind the door. "Stay here and wait until everyone has come through, then slip inside. I'll join you when I can."

"That's your plan?" She laughed, but it came out as a strangled, choking noise. "They'll see me for sure!"

"Don't be such a baby." He patted her head. "It will work out just fine."

She ducked away from his hand. "The furnace room is in the opposite direction of where I want to go." She jerked a thumb toward the other end of the dorm. "The computers are that way."

"So we think, but the water is in here." He tapped his head. "You have to think outside of the box, little girl."

"I'm not a little girl," she growled. How condescending can a guy get? He was acting like he had this whole thing planned from the beginning. "And I can't go in the water. It'll get my instructions wet!"

"What instructions?" He rubbed his hands together. "There are instructions for this kind of thing?"

Monica raised her eyebrows. He was acting like a little kid with a new toy. This was life and death, but maybe he couldn't see that.

She dug into her pocket again and showed him the translated paper. "This. It's instructions on how to shut down the computers. The last ruler—" She grimaced. Her father, someone she would never know and couldn't remember. He wasn't just "The last ruler of Cillineese" to her, but it was so easy to forget. She shook off the useless thought. It didn't need to cloud her mind now. "The last ruler managed to figure out the controls. I don't know how he did, but it's what caused the termination, and it's about to cause this one, too."

The man put a finger on the last paragraph. "It ends rather abruptly."

She held the page close to her face. "Oh, no! Simon never finished translating it. He was working on it when we were caught."

He scratched his head. "Doesn't make me feel very important. That thing holds my life and yours in its hands. Figurative hands, of course."

"Yeah." Monica took the page back and glanced over it. Simon's neat handwriting covered the top half. Notes about different colored wires filled the margin, but only one was circled with a bold stroke. *Purple wire shuts off dome.* She pushed the page into her pocket. "I hope I can figure everything out as I go."

"Excellent. Confidence is a great thing to have." He pressed his ear to the door. A whistle blast shook the room. Blinking, he stuck a finger in his ear and wiggled it around. "They're coming. Stay there and slip in at your first opportunity."

He meandered over to the boy's cot and set his bag at the foot of the bed. The door banged open and almost hit Monica in the face. She held her hand out in front of her and peered around the edge. Six men trooped in. Sweat coated their red faces and rippling muscles. They talked among themselves, grumbling about the condition of the furnace and the water flow. Four boys followed close behind. Their bare chests heaved, and one boy's tongue stuck out as he panted.

Monica crept from behind the door as it began to close. She darted inside, and the latch clicked behind her. She pressed her back against the concrete wall and froze, listening. No yells came from the dorm. They must not have seen her.

Breathing a sigh of relief, she glanced around the steamy room. The river flowed fast and furious from one end to the other. As before, it bubbled and splashed loudly, and a wheel on each side of the river churned the water into a white, foaming torrent.

The heavy smell of burning wood and charcoal filled the room, tickling her nose. She pinched her nostrils together to suppress a sneeze.

As she pushed away from the wall, the door swung open.

The medic waved as he stepped inside. "Hello again." He strode to the water's edge and shouted over the noise, "Come along."

Monica crept to his side, carefully skirting the deeper puddles that populated the paved floor, but the river sloshed over its concrete banks and wet her toes.

"I've lived beside this river for the past few years," the man said. "Usually I work in another section, but I was called here last night for the boy." As another wave swept over the bank, he took a step back.

Monica watched the waterwheels splash around and around. The huge furnace on the other side of the river groaned and hissed a puff of steam into the air. "Now tell me how the river is going to help us."

"Don't you see?" The man clapped. "The water will run to the computers. You can get into the room by swimming downriver! I'm sure the setup would be the same as in here. The computers need a great deal of power to operate."

She widened her eyes. "Swim?" She stared at the river. It sped by, roaring like the lions from the stories. "What if there's no space to breathe between here and the other room? Besides, I can't swim very well. We only swam in still water in the bathing caverns. The waterwheel is in the way, too. I can't get past that."

"There's space above the water level. I've seen it in the other furnace room. And the waterwheel can be stopped for a few moments at a time in case it jams. He rubbed the back of his neck. "I would go for you—it'd be quite an adventure, but it's out-of-bounds for me."

"You're insane," she muttered. "My instructions will get wet." She patted her pocket where the papers lay nestled. "Then it'd be useless to be in the computer room."

"Hold them above your head." The man shoved her toward the waterwheel. "You're the one who said we're about to die. Maybe you should act like it."

She stumbled forward. The wheel splashed noisily, turning an axle that ran into the wall. Green lights flashed on and off where the metal bar disappeared into the concrete.

He pointed at the waterwheel. "If you go, look for the lever under the axle. That'll stop it."

Monica's fingers twinged. She glanced at the bandages on her arms and hand. What other way could she go? The ducts wouldn't work, and there couldn't be any way to the room from the tunnels. The messengers would know about it if there were, and rumors would have circulated back to the council. Maybe the river was the only way to get there. Most slaves couldn't swim well, and none could get close to the computers anyway, so it made sense to hide them in a place with the river as the only access.

He tapped his foot. "Whatever you decide, make it quick. I'm going to the dorm now. I must check on my patient then head back to my other work."

"Thank you." She touched her bandaged arm. "For helping me. I'm not sure what I would have done without you."

"You're welcome." He grasped the doorknob. "Now you can help the rest of us and do what you can to shut that computer off." He opened the door a crack, slipped through the opening, and let it close softly behind him.

As Monica sidled up to the waterwheel, she hugged herself. Droplets sprayed her face and body, soaking her oversized outfit and her bandages. A chill raced down her spine. There was no way around this. She had to swim through here. It was either that or wait for death to come from the dome and the gas.

She found the lever beneath the axle, a wooden dowel the size of a mop handle. A large plaque nailed to the wall spelled out some words in Old Cillineese, the same language as on the original computer instructions. She yanked the lever down, and the wheel shuddered to a halt. Water piled up behind the wheel for a moment before finding its way around the side. Red lights blinked on where the green had been. The overhead lights dimmed, and the fans in the ducts slowed their whirring.

Monica looked at the door leading to the dormitory. Might the wheel's stoppage eventually trigger an alarm? That would make sense. The computers couldn't survive without the power the wheels generated. Still, it seemed that the medic would have mentioned it. Maybe he knew there would be enough time to get away.

She took in a deep breath and stepped toward the wheel. She would soon find out.

CHAPTER 32

"Here goes everything." Monica withdrew the map and directions from her pocket, then squeezed next to the waterwheel, her back to the wall. Her shirt snagged, and her hair caught on splintered wood. When she pulled free, she ducked under the axle and came out on the other side of the wheel, stepping onto a narrow ledge barely large enough to stand on without her feet slipping off into the water.

Holding the papers above her head, she waded into the river. Her toes cramped in the frigid water, sending streaks of pain through her feet as she tiptoed across the rough bottom. The current pushed her to the side toward a dark tunnel in the wall, too dark to see what lay beyond its yawning arch.

As she walked that way, leaning back against the flow, the floor angled downward. Swirling water rose to her waist, then to her chest, then to her chin. Finally, the floor dropped away from her toes completely, forcing her to swim and battle the current.

Kicking, she tried to maintain a controlled float, but with only one arm to help her, the current swept her along wherever it pleased. Short gasps forced their way from her chest. Light from the furnace room dimmed. As she bobbed in the churning foam, the icy water numbed her arms, finishing off any pain that remained.

The river turned sharply to the right. Her body slammed into a wall before spinning back into the swirling flow and hurtling onward. Darkness closed in. Cold penetrated her bones. Kicking harder and paddling frantically with one hand, she lunged to keep her neck and head above the surface. What if the river never ended? What if the medic was wrong and it didn't lead into the computer room at all?

Her heart pounded. Her chest heaved. She bit her lip, trying to keep from hyperventilating. Staying afloat was all that mattered. Battle the water. Fight for breaths. The river had to come outside somewhere, even if there was no computer room.

With jagged walls all around, blackness became an enemy. Her head scraped against the stone ceiling. Her foot smashed into a rock. Squealing, she pulled her knees up, but her head sank below the surface.

Water flooded into her nostrils. She stretched to touch the river-bed with her feet, but they flailed aimlessly. Spluttering, she kicked harder. Her head resurfaced. A sneeze propelled the water from her nose and lungs, allowing her to breathe again.

A wave crashed against a side wall, discernible only by the horrific sound of thunderous splashes. The rebounding surge swept over her head and reached her outstretched wrist, almost lapping her fingers and the papers.

As she rounded another curve, the current sped up, still carrying her along helplessly. From somewhere ahead, the sound of a clacking waterwheel echoed across the water. Of course the next room would have a wheel just like the last. The city wouldn't waste a place to generate electricity.

The noise grew louder. Waves battered the rhythmic clacking, creating a chaotic blend of water and wheel discord. As she careened down the river, she bumped into a wall. Her free hand scraped against the side. Gripping a rocky protrusion, she slowed herself down. She pushed the papers between her teeth and grabbed the stone with both hands. The porous rock sliced into her finger-tips. Grunting, she clenched the stone in spite of the pain. The current ripped by, tugging on her body and saturated clothes, demanding she join the flow.

She extended her leg, searching for a foothold, but met with empty water once again. A sudden surge stripped her away and whipped her farther downstream. Still biting the papers, she fought back. Her feet hit the riverbed, and she grabbed the wall again, this time finding a better hold. Knees quaking, she braced her legs, angling her body to stand against the driving force at her back. Finally, she released the wall and managed to keep herself grounded.

She shuffled toward the waterwheel noise. The paper between her teeth felt soggy, so she took it out with a damp hand. She couldn't lose these directions. They were the key to everyone's survival.

With each step, cold water pounded against her back. The longer her torso and legs stayed submerged, the more the numbness increased. Her joints and bones ached. If she didn't find solid ground soon, her limbs would give way, and all would be lost.

The slapping of the waterwheel grew closer. With darkness all around, how could she find a way to avoid the paddles? She had to feel her way to safety.

She reached out her uninjured hand. Gritting her teeth, she braced for impact. The memory of fan blades severing her fingers shot into her mind. What else was she supposed to do? She couldn't swim back against the current, and allowing the river to carry her headfirst under a body-breaking wheel was out of the question.

Spray kicked up from the river, soaking her face. She shut her eyes. It was too dark to see anyway. Something smacked her knuckles. She yanked her hand back. The wheel must be right there, just a foot away.

She sidestepped to the wall and pressed her back against it. If the setup was anything like the furnace room's, she could inch her way downstream and squeeze past the wheel. There'd likely be no way to stop the wheel from this end.

Her shoulder blades brushing against the sharp wall, she inched along to her right, holding her hand out in search of the axle. Her fingers met with smooth, spinning metal. After ducking underneath, she stood and reached forward again to find the waterwheel's outer edge.

She bit her lip, bracing for impact. The paddles smacked her knuckles once more. She withdrew her fingers until they were just out of reach.

She sidled to the right. Her foot knocked against something hard, pitching her forward. She flung out her hands to catch herself, but they hit the waterwheel. Searing pain shot to her elbows. The paddles smashed against her hands and forearms. She reeled back against the wall, hugging her arms to her chest.

She raised her foot and stepped on what she had hit, a rise that felt like a concrete bank. Pressing her foot down on the firm ground, she stepped onto the bank and squeezed past the wheel.

Dropping to her knees, she gasped and wrapped herself up even more tightly. The bandages had been ripped from her hands and arms, and warm liquid streamed into her shirt.

Her eyes begged for light. They ached and burned as she sat crying. There had to be a light somewhere. How was she supposed to turn off the computer in complete darkness?

The instructions had been torn from her hands anyway, so what could she do even if there was light to see by?

Leaning forward, she rested her head on the gritty concrete floor and closed her eyes. There was nothing to do now but wait for the dome to close. She had failed her family. They saved her life and lost theirs so she could bring freedom to their people. Her nurse, Faye, had done the same, as had others. So many had sacrificed for the one hope they had remaining, a chip-less girl named Monica.

She touched the scar on her sternum. Every chip she'd used through the years represented another person dying so she could live in their place.

There were so many people who had risked so much for her. The boy who cleaned the chandeliers here in Cillineese. He would die. The twins in the stairwell and the little girl to whom she had given the glowing ball. Was she clutching the shining orb now? Cowering in the dark, realizing her sorry fate? Did she know the giver of this gift of light would cause her untimely plunge into fatal darkness?

Monica clenched her fists. She had failed them all.

Something cold and sharp bit into her thigh. The medallion. She fished the necklace from her pocket and clutched the jagged-edged disk in her palm. She had failed Alyssa, too. The grieving mother had given up her life and still managed to save Sasha's chip, but for what purpose? "Go rescue the slaves," she had said, half in sarcasm, yet half in hope that the easily fatigued girl could overcome her weaknesses and perform a miracle.

As the medallion cut into her hand, more memories of Alyssa resurfaced. She hadn't given up when her husband was taken away. She kept going, caring for the daughter she loved, and when her child was stripped from her arms, she cared for an uppity girl who thought she was better than everyone else. Alyssa had hoped Monica would free the slaves, and now she lay helpless on the cold, wet ground, ready to give up.

While the wheel clacked again and again, and the water continued its never-ending rush toward oblivion, Monica gave in to the cold and blacked out.

CHAPTER 33

A low thrum vibrated, rattling Monica's eardrums. Warmer now, she opened her eyes and sat up. Her arms burned as if on fire. The fingers on both hands stung. Darkness surrounded her, like a blanket of pure blackness. She draped the medallion's cord around her neck and rubbed her eyes. She blinked twice. The blackness stayed. What was going on?

Splashing water blended in with the thrum. A shudder ran down her spine. The computer room. This was the computer room, wasn't it? The trek down the river came flooding back to mind. A sob caught in her throat. She wasn't dead yet. She had to live with her failure for a little longer. Without a wristband, there was no telling how much time she had wasted, not in this darkness.

The waterwheel continued to pound in the steadily flowing stream, adding to the vibrating pulse that filled the room. Monica climbed to her feet. Her knees shook, and her calf muscles complained. The sensation of water rushing past still tingled her skin, throwing her off balance.

She hugged herself to quell the tingle, shuddering as she glanced around. How far away were the ceilings and walls? The dark room could be just a small box or extend a mile in every direction.

She stretched her arms out to either side. Her hands met empty space. The air felt still and calm. Dust tickled her nose. She let her hands drop back to her sides. What was the use? She could never find and dismantle the computer in the dark.

A tiny green light blinked on to her left, in the direction of the river's churning splashes. The pinhead-sized bulb flashed, seemingly in rhythm with the clacking wheel. She edged her toes in that direction, never lifting her feet from the ground. If there was a drop-off somewhere in the floor, she didn't want to take the plunge again.

She shuffled forward an inch, then a foot, then three feet. She reached out in front, but her hands again met only empty air. This must be what it was like to be blind. One of the children in her old dorm went blind, and he was terminated within the week. The Nobles' system didn't allow for people with defects. Even Noble children born with disabilities were killed before their fifth birthday.

The green light continued flashing. Monica slid forward another step. She wasn't blind, and she had lived, defying all odds. Her nursemaid and father had made sure of that. The tiny light seemed like a glimmer of hope. Maybe there was still a chance. She couldn't let their city die for a second time. There were thousands, millions of people who wanted to live, who deserved to live. If they died now, it would be her fault.

Her toes touched the edge of the riverbank. The computer had to be on the other side. She lowered herself to the floor and dunked her feet into the water. They dangled over the concrete edge. The river flowed deeper here than in the furnace room. What if she jumped down and couldn't reach the bottom? She could be swept downstream and drowned under another waterwheel.

She gripped the bank ledge with her aching fingers. If she was going to do this, she had to keep up her resolve. There was no time to think about the what-ifs. Her father risked his life to save her from Cillineese. Now she had to save herself and others.

The flow swirled around her calves, bringing back the chill. As she lowered herself into the water, the current ripped across her body as if trying to pull her into a series of violent swirls.

She tightened her grip on the ledge and reached one foot toward the opposite bank. The water batted her leg, her toes unable to touch the other side.

Turning around and facing the opposite bank, she planted both feet and shoved off. As she hurtled across, the river threw her farther downstream. When her palms smacked against the shore, she clutched the side and hauled herself onto the bank.

The buzzing intensified. It reverberated around her head, thumping against her ears. As she lay spread-eagle on the concrete bank, her clothes stuck to her skin, shivers ran through her entire body, and her teeth chattered. The light blinked above her head and to her right.

She rubbed her upper arms despite the pain in her hands. The computer had to be here. The light must be one of its signals. If only she had another glowing ball, she could find her way. Maybe the computer held a switch that would turn on other lights.

Reaching out, she crept forward. Her fingers touched a rough surface. The wall? She ran her hands across the flat, vertical area, every inch stinging her skin. Wincing, she followed the wall to her right, toward the green indicator.

Prickles stung her bare feet. She shuddered. What could she be stepping on? Whatever it was, if she wanted to find a light switch, she had to continue. As her feet protested with every step, the prickles turned into stings, like sharp pins poking her soles.

Cold metal met her right hand. She stopped. Probing with her fingers, she fumbled over grooves embedded in the wall, maybe the outlines of letters. She traced them over and over. What did they say? She tried to keep track of each shape, but they fell away from her memory.

Her fingers followed the border of the metallic sign—a plaque of some sort. That's not what she wanted. There had to be a light switch somewhere. Otherwise, how had the original slaves seen to finish their work?

Her foot struck something smooth and cool, but a quick probe with her toes provided no clue as to what it might be. She shuddered again and continued her search. Several inches to the right of the plaque, her hand hit another metal object, a bar of some kind protruding from the concrete. Her heart skipped a beat. Could it be the switch? Her fingers explored the bar and plate attached to the wall. Yes, it could be a switch. There was only one way to find out.

She tugged on the lever with both hands. The metal groaned and creaked. Bits of something rained down on her head. Still pulling the rough bar, she lifted herself to tiptoes to get leverage. More pieces fell to the floor, hitting her arms on the way down. They stung her wounds, and her hands screamed at her to stop.

With a guttural yell, she jumped high and jerked the switch down. A groan shuddered through the room. The buzzing intensified further. Something glimmered overhead, swaying back and forth. She released the bar and dropped to the floor. What had she done?

Monica's foot hit the object she had felt earlier. As she edged away from it, the glimmer above grew, and the room brightened. Overhead lights appeared in the gloom, hanging from chains that had been pounded into the ceiling. Ductwork weaved among the wire-and-pipe maze overhead. The lights sputtered and sparked but stayed on, still growing brighter.

The green light blinked in the midst of an angled display panel dotted with darkened bulbs. She did a slow three-sixty, her feet touching wires snaking across the floor. Waterwheels splashed and churned the river at both ends of the room. On either side of the river, a plastic barrier shielded a metal box from the exit wheel's spray.

Monica's foot touched the smooth object once again. She looked down. A bone! She jumped back, shrieking. A skeleton lay beneath the switch. Its skull rested on the ground, mouth wide open, its empty eye sockets staring.

She inched away from the brown bones. Bile rose in her throat. Whoever this was must have been lying here for centuries. She set a palm on the wall. The coarse texture brought her back to the task at hand. These computers had to be shut off, or she would end up like this person, sealed in here for hundreds of years with no one knowing what happened to her or even caring.

After skirting the bones, she crept to the display of pinhead-sized lightbulbs, an upright metal sheet attached to a huge metal box. The box sat against the wall perpendicular to the river's flow, stretching from the adjacent wall to within a foot or so of the river and its exiting waterwheel. Across the river, as she had seen earlier, a similar but larger box sat against the same exit wall, though no lights illuminated its front display.

Monica scanned the box on her side of the river. A word in old Cillineese was inscribed under each light.

She glanced back at the staring skeleton. A chain and manacle ran from its wrist to a rusting hook embedded in the floor. The hook abutted a doorway blocked by a brick wall. A plaque to the door-way's right read something in Old Cillineese as well.

She shook her head. Could that be one of the original slaves? Maybe even the person who designed the computers? It would make sense that the Nobles wouldn't want anyone who knew the system to come out of here alive.

Crouching beside the computer, Monica studied the display. There had to be a way to figure this out on her own. All she had to do was disconnect the purple wire, right? Messing something up was certainly easier than fixing it.

She found a crack in the metalwork below the angled display. She slid her fingernails into the opening and with a loud snap pried a panel from the box. A mishmash of wires filled the space.

Poking her head inside, she looked toward the river. A tunnel extended to the other parts of the computer, a conduit for the wires, dipping underground when it reached the riverbank. She tugged on the colorful wires. Red, green, blue, and yellow plastic wove in a tangled mess through the metal tunnel, none of them the right color, but maybe they controlled the chips. She gave them another tug, but they held firm.

When she withdrew her head, a second light came to life on the control board. The once-green orb flashed red. She squeaked. What had she done? Nothing had broken loose. Did she cause the lights to change? Or had something else? Could she have triggered an alarm?

Three more lights came on, two orange and one purple. A strobe light on the opposite bank's computer box flashed red, sending out a pulsing beam that spun in circles, orbiting faster and faster.

Monica glanced back and forth between the two computer displays. Just tugging on the wires couldn't have done that, right? She pulled another panel free from the computer casing but found only more wires. There had to be a control board somewhere. Yet, maybe not. This machine had run for two centuries unassisted, as far as she could tell.

She ripped off a third sheet of metal. Cobwebs stretched between the panel and wires behind it, tearing as she pulled. She tossed the metal into a pile with the others, making it clang loudly.

As she reached into the web-filled area, her hands stung in protest. The sticky webbing adhered to her oozing wounds. She cleared the webs away and found nothing but more of the plastic-covered wires leading toward the river and waterwheel.

She glanced around the room. Maybe the control panel was on the other side, but, if that were true, why would they put the light switch and the plaque on this side? A low, piercing whine emitted from somewhere, filling her ears, drilling into her brain. She slapped her hands against the sides of her head and knelt on the ground, then fell to the floor in a fetal position. The noise grew louder and more intense before finally dying away.

For a moment, she lay quivering. Her ears rang, and throbbing pain stormed through her brain, so excruciating it seemed that her head might explode.

After a few seconds, the pain eased. She crawled to her feet and shuffled back to the board of lights. All twenty bulbs were now flashing bright red. She licked her lips. This couldn't be good. Red was always a bad sign. Danger. A warning.

Then, the vibrating stopped. The hairs on her arms stood on end. Could this mean that the dome was about to close? Would the gas be next?

CHAPTER 34

Rumbling shook the computer room, starting out as a violent shock and then easing to a gentle tremble. When it stopped, Monica peeled away a fourth sheet of metal, the last one before the wires dove below ground. More wires were attached to huge metal panels at the back of the computer, none the right color. At the connection points, varicolored raised dots punctuated the surface. Fans embedded in the metal whirred around and around.

She studied the wires leading to the lights. Who was she kidding? None of the wall slaves knew anything about computers or electronics. They were all banned years ago. Yet, if she could just find the purple wire, she could stop the mass termination, or at least stall it indefinitely.

The lights turned off one by one, as if signaling a countdown. Another rumble echoed the first, this one sharper and longer lasting. Monica shivered in her damp clothes, hugging her bloody arms to herself. This was really the end now. The doors would lower into the tunnels and cut off the messenger routes, and the dome would rise from the ground and blacken the sky, the sheets of metal slowly unfolding and sealing off the city from the rest of the world. Bits of dirt would be clinging to the dome that had rested in the earth for twelve years.

She yanked the panel of lights from the computer, ripping the attached wires and tearing more skin from her fingers. At least she could do as much damage to this foul beast as possible, and maybe the purple wire lay hidden among the others. As drops of blood fell on the exposed wires, she snatched them up and jerked them from their connection points, making sparks fly.

A grinding noise rattled her ears. The rumbling slowed but didn't stop. She wrapped her arms around another bundle of cords and yanked them out of their ports. More sparks flew. The strobe light across the river blinked out.

When she grabbed a thick red wire, her arms shook. Her body stiffened. Finally, the jolt shot her away from the panel, sending her sliding on her backside. What was that? Did the computer have another defense mechanism? Something other than killing the chips that came near?

After crawling back to the access hole, she skipped the hot wire and pulled out a handful of green-colored ones from the connection points at the back. As she grabbed and jerked out more and more wires, the rumbling continued. Moments later, all the wires except the one that had shocked her lay on the floor in a tangled mess, some covering the skeleton and some dangling in the river.

Yet, no purple wire appeared. It simply wasn't in this box anywhere. Maybe the instructions were wrong. It made sense that the most important wire would be electrified. The red one had to come out.

She reached into the machine and wrapped her fingers around the wire. As the heel of her hand touched the exposed end, a shock ripped through her spine. Pulling with all her might, she stood rigid for a split second, then jerked back and fell to the floor, the wire clasped in her hand.

Her whole body shook, and her muscles contracted, pulling her into a tight ball. She lay still. Black dots swirled in her vision. Gasping for breath, she crawled to her feet, her hands leaving bloody prints on the floor.

The entire room spun around her, making her sway and stagger. She rested a hand on the empty computer shell. The lights overhead flickered, but the rumbling continued. She gulped. What else was there to do?

She glanced at the computer on the other side of the river, standing unharmed near the opposite bank. The waterwheels spun even faster than before, their gears now spraying sparks across the water.

Monica threw the red wire on the ground. The purple one had to be over there. She scrambled to the edge of the river. If she swam across again, she might be swept into the wheel. There was only one other thing to try. She checked the medallion's cord around her neck, then, getting a running start, leaped as far as she could. When her feet struck the wet ground on the other side, she slipped, rolled, and banged her head on the computer panel.

Black spots danced in front of her eyes again. She shook them away and crawled to her feet. She had to hurry. If she waited much longer, loss of blood wouldn't matter. She would be dead from the gas that was sure to come.

Her abused fingers poked into a crevice and yanked a panel away, making it swing on hinges and bang against the wall. A layer of dust puffed off the surface and floated through the air. A vent above immediately swallowed the dust, sweeping it from the room.

In an alcove behind the hinged door, fuzzy white-and-black lines danced across a shiny glass screen. She tapped the black glass. Sometimes the wristbands had the same problem and smacking them often cleared it up. The screen blinked off. She kicked the machine, but it didn't revive.

She plucked off all the other panels, revealing a mess of wires just as large and complicated as those on the opposite side of the river. Her head spinning again, she sat on the floor. If the purple one lay buried within the mess, there was only one way to find out.

As more rumblings shook the room, Monica gathered an arm-load of wires and braced her feet against the wall. With a backward lunge, she yanked them free. A pop sounded. Sparks showered everywhere.

After crawling back to the computer, she looked inside. On the floor where the wires had been, a single purple wire, much thicker than the others, ran from the wall to the black screen. Wrapping her burning, bleeding fingers around it, she braced her feet again and pulled.

It didn't budge. It wouldn't even stretch.

Again and again she pulled, grunting, trembling, pleading. It had to come out! It just had to!

Still it stayed intact.

She dropped it and fell to her backside. The rumbling grew louder. The room began to shake. Lights overhead swayed, and the ductwork creaked.

"No!" she shouted, letting the cry stretch out and echo through the room. She couldn't give up now, but how could she disconnect the wire? Time was sifting away, and no ideas remained.

A hissing noise sounded. She glanced over her shoulder. From the river's source, white mist curled into the room. *Gas!*

When she leaped to her feet, the medallion swung at her chest, scratching her burn mark. She snatched it off and stared at Sasha's image. Alyssa's appeal whispered in Monica's mind. *Go rescue the slaves!*

Clutching the sides, she let the sharp edge dig into her skin. Maybe. Just maybe.

She lunged back to the computer, grabbed the purple wire, and began sawing at it with the medallion. When she cut through the outer insulation, a piercing tingle coursed through her body. Sparks rained over her aching fingers. An acrid film coated her tongue, a sure sign that the gas had mixed into the air.

With a final chop, she sliced through. The severed wire sparked and danced in place for a moment before settling into a fading sizzle.

Her body quaking, she struggled to her feet. The rumbling stopped, but the cloud of gas expanded. As her vision darkened, she held her breath. Maybe there wasn't any gas farther downstream.

After staggering back to the river, she slipped the necklace on and squeezed between the waterwheel and the wall. When she dove into the water on the other side, her open wounds shrieked in protest. As she bobbed in the current, it whipped her back and forth. Her head smacked against stone. A cracking sound echoed over the pounding water. Blinding white light flashed in her vision, and pain filled her head, masking all the earlier injuries.

A scream tearing through her throat, she sank beneath the surface. Water filled her mouth and lungs. She kicked until her head bobbed over the foam. A violent heave brought the water surging back up from her airway. Choking and spluttering, she fought off the blackness.

The white mist closed in, though the river continued to sweep her downstream faster and faster. The air tasted bitter. She dove under the surface. The cold water slammed against her head, and her foot scraped against a rock, but the dual shots of pain chased away the darkness in her mind.

Rolling into a ball to conserve body heat, she stayed submerged until her lungs felt like they would explode. Bile rose into her throat, and she threw up underwater. She tried to gasp for breath, but only water entered her mouth, choking her.

Her back slammed into a stalagmite. Grabbing it, she crawled to the surface and coughed. Water erupted from her lungs and spewed from her lips. Then, her breathing eased to a rhythmic flow.

She rested her cheek against the cool stone. Her lungs burned like fire. The white mist rolled down the river and surrounded her again. The acrid taste returned, coating her tongue. She released the stalagmite and let the current carry her away. If she let gas overpower her, she would never find out if she succeeded and if anyone survived.

As the lights from the computer room faded, she fought away sleep. She couldn't sleep. If she slept, she would drown. A warm spot pulsed on the back of her head where she had slammed against the rocks. The pain worked to keep her awake.

The river ferried her through dark tunnels, the mist now invisible in the blackness. She let herself sink until just her nose and eyes poked through the surface. The acrid taste dissipated. The current's speed ebbed and now caressed her limbs instead of pounding her against the rocks.

Drops of water fell from the ceiling, splashing her face. The air grew stale and cold. Mustering strength, she swam with the current. It swirled gently around her, almost nonexistent. She must have entered an underground pool.

Farther ahead, a light illuminated a dirt-lined passage. Monica paddled to the source. A single lightbulb dangled from a chain above a narrow tunnel. She hoisted herself onto a rough, pebbly beach, every muscle screaming as she dragged herself from the dark water. Then she collapsed on the shore and blacked out.

CHAPTER 35

Monica's head throbbed. She awoke lying on her stomach, a dull ache pounding at the back of her skull. Her arms burned, and nausea boiled.

She rolled onto her back and rubbed her eyes. Gritty sand filled the wounds on her hands. A searing pain started in her fingers and crawled up to her wrists. The dirt smelled musty, and the odor churned her stomach, adding to the nausea.

Monica held her hands in front of her. The light above swayed, casting irregular shadows across her skin. All the surface flesh had been torn from her palms. Even the smallest wound revealed pink, raw skin. Blood oozed from the deepest cuts, and a white bone poked through the finger stub on her right hand.

She held back a sob. How could her hands recover? Would she ever get out of this cave? No one knew she was down here. They might even all be dead. If she failed to stop the termination, maybe she would never know. Or she could have succeeded. The rumblings had stopped when she pulled out the purple wire, but what if it had been too late?

She braced her forearms on the ground and army-crawled across the tunnel floor's incline, her head low. Her shoulders cramped. Cries erupted from her chest. She tried to bite them back, but pain forced them out. Dirt caked her wounds, clogging the flow of blood.

As she inched along the tunnel floor, her clothing began to dry. With the air growing warmer, the shivers slowly faded, but with the warmth, the blood flowed more freely from her hand wounds.

She planted her hands on the ground and rubbed dirt into the gouges. The bleeding slowed once more, and she continued on.

A foot in front of her, a solid door blocked her way. She tapped the wooden surface. A light above the door blinked. Red, yellow, green—it cycled through the three colors over and over, a low whine buzzing from the bulb.

Monica climbed to a sitting position and rested her back against the door. It must have lost communication with the computer and didn't know what to do. At least ripping out all those wires did some good.

She rapped the surface with a raw knuckle. Her breath rattled in her chest. Someone had to hear her. She knocked again.

"Who's there?" a muffled voice called from the other side.

She gulped. Someone had survived! She gathered her strength and shouted, "My name's Monica. I'm hurt. Please help me!"

"Wait a minute." Something slammed against the door. "It doesn't open; it's sealed."

"The computers are shut off." Monica scooted away. "The door can't open automatically."

"No, that's not it. The computers can't be shut off. This door is just sealed. No one goes through it. No one's allowed."

"The computers can be shut off." Monica rested her head against the tunnel wall. Her brain throbbed at every word. "The door will have to be kicked in."

"I'll try." The voice faded away.

Something thudded against the thick wood. It hit again, sounding like a shoe against the boards. A crack appeared down the door's center, revealing the heel of a boot.

"It's starting to give. Get away!"

Monica scooted farther to the side. The boot made contact again, and the door flew off its hinges. As splinters ricocheted in every direction, she held her arms over her head, protecting her face.

A man fell to the ground in front of her, nearly landing in her lap. He hopped up and dusted himself off. "There, that's better." He looked at her, his eyebrows lifting. "How'd you get in here?"

She stared at him. This was the same man who had let her through the Cillineese wall on her first trip to the library!

He frowned. "I know you from somewhere, don't I?"

"Yes." She tried to keep her eyes open, but she suddenly felt so sleepy. "You let me into Cillineese the other day on your messenger route."

"You're that girl who almost got me into trouble." He glanced over his shoulder. "I was late for one of my errands. I'm going to be late now, too, but . . ." He tapped his wristband. "My screen seems to be malfunctioning. It isn't getting any coordinates or new pickups. I'll have to stop and get it exchanged."

"That's because the computers are shut down like I told you." She gasped for breath. Why was everything swirling? She closed her eyes, yet even the blackness seemed to spin her around in a circle.

"Are you all right? You're very pale." A cool hand touched her forehead. "And how did you get so covered in mud?"

Forcing a smile, she brushed the hand away. "I'm always pale. All wall slaves are."

"No, pale even for a wall slave." Concern filtered into the man's voice. "You should go to the infirmary."

"They can't do anything for me." A shudder shook her entire body. "Slaves go there to die. I'm not dying."

"Don't be so sure."

Strong arms lifted her into the air. She stiffened. One arm supported her back, and the other cradled her legs. Her heart raced. She couldn't go to the infirmary. Everyone died there. They didn't give medicine to wall slaves. When people went to the infirmary, they died and were incinerated, their chips dug from their skulls and given to her to use.

The man's stride lengthened and smoothed out into a fast jog. He carried her as though she weighed nothing at all. As if working on their own, her arms wrapped around his neck, her fingers linked to keep a strong hold.

Spasms shook her body. Where was he going? She held on tighter. What would they do with her when she died? She tried to envision the scene. Everything spun in her mind's eye. Her thoughts jumbled together. The infirmary. People died, their chips taken. What would they do when they found none in her? An empty girl with no chip. They would cut her open and incinerate her flesh. The flesh would char, and she'd be empty still. Her mind would be gone. Gone where?

"Where?" she muttered.

"The infirmary." The man breathed heavily, the only sign that he felt her weight in his arms. "We'll get there in time, don't worry."

The infirmary. She shook all over again. Some of the slaves said you went nowhere when you died, but how could you go nowhere? Some spoke of a better place in their songs. They said that an angel scooped you up and carried you there, a ride through the air in strong arms. She never paid much attention, nor could she hold the thought now. A fire burned in her brain. The back of her skull ached, and her bones felt like glass inside her limbs.

"Hold on, girl; we're almost there." The man's voice bounced with his steps as they mounted a flight of stairs.

"Was there gas?" She tried to open her eyes, but someone must have sewn them shut. No matter how hard she flexed her eyelids, they stayed closed. "Did the computers work? Did the dome close?"

"The strangest things happened in the last hour." A door creaked open, and the rush of soap-scented air brushed her face. "Nanci? I have another patient for you. I think the gas got her. She's not making any sense."

"My, my, my." An old woman's fluttery voice filled the room. "Where did you ever come across this poor thing? I don't have a spare bed."

"She was in the old bathing caves tunnel, the one they closed off years ago." The man's grip tightened around her shoulders. "She's worse off than some of your other patients. Can't you move one?"

"No, she doesn't even belong here." The woman tugged on Monica's shorn sleeve.

Monica groaned and pulled away. Even the slightest touch sent sparks of pain up her arm.

"She's a Seen, can't you tell?"

"No," the man grunted. "I can just see she's a muddy mess. Almost couldn't tell it was a girl under all this mud, and I'm getting it all over my uniform. What do you want me to do with her?"

"Take her to the Seen infirmary. She'll get much better care there, anyway." The woman's voice grated on Monica's ears. "I can't do anything for these poor folks other than give them fresh air. For a moment the world was ending around our ears, and now it's back to normal . . . if you can call this normal."

Monica stiffened. She barely understood what the woman was saying. Did the dome not close, then? Why wouldn't her ears stop ringing?

"I can't go into the Seen infirmary, Nanci! I'm not even supposed to be here. I'm late as it is, and my wristband isn't working. Besides, I need to check all the tunnels for more messengers. The gas is starting to clear."

"Patrick, don't be a baby. You take that poor girl there right now. Nothing's working as it used to. You'll be perfectly fine."

"I don't want to get zapped." The man carrying her walked again, apparently back the way they had come. "I've seen many a man fall. It gives me the heebie-jeebies to see the sparks fly."

"You'd be dead right now if it weren't for a miracle stopping that dome, so pass it on and help that poor girl."

"Fine, but I don't even know where the Seen infirmary is, and I can't fit through the ridiculously small passages. I'm too big."

"I'll take her then, you big baby." Something hit the floor with a muffled thud. "You can stay here and give the patients water and make sure the fans keep running. The electricity keeps trying to turn off."

The man transferred Monica into the woman's arms. Her limbs felt hard and cold. Monica bit back a cry of pain. Why was everything on fire?

"There we go, little girl. Don't worry. You'll be right as rain soon enough." The woman carried her into the fresher-smelling air.

"Hurry back, Nanci. I can't babysit these kids all day."

"You're a big teddy bear, Patrick," Nanci shouted back. "You'll be fine."

As she climbed a flight of steps, her breathing labored. "You're heavier than you look, girl. Must be all that mud caked to you. What have you been doing?"

Monica tried to open her eyes again. Who was this person carrying her anyway? Her name seemed so familiar. Could she be trusted? Was she really taking her to the infirmary? Shivers jolted Monica's body. She couldn't get warm. The cold seemed to seep into her very bones.

The woman readjusted her grip around Monica's shoulders and knees. "You're going into shock. Stay awake if you can. Can you open your eyes for me?"

Monica tried to do what the woman said, but her body no longer belonged to her. It was as if she was inside her head but had no control and someone else had taken over.

The woman stopped and leaned over. Monica's head brushed the ground. She stiffened. Was this woman going to dump her somewhere and leave her for dead?

Something creaked loudly, shrieking in Monica's eardrums. She groaned. The woman laid her down.

"Hold on, girl. Keep breathing. The poison will work its way out of your system. If you're still alive now, you'll survive." She grabbed Monica's shoulders and dragged her across the ground. "That's been the case with the others."

"Some died?" Monica's voice rasped in the back of her throat. "What happened?"

"I don't know all the details, but don't worry yourself about it, dear. I'm sure you had nothing to do with it."

"I did. I did." Monica coughed. Now even her throat felt like it was on fire. "It's my fault. I should have been faster. I was too afraid at first."

"Save your breath, honey." The woman lifted her into her arms again. "We're almost there. We're in the main part of the palace now."

The humming of voices swirled around her. Monica tried to cover her ears, but her hands wouldn't respond to her commands. Who was talking? Why wouldn't they be quiet?

"What are you doing here?" A distinct female's voice rose above the others. "Who's the girl?"

Nanci's arms quivered under Monica's body. "I have one of your people here. A messenger found her. She breathed more of the gas than some of the others. She's bleeding, too." Her voice trembled to match her body.

"I'll take her." The speaker took Monica into her arms. "You'd better get back into the walls. Master Gerald is on a rampage. He's furious. He's already tried to kill two of us, but the chips aren't responding."

"Aren't responding?" Nanci gasped. "None of our wristbands are working, either. What's going on?"

"No one knows." The woman started walking away. As Monica

bobbed with every step, the woman raised her voice. "The messengers say that everyone in the city who isn't dead is scared silly, but they're coming out of their houses now that the gas is dissipating."

Monica's lungs seemed to close. Her throat swelled. She gasped for breath. She tried to breathe through her nose, but no air got through.

"Hold on, kid." The woman broke into a run and bounded up a flight of stairs.

Monica gasped again and choked. Why couldn't she get any air? She tried to move her arms, commanding them to reach out and take off whatever held its grip on her breath, but they didn't respond.

A door opened. It slammed against the wall. The woman shouted, "Coral! We have a bad case here. She needs oxygen."

"Hurry! Put her on the bed here!"

The woman laid Monica on a soft mattress that cradled her back and sore limbs. Something clamped around her wrists and ankles. Everything danced in circles in her head, and she still couldn't pry open her eyes.

"How is she, Coral?"

"I don't know yet." Coral's voice quivered.

A plastic mask covered Monica's mouth. Dry, sweet-smelling air filtered into her nose and wafted into her lungs. She gulped it down. Her throat opened up and accepted the delicious air.

"That's a good girl. Breathe nice and deep now."

Something sliced away her sleeves. Cold hands squeezed frigid water onto her wounds. The cuts stung. Monica gasped and cried out.

Another strap fell over her shoulders and chest, holding her to the bed.

"This is the worst one yet that's come this far," Coral said, as she scrubbed a spot on Monica's forearm. "The others died before this. Who is this girl? I don't recognize her."

A sharp prick jabbed Monica's skin. Seconds later, the spinning sensation took over, swirling her into a deep sleep.

CHAPTER 36

"**I**s she coming to?"

"I don't know. Her eyelids are fluttering."

"I wasn't sure how she would take the anesthesia after being exposed to the gas."

"It was risky for sure, but she would have died if she woke up and hurt herself."

The words floated around Monica's head as if they belonged to phantoms. A sharp, acrid smell filled her nose. Did someone leave some cleaning solution out?

"She's moving now."

"Yes, I see."

She reached up to grab hold of the voices. They needed to be silenced. Something held her wrist in its clutches. Her chest felt the same compression across her rib cage, holding her to the mattress.

"Help!" she groaned. "I can't move."

"That's for your own safety," the first voice said. "You were trying to tear at your wounds. They were bad enough already without you ripping off the bandages."

Monica forced her eyes open, blinking them rapidly. Two women stood above her. A white light framed them from above, shining through their dark hair.

One put a hand on Monica's forehead. "Her fever's broken." She smiled. "Do you remember me? I brought you here after the wall slave rescued you from the tunnels."

"I remember the . . ." Monica licked her dry lips. "I remember the trip here. The bouncing and the stairs." Her voice cracked.

The woman put a straw up to Monica's mouth. "Here, drink this."

Monica caught the straw between her teeth and took a long draw of water. The liquid soothed her throat. "Thank you."

The second woman backed away from the bed. "I have other patients to attend to. You can see to her, Jasmine."

"Thank you, Coral." Jasmine held the cup while Monica took another sip. "Are you feeling better?"

"I guess so." Monica turned her head to the side. A row of beds lined the white brightly lit room. A body occupied every bed, and Coral rushed from one to another.

Monica turned to the other side. Her own bed touched the wall. "Where are we?"

"The Nobles' infirmary." Jasmine grinned. "Gerald couldn't stop us when he found out the chips weren't working anymore. He was sick himself, and we gave him medical care, but once he was well enough, we shooed him out to make room for the others."

Monica frowned. "What about the wall slaves? Don't they need help, too?" A soft blanket covered her body, warming her bandaged arms and chest. "They don't have any supplies at all."

"They don't?" Jasmine pulled the cup back and put it on a side table. "Our infirmaries don't have much, but we do have oxygen and painkillers. That's all you really need to fight off this gas." She sighed. "If someone breathed in too much, they're a lost cause. We almost lost you. Coral wanted to give up, but I could tell you're a fighter."

Monica closed her eyes. "Thank you." Her head still ached,

but the throb felt distant and muffled. They must have given her painkillers, like the medic in the furnace room had. Was he okay? Or had the gas gotten him? And what about the rest of the wall slaves?

"Are you going back to sleep?"

Monica shook her head. "Someone needs to help the wall slaves." She tried to sit up again, but the bonds held her back. "Does anyone know how many died?"

Jasmine unstrapped Monica's ankles, wrists, chest, and shoulders. "There's no official count. The traders and peasants are scared out of their wits. At least that's what the messengers are saying. We were sure we were doomed." She pointed at the skylight. "The dome started to close, and everything was being blocked out by the metal. Everyone was screaming." She unfastened the last buckle around Monica's waist. "Where were you? You must have missed out on everything."

"I was . . ." Monica held a hand against her head. "It's too hard to explain, but, trust me; I didn't miss out on anything."

"If you say so." Jasmine handed Monica a clean Seen's dress and shorts. "Here, we had to dispose of your old clothes. They were damaged beyond repair." She pulled a curtain around the bed, concealing it from everyone on the outside.

Monica dressed as quickly as her stiff limbs and bandaged hands would allow. Her fingers wouldn't move to fasten the buttons in the back. Should she tell this woman about the computers? She might praise her, or she might betray her to Master Gerald.

Jasmine helped her with the tiny buttons. "There you go." She took Monica's wrists and turned her forearms up. White dressings covered both skinny arms. Dots of blood speckled the outside of the bandages. "You did a number on your hands, too. What in the world were you doing?"

Monica pulled her arms away. The same bandages covered her hands as well, wrapping her fingers so thickly her hands looked like mitts. Her skull still aching, she laid a palm on the back of her head. Thick gauze wrapped all around, covering her forehead and hair.

"Not going to tell me?" Jasmine crossed her arms. "I did save your life. If you hadn't gotten the oxygen and medicine when you did, I think you wouldn't have been long for this world."

Monica winced. She must have hit her head really hard to deserve a bandage that size. "I'll tell you if you promise not to tell anyone else or panic." She put one hand over the other in her lap. They were useless clubs now. She couldn't even dress herself.

"I won't. After what I've seen today, not much will faze me." Jasmine tapped Monica's shoulder with a finger. "Did someone hurt you?"

"No." Monica laid a hand on her hot cheek where a rough patch of skin grated against the bandage. "Actually, some of it, yes." She covered her injured eye, where she had slammed it on the stairs. "I got this when I tripped down some stairs because someone was dragging me." She shuddered. Her heart had been in her throat that entire journey. She had been so certain the council was going to kill her, but here she was. The computers were dead, and she had survived.

"Someone?" Jasmine caressed Monica's forearm. "What about all the other wounds? You didn't do all this to yourself."

"Not on purpose." Monica looked at the crisp, white sheets. How could she explain? The woman would never believe her under normal circumstances, but maybe after the day's events, she would be willing to hear her out. "I cut my fingers on a fan in the air ducts, and the rest happened as I tried to get into the computer room."

"The computer room?" Jasmine laughed and sat at the foot of the bed. "You must have hit your head pretty hard. You know, if someone hurt you, you won't get in trouble for telling me." She unclasped the wristband on her thin, pale wrist. "We're all on equal ground right now. The Cillineese computers must have malfunctioned. We're safe for a little while."

"No, they didn't malfunction." Monica swung her feet off the bed. She needed to find out what was going on outside—who was living and who had died. She needed to find Simon.

Monica put both bare feet on the cold wood floor. "I shut off the computer. The dome didn't finish closing, and the gas—I don't really know what happened with it, but it stopped flowing because of me." She stood but suddenly felt dizzy and had to sit back on the bed.

A puzzled look spread over Jasmine's face. Her eyebrows wrinkled, and she shook her head. "You're just a Seen child. Not even Master Gerald is allowed near the computers. No one knows where they are. You shouldn't take credit for this miracle."

"That's how my hands got torn up. The wires and panels from the computer tore them, and the river to the bath caverns runs through the computer room. I swam to the bath caverns, and that's how Patrick found me." Monica sighed. How could she get this woman to understand? But maybe it wasn't important. It might be better that no one knew.

"Just relax." With a gentle touch, Jasmine guided Monica back down to the bed. "You're stressed from the amount of blood you lost. Some people remember things differently when they're trying to figure out how a phenomenon like this happened."

Monica pushed Jasmine's hands away and slid off the bed. This woman wasn't going to believe her. "I need to talk to Simon. Do you know where he is? Did he survive?"

"The librarian?" Jasmine shook her head. "I haven't seen him since he was last sick, and that was months ago. We searched all the palace rooms, and we brought everyone we found sick in here."

"He was in trouble with Master Gerald when I left." Monica staggered toward the door, grabbing hold of the metal footboard of each bed as she passed. "I need to tell him what happened, that it's okay."

"You can't go yet." Jasmine rushed to Monica and grabbed her arm. "You're not well."

Pain shot through Monica's wounds. She squealed and pulled away. "Don't touch me!" She hugged her arms close and glared at Jasmine. "Thank you for your help, but I really do need to go. I have more to do."

"Where are you planning on going? There's still gas in some of the unventilated rooms." Jasmine and Monica stood nearly toe-to-toe next to the infirmary doorway. "Some of the walls could be impassable. The dome didn't close all the way, so much of the gas escaped, but we're still working on opening the windows."

"I need to find Simon." Monica continued her slow, shuffling walk. Her legs wouldn't respond to her commands.

"Wait!" Jasmine ran to her side. She held out a disk attached to a leather cord. "Here's your necklace. We took it off when we cleaned you up. It's rather sharp."

Monica smiled. "Thank you. Can you put it on for me? I don't think I can manage it myself."

Jasmine nodded and tied the string at the back of Monica's neck. "There." She put her hands on her hips. "But I still don't think you should be going anywhere. You're not well."

"Well or not, I need to find Simon." Monica shuffled down the hall. "I'll recheck the library."

"There aren't any windows in there," Jasmine called after her. "The gas will be terrible. Don't breathe any more in!"

"I'll do my best." After staggering through a hallway, she stopped at an intersection. Scratching at her bandages, she looked to the left, then the right. Where was she, anyway? She hadn't been to this side of the house before.

To the left, a balcony opened up farther down the hall. She chose that corridor and found a stairway to the first floor. As she descended, a chilly breeze wafted across her body. A strange chirping noise echoed through the house, and the rustling of leaves filtered in through the open windows.

Monica shivered. Where was everybody? It seemed like more

people should be around after such a near catastrophe. And where was Master Gerald?

After finding the entry room with the dual staircases, she climbed the steps toward the balcony leading to the library, now quite sure of where she was. Drops of blood marred the marble slab where she had slammed her head. Staying on the opposite side, she looked away. The events of the day must have kept the cleaning duties from being taken care of. Normally, a mess like that would have been wiped up in minutes.

Monica scurried to the library. Her legs responded more readily now. Whatever drug Coral had given her must have been wearing off. Moments later, she reached the library door. White mist floated out from under the crack.

She inhaled deeply and held her breath before swinging the door open. A wave of gas encircled her, tickling her neck and limbs. She threw the other door open and ran inside.

The library felt distant and quiet. She waved the mist from her face. Her eyes stung, and her lungs started to burn. "Simon?" she shouted. Her lungs expelled all her reserves. She darted back out of the room and closed the doors behind her. If he was in there, he had to be dead.

She ran to the Seen dormitory and pulled the cord. What if no one was alive up there and able to lower the ladder? Alfred could be dead. Gerald might have taken his anger out on him.

The ladder dropped to the floor. She trotted up the steps, taking them two at a time. She jumped the last two and landed hard on the floor above. Alfred lay sprawled out by the trapdoor opening. He stared at the ceiling, his eyes glassy.

Turning his head, he smiled. "Monica?"

"Yes, Alfred. Yes, it's me."

"I . . . I got the ladder down for you."

"Yes, I know. You did great." She hooked her arms under his shoulders. "Don't worry; I'll get you out of here." Her forearms burning under the pressure, she dragged him down the first couple of steps. Her bare feet gripped the worn, smooth steps with ease. "The other Seen have taken over the Nobles' infirmary. The chips aren't working anymore. We're safe now." She tugged him down five more stairs. His bare heels thumped against the wood.

"What happened?" He heaved a dry, rasping cough. "One minute Master Gerald was yelling at me, and then he stormed off saying something about Simon. Is Simon okay?"

"I don't know. I can't find him." When they reached floor level, Monica laid him on his back. "Can you walk?"

"I don't know." He rolled to his stomach and tried to push himself to his knees, but his arms collapsed under his weight.

"Just stay here." Monica held up a bandaged hand. "I'm going to look for Simon, and I'll find someone to come back and help you."

"Okay." Alfred lay on his stomach and folded his arms under his cheek. "I feel so sleepy. The gas came through the ceiling, and I started to fall asleep, but then it went away."

"I know." She gave him a smile. "You're welcome."

CHAPTER 37

Pumping her arms as fast as she could, Monica raced back to the infirmary. Her head pounded, and more blood seeped through her bandages. Inside, Coral and Jasmine leaned over a patient's bed, whispering to each other.

Monica rushed in and tugged on Jasmine's arm. "I found someone who needs help. He was in one of the dorms. I need help to bring him back here."

Jasmine followed her into the corridor. "You found your friend?"

"Not Simon." She mounted the marble steps. Her head swam, but she pressed on. "I found a boy. He cleans the Seen dorm near the library."

"Ah, that dorm; I know of it." Jasmine's long, thin legs took the steps two at a time with ease.

Huffing and puffing, Monica sat on the top stair. "I need to rest a minute."

Jasmine crouched next to her. "Where exactly is this boy? He probably needs oxygen. We should get him back to the infirmary as quickly as possible."

"He's just down this hall and to the right." Monica waved in that direction. "I need to find Simon. I have to make sure he's okay. Gerald was threatening him."

"Master Gerald?" Jasmine raised an eyebrow. "He can't do anything to anyone now. None of the chips are working, so don't worry; Simon will be fine."

"I still want to find him. I need to tell him about the computers."

"Ah, yes." Jasmine nodded, her face now blank. "The computers you shut down."

"I did. You might not believe me, but I did." Monica rose and turned down the hall toward the bedrooms. "I'll find him even if I have to search the entire palace."

"I'll go get the boy." Jasmine headed down the hall toward the library.

"His name is Alfred!" Monica called. She crept down the corridor, her left hand on the wall, her exposed fingertips caressing the tapestries. Every thread felt silky smooth. The scenes depicted different crowning ceremonies of the rulers of Cillineese.

She stopped at the second-to-last hanging. A man wearing a long white cloak bowed before eight council members, all standing in the grand receiving hall in Cantral. She touched the fibers depicting the polished marble floors and walls. She had been there once before on a cleaning assignment. The whole room was so enormous it took ten slaves all day to scrub it down after the crowning of a new city-state ruler.

She stared hard at the man being crowned. She needed to find Simon, but this man looked so familiar. He had the same profile as Master Gerald. She stepped over to the final tapestry. But, no, this one depicted Master Gerald, his unmistakable stare giving him away.

So the other one—Monica stepped back to the previous tapestry—couldn't be the current ruler. The man in this weaving stood by a woman with long brown hair and a swirling white dress. She had her head bowed, her gaze toward the ground.

Monica crossed her arms and shivered. She glanced at an open window. It helped release gas outside, but it also let in cold air.

She blinked at the light. The tingling down her spine wasn't just from the cold. These people were too familiar. She had seen them before. She shook her head, hoping to avoid the obvious conclusion, but it forced itself into her thoughts. These had to be her parents when her father was made ruler of Cillineese so long ago, years before she was born.

She sighed. She would never know them. They had been wiped away with a mere command from an unthinking, unfeeling machine. If only she could have helped them then.

Reaching up, she touched the thin threads that wove her mother's face. She tried to bring up a memory of this woman who had given her life, but none would come. The only mother she could recall was Emmilah, the slave woman who had cared for and protected her for four years.

Monica's lips trembled as she turned away and resumed her solitary march down the long corridor. Both mothers had spent only four years with her before she was cast into the world on her own, but she was more fortunate than some slave children. Most of them spent their first few days with their mothers before the women were sent back to work and the children given to caretakers.

She tramped down the carpet in the center of the hall, no longer caring if her feet left smudges on the plush surface. Those children would be assigned to work with an adult until they were old enough to be on their own. Only the luckiest children were overseen by their parents, and she had been one of them.

She gritted her teeth. No, not her. Not really. Masha had been with her parents until the unnamed disease swept her away, and then Emmilah and Iain had taken a newly orphaned Monica in her place. She wiped away a tear. Would they have been so happy to receive her if Masha hadn't died? They wouldn't have had a chip for her, and they would have had to share their food with a Noble brat who cried for her real parents.

Her foot smashed into something metal. She jumped back. The spiral staircase lay inches in front of her. She rubbed her bruised toes. Somehow she had managed to walk all the way down the corridor of bedrooms without even noticing where she was going.

After retracing her steps to Audrey's room, she knocked on the door. Audrey would probably know where Simon was; she seemed attached to the old man.

"Go away!" someone shouted. The voice was deep, probably a man's.

Monica edged away. Could it be Master Gerald? She didn't want to cross paths with him again.

"Who's there?" the speaker called. "If it's one of you Seen come to torment us again, I'll have you know that you will be punished terribly once the computers are fixed. I will explain to the Eight what happened, and I will be put back in power!" The man ranted on. "This sort of uprising will never go without great retribution."

Monica's head throbbed with every word. She backed away another step. Simon could be in there. Gerald likely wanted to keep him close as evidence to show the council.

The door opened a crack. Gerald stuck his head out and glanced to the left, then to the right. Just before he pulled back in, he stopped and stared at Monica. "You've come creeping out of your hole again, I see."

She turned to run. He shot out of the room and grabbed her collar. She whirled around and shoved him away, then kicked him in the shins. He pushed her into the bedroom and slammed the door shut.

Monica stumbled and fell to the floor. Ignoring the pain, she jumped to her feet and scanned her surroundings. A four-poster bed took up one-half of the room, and books and toys lay scattered across the floor. A wardrobe stood at the other end, the faint smell of mothballs wafting from its recesses.

Gerald slid a bolt in place, blocked the door with his body, and crossed his arms over his narrow chest. As his black bangs hung over his eyes, he breathed heavily.

"Daddy? What are you doing?" Audrey lounged on the bed, a book open in front of her. She propped herself up on her elbows and blinked at Monica. "I know who you are. You're Simon's new assistant."

Monica glanced between Gerald and his daughter. Maybe there was a slave's access door somewhere. The Seen nurse wouldn't use it, but a cleaning maid might. The woodwork disguised any hint of a sliding or hinged panel. She tensed her legs, ready to spring for the door.

"She's not really Simon's assistant, Audrey." Gerald stalked toward Monica, his arms extended as if to grab her.

"What have you done with Simon?" Monica growled as she backed into a bedpost. "I need to talk to him."

Gerald stopped, plucked off his wristband, and threw it on the ground. "If this were working, you would never dare talk to me like that, Sierra."

Smiling, Monica started to circle around him, step by step. "I don't have a chip, remember?" She nodded at Audrey. "But I'm sure you don't want your daughter to know about that, do you?"

"Know about what, Daddy?" Audrey crawled to the edge of her bed. "Where is Simon? Are we going to have lessons today?"

Gerald set his back against the door, blocking it again. "I forbid you to tell her." He looked his daughter in the eye. "Don't worry. Lessons will go back to normal soon. We're going to have a new librarian, and you'll have a new nurse, too."

"Is Simon alive?" Monica backed to a wall until her heels touched the wood, one sliding along the surface. There had to be a panel somewhere. "If you tell me where he is, I won't tell her who I am." She brushed past a corner and shifted to the adjacent wall.

Audrey climbed off her bed and grabbed her father's hand. Holding it tightly, she looked up at him. "What's going on, Daddy?"

He patted her head, then turned to Monica. "Go ahead and tell her, then. I want you right here where I can find you when the team from Cantral arrives to investigate this matter. They won't be at all pleased with the amount of gas you released into the atmosphere. The oxygen levels are rather delicately balanced, but I don't suppose you would know that. The slaves are so uneducated."

"Whose fault is that?" Monica's heel met a crack in the wall. Could it be one of the panels? Gerald's eyes followed her every move. Could she open the panel and duck inside before he could grab her? Her bandaged hands felt none of the grainy texture of the wood. With her fingers bound together, they might not be able to work the hidden latch even if she found it.

She firmed her voice. "The children don't know how we're treated until they've been trained not to care. How would you like it if Audrey were to suddenly find herself living as a wall slave in Cantral, forced to do work beyond her years and labor all day until she collapsed?"

"You'll leave my daughters out of this." Gerald pushed Audrey behind him and stomped toward Monica. "Amelia is already suffering because of you. She is under house arrest in Cantral. They're threatening to terminate her if I don't comply with all of their questions and searches."

Monica's hands found the latch, a wooden lever carved into a shape her wrapped fingers couldn't identify. Her hands fumbled with the wood, making it slip through her bandaged mitts.

Gerald grabbed a fistful of her hair, sliding her bandage off as he pulled. "You won't get away again. As soon as I turn you in, things will go back to normal. I've learned my lesson about being too ambitious, but you're still a prize they will pay dearly for."

"Daddy!" Audrey squealed. "You're hurting her."

Monica twisted in his grip. Her scalp felt like it was being peeled from her skull. She clawed at his hand, but he only pulled harder.

"Audrey, she's the reason you can't be with Amelia." He dragged Monica to the wardrobe. "Do you want Amelia to get hurt?"

"I thought she was sick," Audrey whimpered. "You said the Cantral doctors would make her better, and then I could see her again."

He swung the door open and yanked out the little-girl dresses hanging inside. A handful of mothballs tumbled to the ground. "She will get better faster if the Eight have this troublemaker."

"I don't understand!" Audrey ran to his side and clutched his arm. "The books say Amelia needs medicine. Aren't the doctors giving it to her?"

Monica's eyes rolled back in her head. Her scalp couldn't possibly be strong enough to stand this much pressure. Her skull felt like it was going to explode.

Gerald shoved Monica into the wardrobe. When he released her hair, she kicked at his stomach. He dodged and started to close the door. She flung herself against it, making it smack Gerald in the face.

She darted from the wardrobe and ran for the bedroom door. "He's lying, Audrey." Gasping, she fumbled with the latch. "They'll let her come home if he turns me in, but it won't make her better." Why wasn't this working? Her mitts couldn't get a grip on the metal knob. "You know the history of Cillineese. I saw some of the books you checked out for lessons."

Gerald groaned and stumbled slowly toward her.

Audrey scampered to Monica's side. "Yes, what about them?"

"Then you know who the ruler was before your father—his brother. And that he's on record as having only one child, terminated with the city before she was given a chip." The knob finally slid free from the catch, and the door swung open.

"Yes, of course." Audrey glanced at her father. One hand covering an eye, he tripped over a stack of books and toppled to the side, landing in a heap.

"I'm that child—your cousin. I'm trying to make things right." Monica dashed out the door and galloped down the spiral staircase. Maybe Audrey would take the information and put it to good use. If they survived, she could be the future ruler of Cillineese.

CHAPTER 38

As Monica's feet pounded the steps, the metal stairs shivered. She leaped off the last stair and landed softly on the carpeted floor of the open corridor.

Footsteps shook the stairs again. She bit her lip. Gerald must have recovered and decided to give chase. She opened the first door she came to. No vapor filled the room, so she ducked inside.

A solitary open window gave light to the empty meeting room. She pulled a plush rolling chair up to the narrow stone opening. The glass pane had been pushed open halfway. After shoving the window up as far as it would go, she mounted the sill and looked outside. A five-foot drop and a long slope lay before her, nothing compared to what she had been through.

She leaped from the window and tumbled down the hillside. Something poked her with every roll. She pulled her arms in close, trying to protect them. Finally, her head hit against something hard.

"Ow!" someone yelled. The speaker pulled her to her feet. "Are you all right?"

Monica rubbed her eyes with the side of her bandaged hand. If only the world would stop spinning for a minute. "I . . . I think so."

"That was quite a fall." A brawny, suntanned man stood in front of her, both hands on her shoulders. "What are you in such a hurry from? Everyone's celebrating. There's nothing to fear for now."

She glanced over her shoulder. Would Gerald follow through the window? Everything felt so warm, she couldn't think. Her eyes burning, she squinted at the man. "I'm outside."

"Of course you're outside." The man still held her shoulder. "Where else would you be?"

She shuddered. Of course—she had climbed out the window—but at the moment she had done so, she hadn't thought about where she was. She sank to the grass and laid her head on her knees. It wasn't safe out here. Everything was so big and open.

"Come on, girl, we're missing the parties." The man knelt beside her. "Most of the other Seen have made their way out here for the festivities."

"I have to find Simon." Monica looked up and pushed her hair out of her eyes. The man stared back at her. His brown face was coated with dirt and sweat despite the cold air.

"I don't know anyone named Simon."

Sweating and shivering at the same time, she peered at the sky. The piercing blue haze above stung her eyes. A golden orb hung high in the air, beating down on the world.

She shielded her eyes. The sun, of course. Everyone knew what the sun was, but few of the wall slaves had seen the dreadfully bright globe. Squinting, she pulled her thoughts back together. If what the man said was true, and the other Seen had come out of the palace, then maybe Simon had escaped.

"Are you all right, kid?" He offered her a hand up. "Most Seen don't have this much trouble coming outside."

She took his hand, despite her wounds, and pulled herself up. As she stood on the steep grassy slope, her legs trembled. During her life in the palace, she knew only stairs and long, never-ending corridors. She wasn't ready to be outside yet. Her eyes still rebelled at the thought of opening all the way.

"Are you ill?" the man asked. "The village doctor is full to the brim, but you can try to see him, if you'd like."

She shook her head. "I already saw the Seen nurse, thank you."

She forced her eyes to open fully. The flood of images almost knocked her down again. A tall white wall surrounded the palace. A stream flowed by its base, but not like the stream in the furnace room. Crystal clear water trickled merrily through sun-baked rocks, and tall, ornamental flowers lined the water's edge. A heavy, sticky, sweet smell hung in the air, like a Noble woman's dressing room after someone spilled a bottle of perfume.

Trees stood in groves around the garden, and paved stone paths twisted in and out of the clusters. Everything was so bright, she could hardly take it in. The feeble lights in the walls didn't do the sun justice. Even the windows in the palace were tinted, keeping out the majestic glory of the full light of day.

"I just can't keep my eyes open." Monica laughed, blinking away tears. "I know I've seen things like this before, but I hardly remember them. Memories have nothing on the real thing."

"When you sweat all day under the hot sun trying to make this pretty enough for their highnesses, it loses some of that touch." The man pointed at a small gate nestled in the white wall. "That's the way out to the village if you'd like to join the party. It's where I'm headed."

Monica strained her ears, putting to practice all the listening she had done over the many years. The sound of laughter floated through the air. People talked. Children screamed but not in pain as if they were being terminated.

She looked up at the man. "Why is everyone being so noisy? Are they allowed to do that?"

"Who's to stop them from celebrating?" The man grinned. "All the chips have stopped working. Haven't you noticed?"

"Yes, I noticed." Monica scanned the horizon. A gray wall extended into the sky, high above the white wall around the palace. It slowly descended inch by inch. She pointed at the disappearing mass. "Is that the dome?"

When the man followed her pointing finger, his ruddy face paled a bit. "Yes, you didn't see it from the palace, did you?"

"I was in the tunnels." She sank to the ground again. Her limbs still ached from the battering she took in the river. "I didn't see anything."

"The dome started to close, just like in the stories. It blocked out the sky and was almost closed; just a space the size of the palace remained open. Everyone was screaming." He shrugged and looked at the ground. "I must say I was pretty scared myself. Then the gas started coming from the sky. Some people died. We don't know how many yet. Those of us living are just happy we survived."

She stared at his honest face, so innocent, so ignorant of the truth. If only he knew how close their brush with death really was. "I'm happy for you, too."

He frowned. "You say you were in the tunnels? We heard rumors that everyone underground died."

"Most of them did, I think. There wasn't enough ventilation to let the gas escape, but I know a few survived." Monica sighed. She would have to follow this man out into the city if she wanted to find Simon.

Shuddering, she rose to her feet. It had to be done. She needed to tell Simon what happened, that it was okay; she hadn't gotten hurt when he had given up.

"So do you want to go with me or not?" He gestured toward the palace wall. "If I were you, I'd want to get out of here and live a little before squads come from Cantral to fix everything and finish us off."

"Can they do that?" She followed him to the gate. "The chips aren't working, so how can they kill anyone?"

He pushed open the gate and held it for her. A red light blinked above the thick wooden door. "They have other ways. There are rumors about it."

Inhaling deeply, she stepped out of the garden. A dense row of trees a few yards away concealed anything past their tall branches. Lush grass covered the ground, except where a path had been worn away. The dirt trail meandered into the stand of trees and disappeared in the distance.

The man led the way, talking as he tromped through the thicket. "Of course everyone is gossiping about the different ways they could kill us. Me, I'm just happy to be alive now, living for this moment, you know?" He didn't wait for an answer. "I've heard about these machines that can fire a projectile, and it'll rip clean through a man."

"Like a gun?" Monica jumped over a fallen branch. Sticks poked her bare feet. "I read about those recently in the library."

"Perhaps that's what they're called." He shrugged. "For now we're safe. At the rate the dome is descending, the roads won't be passable for three or four more hours."

Monica ducked under a tree branch. As a sharp, musky smell wafted through the air, she wrinkled her nose. "What is that?"

"Just a skunk. The woods here are full of animals. Wait until you pass the corrals. Your nose won't know what hit it."

She shuddered. Didn't they keep things clean here? The palace never held any strange smells. Every room carried the same empty, clean odor of freshly scrubbed floors. "So do you think Cantral will bring an army and mow everyone down?"

"Who knows? Like I said, I'm living for the moment."

When they stepped out of the woods, Monica stopped. A village lay before them, just down a steep incline. Fields and fields of empty land lay beyond the squat houses, expanding for miles before ending at the base of the dome.

The dark brown houses made neat little rows in the city; every street lay straight as a pin. A square in the town's center hummed with activity. Indistinct forms moved around the area, shouting and laughing.

Monica's knees knocked together. She couldn't go out among all that hustle and bustle. The biggest crowd she had ever been in was the early morning scrambles in the dorms. Those were all people who lived in the same situation, who knew what she had gone through. These villagers, oppressed as they were, didn't know what it was like to be a slave. They could be seen by the world. In the palace, that was a special rank.

"Are you all right?" The man stood at the base of the hill.

"Go on without me," Monica called. "I want to take my time."

The man nodded and jogged down the path to the village. Monica walked along the hillside, the grass caressing her bare calves and feet. The crest of the hill circled the palace's man-made wall, lined by the forest of trees, creating a parallel natural wall. She held a hand up to shade her eyes. Beyond the trees, the palace sat on a summit above the rest of the village, an appropriate position—lofty, high, and mighty.

As she walked, it seemed that more houses popped up with every step. The village was brimming with life—real homes with real people. How odd it all seemed, like strolling through a storybook.

When she rounded a corner, a deep trench blocked her path, forming a space for the drawbridge leading to the palace. Stopping, she scanned the surrounding area. The houses extended on and on straight ahead past the far palace wall, as far as she could see. The dome wasn't even visible in this direction.

She gasped. How big could Cillineese really be? The books

spoke of millions. Of course, that was a lot, but how many was it really? How long would a line of a million people be if they stood shoulder to shoulder? They could fill the palace a hundred times over. The houses the villagers lived in were nothing like the palace. Their short, straight walls and plain architecture looked bland next to the grandeur of the white stone palace rising above them.

Monica smiled. Bland, yes. Yet real. Very real.

CHAPTER 39

Monica stood on the grassy knoll between the palace and the city. In the space between two bustling areas it felt safe and secure. The sun beat down, warming her body in the frigid air. The grass released a sweet scent. She breathed deeply and started down the slope toward the city. As nice as it was, she couldn't stay on the hill forever. She had to find Simon, and she needed to talk to the slave council. They would have something to say about Gerald and his fall from power.

She slid down the smooth grass and landed on her feet beside the road leading away from the drawbridge. The palace entrance stood empty, the front doors open, yawning widely as if to suck in an unwary passerby. She skulked past the drawbridge. No guards would likely care if she went by, but Gerald might still be searching for her.

She jogged down the cobblestone road. Empty houses lined each side of the row. Identical windows cut eyes into the front of the houses, one window per house, right next to the front door.

Every house stood silent as she ran past. Her feet made soft pattering noises on the hard rock. Leaf litter blew in the wind, rustling and crackling.

She skipped to a halt outside a house. They couldn't all fit in the one square she had seen from the wall, could they? She knocked on the weathered door. It swung in, already unlatched.

"Hello?" She peered inside.

Five empty mats were stacked in one corner beside a black cookstove. A coat and scarf hung on a spike in the wall. The splashing of water echoed through the one-room house. A waterwheel turned over and over in a big basin in another corner. The water flowed in from a pipe in the wall and drained into a hole in the floor.

Another wheel, this one on legs, stood in the corner. Fibrous threads stuck this way and that off of a hairy brown clump on a spike attached to the legs. She squinted at the strange object. What could that be used for?

Something bubbled on the stove. She inhaled deeply. The scent didn't remind her of anything she had ever smelled before, but it made her stomach rumble. She licked her lips. Dinner last night felt like a year ago, but she couldn't take food from these people.

She shut the door and backed away from the house. The wind blew her hair into her eyes. Laughter swirled in the air. She glanced up and down the empty street. The noise was coming from farther down the maze of byways and footpaths.

"Hello?" she yelled. Only an echo of her own voice replied. Where was everyone? The man in the garden had made it sound like many had survived, but it felt like a town of ghosts.

She wandered down the street. The houses cast shadows across the cobblestones. Every time she entered a shady spot, she shivered in the cooler air. Ahead, the dome stood high in the sky, though the base stayed out of view. As she wove through the empty streets, she kept the dome in front. If she got lost, she would know which way to come back.

When she turned down a left side street, the noises grew louder. The houses were still the same, identical in every way, but the street suddenly opened up into a large square. People danced and shouted in the center.

Shops lined the sides of the square. Large signs above the awnings advertised their wares. The smell of warm bread wafted from the bakery, and cups of a steaming hot beverage sat in a row on the counter of another stall. They flavored the air with cinnamon, a spice favored by the Nobles.

Monica pressed herself against the last house on the row before the raucous scene. She stared, widening her eyes. The women swirled their long, brown skirts as they danced. Men twirled the ladies in patterned circles. Children chased each other in and out of the couples. Their short tunics barely covered their scabby knees, and their toes were blue, but they laughed all the same.

A man stood in the middle of the square. He clutched a wooden stringed instrument. His left hand flew up and down the narrow end of the box. His other hand wielded a thin piece of wood with hairs attached to the bottom half. The strands glided across the instrument's strings, issuing a sweet, syrupy noise. The melody skipped through the crowd and matched the dancing steps of all the boots and bare feet.

Monica's mouth hung open. Her own feet wanted to join in the steady rhythm. She could recall hearing notes like this before. Some of the mothers in the dorms would sing softly to their children, but they were often hushed by tired workers trying to sleep.

She blinked, shaking her mind back to the task at hand. The man said that Seen had come out to the square. She scanned the crowd again. Some men and women in the Seen uniform stood on the outskirts of the party. They clapped along with the music, but none joined the dancing.

Monica stood on tiptoes. The dancers kept sweeping into her line of sight, blocking her view. She took a step forward and craned her neck. Was Simon here? He would like to observe this sort of thing, for his studies, of course.

An older man sat on a rickety stool beside a bread shop. His uniform matched the Seen men's starched black pants and shirt. His white hair blew in the wind. Monica edged into the square. There he was. That man had to be Simon.

Keeping her back to the wall, she sidled around to the other end of the courtyard. No one paid her any mind. She sighed in relief and continued up to the man. It certainly looked like the old librarian, but his face was aglow, and he waved at a passing child. Could this be the sour old librarian who had given up on their plan?

He turned, and their eyes met. He jumped up from his seat. "There you are!" He strode to her and grabbed her shoulders. "Where have you been?"

"What do you mean where have I been?" she hissed as she jerked away. "You left me for dead in Master Gerald's clutches."

As the festivities continued in the square, Simon, his expression calm, ushered her down a side street.

When the party's noise faded, Monica leaped away from him and gave him a savage stare. "You abandoned me!"

"Not at all. I began searching for you immediately." He grinned, showing his crooked teeth. "The moment the dome appeared, however, I knew you had gotten away from Gerald, so I turned my attention to my own safety. If he had found me, he would have turned me in instead of you."

"How did you stay out of sight? Aren't you confined to the library during the day?" She watched his expression carefully. He could be hiding something. If he betrayed her once, he might do it again, though now he had nothing to fear from his chip.

"I sneaked out of the library." The wrinkles around his mouth and eyes relaxed. "Yes, my chip hurt me, but I was able to stand it until they were disabled. I even saved your rat, though not for dinner."

"But you couldn't have known I was going to disable them. For all you knew, I was on my way to execution in Cantral."

"What choice did I have but to hope?" He smiled again. "You certainly had me worried. I felt ready to pass out. And you were a little late stopping the gas. I'm afraid some people died."

"I know." At the mention of death, Monica's resolve to be distrustful melted away. "I tried, but I lost the directions, and I didn't know what controls to use, so I just ripped out the wires. Before I lost the translation, I noticed a note you made about a purple wire. Cutting that one worked."

"Ah! Good. I'm glad to hear that my efforts saved Cillineese after all."

"*Your* efforts? But I—"

"Yes, of course my efforts." Simon pulled her farther away from the laughter and celebration. "Were the computers where I thought they'd be? The air ducts should have been straightforward."

Monica held up her bandaged hands. Dark spots had appeared on some of the white strips of gauze, and her skin stung a little. "There was a giant fan blocking my way into the computer room. It cut off a bit of my fingers. I had to find a different way into the room, but the computers were where you thought they would be."

Simon clapped his hands, suddenly looking like his old self. "Excellent! I knew they had to be there." As she tried to rub away the sting, he stopped clapping. "Um, yes. Sorry about your hands. I didn't think there would be a fan there. Those are usually at the end of a vent into a room, not on the inside of the ducts."

"It must have been to protect the computers." Monica sighed. "There's no way to get my finger back."

"Yes, that is one of the tragic consequences, one of many."

"Too many." She pointed one of her mitts at the merrymaking in the square. "How can they be so happy if their friends are dead?"

"Because they themselves did not die." He took her by the arm and led her down the street, heading back toward the palace. "When you're about to lose your life, and all hope is stripped away, then handed back to you seconds later, you're too happy just being alive to think about others." He released her arm and kept walking. "Just wait until evening. Once the incinerator flames are lit and they have to burn all the dead, then you will see the tears flow freely."

Monica followed him to the palace drawbridge and stopped at the edge of the wooden planks. "Where are we going, Simon? Can't you explain your plans to me before you put them into motion? It works better that way."

He paused on the other side of the bridge. "You seem to have escaped from Master Gerald all right even after the plan was started. You follow orders well."

"I've been following orders ever since my father took me in. I became a slave to save my life." She looked at the ground. "I wanted to find you so you would know I was all right, but I'm done now."

"Done?" He scratched his head. "What do you mean, done? Done living? That seems rather rash, after all you've accomplished."

Monica bit back a smile. Simon was his old self again, the same old man she had known for only a few days. After working with him for so many hours, she had become used to his strange ways. They seemed almost normal.

She shook her head. She had to remain firm in this, or he would convince her to change her mind. "I'm done working for the slave council. You have hundreds, thousands of people now who have chips that don't work. Use one of them as your puppet. I want to live normally. I can do that here. I'll find somewhere to live in the city. I can have a life, not be worried about where my next chip will come from and who will die next so I can take the identity of some unfortunate soul."

Simon stared at her, his brow furrowing. "That was a pretty speech, but I'm afraid it doesn't work that way. No one among these people can replace you, even if they were willing."

"Why?" She crossed her arms despite the growing pain. "Every-one is basically chip-less now, just like me."

"They are chip-less here." He gestured in a wide circle. "Inside Cillineese, everywhere the next city doesn't reach. If one of them were to go to the Cantral border or to the New Kale border, they would be on the computer's scope again and terminated immedi-ately." He unclipped the wristband still clinging to his wrinkled arm. "All citizens of Cillineese are to be terminated if they step outside the city walls, even those who weren't here during the rebellion plans. It keeps everything neat and clean." He rubbed a finger over his wrist-band's blue screen. "There is one girl, however, who is a citizen of Cillineese, and she isn't going to be executed. At least for now." He pulled a cloth out of a pocket and wiped down his band before snap-ping it back on. "And she happens to look almost exactly like you."

"There has to be another way, Simon." Monica spread out her arms, though they flared with pain. "I'm not taking Amelia's place! She's still alive."

"Not for long, unfortunately. I've heard her health is failing rapidly. The Eight are hoping she stays alive long enough to ques-tion her, but the chances of that aren't high."

"How do you know?" Monica shook her head. "How could you possibly know? She's there, and you're here."

"A messenger was sent back to Cillineese right before the dome started to close. He was sent to his death, though, I'm afraid." Simon beckoned to her. "Come along now. We have some things to do to get you ready to play this poor girl's role. You haven't been a Noble for some time now."

She stepped onto the first plank. "Do you know how many messengers died?"

"No, of course not." He sighed. "Are you coming or not?"

She held out her arms and hands. "What about my bandages? They will know right away I'm not Amelia, and Gerald is on the lookout to kill me!"

He shook his head. "Such a little thing. Amelia could have fallen and hurt herself. Some bandages and alterations in appearance could be the result of medical procedures. And don't worry about Gerald. Audrey and he are stuck in Cillineese, and Amelia is in Cantral. They won't be seeing each other for some time."

Simon stood at the other side of the bridge, waiting with his hands behind his back, one eyebrow raised. Monica looked over her shoulder at the empty street. The townspeople were probably still laughing and enjoying their newfound freedom. What would it be like to join them? To not be afraid of being in the open? She could live here. Cantral didn't have enough manpower to search every house in Cillineese, did they? She would be safe. Yet, she would be trading her safety for the potential freedom of every man, woman, and child in the city.

"Monica? We really don't have much time." He nodded at the palace. "Amelia doesn't have that much time. This disease is killing her quickly. She won't last long under house arrest with little medical care."

"But you want her to die." Tears quivered on the edge of Monica's eyelashes, tears of frustration and pain as the medicine wore off. "I've met her. It was hard enough to take Nat's identity after knowing him. I can't do it again. You want me to go from wall slave, to Seen, to Noble, as if it's a skin I can put on. But it's not." She looked up at the sky and tried to blink away the tears. "I got to be out here for the first time since I can remember. I like it. I like the outdoors. I don't want to be shut away again."

"Shut away?" Simon slid a shoe across the first plank on his side of the bridge. "I see. Perhaps I should tell everyone that a certain chip-less girl has decided that her duty toward them is finished because she fears being shut away. They might wonder how this shutting away compares to what they will face. Not only will they all eventually be cruelly terminated, the slavish oppression in the other cities will continue, perhaps increase as the paranoid

Nobles attempt to tighten their grip. Her decision to quit before the task is accomplished will result in a situation far worse than if she had given up before she began. It would have been better for all if she had perished in the ductwork, a victim of the fan blades. Perhaps eight years ago, her corpse should have been the one found in the ducts of Cantral instead of the unfortunate six-year-old who assumed her identity."

Monica stared at the ground. Heat rose into her cheeks. Although Simon was obviously trying to goad her with guilt, every word he said was true.

She planted her feet on her side of the bridge. He was persuasive, but she had to make this decision on her own, not allowing guilt to be yet another slave driver. When she was in the ducts, she decided to stop fearing the dark. She had figured out, with a little help, how to get to the computer rooms. After losing the directions, she had also shut off the computers and saved millions, not being directed by Simon or one of the slave council. She had done it herself.

As pain flared again, she raised a bandaged hand. Wasn't it someone else's turn to suffer?

She looked again at Simon. With his hands stuffed in his pockets, he gazed back at her, tears trickling from both eyes. Exhaling heavily, he shook his head sadly. "I'm sorry."

"Sorry?" Her voice rose barely above a whisper. "For what?"

He shuffled across the bridge, knelt in front of her, and looked into her eyes. "For everything. I have mistreated you, manipulated you, and ordered you around like my own slave. I should be shouting your praises from the rooftops." He took one of her bandaged hands and kissed her fingertips. "You, my dear, are a heroine, the savior of all Cillineese. You have given us hope. We see now that the Nobles' hold is vulnerable. You have loosened its grip of terror. Now all we need to do is find a way to strip their fingers away from our necks for good."

He rose to his feet and caressed her cheek. "You have done well, a noble slave who deserves to be seen by all, no longer shut away, no longer a hidden refugee, a child free to enjoy the warmth of sunshine. You are a faithful instrument, though not faith itself, and faith will never die, never tire, never fade away. Whether or not you choose to take part, we will find a way to conquer our task-masters." He withdrew a thin yellow book from an inner pocket. "Your mother's diary. I secretly translated the first page. I think you should read it."

After handing it to her, he turned, crossed the bridge again, and shuffled toward the arched palace doors, his shoulders stooped once more, the spring gone from his step. Then, he turned and spoke, his eyes focused on the ground. "Decide what you will. I have to go to the infirmary. I need to check on some friends. If you don't join me, I'll know your final decision."

CHAPTER 40

Monica watched Simon disappear into the building. Her feet felt rooted to the bridge, as if they had become part of the dead wood. "Simon," she whispered, but her feeble call fell short.

She opened to the diary's first page. The breeze lifted a scrap of paper, apparently a page Simon had inserted. At the top, his familiar handwriting scrawled out a message from long ago.

My dear Sierra, I hope someday you will read this journal. By the time you are old enough to understand these words, you will likely have already experienced much suffering, and I weep even now for the heartaches, bruises, and tears our plans will almost surely bring upon you. Tyrants will never voluntarily loosen their iron grip. Resistance only makes them tighten their choke hold and crush those who threaten their power. Yet, since they will scan the skies for attacking eagles, perhaps a quiet mouse will be able to sneak past their defenses and penetrate their power structure.

We pray that you, dear Sierra, will be the mouse who will be able to crawl into spaces inaccessible by the big and strong, an undetectable infiltrator who will go where even the Nobles have never stood—the threshold of the cruel enforcers, the computers of Cillineese. Even now your father is risking his life to learn as much as he can about the unfeeling machines—where they are, how to sever their wicked whips. Someday he hopes to equip you with that knowledge so that you will go forth with weapons to help those who desperately need you.

Still, my darling daughter, even if our plans fail to work in the way we envision, remember this. The God of our songs is with you and will never forsake you. He blesses the weak and lowly and will rise up against their oppressors. As the holy writings say, "He pours contempt on Nobles and loosens the belt of the strong."

When you need wisdom, it will blossom within you. When you need a companion, one will appear as if out of nowhere. When you need light, a star will lend you its glory. And when you need rescue, knock on any door, and your deliverer will already be waiting to lift you to your feet again.

Remember, you cannot do this on your own. You will have gifts, but you must rely on the giver. Even if you succeed in breaking one chain, the next will be more difficult, for the tyrants will retaliate with a fury you cannot imagine. You will need a shield sturdier than wood or metal. You will need faith—faith to endure, faith to achieve, faith to survive. Without faith in the one who grants the ability to break the chains, you will end up in chains yourself, another victim who trusted only in her own strength.

I love you, dearest one. If I am taken away from you, I hope you will be able to find Simon, your father's former tutor. I will entrust him with this journal. If he has not lost faith himself, perhaps he will teach you more about the God of our songs.

Tears flowing, Monica swallowed. There was just too much here to take in! Her birth mother, a woman she couldn't even remember, had loved her before she was ever born, and now she spoke from her grave.

She had set the standards for her daughter so high. The hopes were so much to live up to. Millions of people counted on the fulfillment of this dead woman's dreams: Maisy and the other slaves of Cantral—Opal, the Seen girl from the library; Sam, her mother, and the other laundry slaves; everyone from the dorm she had lived in as a little girl; and every slave in every city-state around the world.

Monica clapped her hands over her ears as if to block out their cries. There were so many, so many more in Cantral than here in Cillineese—eight times as many slaves in a palace eight times as big as this one, with eight times as much suffering inside its white walls. Only the slaves she knew came to mind, but there were others. For every one she was familiar with, there were five more in another part of the palace.

She glanced over the page again, and her eyes wandered to Simon's name. She smiled. He had known all along who she was. Why hadn't he told her? Had he not thought she was ready for the task? But now it was obvious. She had done and would continue to do everything they had hoped for. She wasn't a puppet. She was a daughter, a student, and a friend.

She tucked the book under her arm and jumped to the other side of the bridge. The cobblestone path felt cool and smooth beneath her feet, firming her decision. It was the right thing to do—to help these people who had given her so much, who had suffered so much.

Monica wandered into the palace entrance hall. The same stair Gerald had dragged her down swept up to the balcony above. She strode into the center of the room and spread out her arms. This room wouldn't scare her anymore. The outside had opened up a whole new world. She didn't have to fear the open space.

She hugged herself and brought back the last good memories she could recall of her adoptive father. He had comforted her before she had to go meet the slave council member for the first time. He had been an imposter, trying to uncover a plot, but her father didn't know. He had hugged her and told her to be brave. If she was quick and listened to the warning signs, no one could catch her. During the hard times in the walls and in the toughest moments in the river, those precious memories had slipped away, but she would remember them now, along with an addition.

"I don't have to do this alone," she whispered.

Pushing into a confident stride, she headed for the infirmary. Simon would have to help with the planning stages, but this was *her* decision, *her* mission. No slave council or Seen would have to force her to do her duty, and no slave council could stop her.

She looked back over her shoulder to the open door in the foyer. The wind blew it shut with a bang. She bent her lips into a sad smile. The city might be inviting, but it was not yet hers to enjoy. Freedom would have to wait. As long as her friends still suffered, as long as they couldn't be free, she could never rest.

She marched into the infirmary. Alfred lay in a bed near the center of the room, Simon sitting in a chair at his side. He held the boy's hand and spoke to him in quiet whispers.

Steeling herself, Monica crept to his side. There was no backing out now. She knelt beside Simon and touched Alfred's hand. His suffering was her fault. If she hadn't lost hope, she could have prevented all of this.

Alfred coughed under the oxygen mask over his mouth and nose, seemingly unaware of her presence. She gently compressed his hand. She wouldn't be weak again. No Alfreds or Margos or Sashas would suffer again, as long as she had strength to help them.

"Simon?" she whispered.

"You've decided?" He released Alfred's hand and sat back in his chair.

"Yes." As she caressed Alfred's knuckles, his breathing evened out, and his eyes opened. He gave her a faint smile, then closed his eyes again.

She slid the diary into Simon's hand. "I want to help the slaves in Cantral. I'll take Amelia's place and find a way to dismantle the computers."

Simon nodded and patted the book. The faintest glimmer of a tear hovered at the corner of his eye. "I see that my little speech performed admirably."

"Don't try to con me, Simon. I know you meant it. I can see the tear in your eye."

"Is that so?" He brushed the tear away and focused on Alfred. "I'm sure I have no idea what you're talking about, girl. I think you simply came to your senses."

She smirked. "I don't know how sensible this plan really is. I'll be putting myself under house arrest."

Returning his gaze to her, he patted her hand with his wrinkled one. "It's very sensible, and you are just the heroine to pull it off."

"I just want to help my friends." Monica rose to her feet and withdrew Alyssa's broken medallion, letting it dangle at the end of its cord. "I've seen the celebration," she said as it twirled in the light, "the smiles, the music, the dancing. I want to bring the same joy to Cantral. I want to hear the slaves sing."

"Then we will be the minstrels." He laid a hand on her cheek. "Let's get you ready for another journey."

ACKNOWLEDGMENTS

First I want to say thank you to my parents for never giving up on me, even when it seemed like I wasn't ever going to learn how to read. Thank you for encouraging me to pursue a career as an author, even though most people wouldn't recommend writing for someone with my setbacks.

Thanks to my Ferns, without whom *Precisely Terminated* would not be the book that it is. You two are very encouraging and so helpful.

Mangy and Nia, thanks go to you two as well. Without Clean-Place and your encouragement (especially Mangy's), I'm not sure I ever would have started writing for fun, and that's where it all started.

AMG, thank you for taking a risk with a brand-new author and helping me get the best cover possible.

And thank you to the One who gave me the idea—I'll try to make it less subtle next time.

The **Dragons in our Midst®** and **Oracles of Fire®** collection
by **Bryan Davis**:

RAISING DRAGONS
ISBN-13: 978-089957170-6

The journey begins! Two teens learn of their dragon heritage and flee a deadly slayer who has stalked their ancestors.

THE CANDLESTONE
ISBN-13: 978-089957171-3

Time is running out for Billy as he tries to rescue Bonnie from the Candlestone, a prison that saps their energy.

CIRCLES OF SEVEN
ISBN-13: 978-089957172-0

Billy's final test lies in the heart of Hades, seven circles where he and Bonnie must rescue prisoners and face great dangers.

TEARS OF A DRAGON
ISBN-13: 978-089957173-7

The sorceress Morgan springs a trap designed to enslave the world, and only Billy, Bonnie, and the dragons can stop her.

EYE OF THE ORACLE
ISBN-13: 978-089957870-5

The prequel to *Raising Dragons.* Beginning just before the great flood, this action-packed story relates the tales of the dragons.

ENOCH'S GHOST
ISBN-13: 978-089957871-2

Walter and Ashley travel to worlds where only the power of love and sacrifice can stop the greatest of catastrophes.

LAST OF THE NEPHILIM
ISBN-13: 978-089957872-9

Giants come to Second Eden to prepare for battle against the villagers. Only Dragons and a great sacrifice can stop them.

THE BONES OF MAKAIDOS
ISBN-13: 978-089957874-3

Billy and Bonnie return to help the dragons fight the forces that threaten Heaven itself.

Published by Living Ink Books, an imprint of AMG Publishers
www.livinginkbooks.com ✦ www.amgpublishers.com ✦ 800-266-4977

Now Available from Living Ink Books

SWORDS OF THE SIX

(BOOK 1 IN THE SWORD OF THE DRAGON SERIES)

Scott Appleton

ISBN-13: 978-0-89957-860-6

Betrayed in ancient times by his choice warriors, the dragon prophet sets a plan in motion to bring the traitors to justice. On thousand years later, he hatches human daughters from eggs and arms them with the traitors' swords. Either the traitors will repent, or justice will be served.

Now Available from Living Ink Books

MASTERS & SLAYERS
(BOOK 1 IN THE <u>TALES OF STARLIGHT</u> SERIES)
Bryan Davis

Expert swordsman Adrian Masters attempts a dangerous journey to another world to rescue human captives who have been enslaved there by dragons. He is accompanied by Marcelle, a sword maiden of amazing skill whose ideas about how the operation should be carried out conflict with his own. Since the slaves have been in bonds for generations, they have no memory of their origins, making them reluctant to believe the two would-be rescuers. Set on

For purchasing information visit

www.LivingInkBooks.com

or call 800-266-4977

Coming in 2011 from Living Ink Books

THIRD STARLIGHTER

(BOOK 2 IN THE <u>TALES OF STARLIGHT</u> SERIES)

Bryan Davis

Adrian and Marcelle continue their quest to free the human slaves on the dragon planet of Starlight. While sword maiden Marcelle returns to their home planet in search of military aid, Adrian stays on Starlight to find his brother Frederick, hoping to join forces and liberate the slaves through stealth. Both learn that reliance on brute force or ingenuity will not be enough to bring complete freedom to those held in chains.

For purchasing information visit

www.LivingInkBooks.com

or call 800-266-4977